George pulled Carrie to her feet, smashing the wineglass in his rage. 'We're getting married.'

'Marriage? Even if I favoured it, which I don't, you're not my idea of a husband. You're uneducated and . . . I wouldn't marry – what do you call your people here? I just couldn't marry a *guinea*.'

George stood transfixed. Yankees, he knew, did look down on other ethnic groups. But Carrie?

In his rage he slapped her hard on the right cheek, then hit her again with a closed fist. He picked up his jacket and hat and went out into the wind. The fog seemed to be lifting, a wan moon hung high. George heard a man howling in agony. He realised, with dazed surprise, that it was himself.

ALL OR NOTHING

Stephen Longstreet

A STAR BOOK
published by
the Paperback Division of
W. H. ALLEN & Co. PLC

A Star Book
Published in 1985
by the Paperback Division of
W. H. Allen & Co. PLC
44 Hill Street, London W1X 8LB

First published in Great Britain
by W. H. Allen & Co., 1984
First published in the United States of America
by G. P. Putnam's Sons, 1983

Copyright © Stephen Longstreet 1983

Printed and bound in Great Britain by
Anchor Brendon Ltd, Tiptree, Essex.

ISBN 0 352 315822

Many of the incidents and events in this novel are based
on historical fact—one could hardly write about the city
and avoid the intrusion of its dramas and intrigues, nor
view as jetsam that special flavour that is uniquely its
very own.

However, the fictional characters in this story are the
invention of this writer and are not to be taken for any
person or family alive or buried. When actual historic
personalities appear, they do so under their true names.

S.L.

For my granddaughters—
Many wishes for much happiness

Something Before

Somewhere in San Francisco, in what was once a small post office, there still exists a Federal Arts Project mural produced during the days of the Great Depression. It covers three vast walls and is said to have been based on a sketch by Stanton Macdonald Wright. Titled *City by the Golden Gate*, it was produced by several local artists in a style 'somewhat between Giotto and latter-day Cubism'— so wrote a local art critic named Frankenstein. The main panel (over the stamp and registered-mail windows) is a montage of sea and rocks, early Spanish forts, the first erected permanent structures. There is also a busy procession of miners, ladies in hoop skirts and bustles, military parades, stagecoaches, fireworks (celebrating the admission of the state into the Union), even some early autos and a cable car.

On the left wall, the background depicts clipper ships, paddle-wheel steamers, Seal Rock, the Ferry Station. The foreground presents portraits of citizens of note or notoriety: the last Spanish mayor; a Mr Levi cutting out the first pair of his famous Levi's; the Emperor Norton and his two dogs; Jack London; a dishonest mayor or two; the eccentric young woman who rode with the fire engines, the steam-pumper seen in full gallop of rushing horses, backed by the Coit Tower, which the woman had built.

Well forward in the painting stands the figure of a vigorous-looking middle-aged man dressed in the height of

7

late nineteenth-century tailoring, topped by a gray beaver hat, his open Prince Albert hammer-tailed frock coat showing a red waistcoat 'crossed by watch chains from which dangle an elk tooth and a good-sized Klondike nugget. He poses directly in front of a red-stone Roman-styled building whose sign reads: 'THE PACIFIC-HARVESTERS BANK.' Clearly this is the likeness of the founder, Gregorio (George) Taddeo Fiore, whose name will always be connected with one of California's great banking organizations. He points proudly toward the bank with an elegant cane held in one gloved hand. The face shows virtuosity and style, even an amused hauteur. The darkly handsome features are clearly Italian.

On the right-hand wall is an arrangement of tall buildings on a busy, hilly street—Nob or Russian Hill—and in the background some hint of the Barbary Coast, more picturesque than it could ever actually have been. Sail- and ferryboats dot the bay, a distant Alcatraz exists half-hidden in fog. No notice has been taken of the Great Earthquake and Fire of 1906.

In the foreground are society figures. Most of them are known today only to scholars of the various periods of the city's growth, but prominently displayed are Leland Stanford and his partners Hopkins, Crocker, and Huntington. Standing out in the middle of this group is a tall man with the features of a tenacious marauder, displaying casually a large blueprint labeled 'The Builder of San Francisco'. The figure of Moses Kendrick proclaims bold expediency and agitation: coarse, humorless, yet attractive features, a short-cropped Mormon chin beard, a bit of a paunch, clothed in simply cut loose broadcloth.

Missing from the mural is any image of Ramon Velasquez, a descendant of one of the most famous Spanish land-grant families. At the time of the painting, he was president of the harassed, depression-badgered Pacific-Harvesters Bank. His mother had been Irena Fiore, the sister of the founder George Fiore. Perhaps Velasquez was left out of the mural because he was still very much alive.

Or perhaps he had enough political clout in the Federal Arts Project to keep his portrait out of the painting.

Another missing figure, some gossips insisted at the unveiling, was the Chinese girl Moon Orchid. To most citizens of San Francisco, she was a Chinatown legend, almost a myth. But anyone active in research would find she had existed.

By the early 1940's the mural had become neglected, smoke-stained, and in some places the pigments had flaked. During the war years no one thought much about it. But in the 1950's its historic value was rediscovered and there was talk that the mural should be restored. Nothing came of the project, and so the mural grows fainter and more dreamlike as the years pass.

Seest thou a man diligent in his business? he shall
stand before kings.

—Proverbs 22:29

Take ye wives, and beget sons and daughters . . .
that ye may be increased there, and not
diminished.

—Jeremiah, 29:6

Beware of what you desire,
you will get it.

—Ralph Waldo Emerson

1

Mezzo Forte

1

'All women feel guilty in not being born sons,' said the old grandmother Timo to the boy on the stone floor stringing mushrooms by her side. In the village of Empoli high in the Italian hills, it was whispered the old woman had the evil eye and brewed witch's ointment for burning lovers and hot mixtures for wives needing to bewitch well-hung men.

'You are the last male of the Fiores, remember that. And I saw to it you were born lucky. A he-goat gave milk that night and a two-headed snake was found under Father Orsini's house on your baptismal day. A sure sign you are marked for something,' she spat, 'beyond this flea-bitten village market.'

'Is that like the red blot on Uncle Battista's face?'

The old woman struck the boy on the head with the big metal spoon with which she was mixing some pungent potion by the fireplace.

'Damn fool! I mean *inside* you. You come from these surroundings, but be not impressed by those people who lack nothing and lose everything. Let them fart in the wind. You will go far from here and do much. Getting rich is no sin if you know how to flaunt it. Are you listening to me, Grego?'

The boy ducked the attempted tap of the spoon on his head: the old bag of rags was entertaining but still had the power in her hard thin arms. 'Just remember, it's a world of hares and foxes. Dupes and rogues.'

12

'Is Papa a fox?'
'He is an arsehole of a donkey.'

It was once popular in American journalism to suggest that the most successful American citizens were born poor, came from the hard-scrabble soil of honest labor, that they fought their way upward in a system that rewarded hard work, pluck and honesty. When Gregorio Taddeo Fiore first began to attract attention, newspapers and weekly magazines claimed that he came from the humblest peasant stock and came to San Francisco in rags.

Actually, the Fiores were well-regarded middle-class Italians. The family owned an olive press and a farmers' inn—known as a lively place to drink Chianti in raffia-covered bottles.

Gregorio had been born in 1829, the last of ten children, of which only he and his older sister Irena survived. Grego's education was scanty, his father Aldo preferring that Grego make himself useful handling the olive barrels at the press.

The boy was in awe of his *nonna*—grandmother; clearly the village thought of her as a witch. She had a sardonic laugh and the golden-eyed glare of a hawk. Even the padre of the family, Aldo, was respectful to her. He had inherited the olive press from her, and some arid acres where he raised goats.

The boy was her favorite. She would offer special tidbits to him and chant special charms over him. When Grego helped her grind spices for her fragrant sauces, she would confide in him. 'They are all nose-pickers in this village,' she would say to him. 'But you know the signs, my boy. Always do things by threes—*never* by ones or twos. Never travel in a coach with a nun. If you are bold, life will offer itself to you like a ragged priest holding a chalice, and luck *is* contagious. You will cross the seas; you will find the golden world; you will be like Leonardo da Vinci. Thank the Madonna that our ancestor was seduced by the notary Ser Piero da Vinci.'

When he was fifteen, tall and able to handle the ferocity of stray dogs, lift a donkey off the ground, and able to face his father, who had a rum-blossom nose and hard fists, Grego decided to work his way to Genoa. He would get on a ship and find that golden land his grandmother had spoken of when she cast his fortune in the blood of a freshly killed rooster.

His father, full of white wine and spicy sausages, heard the boy out, cursed him over an upturned barrel of olive pits.

'You loudmouthed whelp! Genoa! The sea! I didn't raise any buggering sailor! I'll hang you up by the ears if I hear any more about going off to drown yourself in the sea.'

'I'll run off, then.'

A backhanded blow knocked Grego onto the pit-strewn floor. 'I've got plans for you,' shouted Aldo. 'You'll marry Luigini's oldest daughter, Bianca.'

'But she's cross-eyed and has big feet . . .'

'Someday she'll inherit the Luigini gristmill, big feet and all. Now, go take the wine kegs down to the inn.'

There was no loss in Grego's self-confidence as he got up, brushed himself free of olive pits. 'The day I can knock you down, old man, is the day I leave.'

Aldo made an obscene gesture of thumb and fist. 'Ha, the Pope's farts will blow down this building before *that* happens.'

Grego had already had his hand up Bianca Luigini's dress and liked it well enough, even though she had small teeth and crossed eyes. And he didn't want to marry a gristmill and stay in a forgotten village like Empoli, where kicking a dog passed for excitement.

For reasons that he couldn't fathom, his mind, his attitudes, seemed more than were needed for simply pressing olives or grinding grain. He struggled with a chaos of doubts and desires, some rebel tensions, imponderable anxieties that were not like those of the village lads who mocked Father Orsini, copulated with goats, got flogged by

14

their fathers, and had no idea that there was any more to life than cobbling shoes or driving donkeys. He was as ready as he would ever be. Father Orsini, who smelled of grappa and old fish, had taught Grego to read, to mouth a bit of Latin ('*Diffialia quae pulchra*'); Grego taught himself to add and subtract. He was ready now for larger worlds.

Grego's only confidante was his sister Irena. Three years older than he, she had a wise head, a bold mouth. She, too, rejected the benign ordered dullness of village existence. There was no way for her, she felt, to realize her full potential. Her choices were either to become a nun, sleep on stale straw, and wear out her knees praying on stone floors, or marry a scratching grove-worker and 'get smelly brats'—as her grandmother Timo expressed it—'Every year, a new brat!'

Though they were very close, only Grego seemed to have a future. For Irena there was no harbor, no ship. Just homilies and the complaints of pregnant wives and she soon among them?

In the fall, when the olives were all picked and the grain ground, Aldo Fiore would string twelve-foot nets on tall poles and set them up on the ridge beyond his olive press. Just after dawn, birds moving south to escape the winter would fly into the nets. Aldo Fiore was very fond of roast robins and other birds strung on a spit and browned over a sizzling fire of dried olive pits.

It was Grego and Irena's task to spend the last part of the night on the grass under the nets during bird-migration season to lower the nets to capture the birds that became entangled in the fine mesh. They never ate the birds—it was enough to watch their father crunch tiny bird bodies and spit out the crushed bones.

They did not like the duty, but one did not disobey the head of a family, a strong man like Aldo, with his hard fists. Children, he insisted, had been created from a man's loins by the good Lord to obey and work.

So this autumnal night with dawn about to break, they

huddled together on the ridge, blankets over their shoulders, discussing the varied possibilities of life.

Grego said this was his year to leave. Irena agreed.

'But you must promise when you are rich and famous, you will send for me. Not just say '*arrivederci*' and wave good-bye.'

'Of course. But how can I become rich, and why famous?'

'Timo, and as a witch she knows, says you have the signs on you. The V on the forehead is for Vinci.'

'I love her, but she's old and dotty. Her brain is a dish of donkey dung and turnip greens.'

Irena took his arm in a firm grip. 'You *promise* to think of me or I'll bite your ear off right now.'

She was nearly as strong as he and had a solid sense of her own worth. He admired and feared her. A hard vivacity, a determination filled her voice as she gripped his arm. If there was a country gaucherie about them in their earnestness, they were unaware of it. It did not lessen their grievances in a setting they felt was not worthy of them.

'I promise,' said Grego. 'But here they come; get ready to drop the tops of the net.'

The first hints of dawn—Grego recalled the priest quoting Homer's 'rosy-fingered dawn'—was tinting the far hills. Chalk-colored clouds would soon be visible, and below the leaf-green hillsides of vines, the slopes of olive trees, the little river with its bosky banks would emerge, a riverbank where one sat and fished and had thoughts that one didn't confess to the priest Father Orsini.

'Here they are, poor creatures,' said Irena. 'They're unaware that they are doomed.'

'Cheer up. You may win the Naples lottery; *they* can't.'

The birds, banded in two loose groups, were coming as the sun was about to charge into the sky. The blue overhead was showing itself, dissolving the purple of a night, Grego felt, the color of the inner skin of a plum.

Now the robins, larks, marsh birds, and others were close. The flutter of their wings could be clearly heard, a kind of low trilling of bird sounds.

Then, as if propelled by unreason, a whole cluster of flying creatures piled onto the net with a crunch as their flight stopped. They sent out cries of alarm; wings, bodies, tails were all in confusion and there was an acid odor of droppings, a loose falling away of feathers. Grego and Irena pulled on two ropes. They lowered the top of the folded part of the nets over the confused thrashing birds. The trapping between layers of nets was complete. Struggling sounds of fragile bones breaking, a pathetic drift of feathers, and it was all over; none would continue their flight to warmer places to mate and breed.

Neither Grego nor his sister would club the birds and gather them in bales destined for the inn's kitchen. That they left to Julian, the lame servant at the inn. As they prepared to leave the revolting task, the shrill fright of the birds growing in panicked confusion, Grego lifted a corner of a net. 'There's an eagle in here! An eagle!'

He put his arms into the net, pressing his hand past a cluster of bird life. After cursing and yelping in pain, he pulled out a ruffled, angry-eyed and protesting large bird. Clearly in the rising day, it was a golden eagle. 'Just like the goddamn Prussian kaiser's coat of arms, eh, Irena?'

Grego's hand was cut by the bird's talons and beak as he held its yellow scaly legs. The bird stared boldly at him with its great eyes, its wings trying to beat free of his arms.

'It's torn your hands!'

'*Dio!* Look at the proud bastard, Irena!'

'What are you going to do with him? He'll kill our chickens! You can get at least ten lire for him in the city market down by the big river.'

'Ten! I could get twenty lire, maybe more. Just for feathers for soldiers' hats, for the Bersagliere regiment. Let's put our hearts on his wings, toss him up in the air so at least our spirits will see the unknown this year.'

'You damn silly fool!' said Irena as she began tearing off a section of her petticoat. 'A rotten time to get poetic. Here, let me bandage your hand.'

17

Grego laughed, wondering at his own behaviour and his strength as he lifted his arms and cast the bird into the air. '*Di Pia Facta Vident!*' It flew free for a moment, hovered an instant in confusion, and then began to pump itself upward with the whirling power of its splendid wingspread. The two Fiores stood silently, watching it beat its way higher, merging at last into the full color of the risen day.

From then on the brother and sister had a kind of mysterious shared relationship; for them, a justifiable understanding existed that somehow their lives would change in their alienation from daily village life.

From a ruined castle, on a remaining doorway, Grego found a family crest and the words 'EX-AEQUO-ET-BUNO'— 'according to what is good and right.' He took it as his own.

When Grego was nineteen and about to run off, his grandmother Timo took to her bed. She lay beneath the big black wooden crucifix with a brass Christ resting from his agony with (Grego always thought) an expression of intense annoyance.

The room was full of corded trunks, dried bags of herbs, mysterious bundles. To Grego as he sat with Timo, it smelled of cats, grandmother, and the smoking wick of the little pot of olive oil burning under a plaster image of the Virgin.

Timo motioned him closer.

'Grego, I have had enough of life. I prefer acts of providence to any other kind, and that gives me visions. When I have gone to sit for eternity on the right side of the Madonna, then—'

'No, no, don't talk of dying.' He was still young enough to think he would never die.

'It's something, dear lad, no one can do for you. So when you go from here, there is a little sum. Not much; I've already paid for a Mass to keep me from being forever in Limbo. What's left, that is yours to go away. It is in the base under the image of the Virgin.' She crossed herself under the cup of burning olive oil. 'So, go to your destiny. After all, you are a da Vinci, or a near one. *Benedicat Vos Omnipotens Deus, Pater et Filius et Spiritus Sanctus.*'

She died some days later, after telling the priest how to give her the last rites properly. She was buried on the dry hillside where generations of simple citizens of the town and countryside put away their dead.

Later, at home, Grego, his father, and Irena shared cups of tart Torre Giulia and a bit of antipasto. They recalled Timo—with her gone, all family history seemed gone.

Aldo nodded as if some wisdom had come to him.

'Grego, life goes on—yes? So after the proper period of mourning, Father Orsini will announce your marriage to Bianca. You're not Cesare Borgia to expect a princess.'

'Let Irena marry first.'

'Ha!' Irena lifted a sardine from the antipasto. 'Marry one of these local rockheads who beat their wives and have the drunkard's brains of an addled dog?'

'Then it's to a nunnery for you.' Aldo belched and settled back in his chair grimacing.

Irena picked up a glass of wine and sipped it. Grego studied his sister. Still young, she had a sudden beauty, that sparkling grace that usually passed after the birth of the third child and fatness set in.

'You're not putting me away among the nuns smelling of piss and sick with the Jesus fever! And *marry* in *this* village—no!'

'She's right, Father. They're all clods.'

Aldo flung his wineglass into the fireplace, stood up. He pulled off his broad belt, doubled it in his heavy hands, and waved it in the air.

'I'm going to skin both of you! Bloody your asses!'

He didn't; he was too full of wine. But two nights later he found Grego in the donkey stable taking down a brown straw-woven suitcase that had belonged to an uncle long dead of knife wounds.

'I'm leaving,' said Grego, wiping dust from his hands. 'And if you take off your belt, I'll knock you into the donkey shit.'

It wasn't really much of a fight, Grego told Irena later that night. 'He's getting old and fat and his wind was bad. I hit him only twice, once in the pasta-basket and once in the side of the head with a bit of harness. He didn't even bleed much.'

Grego left his birthplace before morning, carrying the straw suitcase. Irena walked him down to the winding white road that led away from Empoli. He promised again to send for her when he got to America.

'They've discovered gold in California, in pure lumps right at the grass roots. I will send for you.'

'If you don't, I'll curse you with one of Timo's worst spells.' She kissed his cheek and clung to him. 'I have these dreadful curses from her, so if you fail me . . . ' She laughed, wept—a solid, beautiful girl, powerful in her emotions. 'And in return, Grego, I will try to remain a virgin.'

Gregorio Taddeo Fiore went off with a few gold coins, and not much else, in his suitcase. A young man, clever, rather ignorant, with no idea of the world or the human condition, he was sure he could not only survive but also answer any challenge.

The hard shipboard life taught him much about survival—and patience. In fact, it was not until 1851 that twenty-two-year-old Grego saw the port of San Francisco. As the miserable second mate of a stinking Dutch vessel, the *Eel*, he had had enough of the backbreaking labor and long monotonous months at sea. He jumped ship at the first opportunity.

The village of Yerba Buena, where the sea-weary youth came ashore, had only been called San Francisco since 1846, when the American marines appeared on the peninsula, hauled down the Mexican flag at the Presidio, and christened the new city.

George (the 'Gregorio' had been dropped during several voyages along the English Coast) Fiore had learned a workable English from all the time he had spent with British seamen and shippers. So, carrying a waxed-canvas bundle, his entire possessions, he landed, thinking: They will either hang me or in time honor me. Right now my neck is worried.

2

He walked among a bedlam of Chinese, Mexicans, Yankees, Swenksies—some pounding their boots in the muddy street, others on horseback splashing up dirt. Tents and shacks surrounded him, and lively signs beckoned: 'HASH HOUSE,' 'BEER AND SPIRITS,' 'STAR DANCE HALL,' 'HARRIS AND STRAUSS, MEN'S APPAREL,' 'KENDRICK GOLD EXCHANGE,' 'MINERS' ROOST.'

It was all crude but fascinating. These whiskered men in muddy boots and polished top hats, drunks and dogs, Chinese with pigtails and baskets of vegetables. George noticed hard-eyed men smoking cheroots, their waistcoats of Joseph's colors showing gold chains and nuggets hanging from them.

Groups of riders, saddlebags heavy, rode by shouting strange war cries: one rider almost ran George down and shouted. 'Want yer fuckin' head knocked off?'

George didn't, and retreated farther up the wooden sidewalk. He had dropped over the side of the ship without breakfast and his stomach was demanding food. Outside a gray tent with its flaps tied back hung a sign: 'HATTIE'S HASH HOUSE—HOME COOKING.'

He entered, to be met by greasy air, the crackling sounds of frying, saw crowded long wooden tables and benches occupied by an assortment of rough-dressed men feeding voraciously from tin platters and plates, knives inserted into open mouths and intercepted by raillery, all the while spitting out gristle and bones.

A stout middle-aged woman maneuvering a tray shouted at him, 'Sit down, buster, or get out.'

'I'll sit. What do you have?'

'Beans, bacon, two dollars. Coffee, two bits.'

A tin plate of food was slammed down before him after he handed over some of the precious United States coins he had managed to acquire in Panama. His entire fortune consisted of six Dutch gold coins, four English ones, and some Spanish silver disks of which he didn't know the value. The bacon was rancid, but as a sailor he was used to that. The beans were tasty, cooked in some native sauce. He broke off chunks of coarse bread and sopped up the sauce and found the tin cup contained something never closely related to coffee, perhaps acorns or parched wheat. What a marvelous, wild, practical society. The feeding went on, some finishing, others slipping into place on the benches. Whiskers stained with food helped by a whiskey flask—jaws chewing, a great hawking and spitting, mouths in continual danger from the two-pronged iron forks and the feeding directly off the knife blades. On George's right was a huge man with a flowing ginger-colored beard. The man cut a sliver off the plank table and picked his teeth with it. His stare was myopic and complacent.

'Jasus, I can remember when the greasers served you a suckling pig and goddamn drinkable wine.'

George gave up on the coffee. The man looked around him, worked his toothpick. 'Of course, since we vigilantes hanged a few fucking bastards, and drove out some of the hurr-masters, it's settled down a fair bit. You a guinea?'

'I was born in Italy.'

'That's what I said. No offense meant. You gonna go to the gold diggings?'

'Are they far?'

'Up around Hangtown, all along the Sacramento, but shit, they're worked out. Beyond that, to pan for gold you need a grub sack, tools. It's dumb assholes' game and hard work. Jasus, pick-and-shovel panning and flues and long toms, ice water up to your balls, and claim jumpers if your panning shows gold signs.'

George saw many of the feeders carried weapons in holsters in waistbands.

'You've mined?'

'Mined? Me, muck around like some wet rat? My maw didn't raise up no crazy chillin. Martin T. Wilkins is the name. Land and Main Street Frontage. Values double in land plots every two months.' The man nodded, stood up, held out a large hand.

'See my sign by the Embarcadero, cross from the big wharf? Anytime you figure to invest in land, see Martin T. Land, God ain't making it anymore.'

George Fiore sat over the cold coffee until the stout woman thumped his head with her right hand of knuckles.

'Don't go fall asleep here, mister. You get, go on your way.'

What was the way? He stood in front of the eating place watching a Chinese carefully shovel up fresh horse droppings into a pot, with neatness and care, as if he were handling hothouse fruit. Down the street, some loafers with a whoop and holler had tied cans to a yellow mongrel's tail and the animal went rushing down the muddy thoroughfare. There were pistol shots, but no one seemed to pay any attention.

A young man, hardly a man, more like a damaged boy, small, thin, with bare dirty feet, a bruise across one cheek, touched George's seaman's jacket.

'Please, mista, *anglaise?* I no eat longa time.'

George was about to cuff the young beggar, but recognized an Italian accent in the badly pronounced English.

He asked in Italian, '*Ragazzo*, where are you from? Naples? Florence?'

'Sicily. Catania.'

'Long way from home.'

Out poured a story of an orphan, apprenticed to a stone

23

cutter in Palermo ('Christ tear his entrails out'), going on with his cruel master to Mexico to repair a church in Puerto Hermosillo. Being cast off there, coming to California with a cargo of mules, and living on garbage. Bitten by dogs, kicked by the Yankees. Hungry, hungry. Sleeping in barrels, and no *preghiera* (prayer) answered, ready to jump into the bay. His name was Rocco Bordone. He was fourteen years old and could handle tools, cut stone, castrate lambs, and work leather. He wrung his dirty hands and pleaded. He knew a place where for four bits he could get a plate of horse meat, maybe mule, and a stack of tortillas.

George Fiore, like most Italians from boot-shaped Italy, didn't care for Sicilians. They had a bad reputation for using muskets instead of the respectable knife, and were involved in endless feuds and vendettas. But this boy was thin, pitiful, so he have him a half-dollar and fought off the kissing of his hand and the soiled embrace. It was a lesson, he thought; you could easily end up a tramp, an outcast here in this hurrying crowd among strangers. A man had to look to himself. Perfect his English, speak it as a native. Keep a steely precision of mind. He had worn off his soft edges in his time at sea, had been toughened by frustration. Supporting beggars from his meager handful of coins was foolish ...

He slept that night for a dollar, in a clipper ship that had been hauled ashore, its mast cut off, its hull riddled with windows, and flies and fleas were very active in the straw pallets. George decided to find some parklike area and sleep in the open until he started for the goldfields.

Rocco was waiting for him outside the converted ship, big eyes wide in hope of another coin.

'Fuck off,' George said in English, and added in Italian, 'Go drown yourself.'

'You are going to the mines, you will need many things.'

'You pimping for someone?'

'No, no, but most here are dishonest merchants, selling the picks and shovels made of tin, the beans moldy. But I

24

know the heretics, the Mormons, hard men but honest dealers.'

'Lead the way.'

They walked past storefronts advertising games of chance: hazard, stud poker, vingt-et-un.

That is how George Fiore first met Moses Kendrick, in a large unpainted structure with a high false front and foot-high red letters on it: 'KENDRICK BAZAAR AND GENERAL SUPPLIES.'

George had already encountered the Kendrick spirit of enterprise—the Kendrick Livery Stables across from the ship hotel and Moses Kendrick Timber & Construction Company nearby. Kendrick's Bazaar and General Supplies seemed to be the biggest Kendrick operation: a chaotic array of coal oil, dried codfish, coffee, pungent rubbing ointments, and various smells George could not identify. Hung or stacked along rough sawed plank walls still weeping rosin were horse harnesses, assorted picks, shovels, shelves of patent nostrums, medical items, counters of boots, rough canvas miners' pants and jackets, beehive-shaped hats.

In front were red-painted bins full of loose beans, crackers, dried fruits, rice. George was amazed at the plenty. Racks of shotguns, rifles, and pistols, hunting knives, camp cooking gear.

Rocco said with awe, 'They have *everything*.'

Several clerks in gray aprons scurried about serving a pack of hairy men and a woman in a blue dress. There was a tall man with a fringe of brown beard along his chin, no mustache above the sensual lips, the eyes wide, his bulky torso dressed in ample-cut black broadcloth. He seemed amused at George and Rocco's wonder at the various items. His noncommittal expression covered a strong personality, unlikely to be taken in by swindlers or frauds.

'I'm Moses Kendrick. I own the whole shebang, sailor. I can outfit you, but you're not going to get rich in the diggings. Not unless you hit a bonanza, and they're pretty rare these days.'

'I want to try. I had a grandmother who said being a fool is sometimes educating.'

The man shrugged, but showed interest. 'You will need a mule from my livery stable, a sack of beans, some smoked pork and dried apples. Drink coffee? I'll give you whole beans so you can grind them up with your pistol butt.'

'I don't have a pistol.'

'Well, you'll need one where you'll be going. I've a good old Navy Colt .45. All this comes a mite high. There's also a panning dish, and some other fittings, like skillet, pick and shovel, and other things.'

'No wonder I need a mule.' George took out a small leather bag and extracted four gold Dutch coins.

The merchant studied them, shrewdly hefted them in a big hand.

'Oh, about fifty, sixty dollars' worth. Tell you what I'll do, sailor. I'll grubstake you for half the outfit. Victuals, a jenny mule, the tools.'

'What's grubstake?'

'Grubstake? That means I'm half-partner for use of the supplies and outfit. I get half of what you find. *Why* do I trust you? 'Cause Moses Kendricks is fool enough to think he's a judge of people. Most folk I wouldn't trust with a big spit. What were you before you went to sea?'

George gave his name (Anglo version) and briefly sketched his history. Kendrick listened attentively, at the same time keeping a careful eye on several miners spitting amber tobacco juice into a brass gaboon at their feet.

'Look, George, forget the mining. It's sure as sin back-breaking disappointment. You know farm products and have been knocking about the world. I'll set you up with a horse and wagon, and you go out among the Chinese and Mexicans farming along the bay and river and buy up produce, melons and other fruit, vegetables, chickens, a porker. There's a shortage of fresh products in San Francisco. The galoots are all crazy to dig gold. I want to open a big market.'

'As a partner?' George asked.

'Nope. Pay you ten dollars a week and free grub and bed, and give you a bit of an edge in any supplies you buy here.'

'You own a lot now ... No, I'd rather be on my own.'

'It's a free country, Mr Greeley's paper tells us. Yep.'

'You'll still—what you call it? Grubstake?'

'Half. When your back aches and you're eating the jenny mule and drop over near dead, we'll talk some more.' He nodded, smiled, and yelled to one of the clerks. 'Homer! Put together a full miner's outfit here for Mr Forollo.'

'Fiore.'

'Sure.' Kendrick took a three-inch section of rock candy from the jar and handed it to Rocco. 'Shut your mouth around this, boy. Lick it, don't bite it.'

So, armed with a copy of Webster's *Grammar* and Parson Weems's *Washington*, George Taddeo Fiore and Rocco Bordone loaded a mule and, skillet and tools clanging, started for the diggings beyond Hangtown. They joined a steady stream of men, and even a few women, carrying packs or leading mules, some going out by ferry to Vallejo, Oakland, Suisun Bay, some trekking along the Sacramento, others going inland following wagon tracks, all hoping to find their fortune.

Moses Kendrick, at the age of thirty, had followed a feisty elder of the Latter Day Saints, Samuel Brannan, to California. The party of Mormon immigrants was seeking a haven on the Pacific coast to escape the antipolygamist fervor of their neighbors. They arrived only to find the Stars and Stripes flying over the Presidio and the authority they thought they had escaped entrenched in the new frontier. Sam was so outraged that he threw down his hat and stomped it into the dust. Moses Kendrick, on the other hand, saw opportunity and set up a general merchandise business. Brannan, impressed by Kendrick's shrewdness, put up shop at Sutter's Mill, close to the gold strikes; Moses, in a shack made of ship's timbers and raw boards, set up his business near the ferry station. In time, the two

27

new businessmen began to cooperate, becoming informal partners rather than rivals. They began to build new lives in this foreign land.

With self-restraint, Kendrick had left behind two wives in Salt Lake City and come out with Sarah, his most mature spouse, and three husky sons, aged ten to twelve, who helped the clerks in various tasks. Moses was pernickety but honest, and a shrewd dealer in horse trading, livery stables, and other enterprises. Pious, obsessed with morality, he paid a share of his gains to the mother church in Salt Lake City, and Brigham Young blessed his prosperity.

In contrast, Elder Sam Brannan and his flock refused to pay any tithe to the church and became jack-Mormons, as those who left the church were called. Sam took to drinking and cursing, and was so taken with the bawdy world of San Francisco that some said he frequented the brothels of the booming Barbary Coast.

A man of quick temper, Sam felt Moses wanted to end his partnership/friendship with the fallen-away Mormon. Moses' shrewd pragmatism provided a gentle lapse of the first without losing the second, and without hurting Sam's feelings.

One day, Sam, in Moses Kendrick's office, was drinking whiskey, which like profanity and tobacco was forbidden to a true follower of the Saints. 'Oh, our Brother Brigham'— Sam grinned—'has you by the balls and he's squeezing, eh? Hell, Moses, you're a good thousand miles from the old ram, we owe him *nothing*.'

'I owe the church my faith, my share of the tithes. Brother Young isn't without a sting in his tail, Sam.'

Sam sipped his drink, waved an arm in the air.

'Those pious gun-handlers of his? The Destroying Angels, the Danites? Shit, I've got my own vigilance committee. I call 'em the Exterminators.'

'Sam, we may still do business, but I lift no hand against any man. What Brother Young does comes from a word with God.'

'Fair enough.'

Moses took no part in the deadly war between Brother Young's gunslingers and the vigilantes controlled by Sam Brannan. Sam was smart and farsighted, and forced confrontations to his own advantage. He sent out his Exterminators to intercept the Destroying Angels in the middle of the bone-dry desert. There was gunpowder smoke, and blood was spattered on ancient rocks; some shooting, some killing; and the Destroying Angels either went back to Salt Lake City or joined Brannan's flock. Many of them prospered all along the river from Sutter's Mill down to the Golden Gate.

'It's Sam's way, not mine, even if we are brother Mormons,' Moses told a journalist who had crossed the plains to write of the war of the Danites. There were those who said that Moses Kendrick was 'a cold fish with twenty-dollar gold coins for eyes,' who worked his sons—Chass, Tom, and Homer—'like they were niggers picking cotton,' and that Sarah Kendrick took the switch to them when she felt they needed it. In fact, Sarah gave the sharp edge of her temper to Moses himself when he suggested sending for Agnes, one of his younger wives.

They lived in a cottage with a small pipe organ, one block from the store. They had lightning rods, stained-glass windows, and red climbing roses around the veranda. Sarah had hard blue eyes and it was rumored she dyed her hair, but her apple pies were tasty. Moses went his own way, doing business with gentiles and Mormons, Jewish merchants, and even the remains of the Spanish land-grant families like the Velasquezes—land-rich but money-poor, now that the Yankees were taxing them. Moses was neither arrogant nor hostile to new ideas. He was interested in talk of a railroad east, steamships, and huge water dredges to seek out the gold the miners missed picking over the surface 'as if they were looking for lice,' as he said.

He was forever practical. When it was pointed out by an imported New England minister that Moses rented buildings to sinners, drove his rivals to the wall, and sold

29

whiskey he didn't drink, Moses just smiled.

'I am Lot at Sodom with fingers in my ears.'

Some months later,after heavy blue rains, George Fiore and Rocco returned to Moses Kendrick's store. They were soiled and tattered, their clothing covered with miner's muck.

George wearily approached Moses, who was watching his son Homer hammer lumps of hard sugar from a blue-wrapped cone.

'Mr Kendrick, we didn't eat the goddamned mule. She's outside.'

Moses examined George's gaunt face, a two-inch beard on cheeks and jawline. 'A damn fool would have stayed on and starved to death eating rats.'

George put limp buckskin down on the counter. 'It's about two ounces, I will owe you the rest.'

'Don't owe me nothing. When I grubstake a man, I'm taking a gamble big as his. I lose too.' He yelled at a clerk, 'Jake, give the boy here some lemon drops and a pair of pants. His ass is sticking out. Boots, too, before his toes get away. George, come into my office.'

The office consisted of a big black safe with a full colored sunset painted on it and one word: 'KENDRICK.' A rolltop desk, three chairs, and a print of Joseph Smith receiving the Book of Mormons from an angel, and a photograph of Brigham Young in frock coat and top hat, he seated nearly engulfed by half a dozen of his wives.

'No use horsing around, George. You are so poor you can't make change from a matchstick.' He picked up a map from the desk.

'Now, after we bathe you—you got mule stink all over you— I'm giving you a good horse with good hocks, a well-hung wagon. You go out to the Chinese farms and the Mex families growing things in Velasquez land, San Leandro, San Bruno, along the San Pedro Crick, across to Sausalito. Buy me produce. Like I said, fruit, greens, potatoes, eggs if you can, ducks, a few porkers, a heifer.'

'I want fifteen dollars a week.'

'Twelve. Don't push me, sailor. I want to make sure you're a good commodities man.'

'Commodities?'

'The farm stuff.'

'I want to bring my sister Irena over from Empoli.'

Moses Kendrick handed George the map. 'You be as right as I think you are for this job, and I'll advance you passage money against your pay, say three dollars a week taken off. People say nobody ever got rich picking up the half-dollars I drop, but I keep my word. They also say I'm a good judge of character. Well, I'm not always. I make mistakes, like the Lord, *He* made snakes. Oh, I'll pay that boy Rocco two dollars a week as your helper. Come to supper tonight. The next street over, the white clapboard house with piazza. Sister Kendrick is roasting a goose.'

George didn't speak. He stood in his tattered clothing, smelling his own reeking body odor. The sole of one of his boots flapped like a loose tongue. He took the map from Moses' hand and went out, trying to keep the loose sole from flapping. Moses rubbed the fringe of beard and took up a ledger, lifted a steel-nibbed pen stuck in a potato, dipped it in a brown ink, and on a clean page of the ledger wrote in a looping hand: 'GEORGE FIORE *18th Apr. 1852 #1 Hoss. 1 wagon.*'

3

Bathed and barbered at Larkspur's Bath and Barber Shop, decently clothed, George and Rocco presented themselves at the Kendrick house. Sarah Kendrick wasn't the dragon many of the town gossips reported. There was a bit of the New England schoolteacher in her, which had been there since before she made the Mormon trek to Salt Lake City as a convert to become one of Moses' wives.

'Well, now, you speak good English, Fiore,' she said as she passed plates of sliced goose that her husband was carving. There were also steaming mounds of mashed potatoes, golden cobs of sweet corn drenched in country butter, and foamy mugs of cider.

'I've been reading,' George admitted. 'And I learned some English on the coal barges working on the British coast, Liverpool to Dover.'

'Ah, there is still an English accent. The use of a soft A will help that.'

Rocco, wiping goose grease from his chin, said, 'I too learn very good.'

Moses viewed the remains of the goose, fingering his narrow band of thin whiskers. 'The sailor is going to scout out produce for me to put into a market I'm setting up on Clark Street. You two lads, Homer and Chass, will help Fiore run it.'

Homer, at sixteen the oldest son, looked up from a goose drumstick he was gnawing on. He had a sharp foxlike face over prominent teeth: for all that, George thought, there was a cheerful brightness about the youth, an audacious watchfulness.

'Pa, I'd rather clerk or work in the livery and hack stables.'

Sarah cut a huge apple pie. 'You'll do as you're told, Homer. Brother Fiore, you can borrow my Gibbon *Decline and Fall of the Roman Empire*. You being Italian and all that.'

George answered that he'd be pleased to borrow that work of history. He no longer felt so alien and alone, now that he was among such kindly folk.

When Rocco and he retired for the night in a loft over the Kendrick barn, they lay for a long time logy with food on pallets stuffed with dried corn husks, covered with red trade-goods blankets.

Rocco whispered, 'It is a dream. We wake up, all gone.'

George listened to the peep-peep of barn mice some place in the structure, heard the horses below move about crunching corn. 'No dream, Rocco, no dream.' George turned on his side. 'My belly she not a dream, feels right.' He touched the four volumes of the history Sarah Kendrick had made him take along. *Such* thick books, *so* many pages, so *much* print; he had a pervading sense of futility trying to capture so much wisdom. He fell asleep dreaming the books were large enough to float him on the sea, and there onshore waving to him was his sister Irena, yelling *'Poca favilla! Poca favilla!'*

In the morning, after a breakfast of fried eggs, codfish balls, and soda biscuits, Moses showed George and Rocco to a green-painted wagon, an aging brown mare harnessed to it. 'You cross over the bay and just follow some of the roads like marked on that map. Tess here is a bit long in the tooth for a horse but the wagon's solid; a new back axle, got the wagon in a deal with Sam Brannan when we parted as partners.'

Rocco brandished a whip, swished it. 'Oh, good. I make the horse a-run!'

'No, just meander along.' Moses handed George a canvas bag of silver coins. 'Bargain for every batch, offer half what they ask, come up a mite, then if *no* deal, give it up.'

George accepted Moses' instructions impassively. His calm, he knew, was only external, as he slapped reins on Tess's rump and started for the ferry station to cross to the new way of life awaiting him across the bay.

So began, in hope, naiveté, ardor, George Fiore's career as a produce buyer for Moses Kendrick. He and Rocco and the mare Tess soon knew all the dirt roads to the Chinese farms, the Latins' garden patches, pig sties, and poultry yards. He learned to bargain, to laugh down prices, eat sage-flavored liver pudding, drink buttermilk, and shake his head at preposterous deals. He became quick, lucid, and bold, a most knowledgeable produce-farm man. He and Rocco, aided by Homer Kendrick, set up market stalls in the city, polished the fruits, and displayed the vegetables, sides of bacon, crates of geese, ducks, chickens, sometimes a live suckling piglet with one leg tied to a wagon spoke.

George didn't have much time for reading Roman history but he did burrow into the volumes, and taught Rocco how to speak Yankee-style properly. He himself watched his accent and recalled rules of verbs from the Webster *Grammar* which he had worn to tatters at the mines.

He and Rocco shared a room under a sloping ceiling in a house near the market, run by the widow of a Cornish miner; their landlady offered board and room to clerks, city officials, small shopkeepers ('all gentlemen, now, hain't we? No hanky-panky after hours, now, righto?').

George acquired from Moses Kendrick's stock of weapons a Hawkins rifle which he would bring along on his routes to down prairie hens and wild turkeys, which he often brought as gifts to Sarah Kendrick.

She insisted he take a volume of Voltaire or Swift along on his trips. 'Mr Kendrick, he reads nothing but the Book of Mormon and delayed copies of Mr Greeley's New York *Herald*.' Sarah, though a Mormon convert, was proud of her Boston background and the education her family had acquired many years ago.

She saw that Moses' attitude to George was that of a master proud of a good servant. But she sensed that George sought, if not a partnership, at least more freedom to do business for himself.

Moses' own sons had not attended school and had been taught by their mother. 'They are hardly students, beyond ciphering and some spelling. I can't get much into their heads. And Mr Kendrick says God gave hands for work, not to open books. He doesn't care,' Sarah lamented.

Clearly Sarah saw some anomalies of character in this

Italian youth, an unusual drive to educate himself. In him she saw two invaluable qualities: a zeal for self-improvement and a knack for pleasing Moses. There was an instantaneous rapport between this isolated woman and the (to her) exotic stranger, so different from her own sons, so given to the casual perversity of the frontier.

George was amazed at his own skill in bargaining, in setting up attractive market stalls, at his ability to talk down the grievance of some seller or buyer. He had assumed most people had this knack, a flexibility and art of seeing clearly, acting firmly. He soon learned that wasn't so, that he had something special that was constant and functional, that was part of his nature. He knew Moses was watching him closely, and grew resentful, thinking that the Mormon suspected him of cheating.

It was six months after he had begun his buying trips that he ventured farther to the sparse fringes of the desert, lured by hopes of picking up a bargain heifer or two in a ranch he had heard of run by a Dutchman named Borden. George had camped for the night by the roadside, fed Tess a nosebag of oats, eaten a skillet of chipped beef and sliced potatoes, and smoked his pipe. He did not care for the cigars, cheroots, and stogies that most men smoked.

His thoughts were with Irena. He was sending for her soon, saving money at Mr Ralston's Bank of California. As he lazed by the fire, his mind wandered, thinking of women—not any particular woman, merely a hope that one would appear. A physical being, all warm flesh and curves, to keep and love and have *bambini* with. He had tumbled (driven by his 'juices', as he put it) a few tarts, and they were satisfying enough for a young male; but the great love he sighed for was only a misty vision, remote and unreal ... He knocked out his pipe and prepared to sleep. If Rocco had been with him, he might have talked on the subject of love, passion, body games. But Rocco and Homer were building a smokehouse at the market to prepare their own bacon and hams.

George awoke in the cold dawn to a barren, hostile desert vista, the sun just peering over the rocky landscape to the east. He harnessed Tess and drove up toward the Dutchman's ranch, noting the dry scrub, the dwarf oaks, gullies cut deeply into the ravines where cloudbursts and spring floods had come, engulfing everything, then drained away, leaving a parched landscape. He reached for the water bottle under the seat and had just raised it to his lips when there was a sudden flurry of violent action, and the canvas-covered bottle was torn from his hands; he knew at once with a shock that he was being shot at.

His reflexes were quick. He dived under the seat of the wagon and was reaching for the Hawkins rifle as another shot splintered the side of the wagon. The mare quivered but did not move. George went over the far side of the wagon and, crouching, rushed to an outcropping of red rock. There was room for his body behind one big boulder. Slowly, carefully, he lifted his head, and a slug came with a twanging whine from another direction shattering on the boulder. He fell back to think, the Hawkins held at the ready.

It could hardly be bandits; the horse and wagon were not a highwayman's idea of treasure. The silver coins in the canvas bag would not be worth a bushwhacking—not with miners' gold and silver so readily available.

He wriggled quickly along on his belly, rifle held in front, thinking. Then it came to him: he was driving a wagon known to be Sam Brannan's. Clearly Brigham Young had sent out a new detachment of Avenging Angels, who had mistaken him for that son of a bitch Sam, the backsliding jack-Mormon who was defying their leader. There was a thick growth of spicebush, and George moved behind it— aware that there were probably at least two Avenging Angels out there. He had no idea of their precise location, but they had come close, very close.

The spicebushes ended abruptly at a low dishlike drop, heat waves pulsing off the stony sterile ground. About fifty yards away was a veined outgrowth of layered rock, shaped, he thought, like the picture of an elephant he had once seen in a book. Something moved behind it. A man's head appeared; a rifle was clearly etched in the sunlight. George moved slowly forward; he would have to kneel, even move his feet to get off a telling shot. There was a slight rise, and one of his boots stumbled against a large whitish stone, which fell away, knocking against other stones and setting up a clacking sound. The Avenging Angel moved at once, rose, and swiftly aimed his rifle. George was on his feet, darting to the left as a slug moved past him. In one gesture he lifted his rifle and aimed as he had done so many times at home to hit fast-moving small game. He pressed the trigger. The rifle made a loud sharp sound. For a moment, the Avenging Angel seemed to hang suspended in air, then fell. George moved another shell into the firing chamber and went slowly forward, warily looking to the left and right. He was ten feet from the body when it twisted itself around, exposing a head half shot away. There seemed to be no right eye, but there was enough animation left for a palsied hand to lift up a pistol. George, very close, fired directly into the head, and it shattered. Not fully aware of doing it, driven by some reflex of anger, he kicked the body, hearing his boot heel thump into the chest of the now dead man. He was slightly ashamed of how good it felt.

As he bent over, a shot passed over his head and he knew he had stupidly forgotten the fact that there was at least one more killer. He moved. Fell prone between two boulders and waited. From time to time there were shots, but he held his own fire. He had only eight bullets left and he cursed his frugal folly. Off to the right, the mare and wagon were outlined in the bright day, the horse chomping on dry grass. George grew thirsty. The water bottle lay shattered by the wagon. He hunkered down, peering out from time to time. After long dry hours, dusk came, and as the dark fell, he heard something moving about.

An old trick of Italian smugglers came to him. When the lawmen were closing in, the smugglers would toss stones into far thickets to draw the pursuers away from them.

He gathered some large stones and threw them far to the left. There was a flash of fire about sixty yards away. The night flared up for a moment in a small rose of red fire from the barrel of a gun. In two minutes he threw another just past where he had thrown the first. Again the barrel flare in the night, just a bit to the right of the first shot. George fired two more shots in that direction. There was return fire. Throughout the night he fired twice again, and when he had three bullets left, he stopped shooting. There had been no return fire the last two times. There were three possibilities, he figured: the enemy could be out of cartridges, playing possum, or have decamped. As his thirst intensified, he had to fight down panic. Morning would tell.

Just before the sun rose, Goerge circled behind the place from which he assumed the last shots had come. He waited a half-hour, being careful and slow and very wary; he was once frightened by the whirl of some wild fowl rising from a nest of speckled eggs. Then he saw the blue shape, sprawled legs, a body, an arm gripping a Henry Brass Boy carbine. He approached almost on tiptoes. A big, bearded man lay there on his back, mouth open, showing stained teeth. The man had pulled up his blue flannel shirt, exposing a hairy belly, torn flesh, broken bits of ribs. There was a gaping hole from which blood slowly oozed. Some flies had gathered to explore the wound. The man was still alive. He had turned his head, the eyes staring up at George. The lips moved; no sound came. There was a canteen on the sand, and George kicked aside the carbine as he retrieved the precious container. He rattled it and found it nearly full. Unscrewing the top, he drank noisily, gulping water, letting it run from his mouth down his chin to his neck and chest.

He examined the man: nothing could save him with that gaping ugly wound. It had been a lucky shot in the night. George touched the body with a boot toe. The mouth moved again; the eyes rolled from side to side as if signaling some futile hope. George felt no pity for murdering the bastard, no sympathy for whatever religous fanaticism had sent the two gunmen out on this deadly errand. They would have had no mercy on him, he knew. He stepped back and sent a slug into the head of the prone figure, then turned away.

He never told anyone but Moses what had happened, and that night's adventure appeared to be the Avenging Angels' last desperate attempt to do in Sam Brannan.

4

In 1853, the San Francisco commodities and produce merchant George Fiore wrote to his sister Irena:

It has been so many years, and my heart sings with the joy at the thought of seeing you again. I am glad you will have Father Orsini's sister Maria as a companion.

There are three ways to come to the west coast of this America. You can go around the Horn, but that way risks bad weather, and the voyage is very long. Or you can take the steam trains from New York or Boston to Saint Joseph (Saint Joe, they call it); or from New Orleans take a boat up the river called the Mississippi and to Saint Joseph and join a line of wagons crossing the plains and mountains. There is much danger from red savages if you go this way. The third way is the route I want you to travel. That is to take the ship to the Isthmus of Panama, land at the city called Colon, attach to a pack train across the neck of the isthmus to Panama City, where you will board a ship hired by my patron Mr Kendrick to deliver you, dear sister, to my waiting

39

embrace. A young American friend is helping me write this letter to you, to make sure I give you clear directions in English words you can understand. It will be so much easier for you when you arrive. I am pleased you and your traveling companion have been taking English lessons from the English nun. I don't remember Maria Orsini, but I hope she has some trade, seamstress or cook. If as you say she plans to seek a husband, tell her the men are mostly heretic Protestants or Mormons. The Mexicans are in Holy Mother Church, but most poor and ignorant. There are also the China fellows, and they are heathen.

I am doing well—no pots of gold or a glass coach with footmen in uniform, but I have my own section of the produce market in partnership with Mr Kendrick and his son Homer. We go out twice a week to farms to gather fruits and vegetables.

I am also buying timbers from sawmills, all on my own. Also, I am paying for some land in this place. There is good footage on some of the streets being developed now as more people crowd in. The land has been made larger by filling in the bay, building over the hulls of many ships left to rot. Hard to think that just over twenty years or so ago this was a little village of thirty families and called Yerba Buena. Then came the gold and the Americans. Now it is so crowded that Sam Brannan (a local person of business and loud talk) says 'so crowded no room to swing a cat' (American humor). Rocco and I (I wrote you of him, my assistant) have a little house on North Point and there is room for you and Maria Orsini until she gets settled.

Place flowers on Father's grave, pay for a small mass. I did not love him but I feel a son's duty to make respects to his soul.

So come è sempre l'ora.

> Your brother,
> George
> (one time Gregorio)

The city of Colon stank, pigs ran free in the streets, and there were dark men of all shades: Indians, Negroes, mestizos. The roaches shared people's meals and an insidious fever epidemic killed poeple in the night. But Irena, buoyant and resilient, was happy to get off the four-master *De Grue* after the three-week Atlantic crossing. She had been uncomplaining during the difficult voyage—treating the seasick and trying to make decent the foul cabin she shared with Maria Orsini, who retched, threw up, spit bile, clutched her large brass cross, and asked God to receive her without the last rites, for there was no priest on board. Maria did not die. She came ashore, helped by Irena Fiore to the Blue Parrot Inn, where she lay with a wet cloth dipped in vinegar on her head and asked for a priest.

Irena shouted, 'Damn you, Maria, you'll outlive us all! Clean yourself—there's a basin and a water bucket. Wash, do your hair! We both reek like a pigsty from that sea trip.'

'I forgive you your language, your blasphemy.'

'Forgive? No, thanks. I dragged you from a rotting dull arsehole of a village; I'm going to marry you off to my brother Grego, one of the richest nabobs in the land.'

Maria buried her head in the gray pillow. 'They're lust-filled men who—'

'They do what the good Lord meant men to do to women. If he didn't, he'd have us lay eggs. I'm going to meet the mule drivers.'

'Mules?'

'My brother's friend, Mr What's-his-name, brings supplies across this damn neck of jungle, so we are in the hands of his people here. Go comb your hair.'

Maria repeated she was dying and clutched her rosary and scapula. Irena shook her head and went out. A rooster crowed somewhere till someone or something caused it to break off with a squawk. The heat was damp, and Maria wondered why she had gone off on this mad trip. She was a handsome woman of twenty-eight; no one in the village had seemed fit for a husband. She had wanted to become a nun, but as a novice, the food made her ill. The kneeling prayers on the icy stone floors of the chapel gave her colds and filled her lungs with water. It was her brother, Father Orsini, who had agonized over Irena's story that Grego Fiore was now a rich man across the sea, and wanted a good Italian wife, a pious Catholic one. An order from her brother the priest was to Maria like a word from the Pope himself.

So she had sailed—lamenting, dressed in black, carrying two rosaries, and a book of the lives of the saints (St Teresa was her favorite, but she had a leaning toward St Catherine, the one Irena mockingly said was 'cooked on the griddle over a good hot fire').

Maria was attractive, her hair inky black and wavy, her long face handsome if somewhat stern. Her body, that burden, so very ripe, Irena insisted, for many *bambini*. Maria crossed herself. It was God's wish and Jesus' hope to do what husbands and wives did, good Christians together. St Paul had preached, 'It is better to marry than to burn.' She had seen a bull copulating with the family cow, and a pet dog of the village mayor's wife had a habit of rubbing himself against her in great excitement, exposing that pink sliver of a male creature so indecently. A good thing her brother insisted animals have no souls or they would be accursed for the evil of showing their lusts.

Maria was slumbering, damp with sweat, when Irena burst into the room carrying two white wheat rolls and what she called the 'apple-of-pine' of pale yellow.

'Up, up! We leave in two hours. Now eat, taste the apple-of-pine and drink wine.'

'I want water.'

'Not here, my lady. Water is deadly with fevers and gives the grinding in the belly. We ride mules, so take off your corset.'

'Mules! No, leave me here. I hear church bells, I am among my own.'

'Spanish priests fat as capons?'

In later years, Irena loved to describe that crossing of the Isthmus of Panama with a gang of cargo-carrying guides, the tinkle of mule bells, the knifelike sting of insects, the snakes hanging like living ropes from poisonous plants. Every time Irena told it, she added something extravagant, until she too could not recall if what she recounted of the dismal journey was true or not.

'Imagine a Turkish steam house, the air so thick you could almost bite it, skulls of animals and men along the trail, muck up to the knees, thorns with points like daggers. The mules braying, the guides cursing foul obscenities, whipping them, drinking brandy from wine skins. Why we didn't get raped, sold to Indians, cut open, I don't know. Only the fame of my brother's patron saved us, that and St Catherine. There were many such parties like ours; some died of fever on the trail. Yankees, Jews, Spaniards, Negroes, and yet somehow the cargoes, the lines of pack trains, went on. The smell of money creates daring deeds, eh? Often we met parties going the other way, coming from California and talking of wealth gained or lost on gold strikes. Maria would pray at some roadside shrine or grave. But when we got to Panama City and boarded the little steamship, even Maria cheered up. The ocean was so vast, so blue, smooth as a *bambino*'s ass.'

Irena's embellished tales never revealed that she had lied to Maria, and had invented the story that her brother wanted an Italian wife. That he was not aware of her plans for Maria. Somehow, Irena felt that bringing the two together would be a simple good deed. No great explanation would be needed. Grego must be starved for a fine Italian beauty, a splendid head, a magnificent body. Better, she told herself, than whatever Indian squaw, polished with bear grease, he had been mounting. Men did odd things when the urge was on them.

She had hopes for acquiring a mate herself. After all, she was getting long in the tooth, already at the end of her twenties and technically still a virgin. Perhaps a semivirgin. That summer, when she was learning English and also working in the scent factory where rose leaves and herbs were turned into perfumes, there had been the scientist

Julio from Madrid, who mixed the fragrant distillations properly. The two of them had tussled, touched each other, lain under the stars together drinking white Falerno. Perhaps there was a bit of penetration; the wine made it all hazy. She had gone to confession and said prayers, dozens of Hail Mary's, and paid for a series of novenas for her mother and father. How wise and decent of God to offer absolution and hold out a renewed state of grace.

The young person who had helped George Fiore write to Irena was Carrie Seabrook, Sarah Kendrick's niece. Also from old New England stock, Carrie, a non-Mormon, had appeared in San Francisco with brushes, tubes of paint, and a roll of canvas to capture the bay, desert, and city landscapes.

There was in Carrie a streak of the Bohemian which warred with her bluestocking background. She wore her red hair in a careless bun that always seemed to be tumbling down, and her long paint-stained fingers were strong as a man's. Two of them were colored by the nicotine from what she called her 'cigaroots'. She was small, just over five feet. Carrie dressed in what she called the 'Pre-Raphaelite' style. She wore loose clothes, with corsets and skirts that ended abruptly at the ankle rather than trailing behind, as was proper.

Carrie very early had become a 'new woman.' She admired Amelia Bloomer, read Byron. After her father and mother were drowned off Cape Cod in a summer sailing cruise, she outfoxed the family lawyer, who spoke of safe investments. She had gone to study painting in Paris, in Düsseldorf, and finally in London, where she claimed to have studied with Dante Gabriel Rossetti. She had a good eye for color but had difficulty with figures. Carrie had returned to Boston at twenty-five, only to face staunch disapproval of her smoking, her talk of the rights of women, and her occasional taste for gin. She had come out to see the wild country, 'to bathe naked in the Pacific,' and visit her Aunt Sarah.

George Fiore found her fascinating. He did not understand her talk of 'beating down the hierarchy of men' or the sad role of the subjugated woman. To him she was a new kind of personality to be accepted, as so many other eccentrics were, on a frontier where one didn't ask too many questions.

George took her along on one of his wagon trips to buy farm produce, and she painted watercolors at Tassaz Creek, the San Lorenzo hills, and at Eagle Point. He thought her a virtuoso but he confessed to Carrie, 'I don't know beans about art.'

George was amazed, delighted, and somewhat confused by her. Her beauty made her seem almost too innocent for the rhetoric and opinions she carried. There had been no such woman in Italy, certainly not in his village. As for the women of the ports, they had been whores, foul and coarse. He could not resist this creature.

On their second trip together, they sat under a tall tree munching cold chicken and the creatures that passed for lobsters on the Pacific coast.

'You know, George, they're not really lobsters. No big claws. They're some kind of crayfish, I'd say.' She licked her fingers free of the butter sauce, stood up, and stretched with pleasure. 'God, so much space out here, a good place to kick up one's legs and heels.'

'Watch out for the rattlers.'

They drank a native white wine George got in kegs from new vineyards up in Napa country. Carrie lit one of her cigarettes and plucked at a benzoin spicebush. Something was on her mind.

'You're an intriguing man, George. On the other hand, you're a shrewd man of business, as materialistic a man as I've ever met. But there's a wonderful primitive force in you, a sensitivity to beauty and life. You're a natural man, what Rousseau calls "the happy savage".'

'I'll kick his ass; I'm no savage.'

She leaned against him. 'Oh, you could be. Try.'

George had been intimate with too many women not to

45

know what she meant. And he longed for her passionately, with his body and his heart.

But it was the man who always made the advance, the proper gesture to a women who wasn't a whore. It was *his* place to pursue her; his mouth and limbs should seek out hers. That was the natural way with men and women.

He was shocked and thrilled as she wiped her hands on her loose skirt and stepped out of it. She released her blouse's row of buttons, saying, 'I don't like too much palaver about making love.'

George could only nod and feel himself erect. It seemed only right to slip off his own pants. They came together in the wild vetch grass, a strange sun overhead, and nearby, high up, some hawk hunting for his own lunch among reddish rocks. She was an ardent, vocal lover; half her sexual action seemed to be a kind of extreme gutter use of language urging him on, describing her sensation of their coupling, laced with oaths and obscenities that he had never heard before from a respectable woman. Her physical drive seemed to need the whip of foul language.

Still, it was grand, powerful, and he sensed this was something rare and precious to relish, revel in. Her climax at last stopped her vocal efforts and she lay panting under him, a small smile on her face, her eyes closed. He thought she had fainted or died, and when he tried to withdraw from her, she held him down with amazing strength in her arms.

He kissed her hard, almost brutally, then mouthed her neck, now damp and salty. He gently nuzzled her breasts— amazingly white, not large, but ample enough, his mouth teasing her nipples. She was suddenly very still. He found her staring up at him, hazel-brown eyes studying him. She said softly, 'It's going to be bloody allright.'

It was, for nearly seven months. He rented a little house facing the Pacific above Sausalito. Carrie set up a studio there and would stand at a bay window, a cigarette hanging from a corner of her mouth, painting various views in what she called 'Turner effects.' She always smelled of turpentine, her loose smock pale yellow, stained by

46

pigments, her hair lifted into a knot on top of her head, tied with a blue ribbon, pins falling from it.

George would stay two or three nights a week with her in the disordered studio. They made love on a sagging cot, danced naked before flames of driftwood in the stone fireplace while he broiled a steak on a grill.

They drank a lot of wine, and when Carrie was in a keyed-up mood, her painting either a disaster or a great success, she would add shot glasses of gin to their drinking. George was deeply in love, and too possesive. He was, after all, as he told her, 'an Italian, and we are family people. We like to be sure of each other, our family, our place in society and the church.'

'George Sand and George Eliot knocked that jolly crock of false respectability over long ago, darling. They were true women, no matter how they had to sign their work.'

George was aware he was going deeper into an unchartered relationship, one that should be unthinkable to his old-world Italian view. Yet he was bewitched. Marriage, he felt, would bring Carrie down to his kind of reality, soften her radical ways. He couldn't believe that he didn't understand Carrie Seabrook, that he really had no notion of the true girl. He could not accept that her piquant, audacious conversation was not merely a facade. There was a depth and a uniqueness to her, an artist's expectancy. Trying to change her would be like the woman who marries an alcoholic to get him to give up his drinking.

Of her paintings he could make nothing. They were nothing like the gold-framed pictures that decorated most houses: images of castles, kittens in baskets, horses, dogs with human expressions, historical events that had a finish called *real*. Carrie's pictures were not at all like those. Her lumpy human figures and misty landscapes were beyond him.

She never asked what he thought of her work. 'Artistically, darling, you have tapioca for brains.'

He began talking more of marriage, and she paid it no mind.

47

When he tried to get her to listen seriously to his ideas of family life and the future, Carrie would light another cigarette, cough, and shake her head. 'What we have now is good. I don't want what the numb world accepts blindly: eating, shitting, dying, without ever feeling the wonder of being alive. No, not likely for little Carrie. You want to muck everything up with housekeeping, smelly babies, and wondering if the butcher is giving you full weight.'

George didn't understand her at all. But when he heard from Irena that she was at last coming to join him, he decided to settle matters. Moses and Sarah Kendrick were aware of the tempestuous relationship, and unhappy about it. Sarah was upset that George and Carrie were breaking the moral code. Moses too felt the moral issue, but more important to him was the fact that a young man rising in society and the business world of San Francisco had obligations. One could take a mistress after marriage—the town would shut one eye—but it would never condone this bold and open relationship. An ambitious man had better change that.

It was a windy stormy day, the sea crashing against the rocks, when George finally confronted Carrie. She was in a foul temper. It had been a bickering time, and George and Carrie had come to the little house to 'talk things out' over the weekend. It had begun badly when Rocco had packed buttermilk instead of the clotted cream Carrie used in her coffee. The fireplace didn't draw properly because the wind was too strong in its erratic action as it came roaring down the chimney. Puffs of smoke caused them to cough and open the windows a bit. Carrie's mood worsened when she found she was out of her cigarettes. As the sea increased its fury, they could hear foghorns like some loud bronchial complaint—as ships in the fog were seeking anchorage. George and Carrie's mood seemed to merge, then separate emotionally.

They held filled wineglasses and looked at each other. There had been no lovemaking on the sagging cot. Carrie insisted it was her period. George tried to recall dates and failed. They sat, the day dying in the west. Fog seeped into the room, further dimming the large unframed pictures hung about the room. Carrie had been working, her mood gloomy and remote. Finally the silence broke.

'You may as well know. I can't stand much more. No, not you, George; you've been fine, just fine.' Her hand gripped his wrist. 'But soon I'm moving on from here.'

He shook her off, then grabbed her by the shoulders. 'What the hell are you saying? You *can't* leave.'

'I can and I will. I've been thinking of it for days, weeks really. An artist is a vulnerable human being. But there is in an artist some perverse special kind of bullshit conceit, a God-given talent that drives you up a wall.'

'You don't believe in God. Look, Carrie, we'll get married. I don't care about your crazy ideas, because I know you, really.'

She shook her head. 'You *don't* know me, George. I'm going back to London. I want to show the work I've done here. Europe is the only place for an artist. Europe ... I have to know if I am any bloody good as an artist.'

He pulled her to her feet, smashing the wineglass in his rage. 'We're getting married.'

For a moment or two she looked at him expressionlessly. Then she broke free, went to the clamshell she used for an ashtray, picked out a half-smoked cigarette, and lit it. Slowly she waved out the flame of the match.

'Marriage? Even if I favored it, which I don't, you're not my idea of a husband. You're uneducated and—yes, I'm shocked to find *this* prejudice in me. I wouldn't marry—what do you call your people here? I just couldn't marry a guinea.'

She was pale, shaking, perhaps at her own cruelty. In her fingers the short cigarette was dropping sparks.

George stood transfixed, like the steers he had seen stunned by a huge hammer before the final throat-cutting. He felt her rancor touch his body. Carrie's turning on him was so unexpected. Yankees, he knew, did look down on

49

other ethnic groups. But Carrie? He thought of all their intimacies, their amusing indolent games, their physical union, which he had come to think of as love—while in her mind, after all this, he was nothing but a piece of dirt to be shunned. She saw not only that he was hurt but also that he could be dangerous. Badly shaken by what she had blurted out, she was startled by this deep-seated bigotry welling up to form some deep secret place inside her, some residue of New England snobbishness, austere pride.

He moved toward her. 'You cunt!' he shouted. 'You goddamned bitch!' He needed to hurt her, to say something that would cover her with contempt. Now, if he could only leave here, without fully exposing his agony. A gentleman would go with quiet dignity. But he wasn't a gentleman, was he? That was what *she* said. So why should he care about dignity? In his rage he slapped her hard on the right cheek, then hit her again with a closed fist. She fell whimpering against a small table. Brushes and a palette spread with colors fell to the rough planking of the room, onto the Indian rug he had given her on her last birthday. George picked up his jacket and hat and went out into the wind. The fog seemed to be lifting, a wan moon hung high. George heard a man howling in agony. He realized, with dazed surprise, that it was himself.

2

Con Leggerezza

5

That part of the busy harbor where Irena and Maria were to come ashore was serviced by small boats which brought cargo and passengers onto the docks. Maria had become cheerful as she saw the solid hilly rise of the city topped with fleecy clouds, a spectacular backdrop of the activities of the port. 'There seems to be civilization here,' she said to Irena, who was waving at the squawking seagulls as they descended into a large rowboat.

'It's lively.' Irena was counting luggage; several bundles were threatening to burst their cords or escape their burlap-and-blanket wrappings. Under one arm Irena carried the shiny brass Fiore family clock of rococo design topped by a statue of a spread-winged rooster—neck arched, beak open in the gesture of crowing: a gift for Grego.

'I think I see him!'

'Where?'

'There by those barrels. No, it's not him. Where *can* he be?'

Irena searched the crowds for someone who resembled the shabbily-dressed boy with unruly hair who had left the village to go to sea. She never dreamed that the ragtag scamp was now an elegant man in a pale gray swallowtail frock coat and deep violet cravat stuck through with a red-jeweled pin. The greased hair was combed neatly and topped by a brown beaver hat. Moreover, Grego had cultivated a splendid set of mustaches, waxed this very morning and the ends twisted upward like a professional gambler's. Even Rocco, waiting eagerly by Grego's side, had been transformed. Although his dark suit was not new, it was clean and well cut. He carried a bowler hat of amazing hardness, which he felt too conspicuous to wear but was too proud of to leave at home.

'The ladies, the ladies, whicha ones?'

'Any of them, Rocco.'

'The tall one there in the boat, standing and waving?'

'Might be. She'll tip the damn thing—yes, that's Irena.'

He wanted to wave back to her, but didn't. He was much subdued these days; there was a new wariness about him, his features somewhat drawn and the face thinner. But he was stalwart, burying his recent pain, neither drinking more nor lamenting aloud when brooding alone. He never admitted fully the blow to his pride, the shattering of his image of perfect love. He spoke of it to no one, not even Sarah Kendrick, who hinted it would be good to 'talk things out.'

George had come through—weathered the shock, he felt with a better understanding that life is often inadequae to human desires. While he lacked the words, he sensed the ultimate futility of living in hope that others were the equal to one's own emotions. Moreover, a man must have the courage to know he stood alone, that no beneficent power would intercede. George no longer despaired; he had recovered some of the eager pulse of existence, and the early bodily gusto he hoped would also soon return.

Irena and the tall handsome dark woman stood on the wharf, billowing skirts held properly in place against the slight breeze. He stepped forward and Irena flung herself into his arms with a great cry of joy.

This, he felt, *this* was reality. Now things transitory and superficial could be locked away with a minimal amount of pain. A new life would begin, with the love of family and true friends.

'So tall! So handsome! A regular dandy, *e pur troppo bello* ...'

'We've both grown. How was the voyage?'

'Hades! Travel was made by Satan. How do you like my English, eh? This is Maria Orsini, Father Orsini's sister.'

'Younger sister,' said the dark woman with a faint smile, shyly bowing her head beneath its dark straw hat with a bright blue ribbon.

'So, how is the good padre?' He pressed her arm, smiled, took in the fine body, the large cross on a silver chain around a graceful neck.

'He's well,' said Irena. 'Ah, this is the Rocco who fends for you.'

George suggested they leave Rocco to follow with the luggage in a market cart. He escorted the two women to his buckboard, drawn by two fine bays. Yes, he owned them outright, he proudly explained.

His tan leather gloves held the reins firmly as they moved away from the docks, past drays, wheelbarrows, wagons of all types.

The two women looked with interest at sailors, merchants, loafers, busy people with burdens, well-dressed men and women moving at slow pace. Even Maria took it all in with joy, the memory of her seasickness put aside.

'Ah, the New World. Even the people are new,' Maria said. 'And the people with the tails and white-soled shoes? They must be the Chinese?'

George said they were. Maria held a small handkerchief to her face as if hiding most of her featues from the passing town folk. 'Is there a war, Signore Fiore? So many weapons here!' George explained that those armed people were miners and gold convoy guards, although most citizens did carry a body pistol.

'A gun is like a kind of symbol to Americans,' he explained. 'The carrying of arms is a freedom to be proud of. *We* Americans,' he added, tapping a pants pocket where he had a silver-mounted English pistol. 'It's our right.'

'They accept God here?' Maria asked as they passed a white structure topped by a gilt cross.

George grinned and flicked the horse with the tassels of

his slender whip. 'That one is the Protestant God. They don't let him rest on his cross.'

Maria fingered her cross. 'They run free here, the heretics?'

'Mormons, Buddhists … the Red Indians have a Great Buffalo spirit in the sky.'

Maria could only nod in wonder. This was amazing, this lack of the *giusta* faith. But one didn't have to despair. This was good soil for souls; all these lost ones could one day be brought back to the one true faith. Maria felt a stirring of joy. Was it being free of the ship, the shifting menace of the glass-green roaring seas? Was it the thought of the nearness to this handsome man? Hidden under her little straw hat and gay ribbon she felt a kind of glow at the idea he could be her husband. Up until now, for all of Irena's hints, her bold barnyard talk and amusing obscene gestures about a marriage with her brother, it hardly seemed that there was such a man and she could be a wife. She studied his face, a decent enough man by his manner, not cantankerous. If only there wasn't all that business of sleeping together in one bed, that matching of parts, and the calculated probability of seeding her body with *bambini*.

'Mary pity women,' she recited silently. 'One must accept.' The buckboard was approaching a three-story house with white stone steps flanked by freshly polished brass railings. They mounted the steps to two wide pale green doors.

'Mr Kendrick's house. You'll like them; they're my best friends.'

'They are … ?'

'Mormons. They are permitted a whole damn nest of wives, but only one of Mr Kendrick's wives is here.'

Irena winked at Maria. 'And you, poor Grego, have not even one wife. A sad state of things.'

'Try saying "George" not "Grego."'

Sarah welcomed the newcomers warmly, putting her arms around them and kissing them each on the cheek. 'You don't look so travelworn.'

'We are fine,' said Irena. 'What a nice place you have!'

Mormon simplicity had given way to a more luxurious style at the Kendrick's. Colorful braided rugs and pictures of stern-looking church leaders in heavy gilt frames decorated the parlor. Several canaries sang from woven reed cages next to a parlor organ on which sat ferns in brass pots and lamps with pale blue glass shades. Irena could hardly believe such wealth.

Moses led them into the even more opulent dining room, its walls hung with shiny china picture plates showing the cities of the world. There was a stove with German silver trimmings, a table set with linen rings. Irena truly felt heaven would have a rival here in San Francisco.

Maria hunted for holy pictures in vain.

Irena grew bold and asked for the place one did nature's things and was further astounded to be shown to the indoor privy serviced by a water tank on the roof. The Americans thought of *everything*.

They had a huge meal of venison, boiled sweet corn, pear-and-plum pie. There was much laughter and a festive spirit prevailed.

That night, Irena and Maria were in bed in what George called his 'spare room'. They lay in cotton shirts on soft pillows and tried to recall the events, the excitements of the day.

'Ah, Mr Kendrick and Grego-George are merchants, not trash. But did you notice?'

'What?'

'The woman Sarah, she is in charge. There is no ordering her about. She is the equal, as women should be. For the woman is the important one here. If not for women, men would live in ditches, eat out of holes in the ground.'

'God created woman to serve man!'

'What nonsense! Just because some old Jew writes a story of a foolish couple in a garden eating some fruit, I'm inferior to men? Maria, when you marry my brother, a little respect, but don't let him use you for a foot rug.'

Maria muttered something softly. She was exhausted. It

56

was five minutes before Irena discovered she was talking to herself. Outside, a clock bonged deeply. Far off, someone was firing a pistol, a courting cat cried out his desires. Thank you. *Ah, Dio*, thank you that you made the world so full of so much.

They settled in George's house. Irena began working at the produce market on Montgomery Street, selling the tomatoes and the Chinese celery, the golden melons shaped like cannonballs, and the striped blue melons. She would husk fresh sweet corn, biting into a kernel to show how fresh and sweet it was. Irena mastered a horse Rocco had taught her to ride, and she had a divided deerskin riding skirt made after a style she saw in a magazine.

'It's life, it's full living!' she would cry out at supper, devouring the Mexican spiced spareribs, the wild ducks George had brought home.

Maria was accepting, even pleased with her new life. She had found St Patrick's, a church just a few years old. So she contented herself by going to mass and by making lace, a skill she had learned in the convent. The lace sold well to the ladies of San Francisco.

Father O'Hara of St Patrick's was a fat little priest who smelled of fried fish and onions and was thankful that God prevented everything from happening all at once. He listened to Maria's confessions, making comforting purring sounds. Only her dreams gave him trouble. The recurring dream she confessed was of her being without clothes. ('Naked, you mean, my dear girl?' 'Yes, worse, seeing men also without clothing.' 'Showing their parts, you mean?' 'Yes, and a hovering of angels, flourishing overhead.')

He gave her six Hail Marys and Our Fathers, sent Maria away feeling relieved with a sense of grace, lighter and with only a small pervading fear she would end up damned.

One of the nude men who came into her sleep had the features of George Fiore. She was aware that at meals he would glance at her when he thought no one was watching him. He would hand her the best part of a duck breast, refill her wineglass. Later, when she was working on a length of lace, alone, she felt shameful sensations and would clutch her cross. In the market, at Clay and Sansome streets, she bought a large brass crucifix and hung it over the bed. One hot afternoon when the maid was at siesta, Maria dreamed of an altar boy offering the Pope a missal, and both were soon taking off their clothes. Maria awoke in a sweat, feeling the Devil had her by the liver. She dressed and went to find Father O'Hara.

The nuns had warned her of the meaning of such dreams. ('There is nothing for it, my girl, but to go into marriage.')

Maria protested that there was no one in this new country who seemed right. ('Bathe yourself with cold water, not naked but in a robe; avoid red meat, my dear girl.' 'What of wine, Father?' 'The good Lord Jaysus himself, didn't he turn the water to wine at that wedding feast? But shun the brandies and be sure your smallclothes, your undergarments, are loose. Too-tight lacing heats the blood. Two Hail Marys and a bit in the church fund box at the door.')

George too was having dreams, flickering images of the cruel Carrie dressed or naked like a *demimondaine*. The galloping of all his horses down a ravine and he whipping them as if hoping they would crash down Ruskin's Ravine ... rain falling and fruit heavy as bulls' balls, pears, peaches, grapes in clusters, smashing, their juices running into his mouth. He began to wonder if he should marry and shake off Carrie, to rid himself of such incontrollable passions. He had no idea that he was the subject of many conversations between Moses and Sarah, who were not unaware of his restless mood.

One morning, her hair *en papillote*, Sarah served her sons their mush and milk, fried eggs, and rusks for breakfast before they left for school. That done, she sat down and watched Moses cut into a ham steak. 'Yes, Moses, it's like that for a man. His vanity to prove to himself he's still a man.'

'How you go on, Sarah.' Moses wiped his mouth, buttered a hot soda biscuit. 'Are you worried about George going too often to the prostitutes?'

'I mean he's going to take a wife, that Italian girl who makes lace. It's obvious.'

Moses permitted himself a rare oath. 'I'll be goddamned. A woman's mind is sure full of odd furniture. George is much too sensible for that. Why, she's so drab! Must be a couple years older, and I'll bet she's not one for slap-and-tickle.'

'You're being vulgar, Mr Kendrick,' Sarah said, smiling. 'But it's as plain as fleas on a scratching dog.'

'Only gentiles think one woman has everything.'

Sarah sniffed: Moses had two wives left in Salt Lake City.

Though George was in doubt of his emotional state, he did not go to Father O'Hara, saying to himself: 'Churches are for women, God is for men.' But he sensed his control was dwindling and that he had better move Maria out of the house; the odor of her, her lavender scent, the pungent smell of her hair, and the sight of her intimate garments being hung on the line by the maid—it was too much. So he would take the leap. He'd have Irena set up the wedding date and get it over with. Maria would be a satisfactory wife: her splendid body was perfectly suited for bearing children, and clearly she would be a good Fiore wife and make a real home from his house. But was he sure?

Ruthlessly burying his yearning for Carrie and their lost passion, he began to shower Maria with gifts. On her Saint's Day, he bought her large gold earrings with blue stones from a shop on Kearny Street. When the Kendricks celebrated Thanksgiving, George got Maria new French boots with gray tops and pearl-shell buttons. She refused to ride a horse, but would venture out in the buggy, her gloved hand tightly clutching the reins of an elderly horse.

Yet still he dared not propose. He was racked by doubts, until one morning, when Maria was on the back veranda washing her long coils of inky black hair in a basin, he could resist no longer. She was bent over the washstand, clad only in a petticoat and chemise. George seized her from behind, exclaiming breathlessly, 'I think we shall marry soon.'

She grabbed her dressing gown, leaving imprints of her wet hand on its pale blue surface. 'You must not see me like this.' George accepted that for a yes to his offer, and his head ached all day.

Irena took to the city with delight, to the new land, its people, its way of life, all enjoyed with an intensity that, when she thought about it, made her burst into laughter. She demanded a horse and a wagon of her own a few days after her arrival, and drove it fearlessly, night and day, into the countryside. She ate country meals with strangers, fought off the bites of red bugs and mosquitoes, hooting back at the owl as she urged her horse to a faster clop-clop of his hooves on a plank bridge.

She enjoyed 'a good sweat,' hard work, riding: she helped in loading wagons, unloading produce. It gave her a firmness, the deep tan acquired by so much life in the open. People took notice of Irena Fiore, in her split leather riding skirt and blue military-cut jacket. She thought a sunbonnet or a woman's hat ridiculous, favoring one of her brother's flat wide-brimmed Spanish hats. If comment or disapproval of her attire reached her, she would remark, 'Fuck bourgeois decorum.'

Irena's English improved, became 'Americanized,' from taking lessons from Sarah Kendrick. Irena loved to gossip over coffee and cornbread with this transplanted new England convert to Mormon ways. They understood each other: clever women isolated on a frontier. As for the Latin people of San Francisco, Irena's Italian allowed her to talk easily with the Spanish farm workers, brown barefoot families raising maize and silver-striped melons. But she was best with the Chinese field workers, who seldom spoke but kowtowed and toiled, eking out what seemed to her a very strange life. She tasted dishes of rice flavored with possum fat and pinder nuts, and mudfish and eels. Their green vegetables and earth-root plants were in great demand. Irena was a good bargainer and not as fair as George. She loved the adventure of her life, wandering freely, seeing new exotic people, and driving shrewd bargains for Grego.

She became a marvelous rider. Besides her buggy, George bought her an Indian pony, a spotted horse that had a hard mouth and once tried to crush her against a fence. But she mastered him with a firm hand and a pair of cruel Spanish spurs, and soon Chianti (as she called him) seemed to enjoy their rides all along the bay as much as she did. There was a need in Irena, for all her enjoyment and people and of talk, for the solitary moment. She would ride her spotted horse down to the shore past scurrying little crabs, sea spawnings, driftwood, and clusters of cedar berries. She could lie for hours among the fennel and white spider lilies, looking up at the sky and wondering 'next, *what* next?' Her mind roamed from exquisite fantasies and images of copious joys, and then plummeted to pain at the shortness of life, the loneliness in each soul, a deep pain like an incision. But these moods were rare.

She looked at some paintings Sarah's niece had left behind, strong shapes of vast vistas, done not in detail but by suggestions of modulated masses, merging colors, and sweeping outlines. Irena felt she understood the artist, saw the intrinsic, even unbearable emotions the artist had shaped into private sensibilities. From what Sarah had told her, she was aware that her brother George had suffered a deep disappointment during an involvement with the artist. She knew when he was thinking of her, this 'Miss Seabrook'; he would become vague and remote. But clearly he was not one to give in to a lost passion. George had become harder, a bit more wary, impervious to being hurt—or so he seemed to suggest to the world.

The brother and sister were closer than ever and settled into a comfortable pattern. Irena ran the house. There was a barefoot Mexican girl, Conchita Concepcion, to cook and clean the little house. Rocco, grown a bit less thin, took care of the stables, where four horses chewed their corn with side-swaying jaws and rubbery lips. Rocco also took care of the garden and trimmed the fruit trees George planted, testing new varieties of plum and peach, a pippin apple. Lemon trees failed to survive the climate, and he contracted for citrus from what was now called Los Angeles. In spite of American ham and eggs at breakfast, George and Irena still loved a good dish of pasta, and found a wine they compared to Torre Giulia; festive occasions called for *sogliole all marinara* or *fritto misto*. Yet proudly they were eating more and more Yankee style: white lima beans, miner style, with salt pork or venison when some hunter brought it to market, and they had already developed the native delight in eating corn on the cob.

The thriving business consumed their waking hours and dominated even mealtime conversations. 'What's in harvest? The ships will pay anything for it. And we need cheese.' George would light his pipe after a hearty breakfast and discuss the day's prospects with Irena. This morning was no exception.

Irena broke the yolks of three eggs on her plate and forked them up between bites of wheat bread. She ate with relish, but never ran to fat like others of her background, although she was, as she confessed 'perhaps a bit plump.'

'Cheese, we need cheese.' George was working out figures on a bit of paper, determining how much timber was needed for a section of a new project. The city needed ready-built doors and windows, a good supply of hardware, locks, hinges, all ordered from Hong Kong.

'Try the Casa for cheese. The big Velasquez place, Irena, up the coast between Sausalito and Inverness.'

'Very fancy, weren't they, the Velasquezes? Rich, but they haven't been able to pay all their taxes. They'd sell us some of their cheese?'

'Why not? The click of silver also talks Spanish.'

George accepted a fresh cup of coffee from Conchita Concepcion. 'This whole coast was once owned by these grandees. Gifts from the Spanish kings, thousands—no,

62

millions of acres; ruled all the *pobladores*, lived on air selling cattle hides and tallow to ships, enslaving those Indians they could catch to build their missions. Lazy ease. First ruled by Spain, then Mexico.' He snapped his fingers, 'The *americanos* pushed them aside.'

'What are you, Grego, a historian?'

'I'm studying their grape culture, their wine. Once they made a lot of it.'

'I'll ride out and talk to this Velasquez.'

'Tomas Velasquez enjoys his empty titles. A gambler, I hear, always in need of the cash. If his cattle look properly fed, Irena, we might just buy a herd and have his men slaughter them for us.'

'Mr Moses isn't bothered that you'—she rolled her head, searched for the words—'are without him in the new business projects?'

George stood up, placed his napkin in its ring, and walked to the window overlooking the garden where Rocco was tending the tomato plants.

'Between him and me in business, there is an understanding. As I see it, what is his is his, ours is ours, and what's my own is mine. *Capisce?* I wonder sometimes if he knows this.'

'You still don't trust a *yanqui?*'

'Moses I trust. But I must be my own man. And Moses likes to dominate.'

He left without saying any more. Her brother was certainly touchy, Irena thought, since that cold New England bitch thumbed her nose at him.

She had Rocco polish her riding boots, got into the soft leather divided riding skirt, decided on a pale blue blouse, a darker blue riding jacket, and added looped silver earrings. She looked wonderful, she thought as she admired herself in the pier glass, tilting her flat-topped Spanish hat to a more dashing angle. Irena was thinking of taking a lover. None of the men who had been attracted to her since her arrival had interested her. Some were good enough, but as her grandmother had once said, 'The merely good is the enemy of the best.'

Perhaps if there was anyone in San Francisco who knew the old woman's spells and magic herbs, love potions and brews, Irena might buy some. Why not?

6

The simplest way for the conquering Americans to take over the Spanish land grants—their ranchos, vineyards, the acres where their dangerous-looking cattle ran wild—was to 'set up a tax-lien farce, an auction, and sell them to some jackboot Yankee lawyer or speculator with his eye on the good land and acreage,' as Sam Brannan explained. Few of the original owners had managed to hold on to their inheritances.

One family who did was the Velasquez clan across the Golden Gate in what the Americans were calling the Marin district. A ferret-faced Philadelphia lawyer, Matthew Gower, saved most of their holdings. They lost only a few thousand acres in Sonoma, a bit of sea frontage at Rio Camino, a boat yard at Morro Bay, and a good part of their timber around Clear Lake in legal fees to Gower, but had fared far better than the other Spanish grandees.

The last of the direct male line was Tomas Velasquez, aged thirty, whose passions were the good life, gambling, and riding half-tamed horses. He had avoided formal education and could hardly write a line, though he could read with some difficulty. Two ancient aunts had raised him and kept him out of the maids' beds until he was sixteen. When they died, he had a mass said for their souls, arranged for novenas, and promptly began raising hell.

People said that if he didn't die over a gambling table or break his neck in a fall from a horse first, he'd see the Casa Cuesta fall into the hands of the lawyers and the land boomers.

Tomas Velasquez was behind in his taxes, and Moses Kendrick held a mortgage on the best acres near the city, but Tomas seemed indifferent to impending catastrophe. He was a pleasant fellow, everyone said; bright enough at five-draw stud poker, a happy loser, but a man of much self-confidence, and thus had too little ambition to untangle the Velasquez holdings from torts, liens, and boundary disputes. He seemed impervious to the nastiness of law-court hearings, claims against the family lands. He drank too much, although he wasn't a drunkard, and lived contentedly among unpaid scrounging servants and their broods. He existed in a blanket of vagueness and indolence. Everyone agreed he had fine manners, and except when family honor was touched, he was modest and hardly snobbish about his rights by birth and the honors from long-dead kings of Spain.

This one morning, near noon actually, he was hung-over. He hardly recalled the loss of two of his best horses to two aces against his king and jack. He had drunk too much brandy and wasn't recovering as quickly as he had at eighteen and twenty. He had been awakened from desolate dreams by omens of a bad day—the pitched barking of the dogs. He had sat painfully on the edge of the bed, naked, plump, too bemused by the dreams to hunt for his slippers. He once had treasured the sense of waking with no burden of doubts, remembering his aunts' warning of the corrupting poison of too-early-morning thoughts, of the danger of existing between the pressure of so many doubts and the ecstatic awareness of loving. He scratched his ribs, smiled, poured himself a recovering drink. In an askew world with all its foibles, good brandy was a good and true friend.

After a morning of contradictory winds, the California sky was turning the color of heated brass. The harsh sun was bringing into focus the ridge on which the large red-tiled house stood, picking out the green of the boxwood labyrinth, the pastel colors of the neglected rose garden, and the bellies of great terra-cotta pots once planted with seasonal flowers. The weathered brick and stucco exuded a sense of lost splendor.

Tomas Velasquez wandered through the east entrance onto the gray stone drive of Casa Cuesta. He was dressed rather eccentrically for that hour, in a jacket that had belonged to his grandfather and which still had the gilt-and-silver crest of the great house of Velasquez over the right shoulder. He called to the dogs that ran loose inside the walled grounds all night, adding a curse in Spanish, '*Hijo maldito malcriado!*' The happy animals leaped about him, droplets of dew gleaming on their pelts, sensing he had some tidbit for them in the pocket of the worn gold-threaded jacket with its patches of dark leather at the elbows. In a dry season the dogs kept the deer from devouring the blossoms or leaves in the gardens.

Tomas enjoyed the sight of the Pacific Ocean, in spite of his aching head. The twinkling sea was highlighted as if surfaced by tumbling silver coins. Today Spur Rock was visible, a good Spanish omen. He smiled. *Eso es lo que es*. It was a damn good omen. He would bet on a fast horse, put fifty dollars on the nose at the racetrack. A good long shot, say, eighteen or twenty to one. He nodded, talked to the dogs in a mixture of Spanish and Anglo.

'*Hijos de la gran puta*, it is time we won a good race at some damn fine odds, eh?'

He played idly with the expectant panting dogs, tossing each a hard brown biscuit. Tomas liked dogs. The mission father, *hijo de la gran puta*, had once hunted Indians with just such savage dogs when seeking runaway workers from the hard labor of building the missions.... The dogs suddenly stood still, perking up their ears. He saw there was a rider coming up the slope. Closer, he saw it was a woman. The dogs raced to greet her.

Tomas wondered. A creditor? Hardly. Some whore he

had invited? No, she'd come in a hired carriage. The day was brightening, intensifying his headache. He didn't feel like facing visitors.

The rider had passed the rusted open iron gates and was beating at the dogs with a riding crop; the dogs barked and nipped her spotted horse's legs. Tomas felt there should have been a groom or two around to welcome the rider. But the few servants left were out gathering corn to feed the horses, and the stable help, he suspected, were either drunk in the kitchen or fucking each other in some corner.

Tomas advanced, feeling pins sink into his aching brain. He drove off the dogs with Spanish curses. His visitor was a young woman in buckskin riding skirt and a flat-topped wide-brimmed hat half-hiding strong, solid features. Not a great beauty, perhaps, but a damn handsome bit of woman, singularly cheerful for all the dog's attacks.

'I beg you, señora, forgive the goddamn dogs. Welcome to Casa Cuesta.'

'You are in charge here?' She dismounted with the skill and grace of a circus rider he had once seen, tucked her riding-crop under an arm, looked over the neglected grounds, and began to remove her gloves. 'Who's let this place go to wreck like this?'

'Time, señora. Time is the change who rules here.'

'Well, that's your problem. I'm Irena Fiore. I hope your dairy herd is still producing. Who handles the cheese-making here?'

Tomas shrugged. 'Do we *still* make cheese here? I have no idea.'

'Who the devil could tell me? Don't you know your job?'

'Not actually, no. Oh, I'm Tomas Velasquez. Welcome. And perhaps I can find out if the cheese is still being made.'

'Tomas Velasquez? Jesus Christ, I thought you were one of the hired help. That jacket isn't very new, is it?' She held out a hand, and he took it, feeling the strength in the grip, the firmness of the hand itself. A woman to be wary of, eyes just slightly *à la chinoise*.

He suggested they go to the dairy and see for themselves.

He admitted he hadn't been near the place in months. An old man called Julio was in charge of the milk herd.

Julio, a solid old man with a gimpy leg and muttonchop whiskers, showed them into a room smelling of straw, whey, chicken droppings. He brushed a hen off a table, bowed, and got out a wine jug and glasses. The wine was tart but fruity.

'Your own wine, Don Tomas?'

'It may be.'

Julio, who was part Indian, judging by his nose, admitted he had made a little for the servants. 'Six, maybe ten casks.'

Irena asked about cheese.

Yes, they still made cheese. The missions took it, but hardly ever paid. If the carts didn't break down, they sold a hundred pounds or so at times to ships in the nearby harbor. But of late, there had been a surplus, few sales, just cheese-making *and* cheese-making. No buyers but the damn priests, who pleaded poverty, and so the springhouses were full of cheese. A Spanish *bel paese*, a white cheese (*jerez*-flavored), an Anglo cheddar.

He showed Tomas and Irena the great stone vaults, cheese hanging and ripening in cloth bags, great wheels of cheese in storage on shelves. In answer to Irena's questions, Julio calculated that two thousand pounds of cheese—maybe more—was being made by the women, who took their wages in cheese, a few capons, or a sheep.

Irena nibbled on a wedge of cheddar-type cheese, licked her teeth clean, and nodded. 'Don Tomas, I'll contract for all you have in storage, and for all you process from now on.'

'Whatever for?' Tomas, his head aching, was having trouble thinking clearly.

'Four cents a pound?'

'I mean, Señora, *why* the devil would anyone want all that damn cheese?'

'My brother, George Fiore, is a dealer in farm and ranch produce.'

It seemed uncouth to talk so much of business. 'Looks

foolish, no, so much cheese? We have to make it, or the cows, Julio says, are in pain, but ...'

Irena took his arm, smiled, nodded. 'I can see you are a gentleman. So, better to get details over with. Julio will tell you it's best you dispose of your cheese stock. And do you have pigs, piglets?'

Julio said sadly, 'No. The servants were hungry, *de mal grado*, and they ate the shoats and the boar and all the piglets on several saints' days and holy hoidays.'

Irena sensed Julio was lying. She took out a wallet and began to count out banknotes on the table, and she added several double eagles in gold coin. 'This is two hundred dollars on account. You can weigh the cheese here ... oh, if your scales are broken, we shall weigh them. You have pen, paper? Write me out an agreement.'

Tomas looked at the wealth on the rough plank table but did not touch it. The handsome señora had no idea of genteel trading. Julio blew dust off a walnut box and brought out a dried-out ink bottle to which he added a bit of wine to get a fluid ink, and skillfully sharpened the points of two quill pens with his knife.

'So,' said Julio, '*mercado*.'

He offered the pen to Tomas, who held up a shaky hand. 'The hand is in no mood to write, Señora Fiore. If you will fill up the paper; but of course, between people of honor, we do not need such things.'

'Always expect people to have honor, so Moses Kendrick told me, but still shuffle the cards yourself.'

She scratched an agreement rapidly on some yellow sheets cut from an old bullfight poster. 'You have the palsy, Don Tomas?'

'No'—he grinned—'I have been drinking last night. My hand cannot take any message from my aching head to my fingers.'

Irena spoke impulsively. 'Why, you poor bastard. But now the contracts are signed and properly witnessed by Julio. I hope your kitchen has hot peppers, two fresh eggs, a pinch of nutmeg, and some olive oil. This potion will cure

69

the hangover of Beelzebub after he's chewed on brimstone and gunpowder.'

Like a child about to be punished, Tomas was led to the house, where a barefoot cook and a walleyed maid produced most of the items needed. A hen was removed squawking from a nest of brown eggs she had been set on just the day before. There was no nutmeg, so Irena used curry powder in the mixture and insisted Tomas swallow the mess. Later they lounged in deep chairs on the great piazza with its cracked marble flooring, watching the afternoon turn to dusk. Tomas admitted he felt better and she begged him to eat a good meal. He asked her to join him for a late supper; he might handle some broth, and a little white meat of chicken (they could hear the protests of a hen being chased for execution by the lean maid with a hatchet).

Later there was some gossip that she had stayed the night at the Casa, stayed for a week. None of this was true, although she was taken with this slack young man (well, thirty was still young, in a way). She'd be thirty herself soon enough. He was attractive and not given to acrimonious arguments like an *italiano*. His skin was blotchy but would improve if he gave up his brandy. Poor Tomas, he was so helpless, exploited by the thieving servants. Julio must have a pot of gold buried under a stone in the fireplace. As for the cook, somebody was buying the orchard fruit, and had they really eaten *all* the pigs and piglets, the geese, the sides of beef listed in some frayed ledgers? And the damn monks, Irena insisted, should be dunned for all that cheese.

It was an act of mercy, she told George and Maria. 'Somebody has to take care of the old booby, a *paisano* with no business sense. And we get a fine supply of very good cheese. In two weeks we'll have cider. I'm getting him to invest in six shoats and a good hard-working boar. The cattle are lean and wild. George, to handle all that beef, we'll have to hire hands to bring them in and to slaughter. I figure the hides alone—'

George laughed, and he hadn't been laughing much of

late. 'You'll be taking over the whole Casa if Velasquez, the "poor booby," doesn't watch out.'

'I didn't mean booby *that* way. Tomas really has quality. A real gentleman of Spain. More than just being gentry. Something that's rare in our world: manners and breeding.'

'And his noble toes sticking out of his shoes. It's no secret, Irena, the Velasquez family has been going downhill for nearly three generations. Moses holds legal paper against some of the best land in their vineyards.'

Irena beat a fist on the table so hard the breakfast dishes rattled in fear. 'Moses is *not* going to get any of the land. Tomas will pay back what is owed!'

'With cheese money?' asked Maria, working on a lace veil for her wedding, just a month away.

Irena fought to keep her temper. 'There's a cider press, there are orchard crops, there are perhaps thousands of head of cattle. And all those acres of grapes up in Napa. Wineries standing desolate now that used to turn out a fine wine—well, a *fair* wine.

George studied his sister's face. 'Banks control a lot of the wineries, don't they?'

'Mortgaged, but Tomas promises me that he'll put down three thousand gallons this year.'

George pointed a finger at Irena. '*If* he has kegs, *if* he has bottles, corks, and can pay pickers and crushers. No!'

'I didn't ask you yet to advance the funds, did I? But would you refuse your future brother-in-law, eh?'

Maria, in amazement, stuck a lace-making needle into a finger—it bled.

By the turn of the century, Irena's conquest of Tomas was legend up and down the coast. Gossips recounted in great detail how Irena Fiore seduced, overwhelmed, and swallowed up Tomas Ovando Velasquez. Magic? Drugs? Spells? *Quién sabe?* Little of this gossip had much to do with the actual history of an impetuous woman and a man discovering his failings. If Tomas was a victim, he was hardly aware of it. For he, in his casual way, saw in Irena a

71

force, a vitality, that somehow shamed him, but not enough to change him much. Not enough 'to get him off his hunkers', as she told her brother. But enough, Irena felt, to recognize the preposterous way in which he had lived which had led to the ruin of Casa Cuesta and the shocking thievery by his servants. '*Madre dolorosa!*' The carrying off of the crops, the edible farm animals, all gone.'

What had been for years a shadowy and insubstantial world, Tomas now saw through Irena's eyes as hovering near disaster.

Actually, Tomas did little more than listen to Irena and agree, nod, and sign papers, as the first attempts were made to bring the wild cattle down from the hills for a roundup and counting. Irena had the cider press repaired and salvaged most of the fruit.

Plans were made for restocking the pigsties. Julio was sternly warned by Irena, who emphasized each word by beating her riding crop against her thigh. He was told that he could stay on and mend his thieving ways. Otherwise, the sheriff was waiting for just a word from Don Tomas to ask Julio, in chains, for an accounting. Irena had learned from George that to handle people, one had to accept some of the weaker parts of their characters and get the most from their better aspects.

There was still the problem of the greedy Philadelphia lawyer. One afternoon, George and Tomas confronted Gower in his neat pine-panelled office.

Bristly as a mastiff, he had shouted back at them, his square silver-rimmed spectacles dropping to the tip of his nose. 'You come back *now*, after it's all rack and ruin, and ask me why I did this and why I did that? Well, it's all in order, and a sad order it is, thanks to you. I never lied or misrepresented the facts!' He climbed a little ladder like a sailor's monkey, and hurled a huge dusty box onto the desk, where it burst and sent forth a little fleet of ledgers, legal documents, yellowed papers with the seals of Spain and Mexico, to sail over the oak desktop.

'Rust, canker, and mold written out. And I've a tin trunk

some place with all the lawsuits, claims, tax liens, torts, judges' writs. Nothing rapacious, no complacency where there was a legal fight worth fighting!'

George, perfectly calm, didn't shout back. Tomas offered a thin cheroot to the lawyer, who refused. George slowly lit his pipe, inhaled and exhaled smoke.

'Now, sir, Mr Gower, we don't come here to curse you or say things are wrong.'

Tomas added, ' "Disarrangement" is the better word. I was never one to make trouble, as you know, Señor Matthew.'

'Wish you had, my boy. Making squalor of what should be one of the grand estates on the coast, and you've retained title, a damn miracle. Of course, Mr Fiore, you understand my fellow countrymen haven't been purely honorable, only legal in what they have done and are doing to many old land-grant families.'

'I'm aware a court is for law, not justice. Now that my sister is going to marry Señor Velasquez, we hope that the estate holdings will be run along more practical lines. There have been ... well, let's call it "vague boundaries" between who owns *what* interests in the estate. Like the timber rights at Clear Lake.'

The little lawyer rubbed a bald expanse of skull that seemed made (George thought) of parchment and wax rather than of human skin. Gower gave a low prolonged chuckle. 'Ah, you agree with Shakespeare! "Let us begin by killing all lawyers!" Well, I saved that timber from Sam Brannan and Moses Kendrick. I took some slopes as my fee, yes, indeed, and I sold some of the boy's shares. As for the mines, digging into the mountains, that was done to keep most of the kit and caboodle together. You have to see a lawyer's work in the right angle of refraction.'

George nodded. 'Let's hold back judgements until everything is counted out, inventoried. Meanwhile, Mr Gower, draw up a marriage agreement.'

'A *what?*'

George spoke sarcastically. 'You know what we guineas

73

are? Greedy peasants, garlic, *bambini*, dirty feet. We keep our wealth in gold coins, which we hang in coils around the necks of our women.'

Tomas protested, 'No, no, he jests, Señor Matthew. The Fiores are connected distantly to the families of the great Leonardo da Vinci.'

'Who? Never mind, Mr Fiore,' said the lawyer, 'you are too well known for me to listen to your little charade. How shall I word this agreement? Blackstone, Jeffries, my ancient texts, don't speak fully of its colonial American status.'

'As is well known, Señor Tomas's estate is in ruin. So, as is only proper, my sister will have a dowry, a dowry of ten thousand dollars. Set down that in return, Señor Tomas will permit his wife and one George Fiore, her brother, to manage the estates, land, cattle, mills, presses, all other assets, with an accounting, of course, to be given each year. We'll retain you to see that the terms of the marriage contract are carried out. Smooth it over with legal chatter.'

Tomas scratched his upper lip. 'Not being in Spanish, it's all so lacking in nobility, simplicity of spirit. I mean, it sounds like ordering a bottle of tequila. Not at all a holy marriage in the eyes of the holy Church.'

Gower pursed his lips and seemed to want to ask if the bridegroom had been coerced into marriage. These Fiore folks were well enough thought of, for dagos, reputed to be clever and imaginative. Matthew Gower was an Easterner with generations of Protestant and Anglo-Saxon background behind him. The lawyer felt anyone not born of early colonial stock a little below the salt. He was not a bigot, and hoped to rise in politics.

'I shall serve the estate if you so desire, and draw up the marriage agreement. I might add, I do add'—he scratched behind an ear—'that both Brannan and Kendrick will fight what they might see as an infringement of their rights to Velasquez holdings. But that we will face in future court battles.' He gave a small smile. 'Lawyers, you know, are *always* ready with any pretense to sue.'

George decided he liked this little lawyer. 'If one has to eat shit,' he recalled his father saying, 'eat it with a silver spoon.' As for Sam Brannan and Moses Kendrick, clearly the Fiores were drawing away, by circumstance and business attitudes, from the self-righteous sense of moral superiority of Moses and the violent rapacity of Sam the jack-Mormon. For all George's proud words to Irena, Moses had begun resenting George for doing so much on his own, and felt George owed his start and much more to Kendrick. He accused George of smart dealing and 'smart-mouthing.'

'Too soon, too fast,' he had told Sarah. She answered, 'You're a fair man—but your pupil is growing too fast for you, teacher.'

'I'll talk to Moses Kendrick,' George told the lawyer, 'so he'll not think we're trying to cheat him.'

Tomas stood up and tapped his cane against the neat rug of the lawyer's office. 'So all is agreement. Good. I must go now, as I have a meeting to attend.'

George wondered what meeting, but decided it was most likely an afternoon game of poker at the Union Hotel. Irena would soon have that problem on her hands. He felt rather pleased that she would have problems with Tomas; Irena had been so smug about her good fortunes. A woman who suspects she is clever volunteers too many answers to questions she is never asked.

As for Tomas hurrying to his card game, if he were asked by the bishop himself how it had all come about, he would have been at a loss to explain. He couldn't swear if he or she had said the first word on the subject of marriage. But he had no regrets; Irena was a fine woman, and besides, a worrisome situation was now settled.

The relationship between George and Moses Kendrick had been disintegrating into hostility for some time. Moses saw himself as a moral man, fair but hard in his dealings, one who tried not to be ruled by enthusiasms. He tried to be consistent in his application to what he felt were the duties of any man out to improve his standing. He also had a strong sense of what he saw as his territorial rights.

San Francisco—for all its reckless ambience—was growing at a fast pace, land values increasing, speculators putting up structures that rented and sold at fabulous prices. Moses' timber was a valued product.

Moses was not pleased to see George buying up growths of white fir, subalpine Engelmann spruce, and western larch. The two men were inspecting a lumber mill near Petaluma, a mill turning out pine plankings.

'George, you're horning in on my turf. I've been buying Lopez's wood for quite a while now, long before you came up the pike.'

George chewed on a twig of spruce. 'So now you find out I own part of the mill, but I'm offering you a fair share.'

'You're buying the timber stands. I'm paying more for lumber by the square foot.'

'I take opportunities the way you and Sam do. All right, Moses, I'll let you buy at the old price for six months.'

'You own an option to buy Lopez out, lock, stock, and barrel. I want you to let me in on that option, for half.'

'A third.'

Moses fought to keep his temper. Scowling and red-faced, he stalked to his buckboard and in a rage whipped his horse away at a furious pace.

George felt badly about Moses wanting a half-share in the timber business, but he was also sure that Moses would never be satisfied till he owned the major share. George was aware that he himself was changing, developing a subtler perception of how one made one's way among so many men of force and cunning, who often used brutal violence in what was still in many ways an outlaw city. Even the criminal element was enterprising, growing bolder.

Sam Brannan's Vigilance Committee was getting reactivated as the force behind 'law and order.' It ran out of town many of the Sydney Ducks, the convicts from Australia; now and then even hanged a few 'higher than their ass,' to shouts and flaming torches in the night. Popularly known as 'Sam's Regulators,' they kept crime, Sam insisted, within reason.

'The gamblers and madams agree and offer us support. Hell, there is enough for everybody, but not for thieves.' Sam, flashing a diamond ring, a pearl-gray top hat, boots with pick-point toes, explained it to George at a mule sale held at North Beach, after congratulating George on his domestic plans.

'Getting married, I hear, going to run in double harness.'

'It's so, Sam …. You think white mules are lucky?'

Sam looked over the gathering of long-eared animals, the crowd examining them, sellers and buyers making intricate gestures as they raised or lowered prices.

'Well, the jenny mules, they're really gray, not white …. A man makes his own luck. George, you're fretting Moses, *our* friend Moses. Standoffish you are these days, he says, not like the son he figured you for. Come join us all—the Regulators are meeting tonight at my diggings, Battery and Pine streets.'

George raised two fingers as a seller pointed to a mule with one drooping ear.

'Sam, I don't believe in vigilante ways. We have a mayor, law courts.'

77

Sam shook his head. 'Now, listen. *We* are the mayor, the courts, the hangman. Why? The slowness, the indifference of the damn law and the courts. They don't work. Every morning you hear more news of murder, robbery. Courts are fancy assholes of lawyers that shield the guilty. Why, even Moses has approved law and order as we see it. Maybe he's still on the fence, but he's tilted our way.'

The mule seller held up three fingers. George shook his head. 'I thought you Mormons prayed for your enemies, Sam.'

Brannan laughed. 'I do, George, I do. I pray them *all* to hell. The way we Regulators see it, what's called "law" is just a nonentity to be scoffed at. Redress through the never-failing remedy so admirably laid down in the code of Judge Lynch.'

'I heard you make that speech in Portsmouth Square the other night.'

'A good thing is worth repeating.'

'Depends on the definition of "good thing," doesn't it?'

The mule seller held up two fingers and a bent one. George nodded. Sam was getting energy now. 'Well, I hope that tom mule you just bought ain't got the blind staggers like the owner.'

There was no denying the rise in crime: murders; burnings and looting; waterfront robbery was popular and costly. The Sydney Ducks threatened to burn the town if Sam's Regulators molested them. But to George the stringing up of arsonists and murderers only made the law lawless.

That night George awoke to the sound of fire bells and a scurrying of wheels and horse hooves in the street. Rocco was already dressed and wearing the fire helmet and coat of a volunteer of the Monumental Firefighting Engine Company. A few blocks away, the DeWitt Harrison warehouse on Commercial Street was in flames when they arrived, and the steam pumper sending sparks from its brass stack as the hose-line stream of water grew weaker.

The fire was too far advanced and the water supply was failing.

George saw the orange-centred crackling flames consume the front of the building. Cap Martin, chief of Monumental Engine Company, his face streaked with soot, his whiskers singed, shifted the fire ax over his shoulder and yelled, 'I tell you, George Fiore, nothin's going to stop her. Water pressure ain't worth a squaw's piss.'

'I've got thousands of gallons of vinegar in barrels in storage up the street. Will the pumper take it?'

'Take it! It will kiss it!' He turned to the close-pressing crowd. 'I need a couple of hundred of you galoots to roust some barrels from Fiore's place and snake them down here for the pumper to suck up.'

The crowd was in a good mood. A hot fire was better than a Fourth of July, and taking part in the fire activities was a delight. George unlocked his warehouse and Rocco listed the number of barrels of vinegar that were rolled down to the DeWitt Harrison place. The heads of the barrels were knocked in and a line of buckets moved the vinegar into the maw of the scarlet-painted steam pumper. Soon a good steady stream of the liquid went searching into the heart of the fire, the air took on a spicy tang, and Cap Martin did a jig of joy. 'All we need now are some Bismarck herring and a head of lettuce to go with the vinegar! Keep them buckets moving!'

It took twenty minutes and most of the contents of the barrels to put out the fire. The major part of the warehouse was saved and nearly all its contents. Reports circulated that while the city's attention was focused on the massive fire, criminals from the Barbary Coast, mostly the Australian gangs, had been looting the shops, carrying off bolts of velvet, furniture, casks of whiskey, sides of beef, and weapons. There was some shooting by owners trying to protect their property. The crowd spread out to attack the looters. Rocco helped in the capture of an Australian known as John Miscreant, caught with a small safe he had carried from a shipping office on Long Wharf.

Sam Brannan and a group of his Regulators held a quick trial of the thief, and the shouting crowd now became a mob.

George insisted the trial was not legal.

'Well, now, Mr Fiore,' said Sam, lifting his arm to the crowd, 'John here is sure guilty, and he'll hang in two hours.'

George and Rocco, standing near Moses Kendrick, heard the crowd begin a triumphant chant. George knew it was dangerous to protest, yet he cried out, 'Moses, stop them! You have some control over Sam.'

Moses shook his head. 'You want to be burned out?'

'We don't know who started that warehouse fire. Certainly not this thief. He was on the wharf. Moses, have you gone over to the Regulators?'

'There's some things that look wrong to some that end up doing the most good.'

The anxious prisoner, looking about wide-eyed, kept saying, 'Gents, I mean, don't let 'ot minds rush you into things. There's the lore and justice, ain't there?'

'The law!' shouted Sam, shoving the prisoner. 'You've been tried by the citizen's law, and found guilty.'

'Moses,' said George, 'you're not really going through with this, are you? You've never been a cruel man. And I thought you believed in the law, in higher law.'

'I must stick with my fellow Mormons against the rabble-rousers. Even jack-Mormons are preferable to this scum.'

'Gents, I'm me mother's only son. 'Ave a bit of mercy, gov.'

'Who's got a noose?' someone cried from the crowd.

Moses said to George, 'Only a damn fool can't see this is a necessary public action. We can't have these animals tearing our city apart.'

A rope was produced and tied around the prisoner's neck. John and his captors began their march along the crowded street, the mob and the Regulators waving pistols, shotguns, bowie knives. Someone gave the prisoner a wad of chewing tobacco and he chewed, spat, and stopped pleading. Sam shouted, 'The son of a bitch, he thinks the Sydney Ducks will rescue him!'

On the east side of Portsmouth Square the Regulators found a house with a good oak beam projecting and the loose end of the rope was tossed over it. Rocco had found several policemen watching from a nearby alley and brought them over to George.

'Damn it, get that man to the jail and alert the mayor, Judge Pitkin, and Alderman Meiggs!'

'The boys are raucous tonight,' said the tallest policeman. 'They're mean, and if we tried to get them to stop, well ...'

'You're the law, the authorities. Use it.'

'Maybe we need more help.'

'Well, get it, fast!'

There were flickering torches, a picnic spirit, tumultuous excitement. The prisoner, noose around his neck, stared at the hilarious, roisterous crowd. Sam and Moses formed the Regulators into a circle around the prisoner. There were now about a dozen police, whom George led toward the prisoner, elbowing their way through the crowd.

George spoke out. 'The police are here, Sam. He is their prisoner. The Regulators can turn him over to them.'

The tall policeman nodded, eyed the crowd. 'That's right, Mr Brannan. Good evening, Mr Kendrick. Like Mr Fiore said, we are asking for the prisoner.'

The mob hooted, waved torches and weapons, shouting, 'String him up,' 'Get his toes off the ground,' 'Pull 'em to heaven!' Sam held up an arm and with the other arm hooked one thumb through his suspender.

'Now, boys, if you police try to interfere with this here hanging, we'll just have to turn our weapons on *you*. Only some country jake of a mudsill would try to get our prisoner.' The police looked at each other, said nothing, stood where they were. George saw they had a gutful of fear. He stepped forward.

'Sam, you can't do this. The man has a right to a trial. Moses, you're a God-fearing decent man—I know that.

The prisoner's a human being, whatever he's done.'

Sam motioned to three men to get hold of the end of the rope. 'Fiore, we can just as easy get another rope and make it a twin hanging.' George looked about him and saw no sympathetic faces.

Rocco moved to George's side, his face pale and grim.

'Hang the fuckin' dagos!'

'Before you boys hang me, who's going to pay for the thousands of gallons of my best vinegar?'

That brought a laugh from the crowd, and a one-eyed man offered an uncorked bottle of whiskey to George. 'Take a snort of ol' forty-rod likker.' George took no further action; the police suddenly were gone. 'String 'im up!' 'Watcha waitin' for?' The prisoner was yanked up high and slowly strangled, twisting like overripe fruit in the fire-lit night. Rocco took his hand off the pistol butt in his belt.

Sam, half brusquely, part breathless, held up both arms. 'Now, citizens, we have a solemn ritual to perform. Each member of the Vigilance Committee is to grab hold of the end of the rope for twenty second, so we shall all be part of a group effort and no one or two persons can be implicated in bringing this skunk to justice. Step up, boys, put your back into it!'

The ritual complete, everyone cheered, hands were shaken, bottles emptied. The fun over, the crowd broke up, recalling the best parts of the night.

George and Rocco went home. Maria and Irena were up, standing in their long linen nightgowns, frightened and asking for details.

'You did wrong, Grego, to try to stop them—wrong, wrong. We're part of the community. If you don't like the Regulators, shut the mouth, don't speak up against them. Even Moses has gone over. Close your eyes, Grego, and save your ass.'

George, beaten, wearily commanded, 'Go to bed, everybody.'

Maria made the sign of the cross, prayed for the soul of the lynched man.

The coroner's report was issued the next day: '*The dead man came to his death at the hands of and in pursuance of a preconcerted action on the part of an association of citizens styling themselves the Committee of Vigilance.*'

No legal action was taken against any member of the committee. George was never paid for the loss of some thousands of gallons of vinegar. The city claimed it had not issued an official written order authorizing its use to fight fires. The mob soon became individuals again—some greeted George in the street, while a few averted their eyes.

He did not blame human frailty for the loss of the Moses friendship. Moses, he knew, was a calculating yet magnanimous man when he felt himself in the right. But when some disturbing feeling made its presence known, he could react with a ferocious sense of being wronged, misunderstood. Moses seeemed to feel that God (and Joseph Smith) had set up an order of consistency and application that was rigid and unflawed, to which Moses Kendrick alone had the key.

George hoped the tensions of their failing friendship would level off after he and Maria were married; perhaps Kendrick would begin to accept him as a responsible citizen and a householder—with the same concerns that Moses had.

In the meantime, George had begun to depend more and more on Rocco, who matured into a good-natured, strong youth. A sense of being wanted had brought him to maturity, and while he was still dependent on George, he showed an alertness and native intelligence which he readily exercised on George's behalf. He had lost the doglike subservience of the tattered, hungry waif he had been. There was now a touch of menace if he was riled. He was a good brawler with his fists, but as the Regulators grew more threatening, he had taken to carrying a Colt .45; he also owned two shotguns and could handle a Henry Brass Boy rifle as well as or better than most. With typical youthful bravado, Rocco saw himself as better than everyone at everything—including the gentler arts of love.

With his luminous eyes and enchanting smile, Rocco felt himself irresistible to women; he even ventured into the Chinese section, where slave girls were available. But after a few visits he grew depressed and stopped going. He had a strong religious sense and a deep loyalty to the Fiore family. He and Maria went to mass together, talked of their favorite saints. She chided him about his womanizing, asked him to think of spiritual consolations. From the Chinese quarter he brought her large spotted goldfish with fan tails. Rocco had a penchant for the colorful, the exotic; he wore a small gold earring in his left earlobe, liked high-spurred Spanish boots with red stitching, and wore a wide-brimmed Cordovian hat well forward over his brow, his thick black curls showing beneath.

Rocco was always vigilant on the family's behalf. While checking timbers on an Oakland dock, soon after the lynching, Rocco said to George, 'I tell you the Regulators are bothering the farmers, suggesting we haven't the cash to pay on our contracts for their crops. Chung Lee tells me he has even been threatened that if he sells only to you, they will chop off his pigtail. You know the Chinese are lifted to heaven, and if it's cut off—'

'I've heard; but don't provoke. Keep your pistol in your pants. *Capisce?*'

'They will think me a coward. Or worse—an *invertito*, a bugger.'

George laughed. 'Wait till they see you dressed for the wedding. A fop of a *dolce far niente*.'

It had been decided that Irena, as the elder, would be married first, a week after the ending of Lent. As there were no surviving members of the Velasquez family, except some distant cousins in Mexico City, several of the best Spanish families had been invited. The heads of the houses of Castillo, Solveira, Quevado, Cervera, and the few Mexicans who owned a dark suit and cut their hair— Flores, Obregon, Benitez, Garcia. They also invited Matthew Gower, the Kendricks, the mayor, aldermen, and (with much doubt) Sam Brannan.

Irena, even with her wedding day close at hand and the Casa to run, did worry abut some possible retaliation from Brannan and Kendrick. But she was mostly concerned with all the wedding plans. She had been buying from merchants as far away as St Louis, ordering brocaded draperies for Maria, an oval medallion mirror for the Casa, and a gold-topped malacca cane for a wedding present for George. Maria was working on a special high-point lace wedding veil. George and she would be married a week after Irena and Tomas. The servants at the Casa, on the range, and in the vineyards sent a polished brass-bound oak cask of wine with a message burned into it with a hot iron: 'IN VINO VERITAS—*In Wine Is Truth*.'

8

The last mayor and the Alta California *gente de razón* were present at the wedding of Tomas Ovando Velasquez and Irena Giannina Fiore. It all went precisely as planned. Bishop Ordonez de Aliaga—shaken by the sea trip—came up from San Diego to San Francisco to perform the holy rites of matrimony in the Church of Nuestra Señora de Guadalupe. There were a choir and melodic carillon. An odd assortment of guests assembled—grandees mixing with some of George's more humble business acquaintances and Tomas's wealthy gambling cronies. Neither Sam Brannan nor the Kendricks attended. Sarah, however, sent a gift—a set of milk-glass pitchers, cups and saucers.

Irena was in an exuberant mood. She kicked her train of white silk aside as, standing with Tomas at the altar, she looked over the church while the bishop read them homilies on the true faith and matrimonial duties. The pews were well-filled. She turned to Tomas, very handsome in his hammertail coat, dark wine-colored cravat, gates-ajar collar.

'How the snot-nosed "noble" families have thinned out,' she whispered to him mischievously, lowering her eyes to look demure. Maria, the bridesmaid, wept happily.

Tomas, a bit tiddly from the two strong brandies poured into him by George, blinked. He was feeling comfortable and affectionate with this handsome woman. The bishop inserted a bit of Latin: '*Fides et justita ... deo gratias.*'

George and Rocco waited, heads bowed, for the ritual to end and the organ to blare up. George was aware that Rocco had a pistol concealed in the tail of his swallowtail frock coat; the night before, so-called hoodlums had very skillfully poured coal oil on the hay bales of the Fiore City stables and set them afire. Rocco, on guard with Chico and two of his sons armed with shotguns, had fired on the arsonists and a trail of blood led to a North Beach wharf.

George disliked the use of weapons, the employment of violence, the hiring of thugs and gunmen. Such procedures, he told Rocco, led to consequences a sane man fears. Yet Sam Brannan's Regulators, Moses Kendrick, and his three grown sons were enemies who menaced all George had accomplished ... He sniffed the church's odor of heliotrope and fuchsia, smoky candlewicks .... It could become a war—Rocco and everyone else armed, shootings from ambush, bushwhacking, face-offs in bars, livery-stable encounters, or out in the open in some dry gulch, lonely ranch, or farm. It angered George—he was a man who liked neatness, and the use of disordered violence was singularly inept.

As always when troubled, he recalled what his old grandmother had told him when he was a boy: 'One can't pick at life with a dainty hand. Only the dead don't have to take risks.' George gritted his teeth. If it had to be guns, it *would* be guns.

He felt Rocco's elbow touch him; George suspected that he must have moaned out loud, but it was only a signal that the bishop was giving the couple his benediction to end the wedding ceremony. *'Confiteor Deo Omnipotenti … Vestri Omnipotens Deus.'*

George recalled the words from his time as a very young altar boy in the village, the whitewashed interior of the little church, dominated by the larger-than-life-size figure of a dreadfully tortured Christ over the altar, gouts of blood, realistic torn flesh, the crown of thorns digging wounds into the brow, and Father Orsini giving a benediction while the choir boys pinched each other.

'Benedicat Vos Omnipotens Deus, Pater, et Filius et Spiritus Sanctus.'

At the wedding feast at the Casa Cuesta, the servants from house, field and barns formed a brass band aided by dulcimer and fiddle. They played a welcome of Spanish music and a sad attempt—*Madre de Dios!*—at the national anthem of the *Yanquis*. Staggering quantities of food had been prepared. Father O'Hara, viewing the bodies of roast pigs and geese and other fowl, said to the bishop, 'It is a barnyard version of the French Revolution!'

Irena was not the shy bride. She was ordering the servants about, urging the guests to have more wine. Tomas was nodding his head for no reason at all, sipping a yellow wine with more bite to it than he had expected, and smiling at the obscene jests of certain of his *Caballero* card-playing, race-horse-owning friends.

He patted Matthew Gower on the shoulder. 'Matt, elegance without ostentation, that's the Velasquez way.'

'You're marrying a remarkable woman, remarkable, my boy. Look what she's done to your estates in just a few months. Remarkable.'

'Remarkable,' said the bridegroom, then turned to answer an obscene wedding-night jest with an obscene answer....

Irena laughed. She felt flushed, and her body—held in the vise of a new tight corset—was bathed in sweat. She had taken too much wine, eaten many of the little red, green, and white cakes, part of a turkey, and now, gorged, was picking at trout in aspic.

Across from the bride and groom, Maria sat smiling; the bishop had given her a rosary blessed by the Holy Father, and had promised he would procure a flask of water from the Jordan for her. A wedding didn't seem so bad to Maria; her own to George would come soon and she was neither morose nor morbid about it. One had to submit to the wedding bed serenely—as St Catherine had lain down on her griddle to be roasted over the hot coals.

The music was getting wilder as the servants poured the musicians more drink. The air in the great ballroom was getting heavy. Even with the tall windows open the candleflame struggled for air. No breeze was coming this night up the ridge to the Casa Cuesta.

Irena and Tomas slipped away. They were going to a lodge in the foothills of the Nicasoir Valley. It was a fine place, Irena had decided, to get rid of her slightly tampered-with virginity. Also, on the practical side, there was a growing market for wool in San Francisco, and with talk of a railroad in the future, raising sheep on their Nicasoir Valley land could be a splendid way to use the meadow and its slopes.

Rocco came up to George, who was hoping his own wedding to Maria would be as hearty and his marriage as fruitful as he knew this one would be. Irena had already talked to her brother and to Matthew Gower about heirs to the Velasquez lands, to the Casa Cuesta and the vineyards.

Rocco took up a cake and nibbled on it as he bent close to George. 'I've hired London Jim and two of his boyos to see the road up to the lodge in Nicasoir Valley isn't'—he lifted an eyebrow—'troubled.'

'I don't think Sam would do anything against Irena and Tomas. And London Jim is a murderous thug.'

Rocco grinned, wiped sugar from the cake off his fingers. 'Yes, he and his Australian bastards don't fear the Regulators. Hate them. We can use them.'

George replied that he didn't like the sons of bitches, but he wouldn't reject the use of force and violence when it was threatened against him and his. He had never before felt so strongly his blood bond with those Italian hill men, carriers of daggers. In Italy one always found a righteous justification for killing. George had thought he had left all that behind him. Now he wasn't so sure.

'Nothing changes but the hats,' Father O'Hara had once said to George, tasting a surviving bottle of Crema di Timo *liquore*. 'Now, here in this land it's tinged with social status, me boy, the new American disease. It's the restlessness of the buffalo hunters, horizon seekers. It's an absurd time when the lunatics appear in the majority.'

George felt that Father O'Hara, behind the rum-blossom nose and the exuberant brogue, made a great deal of sense. As he would put it, 'All certainties go into the void.'

Now George felt his own feelings were riding off in all directions. He lifted a glass of wine, clicked it with the glass in Rocco's hand. 'New times, new problems.' He laughed as he swallowed, spilling some of the drink down his chin. He lifted a crisp fresh napkin and saw to his amazement— Irena's doing for sure—it had embroidered on it the combined crests of the Velasquezes and the house of the Da Vincis.

The marriage of George Fiore and Maria Orsini was a much simpler affair. First of all, George was not a Velasquez. Then too, George wanted a quieter affair; the Brannan and Kendrick combination was active, threatening the farmers and ranchers who supplied him with produce. There was no knowing in what direction their malice would turn.

Father O'Hara performed the ceremony, Rocco was best man, Irena and Tomas had come down from the lodge; she assured them that she was already pregnant with the Velasquez heir.

Her pregnancy was not at all too soon, she insisted. 'Tomas knew his duties. He who walks on his own land walks with God.'

Before his wedding, George spoke to Maria while they took a ride along the cliffs below Casa Cuesta.

'In this country, Maria, a woman can change her mind.'

'You are a virtuous man, Grego.'

'You are pleased?' He flicked his whip at an ear of the horse pulling the buckboard.

'Of course. It is the Lord's will.'

He smiled. 'It is *our* will.'

'Our will is coming from *him*, Grego.

He looked at her, the large bonnet covering much of her face. He slapped the reins on the horse's wide flanks and agreed. She was a good woman, no vindictive attitudes in her, unsophisticated, somewhat superstitious. That, he felt, did no harm in a woman, and might even be a virtue. For a moment as the horse increased its trot he had a vision of Carrie, the wild fury of their activities in bed. With effort he forced images of ecstasy out of his mind. He leaned over and kissed Maria's cheek in atonement for his memory of obvious delight—gave her a searching scrutiny. She had received his kiss calmly, and George recalled he hadn't kissed her very often. Her attitude had suggested a minimal decency: touch, don't handle boisterously.

So after the wedding and a small dinner at the Casa, the new husband and wife went back to their house. George left Maria alone for a half-hour while he smoked a pipe and walked in the garden, which smelled of fertility, growth. The tomatoes were ripening, the fleshy pink turning to a bright red. He plucked a ripe tomato and bit into it slowly, savoring the juices, the yielding texture.

When he entered the bedroom with its great oak bed, the room lit by two candles, his wife was in bed, wearing a linen gown trimmed with her own lace.

She said in a low firm tone, 'The candles, *please*, Grego.'

He blew them out, got out of his voluminous trousers, and undressed in the darkness. He got into bed and lifted the nightdress up to Maria's navel.... The consummation was simply done, in a congenial but not ardent atmosphere. She lay very still and he had to part her legs. There was a resistance and he had little difficulty penetrating her. George asked if he was giving her pain and she did not answer. For a moment he had feared that he would not come erect, that his thoughts of Carrie would betray him now. But there was no faltering; flesh was flesh. When it was done, he was amazed that she orgasmed violently, clung to him for a few moments in a low-breathing stillness.

He said something, some vague assurance, he didn't recall what.

Maria washed herself under the nightgown at a basin and got back into bed. She was soon asleep. Clearly the marriage had been creditably consummated. George lay awake listening to an owl in the trees beyond the garden hotting as it hunted mice near an old barn.

After a while he got up and stared out of a window. The thing—deed? duty?—was done. He was a husband. There had been a skin-to-skin communication; he had accomplished the duties, privileges of a husband. George had expected a little more in this fulfillment of some divine ordinance. There had been for him little excitement, not as there had been with the *other*. She who had gone away was irretrievably lost. Perhaps this joyless duty was suitable penance for his earlier sinful passion with Carrie. George felt tears forming and fought them back. A bland marriage was the best marriage, after all.

It took him a long time to fall asleep—Maria not stirring. Just before he fell away into the void of dreamless sleep, he heard the owl strike; a final fierce *hoot*, the small sound of a mouse coming to its final end to become in a short time, he knew, a tiny bundle of fur and bones ejected out onto the barn floor.

That was the night the Lopez lumber mill was burned. At breakfast, Rocco insisted they act.

We'll have London Jim and his boyos burn down the Kendrick storehouse.' George tried not to think of events as some unbearable saturation point.

'No, no, Rocco. The bastards will be prepared and it will lead to killings.'

'But goddammit, now the farmers will see they'll be burned out if they supply you.'

Maria came in from the kitchen with a tray of eggs and Italian-style sausage and peppers. 'Is there anything else, Grego?'

'No, Maria, that will be fine.... Now, Rocco, I want no actions. We will go on as before. If the produce is denied us, well, I have other things in mind.'

'Like what? Cleaning the street? Picking up trash under the wharves?' Rocco got up violently from the table, overturning his chair.

'Rocco!'

As the young man stamped out, Maria asked, 'Isn't he hungry?'

George served himself and smiled at his wife. 'Angry men usually aren't.'

He ate slowly, thinking. There are, he thought, two vital crises that shape a life—the search for identity and the molding of integrity.

He had been thinking of changing the direction of his business for some time. He had plans for a venture that couldn't fail. Italian and Hispanic farmers, fishermen, ranchers were having serious money problems. The Yankee-Britannic banks were not given to making loans to small enterprises with little or no collateral. It was a struggle when the fishing was poor, when grasshoppers or lack of rain decimated the crops. The small businesses had to survive until the next herring run or harvesting of a fairly good crop, but they had nowhere to turn for a loan that would carry them through.

Then, too, there were the Chinese, crammed together in busily growing Chinatown. Though they kept to themselves, avoiding trouble, several Chinese had been hung up by their pigtails on lampposts by rioting, drunken hoodlums. They kept themselves carefully invisible, bore abuse silently, traded, imported, ran laundries and little eating places serving their pungent, exotic cuisine. Many were prosperous, shipping their gold coins back to China.

These immigrants would provide George with his most lucrative venture yet. To begin his new project, he would cut his produce business, dismiss London Jim and his hoodlums, and keep Rocco from taking any drastic and dangerous action. George made out a list of fishermen and farmers who respected him and would trust him. The Chinese would be harder to convince; gaining their confidence after years of hostility from the 'White Devils' would be nearly impossible. He did not see them as the city did, as 'stupid coolies.' In his limited contact with them, George had found them to be intelligent, adept at surviving, and crafty businessmen. He knew he would find a way to reach them.

George marched into the Kendrick General Store—boot heels clacking on the wooden floor—smiled at the two shaggy guards with shotguns and motioned to Homer behind a counter. Homer had begun working for his father again.

'Got no gun, Homer. There's no pistol on me.'

'Sure, Mr Fiore, that's all right.'

'I want to talk to your father.'

It took a little arranging, but finally he was facing Moses, who was seated behind his big desk. As George later described him, Moses looked 'like a poisoned pup, sitting there red as a sunset, the way Jehovah must have looked down on the Jews when he was ready to throw thunderbolts. Anyway, he was seeing me face to face, letting me say my bit.'

Moses put a hand under his chin, scratched his beard. 'You've got balls, I'll say that for you, Fiore.'

'We call them *coglioni*. Me, I just want to exist and to support, feed my people. I'm here to say I want peace, peace and amity. I'm cutting down the produce gathering, turning over my market stalls to Chico Vallejo, one of my Mexican workers, for a percentage.'

'What's that to me?'

'I want to call off the war, Moses. You and Sam have got

me in a tangle. Your gun-hands can kill some of us, we with our hired guns can kill some of you. Figures?'

'Figures.'

'Now, I don't want Rocco or myself pistoled. I don't want Homer or Chass or you bushwhacked. We've broken bread together. Christ-almighty, Moses, don't you see where we're heading? It's like touching fire to straw.'

The big man nodded, rose and walked to a pitcher, poured himself a glass of water. 'Thirsty?' George said he wasn't. Moses Kendrick wiped his hairless upper lip with two fingers.

'We don't have to kill you, just run you guineas out of town with a bit of tar and feathers.'

'Run out my wife, my sister, Tomas Velasquez too? He's got political connections, Tomas has—maybe as good as yours—through his lawyer, Matt Gower.'

'I could tell Sam not to tar and feather the ladies.... You don't scarebooger me with Matt Gower's connections.'

The two men stared at each other, at a standoff. Moses almost moved toward another glass of water. Instead, he stepped back to his desk and sat down. George wanted to reach for his pipe, but didn't.

'If I walk out of here with no truce—at least that— London Jim and his gang will lay for you, kill you, and maybe even your sons.'

Moses nodded, said nothing.

'I can't control the Sydney Ducks, Moses, once they've tasted blood. That means you and Sam will have to bring the Regulators into the fight. Murder, lynchings, burnings. The state will have to send in the troops. The whole city, the whole shebang—docks, shipping, everything—could go up in flames. But come hell or high water, I'm not going to be run out, with or without tar and feathers.'

'You're not the reasonable fella I thought you were, George. More like the fallen Lucifer.'

'I thought my coming here was a reasonable gamble to avoid disaster. You want me to kiss ass? I'll do it, but on my own terms.'

There was a long silence. George waited tensely while the minutes ticked by. Moses picked up a steel-nibbed pen and began to probe at his fingernails. When he looked up, the last trace of hostility was gone. There was a slight tremor in his hand, and anguish in his eyes.

'All right, George, I gotta admit the picture you paint chills me. We'll just be killing each other off. I can control Sam; he's in a bad way, his business affairs, his whole way of living. I don't crawl, but I admit I can spit in the wrong direction.' He held out his hand. George took it, hoping his own wasn't too damp. 'It can't be like it was, George, but we can walk the streets without looking over our shoulders.'

George nodded. 'It's kind of warm in here. I'd be pleased to take that glass of water now.

By the late 1850's the poor and immigrant working classes were clustered in small villages along the bay. Not many of the Italians or Mexicans had been successful gold-seekers. They found instead that supplying seafood and farm products to San Francisco made them a good living.

George had observed how they went out the Golden Gate for sea bass and perch, the large sardine. In the bay they raked oysters, and from among the kelp beds they baited crates to lure the West Coast lobster that wasn't a lobster at all.

George watched the port expand, the population grow, and hotels rise over landfill, under which the hulls of sailing ships rested, abandoned and left in the silt. The large fish markets at North Beach swelled with the booming city, and more seafood was needed to fill the increasing demand.

George's first opportunity in his new enterprise was ironic in origin. His relationship with Rocco had been strained when the London Jim gang was fired, and George had made little effort to retain a good part of the produce markets. Rocco had left him to go into partnership with Bico Tamala in his eating place on the wharf. But gradually, as his rage had calmed, Rocco saw with a clearer

95

head that George had been right: bloodshed, arson, and even murder would have solved nothing. The Regulators were too strong and Sam Brannan and Moses Kendrick were respected citizens, men of good standing, while George and Rocco were still considered outsiders.

Rocco and Bico Tamala served fine fish soups, shrimp in hot sauces, the giant oysters, and for those who had a taste for it, squid. If they were to make the small pier longer and expand the kitchen, Bico needed funds. But when Rocco approached the Bay City Bank, the Anglo bankers shook their heads.

'You folks are poor risks. What have you got a lease on? Some wooden piles, two old stoves, and your partner's mother, wife, and two sisters. That's no business.'

'Mr Wilson, it is good food, good fish, *good* business. People say it's the place to eat. We have to turn them away, no room.'

'Sorry, but we're not interested in small loans with no collateral.' The banker, Burton Wilson (an investor in the Comstock Lode), waved a hand toward the door. 'Why don't you ask that Fiore feller? One of your dago friends, isn't he?'

'We had a little disagreement.'

'I hear he's come a cropper since Moses Kendrick gave him the heave-ho.'

Rocco kicked the brass cuspidor beside the banker's desk. 'Someday, Mr Wilson, we'll find your fat *culo* better to kick.'

George was pleased when Rocco came to him. They sat in the parlor of the little house among cut glass and a painted plaster Saint Francis, a collection of seashells, and drank Napa red wine.

'I've seen for some time, Rocco, how the Yankee banks are not putting out any of their cash, at least not into the hands of the little people.'

'You think there is a way to make a bank for the Italians, the Mexicans, the Chinese?'

'A bank? No, not with what assets I have. Maybe I can

become a partner in the boats, the eating places, the grape harvest. Invest in them, take a little share if they can't pay back.'

He took a stogie out of a China jar and handed it to Rocco, lit a pipe. They sat smoking, blowing rings into the air. Rocco repaired the end of his cigar with a wet finger. 'No more Havana cheroots Now you give me Pittsburgh stogies, a dollar a barrel?'

George nodded, grinned. 'I've been hard hit. But I remember Father Orsini trying to teach us wooden-headed choir boys a bit of Latin: *Ne cede malis, sed contra audentior ito.*'

Rocco coughed out stogie smoke. 'What the hell does that mean?'

'Roughly, "Don't give way to misfortunes, but rush out boldly to meet them."'

Word spread that George Fiore could help.

Cesare Spinelli was from the Piedmont. He disliked the sea; the heave and toss of stormy night fishing made him ill. When he found a Spanish ship in the bay with a cargo of linen, and a small stock of grape-vine slips packed in moss and kept damp, he sold his share in the small fishing craft he owned with his Uncle Nicklo and bought a hundred slips of grape vine.

North of the city, up in Napa, there was land on a hillside that reminded him of the vineyards of his grandfather. He could buy it all from a Spanish family for five hundred dollars. The problem, he explained to George, was this: he had a wife, six children, two goats, bedding, three beds, a donkey, and two-wheeled cart. The grape slips were dying. None of the Anglo bankers would give a loan.

Spinelli brooded, his wife scolded, and he kept the vine slips damp. They were showing signs of producing leaves, and then, if not planted, they would die. His wife waved a broom at him. 'At least they'll start a fire to cook a fish stew, *if* we had fish.' They were living off the market leavings, fish and shrimp not sold at the end of the day at the wharfs., and the two oldest sons were shining shoes outside the Barbary Coast whorehouses.

His wife waved her arms, tore at her hair. 'And when our girls, Rosa and Elena, grow up, you'll put them in the brothels? I'm too wore down to be a whore myself. So get the devil's grape stakes out of the house before I break them over your head!'

Cesare Spinelli didn't have the few dimes to go get drunk on the dreadful wine the fishermen drank by the jugful. His spirit hadn't yet been broken enough to mooch a glass of wine, but he could see himself soon hanging around the Green Goddess hoping someone would stand him a drink. This morning, ignoring the vine stock soon going to sprout, he had wandered down by Tamala's wharf, where his son Tony had territory as shoeshine boy. He'd twist the little bastard's ear and grab hold of whatever he had earned that day, and go get drunk, as far on the road to drunkenness as the shoeshining could carry one. Saints and Holy Mother, I have become an evil man, he thought. The boy Tony was nowhere in sight, but Tamala, sweating, wiping his face and bull neck with a red bandanna, was there cursing and commanding two men unloading long raw timbers, pitch still flowing from rough sawed edges.

'What am I doing? Fool that I am, listening to Rocco Bordone. I'm enlarging the wharf. Crazy, yes, and these muleheads are splintering the timbers that I want as rafters for the new dining area.'

Cesare Spinelli was impressed. How was it one was able to build in such times? Tamala sipped from a bottle of wine; to cut his morning slimes, he explained, and offered Spinelli the bottle. They had married cousins and were on a family basis, so Tamala let Tony shine shoes in front of his wharf.

'God is not always a fool, Spinelli. After all, the Pope is an Italian, no? And when he prays, he puts in maybe a good word for his own.'

Spinelli sipped. He was a man who distrusted the Church, the Pope, and wasn't sure about God. He took a good pull on the wine bottle. 'The Pope send the money?' Spinelli was wiping the neck of the bottle with the palm of his hand.

'No. The Fiore. He lent me the money to extend the wharf, buy a splendid old stove from that hotel remodeling on Market Street. Who needs the Anglo banks? May their farts poison their wives' wombs. Go see George Fiore.'

So Spinelli's grape vines were planted on the rolling hills of Napa. George now owned half of a still non-productive vineyard, half of a wharf and restaurant. And his new business was launched.

William Ralston's Bank of California boasted a solid stone facade, marble counters, bronze tellers' grilles, silver cuspidors, overhead hanging lamps burning whale oil, and teak paneling. George, visiting William Ralston, admired the offices. He inspected vaults of solid steel shipped over from Birmingham in England, room-high safes with many dials and bars, painted over with scenes of the city, the bay, Indians, and great vistas of the West with sunsets and clouds, images a bit too romantic, George thought, when compared with the actual landscape.

'Fiore,' Ralston asked, 'going to put me out of business?'

'No, sir, Mr Ralston, just admiring all the fancy trimmings I'm going to leave out. Take a high false front off Montgomery Street with a wooden sidewalk, two six-by-four windows set with small panes—formerly owned by a harness man who had murdered a woman at Nancy Barraclough's brothel.' Some of the Regulators had taken him out of jail and hanged him on what was to become Nob Hill.

George's office walls and floor were of rough-sawed board, the room smelling of leather, stale glue, and mouse droppings. The counter came off a lime-juicer in the tea trade from Canton; Rocco had brought the lamps from a wrecked gambling house where the mob found marked cards and loaded dice. The old iron safe was behind a panel of oak boards, to which was added a larger vault that came up from Panama. Few knew that the locks didn't work and its only protection was a steel bar and a large padlock.

The only thing new besides George Fiore's tall shiny black top hat was the ten-foot-long sign attached to the false front over the windows:

FIORE'S GENERAL TRADING CO.
Merchandising, Bills of Exchange

9

Up the coast at Casa Cuesta, Irena was flourishing as well, heavy with the heir of the Velasquezes in her belly. In the first months of her pregnancy she still rode in her querulous fashion over the range, scolded the foreman of the cattle herds, tasted and spit out the first samplings of the wine Julio was producing. '*Cio non vale un'acca*—not worth a straw. Use the best grapes for the first pressings and keep the others for the drunkards. And don't drink so much yourself, Julio, your nose looks on fire.'

'I am, señora, not drinking *more*,' was his usual protest, to which she gave her usual answer: 'You are not drinking *less*, either.'

Between the two of them there was an understanding, even admiration. Irena felt that Julio had the makings of a good manager, and to him she was demanding (he called her a hellcat) but fair. Her most ardent interest was in rebuilding the Velasquez estate. She had decided that sheep would be the most profitable means, that wool and tallow would bring the best cash return. Shipping would soon be made easier by a railroad connecting the coasts, which was now talked of. 'It has to come. Wool is easier to transport to the mills of New England.' She read with relish Greeley's *Herald, Harper's Weekly* (late as they came) to evaluate the eastern markets—their needs for western gold, silver, leather, wool, southern cotton.

As her child grew within her body, she made Tomas seek out old iron chests, rotting leather trunks for documents of the family, the land grant, its history. Tomas grumbled. He accepted assumptions of social superiority without records.

'It's old paper, my dear, nothing else.'

'It's what you are, what your—*our*—son will be.'

Tomas had learned to admire this driving woman, and if she was less passionate since her pregnancy, he had done his duty as a husband and a good Catholic and their relationship was mutually satisfying. He saw her as a person without sham or pretension (but for her pride in being now a Velasquez). Most of all he admired, and was grateful for, the zeal with which she ran his vast holdings. He had stepped aside and occupied himself with dressing well and going to town to gamble a little (Irena limited his funds). He knew it was best not to drink too much. If he was brought back to the Casa too drunk, his wife would pour buckets of water from the coldest well over him to sober him. She gave Tomas a buoyant sense of excitement, and he did not take umbrage at her self-assertiveness. The estate was flourishing, even if new mortgages were piled on to the hilt, money borrowed from the Fiore Trading Co. spent on improvements.

One morning as Irena was recovering from morning sickness, she explained to her husband, who was eating a meal of *piccioni arrosti*, 'The more one owes, the bigger the success. Borrowed money works hard if one uses it well.' She laughed, feeling her child kick away inside her. 'Kick, darling, kick Mama.'

To keep busy, when she grew too heavy to ride, Irena would rummage among the old family papers Tomas found for her and revel in the past history of the Velasquez family in America. Most fascinating were the papers of Tomas's grandfather, Don Cruz Vizcalno, who fancied himself a scholar and collected notes for a book, *Spain in America*. The history of the family's first Americans was never completed, but Irena found it enthralling:

In attempting a history of Spain in America [she read], I should mention here something about my own family's past, to serve as a personal record of those early days of Spanish domination. The first of us to come to the New World was the hidalgo Bernal Diaz del Velasquez, born in 1493 in glorious Spain, the son of Don Francisco Diaz del Castillo Velasquez and Doña Maria Diaz Verdugo, citizens of the town of Medina del Campo. The family is of noble background, but as is often the case in noble families, had not much wealth, but a surplus of hopes and fantasy.

In 1517, at the age of twenty-three, Bernal decided to seek his fortune across the ocean in New Spain. He is described by one who knew him as 'being of medium height, quick and active in all things, well made and known as *"el galán,"* the elegant.' In 1514 he was a soldier in the company of Pedro Arias de Avila, the governor of Tierra Firma.

Bernal went on many expeditions always seeking his fortune. He was with Juan de Grijalva in 1518, and noted: 'Our leader lost two teeth, the inhabitants killed seven of us, but Grijalva did bring back some golden trinkets.'

So the governor decided on a new expedition—which Bernal joined—in 1519, under the famous and cunning brute Hernan Cortez. They landed for the great conquest of Mexico with five hundred and eight soldiers, sixteen stallions and mares. At Tabasco they fought a battle and our ancestor reports: 'I received an arrow in my right thigh but it was a wound of no seriousness.'

He seemed prone to damage but treated it as a mere distraction. Moving inland, Cortez founded the Villa Rica de la Vera Cruz.

Irena delighted in Bernal, who was described ironically by his descendant as 'a pious young man, taking Holy Communion, the Sacrament of Penance, and acts of Contrition before seeking to plunder.' Clearly he, like herself, took pride in the Velasquez pride and honor, she thought. She would call her son Bernal, among his other names.

Looking up from her book, she saw a horseman coming from the direction of Almonte. It was Grego. She called to the servant, 'Inez, set out wine from the springhouse, and some of the little cakes. *Pronto!*'

George was warm from the ride up from the ferry station, and his horse hadn't liked the boat trip from the city. But he was pleased to see what Irena had done to clear the orchard of weeds and to rebuild the fences around the cow barns.

He sipped the wine and leaned back in the rawhide chair, his sister reclining next to him on a wickerwork sofa, her belly well forward like a giant melon.

'I have been reading of how the Velasquezes came here. In leopard skins over shiny armor.'

'Not in a dirty steerage as we did?'

She sniffed. 'The merging of the Da Vincis with one of the noble houses of Spain is not the subject for jest.'

Her brother swished the wine over his palate. 'Tomas told me the first Velasquez robbed the Indians, enslaved them, and grabbed everything he could.'

'How do you think King David, Caesar, Napoleon began? I've been reading a lot of history, since it's hard for me to get about. Even the old popes led armies.'

George tasted one of the cakes. 'And you lead animals to your own ark, buying sheep, importing a costly ram from Mexico City.'

Irena laughed. 'You've been getting the bills.'

'Damn it, go slowly. Not so fast. You've a winery, a cider mill, herds of unruly wild cattle, a cheese-and-butter business, and now sheep. You can't afford it.'

'Great fortunes are made with other people's money.

103

Wool to make cloth is always in short supply, says Horace Greeley.'

'Damn Greeley. Wool prices rise and fall. The Australians are producing it by ton upon ton. And so I'm the money tree?'

Irena eased herself into a better position, groaned. 'Forget Australia. They have to find ships, cross the wide Pacific. We can freight it east by wagons, and soon, soon, the steam trains will come.'

'So will the Messiah, Mr Norton, the Jewish rice merchant, tells me. Irena, I swear I'm not honoring any more bills for the Velasquez account. I'm not Ralston's big Bank of California, just a small trading company that discounts bills of credit, lends against assets, and verifies and accepts notes against crops and cargoes.'

'Don't cry, Grego, or I'll send Inez for a towel. I'll have five hundred barrels of good wine this year, and I'm cutting timber at Novato Creek. You know the city consumes lumber faster than one can cut it.'

'You've mortgaged all that timber and most of the wine already.'

'Next year Ramon Bernal Velasquez will be here.' She patted her stomach. 'He will see a new grapè harvest, more wine casks, and there are tall trees all the way to Petaluma and beyond. Money? Money is shit that grows roses.'

'So *it* has a name already?'

'It's a he, not an it. And how is Maria? Time, you know, you proved you're not a gelding.' She yelled at the servant girl, 'Inez, get us *café brulats*.'

George smiled and sipped the wine. 'I do have a message from Maria. She is sure she too has conceived.'

'God take thanks!' cried Irena. '*Madre, O Dio mio!* The Orsinis are good breeding stock—wide thighs, able to birth a blacksmith's anvil. There was an Orsini pope, wasn't there, who had a dozen bastards. Cesare, Lucrezia.'

'They were Borgias.'

'Related to the Orsinis. Ah, Grego, we have done honor and will go on doing honor to the Fiores.' She accepted a cup from the servant. 'A toast in coffee, brandy, spices.'

'It's only so far that Maria has skipped a period or two. There's nothing for sure.'

Irena sipped, lifted cup from saucer. 'An Italian woman doesn't skip a period to amuse herself. She collects sperm like a miner gold. Ah, there is Tomas.' Her husband had appeared in the doorway carrying a pair of silver spurs. 'Tomas, it's good news. Maria is bearing.'

Tomas laughed, handed the spurs to the servant, 'Polish them, Inez.'

Tomas enjoyed his wife's exhilaration, as long as he was free to pursue the life he chose. Marriage had fattened him up a bit, George noticed, and he was no longer wagering so much in bets at the Mazourha and Aquila d'Oro gambling tables.

'That news, George, calls for a better wine. I have some bottles of a Chambolle-Musigny type put down by my father before the Indians killed him. He was a calm man; just drank, and like Saint Sebastian, waited for the arrows.'

It was a good wine, and Tomas listened to the talk of pork prices and sheep shearing between brother and sister. Business was an insidious bore to Tomas. But now that no one talked to him of his debts, and his creditors had ceased hounding him, life could be lived without the burden of responsibility. He now had time to train his falcons properly.

He offered to show George his birds, and they went off toward the barns. Irena picked up Don Cruz's history again. She felt strongly that a bit of history gives one a sense that one does moult the past like a grasshopper leaving its old shell for a bolder one—one must pick one's past carefully.

It is clear [she read] that my ancestor Bernal Diaz del Velasquez, a true Christian materialist, was an opportunist who added to all that a sense of grace in accepting his wounds. He had some share of the seven hundred thousand gold ounces Cortez collected from the Aztecs, 'and which was divided among us soldiers, but he, Cortez, made the division with such trickery and cunning that all our shares were very small, and many refused in anger to take them. But I took mine. Besides, I acquired some fine cloth and the warm brown-skinned daughter of a chieftain, a beautiful Indian girl called Sivi Topa. Many of us abandoned ourselves to licentiousness, lewd pleasures until March of 1520.'

Resilience and gaucherie alternate. Twenty years afterward, Bernal is named in Padre Augustin Rivera's *Anales Mexicanos* (Volume I, page 147) as a landowner, horse breeder, cattle raiser in Tamaulipas, married to Doña Maria Salazar Juarros—clearly a non-Indian import. A man of extremes, he appears to have sunk into middle age and affluent dullness.

That the family—fertile in children—spread, was clearly documented, although many original papers were lost in a fire at the first rancho in 1740.

A rather different sort of ancestor was Don Gaspar Pedro de Alvarado Velasquez the Second—a great nabob, a magnificent horseman, a gambler at La Collude los Negros. I, on one visit to his Casa, was amazed by the needless number of servants, mounted men, and the slovenly grandeur of everything. Whole oxen roasted in great pits and the broaching of vast kegs of wine and brandies, the use of silver designs on heavy saddles; all part of the jovial, casual, extravagant way of life. A great show of gold trim on the women, splendid detail on the horses' gear and all the ceremonial regalia in full fuss and colors. Don Gaspar is also the *alcalde*, a sort of mayor. While I was there, some knifings and brawlings took place, while dogs enjoyed the feast along with the guests. A marked difference from Bernal Diaz—or perhaps not so great after all.

George, after inspecting Tomas's hawks, strode back to the house and said good-bye to his sister with a warning that she had come to the end of her credit, 'the bottom of the barrel,

dear Irena, with the Fiore Trading Company.' He rode
down to the ferry, brooding over family and the infuriating
strength of women to get their own way. Irena was a genius
at taking chances, while he was a careful plodder,
reconciled to reason, logic. Or did Irena have that wild
Italian gift of self-destructiveness that one often saw, when
common sense seemed overcome by dreams of great
fortunes? He chuckled as the horse pricked up his ears.
Irena was like Columbus, that sailor madly sure the world
was round and India lay to the west. Columbus was surely a
true Italian.

His threat to cut Irena off was not ill-founded. The Fiore
Trading Company was in a period of reckless growth, too
many of its assets on loan to fishermen, farmers and
vineyards. So he brooded, frowning as he rode away from
the Casa. If the grapes were ruined by a dry season, if the
fish didn't run properly that year, if the credits advanced to
importers were unpaid, he would be ruined. A mere delay
of a day or two in collecting loans, or wine turning to
vinegar in the cask, would mean a monumental struggle to
stay solvent. He cursed and hoped Irena's child was born a
girl.

10

'They are not so much rulers as they think they are.'
    'How can you say that?'
    'Why, because all through history it's the woman who has
the *coglioni*—we just don't wear them dangling outside.'
    'The women?'
    'I have been reading a lot since being tied down here, and

we are the makers of the world who fill it with our children. We are the womb; without that the whole of history isn't worth a belch.'

'Irena, how can you talk like that? Men rule the world.'

'Only because we let them *think* they do.'

The two women were reclining on sofas under the wisteria arbor at the Casa, big bellies weighing them down. They were eating honey cake and sipping dark Italian coffee. Irena relished her body's burden, having studied an anatomy book for facts of her condition. Maria, although behind in her conception, bore the larger burden. She seemed precariously overwhelmed by her huge belly. Rocco had insisted she was carrying twins; he knew the signs. Old Maruca, the midwife, had patted Maria's stomach; rubbed it with a secret blend of *eau-de-vie* and anchovy oil; made the sign of the cross and the ram's horn gesture for a safe and easy delivery. She had tended so many Italian women that she knew their langauge and their rituals, which she combined with her own.

'Whatever it is, Doña Maria, it isn't a set of dishes or a keg of wine.'

Father Zorilla—he of the thin melancholy mouth—her favorite priest, had said it was heresy to use the ritual holy gesture together with the Gypsy sign of the ram's horn, and he gave her a text to read, a life of Saint Catherine of Siena.

Tomas took his approaching fatherhood with casual interest, bringing Irena oranges, costly to import from Southern California, and patting her growing stomach. 'Ah, the new Velasquez, polite little fellow. Does he kick, my dear?'

'Kick? He gives me heartburn, and I'm as constipated as a mule in the dry season. But never mind Tomas, I'll not fail you.'

He gave his wife a quizzical look, wiped her brow with a crepe-de-chine handkerchief. He wasn't as sure as she was that it would be a son. But with Irena couch-bound more and more, he did have some propitious moments when he could slip away to town to a card game, an afternoon relaxing at the Poodle Dog bar, and the joshing of the Emperor Norton, who issued his own money and was charmingly mad.

George showed more interest in Maria's condition. Involved as he was in trade and his private banking, engaging in altercations with suppliers and borrowers, he still managed to see to Maria's whims, hear her fears. She was sure she was to die in childbirth, as had two aunts, or that the child would be bewitched by the envy of neighbors and born dead or with red patches of Satan on his face or brow.

Father Zorilla and Father O'Hara were on call, often eating their meals between blessing the womb—*In nomine Patris et Filii et Spiritus Sancti*. There were, George noted, more holy pictures on the walls, several garishly painted plaster images of Saints Francis and Stephen, and an engraving of the Pope. George, fighting back his irritation at the pious decor, didn't speak out against Father Zorilla, who fed on nearly a whole haunch of carefully aged venison one night.

George continued to feel ill at ease in the female atmosphere created by a pregnant woman in the household. He would go off with Rocco to a cockfight, or go fishing after dark on the bay to get away from the house of female odors, the little smoking lamps lit under statues of the Virgin. He slept alone in a small room, for as Maria grew amazingly in size, she rolled about and muttered prayers in her sleep, crying out at times. Maruca, the old midwife, said Maria was in need of red blood, and forced her to eat rare meat, drink red wine, and said that if Maria didn't follow orders, cholera morbus could get in and the child would be born with donkey ears. '*Mangiate bene*,' she would warn. 'Eat well.'

When George grew worried over Maria's size, he insisted that Dr Silas Welton, an elderly Englishman, come to examine her. Maria refused to let the doctor slide his hand beneath her skirt and only allowed him to tap his fingers on her belly. Dr Welton said it was 'a well-packed pregnancy.'

He still had faith in leeches, bleeding, and cupping. But Maria insisted it was God's problem and refused anything but a charcoal powder, which did seem to help her morning vertigo.

She was transported carefully to the Casa, for the two wives had decided to give birth as nearly as possible, in time and geography. Maria was sure her child would not wait the full nine months, and Maruca and Irena agreed. Maruca had a good room with her rags and flannels, her rubbing oils, ointments, powders, and pills and Gypsy lore. '*Cara, carissima*, trust in the old ways.'

In spite of the physical discomfort, it was a pleasant time for the two wives. Irena, talkative, poor-mouthing men's part in the conception process—'A frontal enema, little more'—Maria working her rosary beads and getting a bit carried away by the strong wine and coffee, remembering her childhood herding geese in the Campagna, stringing mushrooms for drying, listening to church music. As for the present, how fearful this new land was; Americans with their curses, big discordant laughter, and their need to dominate everything by violence.

Irena agreed. 'We let them think big, our men. We give them the notion they rule as lords, that they run things, but it's women who are the true strong ones. We who keep them respectable, shame them to work hard, we who sit on the cash box. We cosset them—tell them how fine they are in providing for their families.'

Maria hiccuped. 'If it's as you say, Irena, don't they know that we keep things going?'

'Their vanity is a blindfold. If it weren't for us, they'd be spending their time gambling, racing horses, lifting the petticoats of whores on the Coast, and shooting at each other. Men, my dear Maria, are born wanderers, hedonists. Woman is the civilizer, the homemaker, the one who pushes them out to do the world's work; it's she who says go show me your skills in making money, doing business.... Who am I talking about? Helen of Troy, Cleopatra, Catherine de Medici, the heretic Queen

Elizabeth—no man was their equal.'

'Where did you hear all this, Irena?'

'I read. The family papers. Sarah's books of history to help my English. You should read too.'

'I can hardly read Italian. The English printing, it swims before my eyes. Oh!' She grabbed her keg-shaped stomach. 'It's moving.'

Irena laughed. 'It's been listening to us. Must be a boy.'

It had been a warm day with soft penciled clouds in a low sky, and night brought a heavier heat and searing lightning scars. Irena, in the midst of a dream about her grandmother's larded hare (stewed in bay leaves and brandy), came awake in great pain as her water broke, soaking the bed. Though she cried out loudly, Maria was sleeping deeply, dreaming she was having coffee with St Catherine of Siena. However, the midwife heard the outcry and came rushing across the hall with her bundles and her flasks.

'Yes, yes, *madre mía*—it's broken, the water. Now remain calm, dear Señora Velasquez, calm.'

'I am calm! Damn you ... Oh, oh! Oh!'

'That's right, swear, groan, curse the men who bring us to this with the expelling of their juices, the flourishing of their parts. So strain, *push!*'

'Stop the talk!' Irena cursed fluently as the pains increased.

Maruca tied a towel to the bedpost, and from time to time probed Irena's belly and shouted encouragement, painting Irena's parts with sweet-smelling oil and reciting Gypsy chants.

The night was canopied in a dark heat, and Maruca refreshed herself with a bit of brandy and also rubbed it on Irena's forehead. The old woman was actually a splendid midwife, an expert, experienced in difficult and dangerous deliveries.

Irena begged Maruca to keep Tomas from the room. He had in fact left at dusk to join some friends in a fox hunt given by the Bayside Club. It was a raucous western affair,

111

not the tally-ho of mounted riders in pinks. The riders ran down a mangy bull fox, and after the slaughter, sat around an open fire under the trees, drinking and feasting.

Ramon Bernal Velasquez was born at three-ten in the morning, forced into the world after one vast heave of Irena's body. Shiny with birth slime and attached to Irena by a cord, the large perfect baby made mewing sounds as the midwife cleared his nostrils. He was yawning politely, and only after Maruca had severed the cord and held him up by the legs and slapped his rump did he protest with one loud cry.

'A gentleman, a gentleman,' cried the midwife. 'A juicy little *bambino*.'

'It's a son?' asked the panting mother.

'All the parts, Señora Velasquez.'

'Let me see him.'

'The midwife presented him legs first. 'Look, he'll ruin many a virgin, by the sight of him.'

He was clearly a very beautiful child, long, slim, well-formed. Irena placed the baby at one well-endowed breast, after which he yawned with his toothless mouth and fell asleep. Irena brushed the light brown air into neatness with a loving hand. With children, you give something to God, she thought.

Maria appeared in her long nightgown, eyes still half-closed in sleep. 'The servants are making so much noise, and ...' She broke off, staring at the bed. 'It's *here*? Oh!'

'Here, and look, just look at this fine child.'

Maria rubbed a bare foot and leaned over the bed. She put out a finger to touch the child, but timidly decided against it. The midwife, after a hearty pull at the brandy bottle, wiped her mouth and turned to Maria. 'Now it's *your* turn.'

'Was it ... was it dreadful?'

Irena adjusted the baby in her arms. 'It was ...' She saw Maria's pinched, frightened face, and quickly went on, 'It was nothing. Like a visit to the privy after eating too many green cherries.'

Ramon Velasquez—not yet officially named—slept on, a drop of his mother's milk in one corner of his mouth.

A month later, before her time—someone had surely miscalculated—Maria Fiore apprehensively gave birth to twin sons at four in the afternoon. First she presented the dark one, then three minutes later the blond son. Both births came quickly and easily, to the delight of their relieved mother, who had felt that the burden in her would never emerge. She was prepared for death, though Father O'Hara had refused her the last rites.

Cheerfully he insisted: 'Time enough. I'll be standing nearby. Don't you fear. I'll not be letting you slip away without the rituals.'

George, summoned from the trading company, was pleased. He examined his sons, inspecting them with almost a collector's covetousness. There were no querulous complaints from Maria, resting in bed. She had asked the servant girl Conchita Concepcion to braid her hair, and now reclined in a pale rose brocade robe while her husband and the midwife fussed over the twins occupying one cradle.

Rocco insisted the babies were spitting images of George, and the father felt that he was not being foolish in agreeing. But to him they also looked like skinned muskrats.

'We'll call one "Alfredo" after my grandfather, the dark one. What do you say, Maria? He has Byzantine eyes and will see in the dark.'

Rocco said, 'They look fine to me.'

Maruca added, 'May they have the long life of an oak.'

Maria wished there were no questions to answer. She had done her God-ordained duty to her faith, to her husband. There had been a light seizure of trembling after the births; she felt as if she were drifting on a calm sea. Now there were only the years ahead to wait for heaven; meanwhile, she would resume her lace making. She drove off the pleasurable memory of their nights together. It was sinful the way she took such delirious pleasure in the climaxes of their coupling. It could give one palpitations of the heart to enjoy such things meant only to beget. Lewdness was the devil's game. She let her mind trail off to the odor of lamb with thyme from the kitchen.

'Maria! I said "Alfredo" for one of our sons.'

'Oh, a good name.'

'And the other?'

'Would you permit "Roberto"? After my brother?'

'Permit! Damn it, woman, it's your right.'

Maria hesitated. Questions could be *so* perplexing. 'You didn't like my brother.'

'Let it be "Roberto" … with "Cesare" someplace in there?'

She nodded and felt tired and said she'd like to go to sleep. 'We must baptize them as soon as we can, Grego, in case the Lord would not want us to keep them.'

The midwife clapped her hands. 'No danger, Doña Maria. I have placed a bit of the shell of a double-yolked egg in their cradle. When a hen is descended from the cock that crowed on the day Jesus rose from his tomb … the hen, she shows it by every five years laying a double-yolked egg.'

George left with Rocco, feeling he was sinking into a world of indulgent female attitudes, the odor of babies, and an excess of old wives' tales. Now there was a duality of purpose in his life. The idea of sons was good, and a stifling marriage acceptable. But he felt a void. For a second or so he had had a delicious vision of Carrie's hair tossing on a warm pillow, of an extraordinary passion with a woman he would never have again. Angry at the memory, he went to arrange for the baptism of his sons: the hell with 'Roberto'—'Cesare' would come first.

11

There was some sober apprehension in George at having produced twin sons. Some men, he had noticed, grew a bit grim behind the joy of reproducing themselves and taking on new responsibilities. But for George his sons were compensation for what was for him a cold, indifferent marriage. There was nothing he could fault in Maria's conduct as a housekeeper or a mother. But as a companion and a bed partner she was merely proper, showing no reluctance, at worst rigidly doing her duty, offering her body for the taking but never volunteering it with joy or anticipation, never in a gust of passion persistent for special attention. Her kisses were neat, not ardent. Her embrace was peripheral and she treated her strong orgasms as a predator that leaped upon her. She feared the depths of her passions, and forced herself to bury them. However, she was honest in what she saw as her duty. There was no pretence about her.

Maria's passionate nature reacted best to the Church, her priests; the 'black crows,' as Rocco called them. All this made home a bit of a trial for George. However, now with the twin sons, he would see to it that there was a more lively atmosphere. As for himself, he would accept things with an unruffled complacency, now that he could see life at home and in his enterprises in a steady ascending curve.

They decided to baptize the three babies at one ceremony. To avoid any protracted argument as to which of the two family priests would conduct the event, Father Zorilla would take care of Ramon Bernal Ignatius Fiore del

Farruco Velasquez (Irena had wondered if 'Da Vinci' might be slipped in, but was persuaded against it). As for the Fiore twins, the older (by three minutes) was to become a Christian as Alfredo Ercole Taddeo Fariano Fiore, and his brother would be named Cesare Roberto Angelo Fiore.

The day before the special mass planned to celebrate the newly anointed, Rocco came rushing into the trading company, where George was lifting a dozen mirrors framed in guilded scrolls from a sawdust-packed crate.

'Rocco, get a broom and sweep up this straw.'

'Something has happened at the church, at St Patrick's!'

Before George could reply, Father O'Hara ran in, breathing hard.

'George Fiore, it's like some omen! It's an abomination!'

'What? *What?*' George put down a mirror and turned to them.

'The birds,' said Father O'Hara, 'those filthy creatures.'

'Hundreds,' added Rocco. 'At least hundreds. Maybe thousands.'

'Where?'

Father O'Hara sat down, fanned himself with a loose sleeve of his robe. 'At St Patrick's. A few I'd noticed before, and I didn't mind. But last night, through some hole in the roof they have come in, leaving their droppings over the altar.'

'It's the Devil's doings,' said Rocco. 'The church is bewitched.'

George picked up his hat, set it firmly on his head. 'Show me.'

'We must use exorcists,' continued the priest. 'There is a friar in San Diego, Brother Jablonska, who has studied the cabal in Poland. Paracelsus' *Divina Particula Aurae*, incantations, special prayers.'

The report of the birds' invasion was all too true. The church ceiling seemed plastered with birds, swallows and terns. Some fluttered about, a few bolder ones swooped over the altar and added their offerings to the holy images.

'We must exorcise these devils!'

'Nonsense,' said George. 'They're only birds, and if you know birds' habits, you can get rid of them.'

He put a hand on Rocco's shoulder. 'Get us to the Casa Cuesta. No, first go round to the Poodle Dog and see if Tomas is there. If not, ride to the Casa. Tell him we want to borrow two of his best peregrine hunting falcons.'

Father O'Hara beat his chest with his fists. 'Killings! Here in holy church!'

'Just open the doors wide and open all the windows. The sight of the hawks will clear the birds out like magic.'

It certainly worked. As Tomas released the hawks inside the church, the invaders panicked. The din was incredible as they escaped in groups, in columns, in battalions, beaten against the walls in their haste. The flurry of wings was like the roaring of rushing water. Tomas, who had come along with heavy gauntlets and long leather thongs, smiled as the church was cleared of the birds.

'Marvelous, eh? Trained to the attack, my tiercels. Never have they seen such a collection of prey.'

Rocco said, 'One of your hawks followed the birds out of the window. A big blue-and-gray one, way up front.'

'Goddammit! Pardon me, Padre. That was Nero, my best peregrine.'

Tomas insisted Rocco help him recover the straying falcon, but Nero was never recaptured. Later there was a wild story that he had mated with an eagle and that one of his brood had carried off a human chld.

The christening ceremonies began auspiciously. Father O'Hara was serious but not somber (he had had a tot of brandy in his vestry) as he anointed Ramon Bernal Ignatius Fiore del Farruco Velasquez with the spot of holy oil, the ritual gesture of a touch of the wafer to the tiny mouth, and the final sprinkling of drops of holy water, as he recited the Latin. Ramon was in a long blue gown, and he stared up at the priest during the final 'Et Spiritus Sanctus.' Tomas thought Ramon yawned, but Irena insisted it had been a smile. The twins—both in pure silk chiffon robes—responded a bit more actively to Father Zorilla's touch.

Alfredo twisted about in Rocco's arms, and Cesare (Maria was surprised to hear the priest reveal 'Cesare' as the first name rather than 'Roberto'), in the arms of his godfather, Tomas Velasquez, let out a howl when splashed.

The pews were filled with prominent Italian and Spanish families, and some Anglos—among them Matthew Gower in a red waistcoat. None of the Kendricks or Brannans came, but the church was thronged with vineyard owners and workers, fishermen, and some of the servants not needed at the Casa to prepare the fiesta. In the back row sat Maruca, the midwife, in a dark dress clearly not made for her but cut down from a former owner. A black lace shawl sheltered her head and a string of red coral beads circled her neck. At the priests' final gesture that brought the baptisms to an end, she muttered an old Gypsy chant very low:

> Man is the dream of a shadow
> Set in the shadow of his hooves
> Send life, all fire and quicksilver
> Let the stars whisper changes.

Keeping her hands low and out of sight, Maruca put her two fists together and extended the thumbs outward in the sign of ram horns. The guests surged forward to look at the babies and congratulate the parents. As Tomas remarked, 'Now they are safe from hellfire and Beelzebub!' They crowded around the holy-water font near the funerary plaques by the doors, and everyone dipped a finger to cross his forehead. Then they moved toward the carriages, surreys, buckboards, and buggies for the ride back to the Casa Cuesta.

At the Casa, a feast was laid out on the porches, the terrace, and the lawns. A whole steer was roasting over piñon-wood charcoal in a pit dug in the garden. Two flutes, a fiddle, and a guitar made music. Toasts were drunk and fine wine was brought up from the cellars. Irena, who had changed to yellow silk, announced: 'These roast turkeys are fitting to be served here, for we are full-fledged Americans now! No? *Yes!* And I drink to the generations of the house of Velasquez who founded Casa Cuesta. So feast! There are *vino fino* hams in red wine, *pescada a la española*, and for the Italian birthright of the Fiores, *scaloppine* and *fritto misto* with *gnocchi*. Also whiskey. And for our firstborn I say *di giovanezza il bel purpureo lume!*'

Rocco, with his hand under the skirt of the servant girl Conchita Concepcion, translated this as 'may pretty lights show the babies the way to a full life.'

Tomas was moving about among the guests, laughing and bowing, kissing the married women on the cheek.

He offered a toast of his own: '*Dios que da llaga, da la medicina*. God, who gives the wound, also gives the medicine.'

George noted to himself that the toast didn't seem to fit this joyous celebration. Everyone was feasting and drinking. Maria had been handed two glasses by Matthew Gower and by Father O'Hara, of what she thought was wine, but was actually a heady liqueur, Crema di Timo. The three of them were discussing, with much laughter and refilling of glasses, the serious problem of *why* God made fleas and snakes.

'Ah, Mrs Fiore, He, too, nods at times.'

In the garden Julio and two helpers were beginning to slice the hot roasted steer, filling plates amid shouting as they kicked away the dogs. Maruca, bolting her second portion, began to choke and gasp on an extra large portion of hot greasy beef. Her eyes rolled, she sank to the ground, clutching her chest. Several people began to pound her on the back as her face slowly turned blue and her limbs twitched, while all the crowd gathered to give advice, lay on hands, and beat on her chest. Father Zorilla, located in the arbor, came in a hurry, crucifix banging on his knees, and gave her the last rites. But she was already dead.

The mood of the day, which had started with such joy, changed now to a sad reflection on mortality, and people quietly began to leave. There was some whispering that the

119

midwife Maruca had also been a witch, could produce miscarriages and cause men to become impotent by the use of the evil eye.

In a small room off the great hall of the Casa, the three infants slept on a pallet. Nina, the small seven-year-old daughter of the cook, sat waving a palm-leaf fan over their heads to drive off stray flies. Alfredo opened his eyes, then his pink toothless mouth, and yawned. Nina carefully lifted the baby's christening robe and looked at his parts. She touched them with the fan saying *Dio vi benedica*—God bless you!'

For years after, many recalled the day of the baptism only as the time when the old witch Maruca was taken by the devil back to his abode.

Later the same week, George went to see Martin Scully, an old Irishman who was a sign painter as well as a carriage striper. George showed him a sketch of what he wanted done.

'It's extra for the gold leaf, sir. For a nabob, a real gold job.'

'Do your best, Scully.'

That night, while the babies howled and Maria got up to feed them, George lay awake, his restless mind teeming with ideas and fears: I'll cancel the sign in the morning ... no, I'll go ahead with it ... why am I so unpredictable? ... why my urgency to do this? ... yet it's been a long time I've been thinking this way ... seeking sleep in mindless matters. They've stopped crying ... greedy little pigs, and Maria, for all her slim shape, has plenty of milk for them ... Why does the sight of her filled breasts make me sick? She's a good wife, it's just the enthusiasm has gone out of me.... I'm worried about that sign ... I'm being too audacious ... or too careful in the night ... all the things that can go wrong, all the laughter this can bring down on me from the Anglo bankers, the commodities dealers, the *Yanqui* speculators ... never mind, try to sleep before the babies wake again ... I have seen so much, worked so hard ... have doubts ... been burned by dolorous love in the past ... now nothing is insurmountable … even death, dogma says, is not the final blow. How ridiculous night thoughts are … one doesn't slough off the past, it comes back to you from sleep.…

He fell into troubled sleep near dawn and was awakened by Maria telling him Alfredo was born with a tooth, she had felt it at the morning feeding. It was an omen, she added, to which George replied he hoped so, he could use a good sign from above.

Three days later George stood in front of the Fiore Trading Company, its original sign on the dusty street, as Martin Scully and his helpers raised up a new sign, a larger one with gold letters on a black background, letters two feet high, square, and plain. George had insisted he wanted none of the popular curlicues or ornate designs—no fancy trimmings.

Scully, precariously balanced high on a ladder, held one end of the sign against the front of the building.

'How about here, sir?'

'Fine, fine,' said Rocco. 'Even a blind man can see it.'

'A bit to the right,' said George. 'That's *it*.'

'Nail her in, me boyos!'

A small crowd gathered, a boy with a box of apples, several women who had been shopping, two of them followed by servants carrying their bulging baskets.

George stepped back and felt as if his heart were going to burst. There it was for all to see: THE PACIFIC-HARVESTERS BANK OF CALIFORNIA.

Rocco cheered and began to do a jig he had seen a black-face minstrel show nigger perform. George shook his head. 'That's no way for a banker to act, Rocco.'

'Very suitable,' said a portly gentleman, looking up at the shining gold sign. 'More gold for my kingdom, as it should be.'

George turned to see a short stocky fellow with a Napoleon III mustache and beard.

'Good morning, your Majesty.'

'Good morning, Sir Fiore.'

'The Imperial dogs look fine today.'

It was only proper and fitting, many San Franciscans felt, that their city should be picked as his residence by the Emperor of the US and Protector of Mexico, Norton I. A former rice merchant, he was not a king by any hereditary right or by victory in battle, but self-annointed royalty. He was escorted around town by his two dogs, Bummer and Lazarus. The Emperor wore a self-designed uniform combining the best features of the American Navy and the Army, full-dress royal regalia. On his head ws a high beaver hat festooned with three colorful feathers, held by a shiny brass clasp. The Emperor Norton, as befits an absolute monarch issued his own kind of money, a friendly printer running off cash certificates of different denominations, all bearing the title 'NORTON I, EMPEROR OF THE UNITED STATES AND PROTECTOR OF MEXICO.' The San Francisco merchants, bartenders, and cabbies accepted this kind of money with a smile. There was no record that the government of the United States ever took any action either against his claims to the American throne or against the issuance of cash certificates in competition with the US Mint.

George held out a ten-dollar bill. 'I wonder, your Majesty, could I change this for the true currency of the realm?'

'Happy to, Sir Fiore.' He pulled out his own crudely printed money and took George's offered bill. 'I accept Washington's right to issue money.'

'Very generous of you, sire. Good day ... good day, Bummer ... good day, Lazarus.'

'You may lunch with us at the Palace.'

'Very kind of you, sire, but I have business to attend to.'

The Emperor moved Bummer's leg away from a potted palm. 'I don't object to my subjects being in trade.'

Irena, who never gave a panhandler a dime, insisted, 'They ought to lock the old nut up. Givs the city a bad name. Makes us a laughing stock.'

'No, Irena, he's a kind of city pet. He's harmless and I like him.'

'You would, Grego. Every wino in a doorway can get a

handout from you for a snort of whiskey.'

The self-proclaimed Emperor was originally a British Jew, Joshua Abraham A. Norton. He never claimed any connection with the ruling House of Hanover. He was plain Mr Norton in San Francisco, perhaps as a younger son sent out to the colonies to make his own way. He had started a business into which he was reputed to have sunk forty thousand dollars. He was ruined by bad luck and bad times and disappeared from the streets of San Francisco. When he reappeared, he was no longer J.A. Norton, merchant, but Norton I, monarch. His bearing was calm, proud, and perfectly regal. He remained a kindly, cheerful, chubby figure, democratic, gossipy, interested in his city and his kingdom—a perfect monarch. One of his first actions was to present a check for three million dollars at Ralston's Bank of California, 'to build a bridge over San Francisco Bay.' That proved he was nutty, people said, smiling. imagine a bay bridge! The check drawn on the royal treasury was never cashed.

George told Rocco, 'I keep thinking, with a little less luck and a cog loose in *my* head, I could be like Emperor Norton, not dealing with a full deck.'

'Not you, George.'

'I dream sometimes I'm him.'

'Just keep handing him a ten-spot now and then against the evil eye.'

3

Grazioso

12

First you are five and then you're six and Uncle Rocco brings two ponies on your birthday, one for Alfredo and one for you, Cesare (already being called Charlie, not Cesare, which is a name the other boys laugh at and yell 'Sees-Her-What?'). Being Charlie Fiore is very good: you and Alfredo are twins—he wants to be called Freddy and no longer wets the bed. It's good to go into Papa's bank and look at them count the money. Uncle Rocco says money smells, but it's not so; even the gold coins you get on your birthday smell of nothing at all. Papa has this fine pointed mustache which tickles when he kisses you and calls you snotty kids and hands over lemon drops which he takes from his desk where there is a pistol he never lets you touch and he says he's killed hundreds of bad people with it.

Mama never teases, but dresses in black and goes to mass and there are priests in the house at all hours and in the little chapel Papa has built for Mama in the back of the garden of the big new house on the high hill. They talk funny and get on their knees and know all about hell, which Uncle Rocco says is near Los Angeles.

Cousin Ramon is good to play with. He has a rugger ball and a gun carved out of wood by Young Julio and painted black. Young Julio showed us kittens being born in the stable. Alfredo cried when he was told by Young Julio—he's ten—that we came out of Mama's belly and that Mama and Papa had made us shagging together. Alfredo said no, no,

*and being big and strong even at six, he bloodied Young
Julio's nose while I kicked him in the shins. Ramon just
watched.*

*Ramon just saw that his cousins were 'city ginks'. Young
Julio said they didn't know 'shit from snow.'*

*Aunt Irena is a fat lady and very strong. She could crush
walnuts in her fingers. She gave us crackers—with Brie and
little cakes—and felt our muscles and said, 'My, they are
men, aren't they?' Uncle Tomas smells nice of hair tonic,
which smells a lot like Papa's party whiskey. Uncle Tomas
tied some young chickens to stakes and set his falcons to
attack. Alfredo was sick (again.) Uncle Tomas said, 'Now,
observe, that's the way life is; we eat each other and God eats
us.' Mama said Uncle Tomas 'is not in a state of grace.' He
took a pull on a flask of medicine he said was for his gout.*

*The Casa is fun to visit, sliding on the wet cheese-house
floor, watching the machinery of the winery and cider
presses, chasing the sheep on the slopes. When the maid
tucks me into bed, she says, 'Sleep well, Cesare,' though I
never think of myself as Cesare. I lie in bed listening to some
distant guitar played by a servant—sad, sad, nice music, and
the grown folk are up late talking about deals, land values,
and marriage and scandal and the wrong kind of love and
'who was the father?' They never talk of toads or turtles, of
learning how to find out that marks are letters and letters
make words and a string of words make sense.* I WILL EXALT
THEE MY GOD, O KING ... USE WHEELER'S WAGON GREASE.
*Uncle Rocco once said God was a horse's ass, and Mama
said God sent his own son to save us all, named Jesus Christ.
Young Julio always says 'Jesus Christ' a lot, but Mama says
it's not the same Jesus....*

Rocco Bordone had by the early 1860's matured into a
handsome young man, with a weakness for low society.
'George's shadow,' some called him, but he was really
more a junior partner, able to handle a multitude of
vexations. He knew the money business and how to
manipulate funds and people. George was distressed that

Rocco's keenness of mind could manifest a cruel streak when angered. Yet Rocco could often be discreet where George would frankly speak out. Rocco had an orphan's sagacity, a wariness with little faith in mankind, and a tacit distrust of any too romantic attachment to women. He was an ardent and practical sensualist who could not resist passing involvements with women—usually dancers and women in what passed for fast society on the hills where mansions were rising and a handsome young Italian with curly hair and expressive dark eyes was in demand.

'They are all alike, women. Fun, satisfying, spicy.'

George was amused at Rocco's sentiments. 'Spicy? You sound as if you were taking inventory of a sausage shop.'

'Stand them on their heads and they all look like Russians. And they all like silk, the touch of the stuff—notice that? Speaking of silk, I've been in touch with this Frenchy, Louis Provost, down Angeles way. He's got this place called Jurupa Rancho and has set up a silk company there.'

Which is how the two men came to be driving along the back country behind Oakland to look over some land Rocco felt they should consider. It belonged to a Lopo Maniz who had once approached George to back a pork-processing plant and who now wanted a loan of ten thousand dollars.

George laughed. 'To sell certificates in a new scheme, beautifully printed for the shareholders—you're going to grow silk on the moon now, I bet.'

'You process, not grow, silk here. The California Association ... Why, hell, George, the state legislature already passed a law with liberal bounties to stimulate the culture of silk in the state.'

'You can buy any politician with a handful of walnuts. Silk!'

Rocco was sweating—none of this was going as he had planned.

'Rocco, too much attention to women gives you these crazy ideas.'

128

Rocco pulled a paper out of his pocket. 'It's not crazy. Provost is already growing silkworms near San Jose. I'm buying silkworm eggs from him at six dollars an ounce. Here's the contract. And I'm getting back from the state big subsidies for growing mulberry trees.'

'Mulberry trees? That just *proves* you're crazy!'

'The worms, George, they eat only mulberry leaves. Down south, farmers are changing from growing grains and oranges to planting mulberry trees. You can get a subsidy from the state for the number of cocoons you produce. The little houses the worms live in.'

'Worms are only good for fishing.'

Maniz's adobe house was in a little valley with a stream. He was white-haired, a serious man, poor but audacious. His wife was half-Indian, and around them was their brood of at least a dozen children—picking noses, bare feet kicking up dust as they sported with dogs and several goats.

'Ah, señor'—Lopo played the host—'a little wine perhaps?'

'Cool water would be better, Lopo,' said George, kicking at a lean, sniffing dog. Lopo tried to hide his expectations as George sipped the cool well water. 'I see you've done a good land clearing, cutting brush—sumac, dwarf cedars, all gone.'

'I'm ready for the planting.' Lopo eyed Rocco as if waiting for Rocco to back his statement voiced in quavering tones.

'But where,' asked George, 'are you planning your pigsties, the butchering tables, the smokehouses?'

'Didn't Señor Bordone explain?'

Rocco seemed embarrassed. He took out a cigarillo and lit it, waved off the smoke as George stared at him. Something very fancy was taking place. Rocco was clearly maneuvering toward some daring project. George recognized Rocco's knack for finding overlooked avenues of investment, but he also fell for some harebrained schemes.

Lopo said, 'A drink? *Aguardiente?*'

Rocco took the cigarillo from his mouth. 'Lopo and I are *not* going to process pork. There is something more exciting that will turn all these acres to gold. Like the *yanquis, el patrón*, we, too, are to be rich.'

George turned and started for the buckboard. 'You bastards are going to raise silkworms! I figured, Rocco, your brains were turning to steer dung when you started that talk about this Louis Provost and his lamebrained silk association.'

Rocco was shouting as he followed him. 'With the worm eggs selling soon at ten dollars an ounce, why, an acre of mulberry trees can bring in two thousand an acre from the sale of the goddamn worm eggs!'

Lopo added, speaking softly, 'We got coming one thousand mulberry from a gringo dealer to start. They grow damn fast, six feet in six months. But we need the loan.'

'Forget it. I would not put up ten thousand dollars to sell seats to the Crucifixion with the original actors.' George was outraged at being dragged out here for as stupid a scheme as he'd ever heard.

Rocco shouted, 'I've got money, I've got credit! I'll get a loan from the Bank of California. They're progressive. All the silver kings, Flood, O'Brien, Wallie Sharon, the bank trustees there, are men with vision!'

George whipped up the horses, a pair of bald-faced roans that he usually drove with skill, now recklessly galloping through the bracken and ground pines of Lopo's land. He cursed Rocco's arrogance. Perhaps, he thought with some shame when his temper cooled, I don't want him to make progress on his own. But this is too great a risk. *Silkworm eggs!*

That evening when Maria asked if Rocco was coming to supper, George patted the heads of his two sons, Alfredo and Cesare. 'We'll not see him for some time.'

'You've broken up once again?'

'We saw a reason today to disagree.'

Months later, to the amazement of established businessmen and solid brokers, the silkworm business

130

boomed. It spread like wild weeds. Crops of grains and fruit-bearing orchards were destroyed, plowed under, trees were cut down, and slips of mulberry stock planted. From Southern California to the areas of Gold River, speculation in silkworm eggs raged. The state continued paying heavy bounties, and the politicians managed to divert the flood to little dishonest channels of their own.

George sat with William Ralston, president and founder of the Bank of California, in the steam room of the Neptune Swimming and Bathing Club on the bay.

William C. Ralston was to George an example of how a banker could succeed. Ralston had been raised on midwestern native stone and fed on Mississippi steamboat food. He had been a hired hand on the side-wheelers as a young man, and was twenty-three in 1849 when all the talk was of California gold. He left the steamboats of New Orleans and went to Panama, a fever jungle of 'gators and murderous Indians. Ralston ended up on the Pacific side of the isthmus as a boat agent in the momentous rush to the goldfields.

He was just at his prime, six feet, two inches in his yarn socks, and already weighing two hundred pounds, most of it pure muscle. West Coast shipping was going to sea with anything afloat, and Ralston took four hundred passengers out onto the Pacific from Panama to San Francisco in eighteen days on a side-wheeled Mississippi riverboat. He liked San Francisco and adopted it. By 1856 he owned mills and factories, boats, wineries, canneries, shares in the railroads, and his own theater and bank.

Rocco insisted that it was Ralston's parties, his luxurious way of life, that gave San Francisco class. In fact, Ralston loved the hill city. When he decided to build his great Palace Hotel, he planned 96,250 square feet of rococo Victorian aesthetics, crossed with the elaborate chic of Louis XV, which cost him five million dollars in gold. A fireplace in every room and 'marble enough to make Michelangelo drool with envy,' as he put it. He built four hundred and thirty-nine bathrooms for only twelve hundred guests. The Palace covered a full city block with tiers of bay window, miles of hissing steam pipes, baroque cast-iron radiators, parquet floors of golden oak, lush carpeting. The lobby was paved with silver dollars set in concrete 'so people can get the feel of money from their toes up,' as Ralston explained to George.

Although their tastes differed so vastly—George had no need for the conspicuous display of wealth in which Ralston reveled, so their homes and businesses were at opposite ends of the spectrum—their respect for one another was enormous, and their friendship solid. Each looked forward to meeting the other at the baths for a relaxing, invigorating session in the steam room and a friendly discussion of mutual business concerns in the relaxed atmosphere.

'I still don't see how you lent Rocco and Lopo money to grow worm eggs,' George said to Ralston, mopping his forehead.

The banker dampened his ginger whiskers, wiped his wet chest. 'My dear George, I take risks, but small ones. This worm thing has just started. In six months, a year, you'll see buyers coming out to buy our rolls of silk—yards and yards of the stuff. They won't have to go to China, Japan.'

George looked closely at Ralston, the only Americano banker he trusted.

'You're bullshitting me, Bill. To make silk—I was reading up on it, which you half-wits haven't bothered to do, I see—you have to kill the moth inside before it tears open the silk cocoon. You put it in hot water to kill the moth, and you need experts to unwind the long silk thread.'

'That so, George?'

'Don't be so damn snide. You're a smart guy, Bill. Nobody is winding silk threads. They're tearing open the cocoon to get the eggs. I hear the eggs are actually worth more than their weight in gold. So for the moment, people are paying out big cash for cocoons that can't produce silk.'

'Right as rain, George. No shyster lawyer could put it better. But you only ride with the speculators on the rise, and when things collapse, you make sure you're long out of it.'

George took up a towel and began to wipe his head and face. 'It's sold as a new gold rush, a bonanza. But how many poor bastards who dug and panned, starved on their claims and got shot at, ever hit it big?'

'Enough to bring the crowds to set up new towns, bring in markets, shops, and, yes—fatten banks, eh? Ever hear of the tulip craze in Holland a hundred or so years ago?'

'No. Maria knows more about flowers, and my sister Irena sells hothouse plants in town.'

'No, no, this wasn't for smell or decoration. Tulip bulbs are raised for color, texture; suddenly, for no reason, the Dutchies were paying big money for rare bulbs—for fluted scarlets, black ones, blended rainbows. Speculators were paying hundreds, then thousands of guldens for a bulb. It was crazy, loco, I tell you. For *what?* You couldn't eat the damn thing like an onion. It didn't last but for a season or so. All Holland went dipsy, daft, buying bulbs at fantastic prices.'

'What happened? You can buy tulips at the ferry station for a dime a bulb.'

'Suddenly everybody was loaded up with warehouses of bulbs and no one was buying. No one could sell. Busted.' William Ralston gave his famous silent burst of laughter—a whole expression of uproarious laughter convulsed his face, but completely soundlessly. 'They tried to eat them in salads, feed the hogs ... Me, I'm riding the boom in these damn worm eggs, but I'm not hoarding them. Double their value by the ounce, and out they go.'

'You know, Bill, with the farmers and ranchers planting mulberry trees, there are going to be shortages in staple crops, shortages of horse feed, supplies to gristmills, vegetables. All are going sky-high. Apples, wheat, corn, grapes—that I know. Worms, *no.*'

George did well, contracting for futures in hogs and grain. But he had to send wagons far afield, for around the city, up the coast, and down to San Diego every grower had become a worm-egg farmer. He made no loans to worm growers.

Among the newly rich were Rocco and his partner, Lopo, now a *caballero*. Lopo bought diamonds, put his dozen or so children's virgin feet into painful shoes. He bought a carriage, a top hat, boxes of the best Havanas. He confessed to Father O'Hara that he had fornicated in ornate whorehouses on the Coast with blond Protestant whores and redheaded Polish Jewish *nafkas*. He bought a great English Queen Anne silver set and the children made mud pies in the silver bowls. His wife grew so fat she wore her first corset, and three of the eldest children had to lace her in and tug and tie off the strings of her whalebone stays. *Madre de Dios!*

After a day of trading, Rocco and Lopo were usually found at the Poodle Dog Café or at the bar of the Palace Hotel, cheerfully bragging of the day's progress.

George, taking Alfredo and Cesare for ice cream at the Palace, eyed the elegant tailoring, Lopo with two butter-gold watches gold-chained across the heavy stomach of his yellow silk waistcoat.

Rocco offered a gloved hand. 'Come on, George, why be angry?'

'I'm not angry,' George said taking the proferred hand. 'Not any more. With worm eggs selling at ... what—twenty dollars an ounce?'

'Uncle Rocco,' said Alfredo, 'I can dig worms.'

'You came into worms too, Señore Fiore?'

'Only through the rise in produce—pork and grain.'

'Your sister, Señora Velasquez, is a hard woman. She is growing acres of mulberry shoots, but only for cash will she sell.'

'As she says, nobody gets rich picking up silver dollars she's dropped.'

'We could use,' said Rocco, 'five thousand more trees, but we're putting the cash into eggs for the next rise in price.'

'And what about silk spinning?' asked George.

'That? Oh ... How about joining us in a blue blazer?'

'Why not ... You boys stay and finish your ice cream.'

The bar was crowded by speculators making deals, enjoying their success.

'Jerry, three of your best blazers.... Spinning the stuff? Lopo and me, we're just having some Chiney woman test out the spinning. A few yards. We're going to make us an American flag, *all* pure silk, California silk. To fly over the Capitol dome in Washington.'

'A toast, then—long may she wave.'

George knew something was wrong with the worm-egg boom when Tomas told him that Irena was digging up the mulberry shoots and planting corn.

She had asked Rocco how much silk he was spinning and he told her six yards only. Then she said, 'The mulberry trees are worthless.'

George shook his head. 'I bet Irena makes walking canes out of them.' The others agreed she might.

But in the spring they were still planting trees, buying and selling worm eggs, and the talk was of soon another rise of five dollars to the ounce.

In the summer someone figured out that one hundred million silk-worm eggs were on the market. Too much, too many, and the price fell *if* you could find a buyer. By this time the political boys had pretty much looted the state treasury, and in September a law revoked the subsidy to the egg and tree growers. Eggs fell to four dollars an ounce.

Egg prices went down, down, and with no more state funds to pad the game, the speculation boom burst. Lopo Maniz died from overwork on his silk plantation and most likely from the damage of capricious speculation.

The Daily Star shed a few tears at his passing. 'His place cannot be filled. A greater misfortune could not have happened to this locality, nor to the state at large.'

At the same time, millions of silkworms and mulberry trees were dying of neglect. Desolation hit thousands of acres, and hundreds of worm-egg farmers were ruined, while wily speculators who had dumped their holdings early counted their piles of gold eagles and double eagles.

George noted that not one yard of commercial silk was

ever woven during the worm and egg boom. The only bit of true California silk produced was the American flag, intended to be flown over the Capitol dome. No one was ever able to discover if that banner had actually been flown there.

13

The state of California slowly shook itself—as Irena put it, 'like a wet dog'—after its involvement with the silkworm craze. There were admonitory fingers, patronizing pity, bankrupts, failed farmers, foreclosures by banks. Some had heart failure like Lopo Maniz; in San Francisco there were three suicides. George's bank and trading accounts had suffered, but he was in no danger. He had overpaid for produce, but could sell off most of it with some small losses. Money due the bank would be slow in repayment. The fishermen who borrowed had done well. But those farmers and ranchers who had gotten the mulberry-tree madness had at first made money in selling trees and worm eggs, and then most of them had been caught by the sudden collapse of the market. George was helping many here and there, advancing money to buy seed grain, plow horses. He would go out to watch the mulberry trees being uprooted, piled up, and burned in flaming desolation.

Irena came to the bank with her son, Ramon, a serious, alert child with an amusing way of showing interest in things like the letter press, the files of ledgers boxed in yellow cardboard shapes. Given a pencil and some paper by Uncle George, he drew horses, pigs, sailboats, while his mother, steel-rimmed glasses on her nose, went over some sheets of

figures with Uncle George. She was getting fat, but was still a very attractive figure.

'At such times lunatics make madness popular. What I'm owed, Grego, and can't collect, I forget. I did mostly a cash business.'

'You are now as foolish about wool as Rocco was about silk.'

Irena put away some sheets of accounts in a leather bag. 'You can eat mutton, chew on lamb chops, but not even hogs will eat moth eggs. I haven't enough cash on hand to buy any big herds, unless …'

George shook his head. 'Not a thin dime can I spare you. I'm going down to Los Angeles to see about oranges. They are growing acres of them. You know what I can get for an orange here?'

'Ten cents each. I've bought some, little rocks the color of turds.'

'Those I'm after are from the Rodman Rancho groves. Big yellow juicy fruit. And I want to take the stagecoaches down the coast, visit the mines, try to get silver deposits to handle, maybe.'

Irena searched her brother's face. He seemed wrapped up in some private contemplation, some pleasant, happy diversion.

She moved an elbow into his ribs. 'I think you've got a woman someplace,' she said without malice.

He stared at her, sat erect in his chair. 'Why the devil do you say that?'

'I can smell these things. A kind of frenetic physical impatience in you. You forget we had a witch in the family.' She took out a little black cigar and lit it. 'I'd say Maria isn't the best thing in bed since your house became full of priests and holy pictures in every room.'

He didn't take her remarks unkindly, just sat poker-faced. 'Keep your ideas to yourself, Irena. I don't pry, do I, into your games with Tomas?'

'He's a dear man.' She inhaled, exhaled. George suddenly noticed how the years had touched her. She now

needed glasses for peering nearsightedly at columns of figures, and had less respect for the local society than ever. Some thought her an *arrivista*, trying to recall the glory of the Velasquezes, a woman with a loud mouth given to effrontery and insolence. 'Tomas I understand. The genteel good breeding before me had softened the stock, Grego, and we Da Vincis are giving it vigor, strength.' she fondled her son's black ringlets, kissed his cheek. 'Tomas can't help liking games of chance, a tipple, even a tired eye for a female haunch. I am the forgiving type, if it doesn't go too far into scandal.... We *are* getting older.'

'Yes ... older.'

Ramon drew a dog, turned it into a cat with pointed ears and a long tail. 'Papa, he dances and sings funny sometimes.'

'Yes, my darling *bambino*, a graceful man when in wine.'

The door opened and Rocco came in; he was not one to knock. He looked a bit rumpled, his finery in need of cleaning and a hot iron. He hadn't shaved for a few days, his bowler hat sat well back on hair in need of cutting. He smiled at the brother and sister, the harlequin smile of a naughty child.

'Ah, Irena. Ramon, how good to see how you've grown.' He kissed Irena's hand, which he grabbed.

She directed a mock slap at his head. 'God, you look like a polecat's shithouse.'

'No cat would have me. Give me a cigarillo. I've mislaid my case.'

'Uncle Rocco, look—a cat.'

Rocco lit up and looked at George, who hadn't said anything, but sat well back in his chair as if watching an actor sweat over forgotten lines.

'I'm here, George, the prodigal son. And you have to hear me out—not offer me any fatted calf.'

George pursed his lips to keep from laughing at the sight of Rocco trying to act humble. 'Never mind the fancy words. I expected you to get out of town, flee on a steamer to Mexico or head for Canada.'

138

'I owe everybody,' Rocco admitted, watching the child draw. 'I'm in debt twenty-five thousand dollars. The Bank of California has my note for half of that. The rest?' He made gestures north and south. 'Irena, you understand how things can happen—the devil biting your ass.'

Irena held up a hand, palm forward. "If you have no assets, you addled fool, then creditors can go whistle up their *culo.*'

'I have assets that they can take, you see. Not cash, of course. Lopo's land. I have a mortgage on it, took it when he wanted to buy more fucking worm eggs. I can foreclose now on his—Christ rest his soul—acres. Still fine land. I want to plant grain, put in orchards ... but the Bank of California, my creditors, they will take it away after I take over the place.'

Irena asked, 'What about the widow, the children, you bloodsucker? You'd take everything from them? Serves you right.'

Rocco appeared amused, playing with a steel-nibbed pen on the desk. 'Irena, you'd take the pennies off a dead man's eyes if he owed you money. Anyway'—he turned to George—'can you readjust my debts, get the others, the banks, off my back before they seize the Lopo acres for claims against me? Who else can I turn to? I can't even get credit for a drink at the Palace.'

'You mean, Rocco, will I pay off the bank loans and you will owe me the money? No. And I'm going south—no time to unwind your problems.'

Irena rolled her head to one side. 'I can't help you either. I was just now talking to Grego about loans to buy more sheep.'

Rocco sat looking at his unshined boots—his last two bucks spent— and began to whistle, eyes closed. There was no resentment in his expression when he spoke. 'There are bandits on the roads. I'll get guns and learn their trade.'

Ramon looked up and aimed his pencil at Rocco. '*Bang! Bang!* You're dead, Uncle Rocco.'

'That's right, Ramon, kill your unhappy uncle.'

'I was *just* playing.'

Irena pulled on her left gold earring, a habit she had when in thought. 'Grego, let's help this banty rooster. I might offer the Bank of California the new wine soon in casks against a loan of half of what Rocco owes them. And you make some sort of deal with William Ralston there to take care of the other half of Rocco's debts.'

Rocco shouted, 'Ah, you are good *compadies!*'

George gave his sister an intense look. 'What are we? Preachers selling salvation? Before there is hymn-singing, why this generosity, Irena?'

'The goodness of her heart!' Rocco kissed Irena's hand, and only moving her head out of range saved her from a kiss on a cheek.

George stared from one to the other. Irena put out her cigarillo in a brass ashtray with a flick of her thumb. 'In return for that help, Rocco, you turn over to us as collateral your rights to the Lopo rancho and its assets. And—'

'Of course, of course.'

'As commission for all this, when you pay off what you'll owe us, we will own half of the rancho as your partners.'

Rocco took off his hat and threw it into a corner.

George said, 'Irena hasn't lost her touch, has she?'

'But listen, that's unfair. I mean, asking half the ranch for helping someone.'

Irena stood up, took her son's hand. 'Come, Ramon. And, Rocco, just let Grego know if you really want our help.'

Ramon gave Uncle George a drawing of dancing fish and he and his mother left. Rocco sank into a chair, too shocked to recite his grievances. George poured whiskey into two shot glasses.

Rocco drank, his face suggesting he was sipping hemlock. 'She's better than any bandit with a brace of pistols. But draw up the papers. And don't worry about the widow Maniz and her damn brats. I'm giving her ten good fertile acres and an adobe house down by the creek. She'll grow market produce like they did before. They'll "cut the mustard," as the *yanquis* say.'

'You've a big heart, Rocco. You'll stay afloat like whale shit in the bay.'

Rocco pointed to the whiskey decanter.

When Rocco was gone, George sat at his desk, papers he should go over pushed aside. Damn Irena! *How had she known there was a woman?* He had thought any subtleties of a relationship with Rose Rodman had been carried out with prudence and decorum.

Rose had appeared in San Francisco just three months before on the coastal steamer *West Star*. A widow of one year, Rose was in her middle twenties, tall, with hair of soft mink color worn in a wraparound braid. Her eyes were gray-green with a gemlike gleam, large eyes hooded by long lashes. Perhaps he only thought he saw all that at once. Her late husband, Avrom Rodman, a German Jew, had planted a hundred acres of oranges near Los Angeles and was just beginning to ship them to San Francisco when he mounted a rambunctious horse sold him by a dealer from below the border. The horse threw him, stomped him, and a prayer for the dead of Israel was said in his memory in the small Amora'im Synagogue.

His widow had sent a message to George that she would like to have lunch with him on Tuesday at the Palace Hotel. He was puzzled and intrigued. Ladies did not usually invite men to lunch. Was this for business or …?

On the appointed Tuesday he found her seated in the small red velvet dining room, wearing a small hat with a veil that failed to cover her eyes. Her long body was stylish in a dark green gown, a black band on the left arm.

She was the only woman waiting alone in the dining room, and George introduced himself. The headwaiter bowed, sat them under a cascade of ferns in hanging brass pots. George asked if she cared for a drink; she requested dry white wine. He ordered a bottle, explaining that he owned shares of the vineyard from which the grapes came. She pulled off her gloves and said she was bringing order into poor Avrom's estate and had found some billings for

141

oranges from the Fiore Trading Company. There were two hundred lugs of fruit he could make an offer on.

He said, 'First, Mrs Rodman, to food, then to commerce.' He recommended the brook trout and later, as they sipped wine and ate, he studied her, all her facets so beguiling at this first meeting.

'You see, Mrs Rodman, if the company takes that many oranges, the price will fall. I'll take twenty boxes, which we can sell to the wholesale markets at, say, seven cents each, and they can sell to the public for a dime or twelve cents. The bank no longer sells produce direct to the customers.'

'I see—so I don't think we can do business. Do you know Homer Kendrick?' He said he did.

She wore no rings and her nails were cut short. It was a strong tanned hand, yet slim.

'Mr Fiore, I've got acres of orange trees, lemons, I can't just piddle away a few boxes to your bank. I need volume. The more anyone sells up here, even at lower prices, the more profitable the volume will be. Will you introduce me to Homer Kendrick?'

Of course, he saw her point. He asked how long she would be in town, for he'd have to think over her orange problem. Would she care to see the play opening tonight at the Empire? Some English company was performing *School for Scandal*.

He took her to dinner at Armand's, a little French eating place. She enjoyed the play, saying the theater in Los Angeles was disappointing. He saw her to her hotel and they sat in the lounge drinking small brandies. At last Rose—they were now on a first name basis—stood to say good night, adding that it had been a fine evening. He agreed it had been, as Tomas would say, *muy simpática*.

George knew he was in trouble; the whole goddamn situation that had developed with Carrie was surfacing again. He was sure as shooting in love with this young widow with the startling eyes. His serenity, his belief that he was beyond the frantic emotions of wild passion, was evaporating. *Con cojones, pero conjones,* as the damn natives say. Was he resigned to this indulgence? It was a drive within him, head, heart, and reins, as someone had expressed it, this brusque intrusion of something he had hoped never to feel again.

In the next few days they talked of orange groves, of horses, of the growth of the West. They pressed hands on parting and he lightly kissed her (the butterfly touch), but going further would have been a felicitous error. She would not have played the shocked maiden or the proper offended lady, he thought. More likely she would have slapped him, or even worse, have laughed at him. There was too much independence in the woman.

On the third day he drove her in his gig through the country around Lake Chobot. They ate at a good inn under an arbor: lobster in a mustard sauce, pigeon pie, drank a fair rosé. He did kiss her—this time a message of passion— and she looked at him and shook her head. She seemed to him like a bell that one struck and got no resonance.

'No, George Fiore. I'm not seeking adventure. Yes, I'm a human being, a widow; the shock is not strong anymore, but I have problems. I seem to have the stance of a ready woman, a widow to suggest bed to every male peacock.'

'Please, Rose—'

'I'm not sure which direction my life will take.'

He used his napkin to wipe one corner of her mouth. 'Rose, neither one of us is a damn fool. There is in me a kind of little tin whistle; when it blows, I'm sure as hell I'm near something real, vital.'

'What a clever whistle.'

'How are your signals—inside?'

She dipped fingers into her water glass, dried them. 'The back of my neck gets hot. I think we better drive back to town. I don't like the games we are playing.'

'Rose. You know I'm married. I have children. I'll never lie to you as to what I can offer.'

'Please, no confessions.' She stood up and began to gather up her gloves, slap them together. 'You're a Catholic, I'm a Jew. One more barrier.'

143

'Those are labels—like we put on smoked fish. And I'm a man and luckily we're still young enough. Be honest about this trick nature is playing on us. *Christ!*'

In the stable area by his buggy he grabbed her around the waist and held her close and covered her mouth, savoring her, feeling her body. She raised her arm to hold him off, and they stood there enwrapped, suddenly merged.

In the buggy, the roans going at a good pace, she put up one hand to straighten her hat, smooth her hair, make order of disorder. 'I dislike you, George, for what you did, because I knew I'd like it.'

'Good girl.'

'But listen to me—don't drive so fast. I haven't decided. Not here, so far from home. I'm repulsed and attracted—both. I'm a slow thinker, I want to wonder a bit about us two fools. I've never really felt this way—it's like a sickness.'

He stopped the roans in a clearing. They got out. He fell to his knee and held her by her thighs so she almost fell against him. They talked, he in this low position, she looking out toward the opposite hills. They talked of their love, their fears of passion—the ache and pain of love, of physical attraction. Of each other. She found him, she admitted, more attractive than she had found any other man. But his determination frightened her, her own emotions were still unsettled, her widowhood still too new. In Los Angeles, placid readings of Fielding or Dickens had been her life. Her intellectual life had been nonexistent with her husband. He had had a hard youth of freighting wagons to Santa Fe and Denver, establishing himself in San Diego as an importer of ironware and plows, and then expanding into land deals and the planting of citrus, with small hope of a large market.

As they drove back to the ferry station to get across the bay to San Francisco, George talked of himself, of his marriage. He did not blame Maria for its failure; he should not have married her with such bland lack of feeling. It was duty he had felt; and he touched on Carrie, and the

144

gregarious life-style of his past. The extremes of emotion he had experienced had left him more mature, if no wiser.

Rose had picked wild lupine on the roadside, but they had become crushed and faded by the time they got to the hotel. They kissed at her door but she didn't let him enter her room. He knew she was denying her emotions.

For a week they explored the distant bay areas, avoiding the Velasquez holdings, dining in obscure cafés on Spanish and Italian food. Not all impulses were held back. He kissed her naked breasts—she relieved his tensions one night into a lace handkerchief. He got to know her better— her routine. Rose insisted on a daily bath, clearly an eccentric of uncommon ingredients. Her favorite flowers were begonias. Her eyes seemed to be hunting for something in him. She would get angry at him if he appeared prejudiced in some small way and lost his self-restraint. Yet she was very good to be with. Her sun-touched skin suggested airy space and open country. Rose had a sense of mischief, a desire to hurt at times, teasing him about his hard collars, his pocket talisman of a rare Greek coin, a dried horse chestnut. He was amused by her keeping a napkin in front of her mouth when she spoke at meals. George wondered at those moments near dusk when she stared into space and was lost to him and the city. She would be verbally passionate, ingenious, persistent when she wanted him to agree with her. She remained for him baffling, beautiful, intelligent, yet he would at times feel full of fear at the ridiculous extremes with which he loved her. When not with her, he luxuriated in lengthy dreams, then was often caught up in melancholy self-castigation.

They took to venturing into Chinatown, where George had made friends among some of the *hong* merchants, clients of the bank. They ate pungent *bo lo kei*, drank the *moi kwai lo* rosé wine, tore apart succulent spiced roast duck with their teeth.

She would not sleep with him, allow complete sexual satisfaction. Even as they took some liberties with each other's bodies, she insisted he must come down to her groves near Los Angeles, where they would decide about a relationship, or at least talk it over in earnest.

'Darling, I don't think much will come of it. You are here, rooted like a ten-year-old orange tree, and I'm down there, such a distance away, and the hardship of travel will—'

'I'll come in a few weeks.'

'Your family, your bank?'

'The family knows my ways. I go where I want. The bank is in fine shape, after that damn silkworm matter. I have two fine men as cashiers, and I want to get away for a while. Rose, I've read that people lose their heads, even empires, over love. I never shall. I will cherish you, admire you, worship you. God, I sound like a bad novel.'

'That's not enough for me.'

They were on the Embarcadero watching a three-masted greasy sealer come up the Golden Gate, a vindictive wind ruffling her stained sails.

'George, I suspect that all talk between people in love sounds like a bad novel. When only two people hear it, why, it's fine ...' She looked about her and kissed his ear. 'I'm leaving tomorrow on the *West Star*.'

'So soon. And how far have we gone? Do I know you?'

'I'm no woman of ice. Yes, yes, Mr Fiore, I have obvious frailties where my body and mind are concerned. I've been afraid I'd make some passionate commitment to you.'

'I promise in a few weeks I'll—'

'George, let's not make this a sad parting.'

They said a great deal more to each other, he trying to push beyond the wall of her firmness. And, he suspected as he helped her aboard, it all sounded too simple, too much like platitudes in the novels he had once begun but never finished.

He had bought a necklace of green jade in Chinatown, the pigtailed merchant assuring him it was from the T'ang dynasty and had once belonged to the Emperor Tai Zong's favorite concubine. He gave Rose the gift and in her cabin

146

they shared a last embrace. He thought he saw tears in her eyes, but in the dim light below deck, he couldn't be sure.

Later, at the Poodle Dog, he drank bourbon and felt that the world around him must know he was acting the fool. At least, he comforted himself, no one could call him a fool in *all* regards. And if he was being a fool about Rose, he'd have to continue that way—he could not give her up and he couldn't change his feelings about her.

14

George Fiore, feeling much older than his thirty-odd years, started south for Los Angeles after a woman in her middle twenties. He did wonder why he was being so foolhardy, chasing the widow with luminous eyes and a taut, often disturbing individuality. The bank, he told himself, was in good hands with his two cashiers—David Zimmerman, a solid German, and Frank Pagano, product of a Naples father and a Boston mother. Besides, as a buoyant but stern force, there was Rocco, who would report directly to Irena. George had to admit, as the rocking coach and its six passengers and four horses went jolting and rolling along, that Irena was most likely harder, wiser than himself in many matters. She often objected to his view of humanity, his preoccupied sense of business morality, but was surer of herself perhaps because of her limited approval of mankind.

Despite the jarring stagecoach, it was good to be traveling to new landscapes and to see how the state was growing. It was bursting with new immigrants, ranchers, old Indian fighters marked by arrow wounds, all settling homesteads, planting, raising children and livestock.

The inns George stayed in were not given to much luxury, with their outhouses out back, and where you were fed singed meat on greasy tin plates, and a coffee that one driver insisted was 'half tar and half wildcat piss—that's the tasty part.'

There was still a lot of wilderness for the coach to move through, wild crags which would be leveled or gone around by the railroad. 'That fella Collis P. Huntington and his gang of swindlers are talking of building, raising land values, but so far,' said a Wells Fargo guard, 'bandits are often on the road, just lask week held up and frisked the coach passengers. Yep.'

Near San Miguel, a whiskey drummer told George, 'Oh, yes, there was this Mex some years back, Joaquin Murieta. He used to run wild all along the roads up to San Jose. These greasers can be mean hombres.'

'We've had Yankee bandits, too.'

'Maybe so, but this here Murieta, he got catched and deep-sixed. They cut off his head, and you could see it in a glass jar of whiskey right in the window of Higgins Saloon up on Clark Street. It was there for a long time. Ever take a look at it, mister?'

George's mind was not on travel gossip but on Rose; he couldn't get very interested in bandits of years ago. It could have nothing to do with him anyway. The coach rattled along, its passengers peacefully oblivious of what lay in store at Coyote's Hole Station. A miserable enough structure, the station stood at Walker Pass, where it merged with the Los Angeles bullion trail that brought silver ore from the Cerro Gordo mines into the city for shipment north to the refineries.

Early that morning, caballeros Tiburcio Vasquez and Cleovaro Chavez opened an attack, firing their rifles into the walls of the shack. Vasquez yelled, 'Everybody come out or I burn place down!'

Billy Raymond, the station keeper, was not present, having gone to the privy, but his wife and a half-dozen mule hands and horse drivers made for the door. Vasquez announced himself by name as the famous *bandido*, as his ego demanded. 'Tell everyone come out. I am going to rob stage.

Six men and Mrs Raymond came outside, their hands in the air, and Vasquez's lieutenant, Chavez, covered them with his Henry rifle. Vasquez collected weapons and whatever they had in money and jewelry. Three men appeared from the station stable where they had been bunking, and they too were forced to turn over their valuables. A drinking party had been going on in the stable, and there were two drunks not fully aware of their danger. One of them pulled out his revolver and fired off a wavering shot at the bandit. It missed, but in return the drunk got a rifle slug in a thigh. Vasquez proudly said he could just as well have killed him. 'So next time I order, obey.'

The whole group, minus the wounded drunk, was sent off to lie low in the sagebrush behind the station and warned to remain still. The bandits sat themselves down to wait for the stagecoach.

It was two hours before a cloud of ocher dust showed that the stage was about to enter Coyote's Hole Station. Four tired horses pulled the Concord coach, having come a hard haul from the mountain camp at Havilah, the Cerro Gordo mine.

Leaping forward with his rifle, Vasquez cried, 'Stop! Hands up!'

The driver braked the coach to a full stop and the passengers were ordered out. Four passengers came out without protest. One—a Mr Belshaw—gave up five dollars in coins and ten thousand dollars in mining stock but held on to a pair of new gloves. He pleaded that in this foul weather he needed them to keep his hands warm. Vasquez shrugged, smiled, held up two dollars of the passenger's money. 'I buy them—give you two dollars for them.'

George Fiore was the last to leave the coach. He looked at the two bandits and handed over some gold coins, a small packet of greenbacks. He felt the scene tantalizingly dangerous.

'That all you got?' asked Vasquez.

'You can see.'

The driver said, 'He's a banker—his cash ain't in his breeches, but in a bank.'

George had a money belt next to his skin with fifteen hundred dollars in it, carried in case an interesting deal arose.

The bandit looked at George and smiled. 'The watch, is it good, Señor Banker?'

'Silver, but it runs well.' He handed over chain and watch. He felt the bandit poking a pistol under his jacket where it showed a small bulge. 'What that, Señor?'

'A gift for a lady.'

'Show this to me.'

It was a small, delicate gold lady's watch, double-lidded, packed in a cotton-filled silk case. Embossed on the outer case, Diana the Huntress and her dogs pursued a deer, and below, engraved letters which the bandit examined with care: 'THE ROSE OF SHARON. AMORE.'

'What say? I don't read so good.'

'Just the offering with the lady's name.'

'Sonabitch, fancy. I keep for her.'

George looked at the other passengers, the driver, and the iron box guard, who had not reached for his shotgun. George shrugged. 'If we ever meet again, I'll buy it back.'

The bandit slapped George on the shoulder. 'You fine fella, Señor Banker.'

'Yes, fine fella,' added Chavez, the other bandit.

'Now I think we open iron box.'

The real hope for booty was the Wells Fargo box. However, when forced it contained not coins or bills but only a set of heavy calf-bound lawbooks, in transit from one lawyer to another. Vasquez, a bit confused by this, cursed the law even more than was his usual habit, then smiled broadly as he carried off Mr Belshaw's new polished cowhide boots.

Now that it was safe, a passenger began to gather up the

mining stock which had been scattered all over the landscape. Mr Belshaw commanded that four freight mules be harnessed to the stage to replace the worn-out horses, and soon they were off to spread the alarm that Vasquez was in the region.

The driver rubbed his gums with a snuff stick. 'Your lucky day, gents. He usually kills one of the passengers. He's dumb enough to think that's good luck. Wells Fargo will raise holy hell over that busted iron box.'

George regretted the loss of the gold watch he had ordered from St Louis. Yet he was alive; he might have been killed by that Hispanic degenerate in the bandit's anger at finding no great loot in the strongbox. George felt some tattered piety left in him and gave thanks to God, and saw no harm in crossing himself.

Hours later he and Rose lay together naked in the big bed, having made love skin to skin, come together to a panting climax. There was a wind blowing outside the draped window of the ranch house—a wind she said was called Santa Ana. It came from the Mojave desert, a wind that drove some people and animals mad.

They had gone through their first passionate entanglement of limbs in a wild fury of mouthing, feeling, grasping, and then they had merged. He didn't think of it as penetrating her but rather as a unifying of bodies and blood, ending in that little death when everything is suspended, the final catalepsy that left little breath in the lungs. Then a sighing of recovery, the coming back of intimate odors—female, male. Bodies winding down, almost as if the audacious had turned to nonchalance. He did not feel the sadness and letdown that usually followed his orgasms. In village wisdom, it had been said, 'Only priests and mules are not sad after fucking.' No. He tried to move from her, but she gripped him tight around his torso, her long legs locked behind his back. 'No, not yet.'

Reality, he thought, is not out there in the wind, it exists in these two bodies. He kissed her bruised mouth—there had been brutal moments between them. She had raked his spine with her nails; he could taste blood from the swelling on his lower lip where her teeth had caught him in a moment of loaded tension in that last explosive culmination. There would be bruises on her arms, over her hips.

In the night outside, some small animals or night birds stirred in the groves of oranges—he had never seen so many exotic trees. The Santa Ana wind was too warm to dry their sweat. They had expressed ardor, pleasure, in few words. After a while they fell apart, the sheets, the pillows damp. Rose went behind a screen from where there soon came the sound of a chamber pot in use, the splashing of water in a basin.

'George,' her voice seeped from behind the screen. 'Come wash yourself. That damn wind brings out the sweat.'

He said not only the wind does that, and found her behind the screen toweling that marvelous body with vigor. George was no great expert on painting, but he had seen in some Nob Hill houses copies of Titians, Rubenses, Rembrandts, and other paintings of nudes. So he had a sense of the possibilities of the female body—and Rose surpassed his every fantasy, her breasts firm and high, the nipples strawberry-colored in the light of the hanging lamp. Her torso somehow seemed longer than most women's and the ample curving of her hips and thighs aroused a fresh gush of desire and he could not resist exploring again her inviting pubic triangle.

He asked, as he kissed each breast in turn, 'There's a stream behind the house? Why don't we—'

'Swim in the night?'

'Swim,' he answered.

She laughed, held him close, he not denying himself the pleasure of tracing her body from point to point with probing fingers.

A clock struck three times in the night. In the back of the great U of the house, moonlight etched in an expanse of native flowers beaten by the hot wind. Beyond was a grassy bank and a drop of three feet into a slow-moving stream over a sandy bottom. Soon dawn would encroach and the day come up like an ambush.... These things of the flesh are best done in darkness. They ran, two pink shapes, and dropped into the stream. It was a cold shock to them, for the water was snow runoff from the mountains, and so it retained a tonic chill even in the Santa Ana. They splashed about, swam, and hugged, and Rose cried out, 'We are born in water!' embraced George, and sank. She came up sputtering and tossing her head free of water. Numb with cold, they climbed ashore to a stretch of bank worn away by time, where reeds and tall grass had grown. They lay back, looking up at a sky sugared with stars. But there was nothing very real in the night heavens, nor was there any link to that other world, the pretenses of daytime life. George lowered his head from Rose's breasts to her stomach, paused at the navel, then lower still. His tongue entered between her thighs, active and satisfying, and all life seemed to surround them with the soughing sea. Rose dug her heels into the earth, arched her back, cried out words they could not later recall.

If George was acting mostly as a lover, he was not unaware of the inordinate commitments the late Avrom Rodman had made to citrus growing. Plainly he, too, had been looking forward to the railroad some day going south—the one Collis P. Huntington was promising to start as he bribed Washington politicians to bring in official measures to support the line to Los Angeles and San Deigo. The new rails, said the land boomers, would someday bring the citrus market closer and make it a practical investment. Even a transcontinental rail line.

As Rose drove George—she was proud of her driving skill in her sporting gig—past row after row of deep green trees bearing the golden fruit, he sensed this woman, so sensitive under a hard surface and given to elations and exhilarations, was also in command of this huge fruit and cattle business, really in command of the enterprises that had enabled the ranch and orchards to pay the debts with a huge mortgage and notes to the Hellman Bank of Los Angeles.

They talked of the problems of the Rodman Rancho's obligations as they drove to town. Los Angeles was hardly yet a city, still dusty, its central plaza overrun with stray dogs, shipping what products it had out of the San Pedro harbor, twenty miles away by a tin-pot rail line from city to port.

'Your banking arrangements are poor, Rosie. You've got to consolidate all your loans, notes, mortgages into a clear statement of debts.'

She grinned and flicked her whip on the dun flanks of the horses clipping along, raising a great dust behind. It was the dry season. 'You're spoiling it, George, for bankers to take advantage of people.'

'A good banker strips his victims only down to their skin. There is no interest in bones.'

They were passing smaller orange groves, side roads that showed a carriage or two, some drays hauling timbers, buggies, buckboards.

Rose pointed with her whip to a long series of buildings. 'Banning's stagecoaches. He's been sending mud wagons and freighters, six- to eight-mule-team rigs east into Arizona. He was the man behind the dream of a Los Angeles and San Pedro Railroad to the sea.'

'Twenty miles of track isn't much of a railroad to dream about.'

'What is?' She put a gloved hand in his. 'Mister, we've sort of been living above this, as if the real world doesn't exist. It does. As Marvell said, "But at my back I always hear Time's winged chariot hurrying near."'

George replied that he knew all about reality, and someday soon he would have to go back to his base, to San Francisco, and to what still had to be settled between them. Could anything, she asked, be settled?

It was time, he knew, that he took an accounting of himself, of his place in a hard strong world with its core of corruption. Had he come to trust and rely upon only

154

himself? Did he have too high a regard for himself? In fact, was he as true to himself as he thought? Did he push aside most criteria, values, avoid disenchantment?

Perhaps he was as full of deceptions as the next man. He had worked so hard, taking so many chances; never had he been deceitful or let the disenchantment that destroyed so many seep inside his isolation. That is perhaps why he needed Rose so much—to temper the need to watch himself, observe himself, seek out some inner weakness.

So far, I have acted out my life, he thought. I have self-regard. I admit a good opinion of myself, as does my sister of herself. Could I at middle age, in this love, be rushed toward destruction, an inevitable ruin? The way Sam Brannan ended up—a derelict, a ruined man pointed out as a mockery of what he had once been? Am I, too, an outsider, facing hostile forces, human deceit?

Suddenly here in Southern California I don't know. Rose seems aware of this other self and must see the absurdity in my life. I sense a desperation in this love too full to grasp, to hold on to.

15

George showed little of these introspective moods to Rose.

They made love in the late afternoon and at night, sometimes in the morning, and the maid brought in the breakfast tray and lowered her eyes, suppressing a giggle. There were no secrets at Rodman Rancho; the vine workers, the house servants, the field hands, and the fruit packers were all interrelated, interbred families from Mexico named Sandovals, Quintanas. Few spoke English.

They played and sang love songs to guitar music. Rose's late husband had preferred Mexican-American hired hands. They had, he had insisted, a lazy loyalty to the *rancho*. So what if they loafed and stole a bit, got drunk on church holidays? They did have a pride in being on the place. Rose ran things with a firm hand, the buildings were whitewashed after the rains, the horses shod, the wild cattle driven down the hill to slaughter in season 'when the first cold wind kills the flies.'

Rose was waiting for some clarification of their relationship. She had made it clear she would not give up the *rancho* and the citrus orchards; George, too, had been frank. He would not, could not, part from his wife and his sons, because one of those scandals could even harm the Pacific-Harvesters Bank.

They avoided any fuller discussion of their situation. They went to the Merced Theater to see a performance of *Rip Van Winkle*; visited Buffums's saloon so Rose could show George a gathering of the town's sporting gentry that might rival the Poodle Dog's. They dined at the Bella Union, the best cuisine El Pueblo de los Angeles could produce.

They went picknicking in the mountains, they relaxed. She told him of herself, her family background.

'Avrom Rodman, my husband, was a German from Ulm in Württemberg, from a very proud Jewish family. But in some grain speculation they lost everything. Avrom was only sixteen when he came over as a groom with a cargo of horses. That was in Boston: he became a tinware merchant selling on the farm roads from a wagon, got out here, loved the land, brought over relatives, set them up as tinware peddlers. They roamed the West, settled in Arizona, New Mexico. Ten years ago, Avrom, growing old, saw oranges and lemons as a crop with a future, so—'

'Why did you marry him?' Reclining under a live oak, they were sipping from the second bottle of wine.

'Why do people marry? Admiration? Security?

156

Companionship?'

'You jump over "love."' He handed her a fresh glass of wine from a bottle that had been cooling in a rushing stream close by.

'Let me tell you about *my* family, George. They came from Spain in 1540. Although they were *hebreos cristianos*, Hebrew Christians, the damn Inquisition was burning a lot of them at the stake. Yes, burning them in *auto da fés* so it could seize their estates and, of course, save their souls— fried, baked souls, no matter. The Carvajal family and the Moraleses, they married, became Jewish conquistadors, killing as many Indians as the true dons in Mexico, and setting up estates, very big *ranchos*, breeding wonderful horses, making wine. My ancestors in the New World were true *hidalgos* but still *marranos*. Even if *nuevos cristianos*, still secretly suspected of the ritual practices of orthodox Jews.'

'I'll be goddamned,' said George. 'Never knew of this in history books. It's all Cortez and blood and gold.'

'History, dear George, is usually the lies we've all agreed upon. So, yes, my family, the Carvajals, had to move on a few times. Even so, several of our relatives went into the Holy Office flames during any season of torture and murder in Mexico City in 1570. It was the bad year.'

'A long time ago'—Rose was talking as if addressing the mountains—'the grandson of the first Carvajal in Mexico had a huge *rancho* at Panuco. But the Jesuit hounds of the Inquisition came racing after him, and he, warned by fellow *marranos*, moved his family and his herds north to Zacatecas. Later, his sons and daughters went to Monclova. By my grandfather's times, we had crossed the Rio Grande and were in California.'

George looked into the luminous eyes of the woman; they seemed to be staring at something far away. Something in her trancelike mood set her mouth into a sad, preoccupied smile. Rose seemed to shake herself loose from the past and gave him an apprehensive glance.

'Forgive my mindless gabbing.'

'No, no, go on—I'm fascinated.'

'My father was ruined in the hide trade. The Rancho San Rafael was ours then. Thousands of acres and great herds of wild longhorn cattle. They were raised for their hide, and that in the end ruined the last Carvajals in America. He had contracts with Yankee ships from New England that came around the Horn to buy the hides. They would pay for each of the hides when they came back the next year. They were trustworthy New Englanders. But for some years there was no payment—a money panic. There was no great need for hides then, so the firms that bought from the shippers held back payments and, being dishonest, decided to go bankrupt.'

Rose looked about her, placed her hands behind her head, and gazed up at the robin's-egg-blue sky. 'Give me a little more wine.... I was eighteen, away at school in Havana when the ruin came. We were also owed money by some tobacco people who were burned out, and I had a letter from an aunt; my father in his prayer shawl, and the little boxes on arm and forehead, had said a long prayer and then ...' Rose lowered her head. 'They buried him in his prayer shawl in a plain unpainted box as called for and a ritual *shivah* took place.'

'Yes, I've heard, a ritual mourning.'

'Avrom came out to the auction of what was left of the estate to buy some of the farm machinery being sold off. No, he didn't buy me. I was a willing girl, *anything* to get away from that doomed place. I had two sisters. Hannah and Sarah. They went to relatives in England.'

'How old was he?'

'Avrom? He was forty-five at the time. A good man, a widower, a solid man. He wanted a second wife in his life— he had no children. After years of moving about, he wanted a family. I had a dread of intimacy, and he had little sex drive, like so many men who are obsessed by business concerns. In bed he was, well, tepid. He did manage to produce a baby. It was born dead. '

George took her in his arms and told her she didn't have

to go on talking in this self-lacerating manner. They didn't talk much of anything the rest of the afternoon. They returned to the *rancho* even more in love, with a better understanding of their backgrounds and their situation. They decided that George would go back to San Francisco in a week, to assess what depth there was between them. He swore things would work out, but Rose felt less hopeful that anything could actually solve their situation. Somehow he was aware her detailed recall of her forefathers' past had introduced a great doubt into their relationship. It was their first real quarrel. He said she was a hard bitch when it came to emotions, her own included, and she said, yes, to be hard on oneself is often one's *only* strength. And so it went on in the bedroom and in the dining room at the *rancho*. A lamp was smashed, the servants kept out of the way. Finally, in an intensity of sorrow and passion, they made violent love, accused each other of lack of faith, and asked for forgiveness.

Next morning, they ate breakfast on the terrace, drank brandy, ate their rusks and shirred eggs, offered each other slivers of food with greasy fingers, chewed, and kissed. The house servants agreed that all *gringos* were *locos*.

But this domestic drama lost interest among the Hispanic servants and hired hands when news came of the capture of the *bandido* Tiburcio Vasquez, the hero of the Mexican-Americans. No keeping them in the house or in the fields; they rushed to the city jail. The fruit packing stopped; horses, mules, and donkeys remained uncurried. Everyone in town wanted to see the drama first hand. Officeholders, clerks, council-men, loafers, political freeloaders, all ran into the street when they heard the news. Sure enough, in the jailyard, in a wagon, lay the bandaged figure of the 'Terror of California.' He seemed rather small, not at all the ferocious bandit of legend. In fact, he was rather mild-looking, with a bit of a mustache, a neat chunk of beard. It seemed to many a sellout of a dream to accept this man as 'the desperate brigand who had ruled the highways for years.'

159

In a cell, the bandit was formally introduced to Sheriff Billy Rowland, and a bottle of prime whiskey was produced; glasses were filled and Vasquez showed charming manners. Lifting his glass of the potent bourbon, he offered a toast with true elegance: 'To the president of the United States!'

The bandit was on his way to becoming a folk hero. Those privileged to visit his cell observed how brave he was—not a flinch or a moan when the county doctor, a notoriously clumsy man, probed the wounds. The physician also commented on the bandit's courage and told the sheriff, 'Why, he's still game for a long day's ride.' The sheriff reserved his reply.

How had the capture come about? everyone was asking. Rose and George got the correct version—or perhaps just the official version—from Sheriff Rowland himself, over a supper of venison and wild duck at the Rodman Rancho. Sheriff Rowland enjoyed dining at Rodman's Rancho. He politely picked his teeth behind a napkin. 'Played possum myself,' said the ruddy-faced sheriff. 'I stayed on in town when we got the tip, and sent Undersheriff Johnson out with the boys. You folks are welcome to visit the *bandido* in the jail. Always a crowd there. Kinda hero to the Mexes.'

George said to Rose, 'You might as well give in. We'll go see the hero ourselves.'

'Hero?'

'I've met him. He stole a watch I was bringing down for you.'

'Maybe now he'll give it back.'

'If he remembers me, the hero of the jail.'

'The trial will be better than a play.'

'He's going to be tried up north. They have a few murder charges waiting.'

Two days later, George did. Rose didn't want to go, she had some shopping to do and wanted to check a cargo of boxed oranges whose transit to the port was being delayed.

'I just don't care to see a human being exposed as a circus attraction behind bars.'

'He seems to be enjoying his fame.'

Rowland himself cleared the jail hall of reporters and citizens, including some adoring women bearing flowers and home-cooked dainties. The bandit was wearing a borrowed frock coat and a clean shirt. His long hair had been combed and its natural curls greased. He sat in a chair in leg irons, smoking a thin cigar. He smiled and pointed to a bench. 'I know you, the Señor Banker fella?'

'That's right, I'm not sorry to see you here.'

'Is nothing, just scratches. You mad I take the watch?'

'It was a special gift. But they'll hang you for some killing done up north.'

The bandit looked about him, rolled the cigar around in his mouth. He leaned closer to George, who had seated himself on the bench. 'I tell you, every time is a killing, they say this greaser *bandido*, he do it. To law people, we all look alike.'

'They've got witnesses.'

'Witness you buy. Listen, banker. I want to buy justice. I got ten thousand dollars hid away in dry well in San Jose. You, my bank man, take it and buy me a judge.'

'No, Vasquez. The law isn't perfect by a long shot, but I'm not going to bribe a judge.' He stood up. 'You'll get what's coming to you.'

The bandit smiled. 'As Dios says, we all die. But the little watch, the sheriff he has it. For you.'

'Thanks.'

'Maybe you get me better cigars?'

When George told Sheriff Rowland about the bandit's idea to bribe a judge, the sheriff laughed. 'Son of a bitch, he thinks he's in Mexico. Anyway, he told Johnson he had twenty thousand in gold hidden in a cave near Monterey and he told one of the posse he had a fortune in pearls and diamonds hidden in a hollow tree outside San Diego. What a bullshitter, all to bribe a judge and jury.'

'He told me you've got the lady's gold watch he took from me at Coyote's Hole Station.'

The sheriff opened a rolltop desk and hunted in the

161

debris of pistols, loose cartridges, reward posters, and a bag of peppermint drops, until he brought out the watch and its thin chain. 'This be it?'

'That's it, Sheriff. I'll get a bill of sale and—'

'Hell, no, Mr Fiore, you take it. You, a man whose meat I eat, I trust.'

'Mrs Rodman's food.'

'Yep, nice, the widder.' He dug an elbow in George's rib section. 'This Rodman was a right good Jewman. Made a nice spread of his place and set out all those damn orange trees.'

'California oranges will become famous, Sheriff.'

'Maybe …'

'Well, thanks for the watch.' George went to meet Rose.

She was delighted with the gift, holding the watch up to the sunlight, admiring the gleam of gold. 'We must send this poor fellow some jam.'

'He's getting enough of everything from admirers now.'

The day before George was to take the steamer from San Pedro to San Francisco, the bandit Vasquez was rushed in a closed hack, by the sheriff and his two assistants, for his own trip north to a judge and jury that would see he was properly hanged. Sheriff Rowland told George, 'Had to be on our toes with that customer. Never know if his old sidekick Chavez and some of the old gang wouldn't have tried a rescue.'

George made one last effort to get Rose to sell or lease the Rodman ranch and orange groves and come north with him. 'Unless you're a very big combine, it's too costly to mature the groves. I've been looking into it with people at Hellman's Bank.'

'I've got a good start. I'll buy more land, plant more.'

'But it takes seven years for a tree to begin producing prime fruit, and it has to have the right hardy sour rootstock, whose fruit was not worthwhile, to graft onto the sweet orangewood. Many a would-be orange farmer is the victim of some sharper or drifter selling him willow saplings for certified orangewood stock.'

162

'George, I've acres of fruit-bearing trees, and the young stock will soon bloom. A twelve-year tree offers up a thousand oranges a crop. A bearing orchard is just like finding money in the street.'

'Hardly that, figuring the cost of land, twelve years of nursing the trees, trimming, and costs of fertilizer and spraying.'

That last night, they had made love sadly. Gone were most of the runes of some sacred magic. There was low, soft talk of faith, of believing, and as they lay together near dawn, George could feel the beat of his blood circulating inside his ears. He felt he was caught between depressive qualms and an emotion to which he must be protective and sympathetic. He owed it to this woman in his arms, the warmth, solidity, the odor of her. He might be in error about all the actions involving him with Rose, but never in doubt. It hadn't been all uninhibited joy, what Rose had at first mocked as one of those *affaires de coeur*. For all her passion in offering herself to him, she still remained somewhat elusive, obstinately independent. Had he ever reached to her intimate and private core? Did she have insights and sensations, a feminine subtlety he would never fully touch?

He was a man facing human relationships new to him, a territory outside his usual daily domain of business ambition. What had he wanted? A pleasing girl who could be pleased?

Rose came with him to the boat. They stood on the pier among hurrying people carrying carpetbags, seamen tossing ropes and hauling aboard trunks; a tide sucked with indecent sounds at the piles of the pier.

George felt it was not real in this lime-white sun, the plume of black smoke curling up from the ship's stack. It was more like a scene from one of the operas he had seen in San Francisco. Lovers facing each other, burdened with love, bodies exuding musical passion. But opera could break out in song, heavy notes going high across the footlights.

Rose was in blue taffeta, a circle of a small black trimmed hat perched well forward on hair framing a face aggrieved at this parting. Yet there was also a kind of timidity, not at all like her. A shared feeling, he thought, that now something is moving away from both of us.

The ship's siren was blasting at nervous intervals. A bell rang, someone dropped a crate of grapes and it burst open; people and sailors stepped on them indifferently. Men began to move about the gangplank. George kissed Rose, almost brutally, and she dug her fingers into his back. Later, he recalled there had been little said between them at parting. He had whispered:

'Things will work out, my darling'; and she had answered:

'We can only hope.'

A last hug, and a bruising meeting of lips, a tugging apart of interlaced fingers. No tears, no tears.

He stood at the rail as the steamer met the coastal swells of the Pacific, and the umber-and-violet coast blurred. He thought of how in the past, before meeting Rose, he had thought of *la donna che non si trova*—the woman one never meets. Now he had met her, and was parting from her. For how long? Life could be such a kick in the ass. He was aware that a shower of cinders was falling on the deck from the smoke-belching stack. The ship tilted; he had a slight seizure of vertigo.

Things could work out, he thought as he recovered. But there were problems at the Pacific-Harvesters Bank. There had been several urgent letters from Rocco and Irena. He seemed to be balanced between some great coup and a sense of failure. The Chinese *hong* merchants he had cultivated, Rocco wrote, would not deal with anyone but Mr Fiore. They kowtowed when he served them, but became silent slant-eyed masks when anything seemed to hinder their ritualized dealings with the 'round eyes,' as they called the Americans. Rocco and Irena must have acted patronizing. Then there was that other matter of his being greatly extended in loans to the vineyards and wineries. No other bank cared to become involved with the many small growers whose vineyards were frugal family affairs.

The Pacific-Harvesters Bank was overextended in this too dry season. To make matters worse, some fungus was loose among the vines, and growers would have to survive the grafting of new immune stock to old roots. And would he, could he, bail out the failing wineries?

Good or bad vintage, it took three years for a vine to begin to produce mature grapes and four years before the acres of vines could show a profit. The grower had a big investment, for he usually processed his own wine, and the cost of even the most primitive wine presses, the building of storage cellars, and the casks made the wine industry something only a man with cash on the barrelhead (or credit at the bank) could make a go of.

For better or for worse, it was certainly time to go home.

16

As the Fiore and Velasquez cousins turned seven, then eight, the War Between the States (as some called it), the Civil War, still raged. It was 1863.

Their lead soldiers increased to whole armies. Long lines of ancient warriors, red-coated Britons, French horsemen with lances, cossacks, Japanese samurai—all served, laid out on the ballroom floor at the Casa, to represent the Yanks or the rebels.

Tomas would sometimes play with the lead soldiers, too, and show the boys how the battle of Waterloo was won. '*Merde!*' cried the Imperial Guards. 'Hurrah the Emperor!'

But best of all was playing at George Washington's war.

Ramon didn't mind being Cornwallis, as he figured he got the best-colored soldiers, all scarlet and gold and bearskin hats. Charlie had a big map copied from one in *Harper's Weekly*. He colored army lines with crayon, the rivers, and stars over the forts, a big yellow sun over Washington. And a gold star where Papa was a major in a place on the Father of Waters, as Charles lettered it—the Mississippi, the place called 'Vicksburg.' How had Papa come to be there in such a fine uniform, a double row of buttons, a sword with a sash?

Irena Velasquez kept herself busy at whist parties given to raise money for the wounded soldiers' fund and to provide gruel and old clothes to the freed darkies. Studying her whist hand, she would say, 'Men love war; they only fear getting hurt or killed. Otherwise, they're free of the watchful eyes of their wives, family responsibility. Someone feeds them, someone tells them what to do. Not to think, just go unshaved, go filthy, get drunk, brag and tell lies. That's the *real* picture of war, what a man admires in a war.'

But if she knew you well and she had had a few extra tea-and-rums, she would slide her big body over, half-hood her eyes, and tell some of what actually had sent George Fiore within dangerous proximity to the enemy.

'You want to know about how my brother George went to war? It was Senator Moses Kendrick. That's right, the old blowhard is a war senator in a big shiny top hat, a piped waistcoat, his side-whiskers longer and touched with white. George always felt he owed the old bastard something. Even if, well, there had been trouble between them. Remember Sam Brannan? He went to being a pauper and a drunk. Became dirt. But he was the one drove a wedge between George and Moses Kendrick. So the senator sweet-talked George—they had need of him in the army, the nation was in danger, and George could be a dragon slayer. Bullshit, of course, *non me ne frega un cazzo!* But you flatter even a smart man and you can put a nose ring on him and lead him around.'

That was hardly the full truth. At the time, George could not make as many trips to see Rose Rodman as he wanted. There was the bank to watch in a time of duplicity and war debts. And there was the family: even Maria would begin to wonder why he made so many trips south. George's mood, his nerve ends, seemed to quiver in a sullen petulance. They only received some solace when he met Rose, but he was never fully satisfied. He felt that only God actually fathomed him, and he was having a hard time carrying on a belief in Him. And one day there was Senator Kendrick in a good black broadcloth frock coat, twirling his watch chains over his paunch, there in George's bank. Next to him stood Captain Homer Kendrick in tight blue tailcoat, rows of buttons well shined, as were his spurs, with a sword in proportion to his lean tall body, a serious officer's face under a peaked cap with crossed swords.

It was late afternoon, the gas flares behind the cut-glass bowls burning yellow-orange. Rocco was off to meet some woman.

'You may be surprised to see me here, George,' said the senator.

'I don't surprise much anymore. Sit down, gentlemen. Cigars, a dram …? Homer, you've grown.'

'I have, sir. I'm attached to Custer's horse force, on leave.'

'The boy took a ball in the shoulder in the Shenandoah fighting.'

'Nothing, really.'

George eyed father and son. Why the visit? Were they here to collect for the soldier's wounded fund, or a charity shipment of flour to the frontier for those trapped in the war? The old bastard had tenacity, pride, but he could be *simpático* if he wanted favors. And he seemed now ready to bend his usual cool passivity.

'It's this way, George. The war is all fucked up. Lincoln can't find a general who will soil his nice clean army and fight. British industry is starving with so little cotton getting past our blockade. They're ready to come over to the Rebs'

167

side, declare war, if ...'

'If?' asked George, reaching for a filled pipe.

'If the rebels mount a solid major advance into the North and envelop the Union armies.'

Homer put his thumbs over his sword belt. 'It looks as if Lee is moving across the Potomac, maybe soon, with seventy-five thousand men.'

'Talk, rumor at the bar of the Poodle Dog. But even so ...'

'We need you. I talked about you to the War Department. I told them what we two once did out here.'

George felt no interest in resurrecting the past. 'What the hell for?' He had his pipe lit, and his mind was working furiously. There were some delicate nuances in the air, the old bastard!

'The war can change if Lee is stopped and Grant takes Vicksburg, and he can't. Been there almost a year. He has no supply columns; he is living off the land, what ever he can find. He needs an expert man, a good man to organize his foragers, his wagon columns, steam trains, his transport.'

Homer dug his spurs into George's carpet. 'And you've done it, gathered produce, cattle, pigs, organized mule teams. I worked for you and Pop here.'

'I'm a banker now. It wasn't any pleasure. Boiling sun and freezing in the rain, gathering crops, forage, meat.' He tried to sound phlegmatic, impassive.

'War isn't easy,' said the senator, crossing his legs. He no longer wore boots, George noticed, but elastic-sided shoes.

'Cards on the table, George. You've been offered a major's rank to move supplies out of Los Angeles, Williamsburg, San Pedro, east in wagon trains for the western garrisons. And then move on with men trained as foragers to join Grant, to solve supply problems. Starting with Los Angeles.'

'Los Angeles?' said George. 'Packers and horse handlers, wagons?'

So George went to war, to spend a few weeks with Rose.

And why not? His mind was drawn taut by his emotional problems. For the first time the bank seemed dull, and perhaps too prosperous in wartime economy. As Rocco had said, 'It's coming in so much and we're relending it at such a high interest, it's no fun anymore.'

He did put a six months' limit on his service. So, trying not to think of the faults in his logic, he ordered a uniform and before he left, his son Fred tried on his army hat and Charles belted on the new sword. Everyone called them 'little Yanks.' Maria said nothing; she understood the finality of all he did. She was rapidly becoming interested in whist, to which Irena had introduced her. Irena told him he was a fool, but he sure looked dashing in his uniform. Rocco also wanted to enlist, but George wanted Rocco to help Irena run the bank and to keep him informed, via telegraph, of any crisis.

He left for the South with a sense of wary hope and a touch of adventure. Most of all, with a kind of bewilderment at the treachery into which his glands and emotions were pushing him. When he got to Los Angeles, Rose was elated and wept a bit, saying she didn't like the smell of soldiers. They were very close during those precious few weeks together. George managed to reorganize the supply mess of the local quartermaster and to sort out some hard army men, part rogues and part excitement-seekers, happy to escape from garrison duty.

The day before he left, he said to Rose, 'I'm in no danger. Not with scrounging for supplies. But one doesn't really know, does one? I want to settle things when I come back. I know these damn partings and our short times together are eating into you.'

'Don't, don't,' she said. 'It's as if my whole body is a stranger. I'm worn down by discretion. No more talk; just *be*, just love me. Hold me, hold me!'

George felt as if his life was moving in a circular orbit, but he could not see where the track was leading him, except to war. His sense of accomplishment seemed blunted. His ability to see clearly was gone. He left Rose after a last night of fierce passion. In the morning, he rode out on a half-tamed hard-mouthed horse and watched expressionlessly as the great train of wagons moved east. Ahead were mountains, deserts, and perhaps outlaw raiders calling themselves Confederates. He was not a skilled horseman, but he held the mount steady, appeared calm for all the knot and agony and intensity in his gut.

Foraging for the army differed somewhat from his early forays for Kendrick.

'I'll tell you this, Major,' said Lieutenant Tom Floyd. 'God may not help those who help themselves, but you'll notice he don't stand in front of you with no flaming sword and say, "What you got there?"'

The two men were seated on railroad ties beside an army supply shed, eating a hot mess of broken-up hardtack and salt pork from a spider skillet set on some smoldering hickory embers.

In the hard, wet spring of 1863, Grant was still besieging Vicksburg. The army sat there on a loop of the Mississippi. Forty thousand Union troops had been there since December the year before, and reports said the inhabitants of the city were down to rat fillets and mule cutlets, while the Union regiments sat along bluffs, bayous, and plantations gone to wrack and weed. An army with no lines of supplies, not getting much food or comfort from riverboats herded by the ironclads firing back at the city. So Major Fiore's men were foraging, and were down to rancid bacon, weevily hardtack, horse corn, the last of the coffee, and whatever chicken or bit of wild game the soldiers could scrounge.

His six months' service was now in its eighth month; in the army, such appeals got lost, and mail was rare.

The young officer Tom Lloyd, a good man but tired, said, 'The politicians drinking hot toddies in the Willard bar in Washington, they're calling Vicksburg "the spinal column of America." And as one fat-ass senator in a stovepipe hat figured it, "Break their back there and the damn rebels will die a quick death cut off from their allies in

170

the West."'

George felt Vicksburg would refuse to surrender. He knew the rebels still held 250 miles of the flood-brown river down to Port Hudson's Louisiana sandbars, snags and all, a transmission belt between their east and west. All around Vicksburg you could smell the dead and see the raw earth mounds thrown up by shelling and tunneled-out mines set off underground. But the city remained on top of the bluffs, with heavy fortifications, big guns. On the east bank of the river, its formidable batteries spewed iron and fire out to red-clay hills and riverside trenches, canebrakes, bush and ravines. George hated the sight of the Stars and Bars always flying, or rather drooping, in the warm spring weather. Nothing brought Vicksburg's capture nearer, even if Grant had had the cursing work gangs of soldiers, river sailors, and Negroes trying to dig a canal around the city to force the river into a new bed. He had cut levies and sent gangs mucking about in the bayous. The city held, starved, and its flags flew.

Now, in April, Grant sent George out with a regiment to where the Vicksburg–Jackson railway line met the New Orleans & Jackson Railroad. He hoped to take the rail junction at Jackson, where the rebel supplies of food came through. If the junction was lost, Vicksburg could not be supplied at all by rail. Grant was also moving his muddy forces and bronze cannons south to take the city, some speculated, from the water side.

Major Fiore was at Hard Time Landing. The rebel supplies were myths. He was assembling captured wagons in hopes that Admiral Porter's gunboats and the transports that had run the Vicksburg batteries downriver would have a supply of iron T rails and hook spikes to keep what rail lines the Union had operating in the newly captured territory. Privy gossip was that Grant was coming from all directions, tightening the stranglehold on the city.

George attended a staff meeting. The stumpy little general put it to Sherman, as below soldiers moved down the country pike past burning barns, 'We'll carry what rations of hard bread, coffee, and salt we can and make the country furnish the balance.'

'I hope so, sir,' said George.

And a slim balance the army and George found it, though he was now a skilled scrounger with a hawk's sharp eye for what could be eaten, drunk or carried off. His chief assistant, Lieutenant Floyd, was courageous under fire, and feared at times the wrath of God. Just over six feet, he seemed shorter, being so broad. A long delicate nose, irregular oversized teeth, amusing face, with washed-out greenish eyes.

George took over three captured locomotives. He bossed the flat cars loaded with horse corn and oak barrels of salt pork. He dreamed of Rose, of the bank, of his twin sons, Fred and Charles.

Grant attacked in July and he called into the ranks every man he had, including George. On the twenty-fifth, the Union engineers exploded a huge mine under a major rebel force and the whole siege became a viselike ring of attacks on Vicksburg. Yet the rebel flag could still be made out as it hung over the city's courthouse. George was with Sherman's XV Corps out front, sweating and advancing fearfully through broken woods toward fortified bluffs. Insects attacked mercilessly, the summer sun blazed overhead.

'Christ,' he said, waving his men forward, 'get it over with.'

It never made much sense to George, the bloody battle for the city. He couldn't fit the bits together into any whole picture of that day. All he knew was he was winded and terrified. Seeing men die, turn to dog meat, he was shaking when it was over. Part of the city was burning. Grant had taken Vicksburg! George went down to the river and just sat there on a log, his joints sore, his feet sore. He watched the water running by; twenty feet out a snag was sticking up, and there was a body caught in the snag. Upriver, gunboats were no longer firing. The sun going down in the west made red ribbons on the water. He had fever—one of those obscure river fevers. Lieutenant Floyd limped down to him, his boots in his hand. He pulled off his striped shirt and soaked it in the river. He had a brown torso and a long red scar over the left shoulder blade. His worn pants had the yellow stripe of regular cavalry. He looked out at the body caught on the snag. 'Must be a reb.'

'Yes.'

'They gave up.'

'Yes.'

'Yep, Vicksburg. We just starved them out. They been smoking sumac leaves for tobacco and eating bread made from pea flour.'

George felt the fever shake him. He rose, picked up some flat stones, and began to skim them across the river surface. When he was a boy living in the village, he used to skim stones across the stream. His grandmother would fix him a broth with bread soaked in it, feed him with a big tin spoon.

Lieutenant Floyd flapped his wet shirt in the air. 'It's Fourth of July! No more fighting.'

'Rumor is, Lee is invading the North through Pennsylvania.'

'Well, there's whiskey and singing out by the sutler's carts, just up top of the ridge. It's rotgut, but it's whiskey.'

George didn't feel much like celebrating. He had maybe killed or badly wounded two or three of the rebs. Just after they got past the first trench and were into the fort, it was mean. With his sword he shoved into the bodies at least twice. He could use a drink, a slug of corn pressings, rotgut or not.

The two men found the sutler's cart, one with a group of officers buying meat pies and fruitcake and tobacco, and from under some canvas a tattered soldier was pouring out whiskey from crocks into tin cups. George stood against a tree trunk sipping raw crack-skull whiskey flavored, he suspected, with pepper and chewing tobacco. Horse soldiers and gunner crews were leading their horses down

173

to a stream. All around, soldiers were shouting and slapping backs and talking of who was dead and who was wounded and who had shot himself in the battle. After all, it was victory; it was the Fourth of July. U.S. Grant and the rebel General Pemberton had sat down together and said this part of the war was over.

'You don't look good, Major.'

'A touch of river fever, I guess.'

In some delicate equilibrium, there was the void … it was spinning … he felt he was the sport of forces outside himself and space was endless and warm … severe voices were hostile … distant … and he kept falling and rising … then all was solemn and soothing but for a great thirst, his whole life with no reticence, no shame, seemed to press in, then ebb away….

He opened his eyes to find Tom Floyd, a study in anxiety, looking down on him. He was in the hospital amid the stink of unhealed wounds, dead matter, stale blood.

'Dammit, Major! Alive and kicking!'

George wanted to scream up from the diaphragm, tried to talk, but he seemed too dry in the mouth to force his vocal cords to respond. All he could hear himself utter was '*Ah-ah … har-har.*'

'Jesus, twice they moved you over to the burial-squad sections. You had it bad, a hard bit, Major. *Real* hard.'

He managed to reconnect his voice to his mind. 'Tom, ah, ah, what, *where?*'

'Ha? This is the military hospital in Cairo. You got what they call downriver fever, malaria.'

'How long have I …?'

''Bout three weeks since you come apart near Vicksburg. You sweated, shook like a loose barn door, chills, and you were talking something all mushed up, muttering like and calling for someone.'

Tom Floyd flushed, pulled on an earlobe, looked away to where a male orderly was holding a basin into which a soldier was coughing up something. 'Well, it was … I don't

174

know, Major, I just don't remember.' The young officer let go of his earlobe.

George changed positions—it wasn't easy—felt his lungs were filled with a hot gas, his brow was damp, but he felt fully conscious ... nearly, anyway. He could grasp the present, the butcher-shop odor, Tom; all else between the time he felt the earth come up to strike him and then fall away a mile beneath the surface was vague, fuzzy, translucent unconnected images.

'You're detached from service, Major, can go home. Too sick to return to duty. Why, you must've lost thirty pounds easy.'

George held up a hand. The naked arm was thin, pale; he could not control a tremor. He touched his face, found new hollows under his thrusting cheekbones, a sagging of loose skin under his shaggy chin. There was quite a beard.

'I'll be back to fill you in, Major ... Me? I got me some shell fragment in the right calf. Gimpy, but no real damage, just a little limp. Anything I can do?'

'Shave, I mean, this fuzz, it ...'

'Do it myself for you later. These orderlies are pig gelders.'

'Anything ... letters?'

'Some coming in, the ironclads bring in a few packets. As for your gear, I got hold of what I could. And the war, it's all fucked up now, Vicksburg's taken, and the soldiers moving over the mountains and up the Ohio River to the east. Lee got whupped in Pennsylvania.'

George lay on his back, flexing his arms and legs after the young officer had limped off. It was all so furtive, unreasoning. He must retie himself to the other life, to all he had once accepted—the twin sons, Irena, Maria, Tomas, Rocco ... they seemed a bedazzlement of faces and voices. As he tried to sleep, a nearby medical voice said clearly, '... slug entered the scapula, penetrated and lodged in the thoracic cavity. I'm afraid that ...'

Not everyone was lucky enough to get malaria. He dozed half in and half out of the world, and a short wide doctor with an anxious geniality was taking his pulse.

The doctor had a Maine accent, or what George thought of as a Maine accent. 'Perceptible improvement—much. A close thing, Major. By god, there were two times I was sure you'd fill a grave out there in the back pasture.'

'Thank you ...'

'That young louie Floyd did more than I did. Kept putting wet cloths on your burning head. Bathing you.'

'I had no idea. When do I leave here? I want to ...'

The doctor tapped his fingertips together, looked at George over his silver-rimmed eyeglasses. 'Weak as a blind kitten. Just rest, rest. And when you go, I'll have the young Louie go along. He's with a game leg, now a bit lopsided, and he's going out of here himself.'

George still didn't know where he was. Cairo? Ohio? What had happened? Not at the end of Vicksburg. He was leaving this stinking collection of beds and death, that Mexican-meat-market odor of stale raw flesh.

He spent most of his time dozing, feeling that if he didn't hang on to the spinning earth, grip it firmly, he'd slide right off, shoot like a projectile into space. One afternoon he awoke to find Tom Floyd standing by his bed, holding a pitcher of buttermilk from some springhouse, beads of cold moisture sliding down its surface.

Under his arm, the officer held a rolled newspaper and some letters.

'Ice-cold, Major. Nothing like buttermilk.'

'Letters,' George said hoarsely.

'Yes, letters. Damn mud scow of an ironclad brought downriver some bags from St Louis.'

George held out his hands. Tom Floyd put three letters and the rolled newspaper into them. 'There were a kind of cake, too, mashed flat and full of ants.'

George shuffled the letters after tossing aside the newspaper: Irena's bold writing, block-shaped; Rocco's crazy script, always running uphill; and ... *yes*! The generous, beautiful, curved inky letters of Rose. Thicks and thins shaded with ornate curves.

'Better drink the buttermilk while it's cold, Major.'

George's fingers seemed too weak to open the sealed flaps.

'Damn! Tom, you open this for me and I'll make you a banker.'

'That sure would be generous. You mean it?'

'Yes, you come west with me. Hurry.' He was as yet too weak, and he sensed he would pass out in his weakness if he didn't grit his teeth.

Tom handed George the unfolded letter. George took it, his hands shaking. It was dated three weeks before.

My dear love,

May this find you, and find you safe, and me in your thoughts. Two days ago I gave birth to our child. A girl, six pounds, three ounces. I kept thinking of a poem: '*How many are born to sweet delight.*' If you agree, I will name her Maude after a favorite aunt who saw to my education and schooling. If you have another name that comes to mind, someone you feel you owe a memory, we shall, when you come back to us, take up the matter. Oh, George, George, right now there is too much space between us; what a fine child we have made, pink skin, a good feeder, a retroussé nose. If only you were here, if only I were sure you were alive. The accounts of the Vicksburg/Gettysburg battles have been fearful. I have taken up praying to Hebrew Gods in my ridiculous fears for your safety. Be spared to come and see what we have made.

　　　　　　　　Much love and a bear hug,
　　　　　　　　R.

17

On San Pablo Bay, in 1817, the twentieth mission of the Holy Church was built, the Missión de San Rafael, north of San Francisco. San Rafael itself was a town of pleasant houses, with an older native section that raised poultry for the city's needs.

Petaluma—the original Indian word for 'Beautiful View'—was a ridge above San Rafael, with only three houses set far apart. The best view was from Bay Cottage's terrace, set in a garden of Jacqueminot roses and dwarf cedars. A young widow and her infant daughter had taken the place, rented it through the Pacific-Harvesters Bank. There was a servant, an elderly Hispanic woman with an Indian face, named Lupe. She also acted as baby nurse, did the cooking, and set out a vegetable garden of Mexican peppers, tomatoes, *ensalada* greens, and sweet corn behind the house.

Two or three times a week a man no longer young, looking as if recovering from some illness, would arrive at the house, having driven there in a buggy from the San Rafael livery stables. He brought gifts, packages of food, bottles of wine, *aguardiente*, anchovies. He would hug the baby and admire its weight, the cornflower blue color of its eyes. He and the widow would walk through the garden arm in arm, while Lupe would put a chicken to roasting, set out wine glasses and cakes on the terrace table, and plump up the pillows in the bedroom. Sometimes the man and the widow would drink and nibble at *chimaja* cakes, look over the bay. Sometimes they would retire to the bedroom for an hour or so. The señor, a *gente de razón*, was not well, and Lupe hoped he was not harming himself with so much lovemaking. Lupe had had many husbands, most without the help of the Church, and she knew how easily a *caballero* could kill himself with the making of the love.

'Ah, little one,' she would say to the baby in its cradle, as she mixed the batter for the corn fritters and kept an eye on the roasting chicken over the piñon-wood coals, 'someday you'll turn men's heads yourself in shared pleasures.'

It had not been as difficult as George had thought to get Rose and the baby Maude to come north, settle on the bay near San Francisco. At first, Rose had wept when Tom Floyd appeared with him at Rodman Rancho. George looked so shrunken in his army greatcoat, his face lean and lead-colored. His eyes seemed larger, set deeper; she recalled a poem: 'Goodbye in fear, good-bye in sorrow, good-bye and all in vain.'

'My darling, my darling,' she had cried, holding him close when Tom had helped him down from the hired rig.

'There, there.' His voice seemed lost in his chest. 'I'm fine, fine.'

'You're alive!'

'Just about,' said Tom. 'Oh, I'm Tom Floyd, served with the major.'

'Sorry, Rose. Yes, Tom's been nursing me on the way west.'

'But George, you're wounded, are you—?'

'Malaria, lady,' said Tom, grinning. 'The major sure missed you.' Though George was not given to confiding much beyond the barest outlines, Tom knew something of the situation from George's fever deliriums.

This first reunion was one of tears and George's assurances that he was alive and well. Finally they grew calm. Tom went off to stable the horse and get something to eat in the kitchen. George saw his daughter of a few months, sucking her thumb, staring up at him, not at all upset by this pale, thin stranger looking down at her.

'She's so *small*.'

'George, they all come small at first. Maude is just right in weight and size, making fine progress.' Rose opened her chiffon gown and exposed a plump firm breast. 'I'm a splendid provider.' She picked up the baby, held its head against the breast. 'Feeding time. Maude is a little glutton. Like her father when he—'

'I once did so many things.'

The baby fed with a liquid sucking sound, and George sat down and shook his head. 'Never thought for months any of this was real, was here.'

Rose wiped a drop of milk from the side of the child's mouth. 'The war is over for you.'

'It is for Tom, too. He limps. I'm taking him into the bank. It's not just I wouldn't be here if he hadn't taken notice of my condition, the damn malaria, and seen me through the hellholes of hospitals. Tom never had much of a chance to be anything where he came from but a hard-scrabble failed farmer ... and ...' He suddenly gripped one of Rose's arms. 'Now we can't be separated. You're coming north.'

Rose gently caressed the feeding child. The baby stopped feeding, withdrew its mouth, and was staring at its father.

'You're frightening your daughter.'

That night the two lay together. He was still too weak to make love, just grateful for her encircling arms, knowing this was real, was solid. He awoke when she left the bed twice in the night to feed the baby—Maude, daughter of the woman he loved above all things in the world.... Some small clouds did fog his pleasure—his deep affection for Fred and Charles, his sons; respect for his wife, Maria; and *what* had happened to the bank? He had planned to be away only six months, and now how long had he been gone? His head ached when he tried to figure it, and before morning he had a residual malaria attack, shivering under blankets, teeth chattering. Rose and Tom attended him, rubbing him with spirits and wine, heated bricks wrapped in blankets. Rose feared his dying ('Two things, Lord, I require. Love's name and flame to wrap my soul in fire,' she

wrote in one of the few poems she showed to George.)
Damn all poets!

It was George's recurring attacks every two or three days
that convinced Rose she would have to make a move to San
Francisco. In her eyes, he was clearly dying. She told Tom,
'He's a ghost. Another attack and he will be gone.'

'Well, Mrs Rodman, he's not as puny as all that. He's
buckskin-and-gristle-hard. He came through the hospitals
and the real bad fevers. I mean, these chills, just nothing.'

'He's lost so much weight, walks without that bold, sure
stride, that vigor he had.'

She told George that afternoon that she could lease the
ranch and the orchards to Nat Fowler, a vice-president of
the Hellman Bank, who had been after her for some time to
make a deal. With the baby, she hadn't the time to
supervise the hired hands. Besides, it was financially
beneficial for her to do so, given the loans she had been
forced to take out from the bank.

'You'll never regret it, Rose.' George lay back on a deck
chair and let the sun bathe his drawn, pale face. There had
been early fog but it had burned off by noon and the sun felt
like an essential gift, he had such a need for it. He felt an
extraordinary consciousness of how precious life could be
and how the endeavor to endure was seeping back into him.

'The bank has this house at San Rafael, north of the city.
We foreclosed on some oyster pirate. You'll be so near, and
I want to watch Maude grow.'

'Stay here another two weeks, a month; you need time to
recover fully. Don't go back and rush into things just yet.
No, dear, I'm not jealous or delaying you. It's just....'

He reached for her hand, held it, his eyes
closed. 'Everything depends on me going back now, right
away. Happiness may not be bought by money, but it often
jumps out the window if you haven't got any.'

Rose knew she could not bend his will; he'd give just so
far. Finally her fear that he might have a serious relapse
spurred her decision to turn over the Rodman Rancho to
Nat Fowler. Packing wasn't a problem. Getting a berth on a

ship sailing north was a bit of trouble with war cargoes, officers, and men getting the space priorities; but George sent a telegram to one of General Sherman's staff officers who recalled what a good provider Major Fiore had been. The army provided military passage for George, Mrs Rodman and baby daughter, Tom Floyd, and a servant, Lupe.

The child stood the sea trip well. Tom took care of the settling in at Bay Cottage on Petaluma Ridge. On the big perfumed oak bed in the bedroom there, still smelling of fresh paint, George made love to Rose for the first time since his return. Sweet physical love to his Rose of Sharon. It was tender, it was passionate, it was not violent; but he promised her it soon would be as strong and savage as it had been before. She said if he had a fever attack because of his ardor, she would nail up the doors and windows and never let him in. And he answered with something he had read, "'Men have died, but not for love.'"

'I don't want a dead man in bed with me.'

'Never felt more alive.'

She wiped his damp brow with a corner of the sheet, kissed his shoulder and too-prominent collarbone. 'I want you to take cod-liver oil.'

'Goddammit, Rosie, that's no thing to bring up now at my romantic moment.'

'I'm practical. I'm giving Maude a little bit of it each day, and you'll have your two spoonfuls, at least when you're here.'

He thought, amused: Oh, fine, I have a demanding wife at home and a bossy one here.

His homecoming to his 'proper' family had been strange. What emotions he recalled of his life before Rose were fuzzy. He recalled an old adage he thought appropriate: 'The same water does not pass by twice.' Maria had changed under the spell of Irena's whist parties; there was now, to his surprise, a tendency to frivolity, for all her pious beliefs and handling the beads of her rosary. The house was in order, his sons, Fred and Charles, were neatly dressed, full of spirit, and able to read simple texts and mark up the house with crayons. Rocco had blossomed into worldly sagacity—and better tailoring. He wore his hair well-oiled, attended to a mustache with twisted ends. His dark, large eyes seemed to suggest a Rabelaisian temperament. But he had run the bank well. He gave up the use of George's desk, sat in jovial pleasure facing the returned founder and president.

'You can't kill a dago, eh, George?'

'Everyone is easy to kill, Rocco. A little hurt here and there, a cannonball taking away your head, the swamp fever, the malaria, the yellow jack ... we are fragile stuff, Rocco.'

'You're back, that's important. We are up to our ass in a big wool market. Irena has held off giving loans against wool in storage, even if she has big, big flocks of baa-baas and is clipping them down to the hide.'

'She isn't one to lose her head.'

'She's not greedy; she just wants *everything*.'

'Not only that, she goes out to the racetrack—even Maria bet on a horse. Maria! Who would have thought?'

'The priests still come to feed their faces?'

'Some. Father O'Hara is dead, I hear.'

'A jolly good death—a bit of the juice of the grape, while preaching of Pascal's *Pensées*, which no one seemed to know about, he fell tail-over-teakettle across the altar, the wine chalice, and wafers. Marvelous way to go, made a great impression.'

'Fast, anyway. This Tom Floyd I've turned over to you. He's got a sense of loyalty and a good mind.'

'Raw and ignorant.'

George said simply, 'Like young Rocco Bordone, a filthy, hungry street kid. Lice in his hair, barefoot, ignorant as whale shit. No one saw any good in him, not worth feeding or buying shoes for. Have you any memory of *him*, of what became of Rocco Bordone?'

Rocco made a mock gesture of covering his eyes for shame. 'All right, I'm talking like a real bastard. I'll see to

183

Floyd. If he can add two figures together, I'll start him assisting a teller. *Scusi*.'

'*Grazie*.' George smiled (he was smiling more now). 'I'm going to open a branch bank in Los Angeles. Lots of doings, big doings there. Two banks already there, big successful ones. I want to crowd in, make it three. You're going to manage it after it's set up.'

'A title?' Rocco asked (as usual, he felt only God fully fathomed George Fiore).

'Vice-president of the Pacific-Harvesters Bank of Los Angeles. No, leave off "Los Angeles", just one of our banks.'

'The Pacific-Harvesters Bank.'

'Yes, neat. Say "thank-you."'

Rocco took up a bowler hat, rubbed the palm of a hand arounds its bowl. 'Thank you, Mr President. You're feeling better when you talk of another bank. You *are* happy, Grego?' Rocco rarely used the old name of Grego, only when emotionally affected or when he was being sly.

'Do I look it?'

Rocco looked into the hat as if seeking something. 'I know how things are.'

George said nothing. He picked up an unfilled pipe, put it in his mouth; smoking, lighting a pipe, still gave him a shortage of breath.

Rocco, watching his reaction, made the Italian gesture with thumb and forefinger of *ha-ha, we know* ... 'Vice-president!' he added, and went out chuckling to himself.

George sucked on the empty pipe. Rocco could be discreet. Right now, George had his mind on early loans that the bank had made on wool in storage. He looked over the records and found Irena had kept such loans small and of short term. The unbridled spirit of wartime gambling, wartime prosperity, had made too many people reckless.

William Ralston of the Bank of California told him, 'Speculators, boomers, confidence men, shady lawyers; are there any other kind, George? Activate the whorehouses, the saloons, the racetrack, more new money. Yacht racing

184

in the bay, even some of the Nob Hill folk importing French chefs, who often turn out to be Dutch or Italian, even Poles.'

George met Matthew Gower, the old lawyer, at the Palace Hotel. He seemed a bit more stooped, more wrinkles on his leathery cheeks, but the eyes under hairy, caterpillarlike eyebrows were as alert and cynical as ever.

'Wool eh?... I'll have a good four fingers of Killmarnock Scotch, they stock it for me. I'm not a rye or bourbon drinker.'

'I hope this new buying spree is not like the silkworm-egg madness.'

'No, it's wool. You can feel it, smell it, make cloth, dye it, cut it. It's a useful commodity, but as with everything, greedy men see ways to exploit it for unholy profits.'

'Come on, Matt, we all like profits. What's the true situation here and in Los Angeles?'

The old man sipped his Scotch, smacked his thin lips.

'Would you believe that only about 650 thousand pounds a year were collected? Now there is probably three million pounds a year combined, piled up here and down in Los Angeles.'

George whistled. 'That much?'

'The New England mills need wool. Speculators rush in to make a good thing of rising prices, and dealers offer twenty cents a pound. Merchants and middlemen do not wait for any shearing season to denude the sheep, but begin to buy up wool futures with the fleece still on the damn animals' backs. Wool is warehoused by dealers who wait for the eastern millionaires to come begging for bales of wool at any price. "Supply and demand" is what the speculators gathered at the Palace Hotel bar call it, as they enjoy their Pico punch. "Extortion," the millowners yell as the textile-factory wheels and looms slow down. Harassment, offers and rejections. I'll have another Scotch ... all this dry business talk makes me thirsty.'

'New wool, it keeps growing on the backs of millions of animals.'

'Even the farmers, the flock owners, have joined the speculators, George. Anything resembling wool sells. Short staple stuff from Southern California, full of dust and burs, is selling off the Golden Gate at forty-five cents a pound. Speculators in Los Angeles offer as high as forty-nine cents a pound, as the grazers hold back their shearings at even that price. The sky's the limit in wool prices.'

'But, Matt, I keep seeing enormous flocks of unclipped sheep, eating and alive.'

'There is no real shortage. The growers see money, not wool fleece.'

'I'm a banker and I see my profits elsewhere. You have my text on opening branch banks. Draw up papers for my bank in Los Angeles—it's time to make it legal. The Railroad Act of Congress in sixty-two is setting up twenty-five million in funds and five million acres in public land to build a transcontinental railroad—which means, after war delays, it will reach Los Angeles as soon as the Huntington gang figures out a way to steal most of the funds. The whole West will be tied to the East in shipping and bringing people across the country. I want them to have places to bank.'

'It's a grand swindle, George, that railroad act. Huntington and his friends will suck the US Treasury dry!'

'But we'll have a railroad south.'

At the Casa, George found improvements—two more windmills to supply ground water not only to the barnyard but to the house. Irena had grown wider, her graying hair hidden by a touch of chemical coloring. She was never without her diamond earrings. But she could, she swore, still get on a large horse and go galloping off to curse out some overseer, her foreman son Ramon following behind on a pony.

Tomas was in Spain.

'In his indiscreet maturity, that's Tomas,' Irena explained to her brother as they ate ices under her favorite wisteria arbor. 'The Velasquezes lost a lot of land holdings south of here because a lot of the necessary papers were missing that would have proved their claim. Well, Tomas is in Madrid, at the archives, looking for the originals of the royal grants. I only want what is mine. I mean, what is ours.' She laughed. 'I like living "high off the hog," as we Americans say. Ramon is going to have Casa Cuesta as it once was, a great rancho.'

'You have enough land, Irena, and thousands of sheep. What is this damn wool market?'

'Mad, mad, mad. I'm selling wool off sheep that aren't even lambs yet. Futures.'

'That's wise?'

'You think not, George?'

'Sell all you can. The war is going to end soon. Lincoln has found a general in Grant, and Grant has ordered Sherman to march south through the belly of the interior, tear the confederacy to bits, without mercy, a burning wreck and ruin. Grant is moving toward Richmond, and Lee's armies can't be fed or supplied. So once the war ends, markets will collapse in leather, wool, steel—all items special to the needs of war.'

A few saw it as clearly as George Fiore. The mills and eastern buyers moved warily, not rushing in to buy at the inflated California prices. They had a shrewd sense of self-preservation.

George visited Rose and Maude at least twice a week, but also managed to get up to the Casa as often. He was closer to his sister than his wife, who puzzled him.

'What have you done to Maria?'

Irena laughed, spooned up pink ices. 'Brought her alive. I'm buying some racehorses. I've taught her to handicap. Well, nearly. Do you mind if she joins me in owning a racing stable? It's up to you.'

'Yes, I mind, Irena. A banker can't keep horses for betting. But if you have a sure winner, someday, put down five dollars for me.'

'Win, place or show?'

'How the hell would I know? Does Maria seem all right to you?'

'She is a wife—and all wives' husbands are bastards.'

187

There was something deeper and more solid in Maria, some quality he had never before suspected. To her, he saw, being his wife was the paramount duty in her life. The Church had proclaimed it, and she accepted it. Even if a man was weak, woman was there to wait, to raise the children. Not meekly, but with a kind of pride that she was the strong and steady one, the faithful one. Maria cherished her role.

George had grown to respect her for accepting him as he was—whatever private doubts and fears she might have harbored. He dreaded the day when some suspicion or hurt would cause her to rebel or to confront him in anger. But she never said a word. Only occasionally did he catch a look of sorrow on her face; then he would feel that, as his sister had said, there are times when all men are bastards.

Maria seemed pleased to have him back. They did not sleep together; there was no physical relationship and he was relieved at that—until one night three months after his return, when he was torn out of sleep by Maria flinging herself on him, muttering endearing terms, even indecent ones. She was demonstrative, determined somehow. He, half-asleep, let her roll on him and pull him over her, and they were copulating. He didn't think of it as making love. No, no, not love as he knew it, as they both climaxed like sealed fountains come suddenly to overflowing. In the morning nothing was said, and she did not come to his bed for another two months.

It was an ordeal, a task for his body. In some foolish way he felt disloyal to Rose when Maria demanded this version of marital fidelity.

The wool market came to its own climax. Tom Floyd came running into the bank one noon and up the stairs to George's office. He was flushed and was waving his arms. 'Major! Just been down by the Embarcadero.'

'Taking a walk, Tom?'

'Ships sighted in the Golden Gate from Australia.'

'Australia?'

'Word is they are loaded down with wool.'

188

'Well, that busts the balloon,' George said.

The dealers had overlooked the Australian wool potential. And then suddenly it was there, ships with large consignments of Aussie wool piling up on the San Francisco docks, to be bought up quickly by the mills, and good riddance to all those greedy bastards stuck with huge holdings in California wool.

Wires went out to middlemen—'BUY NO MORE CALIFORNIA WOOL AT ANY PRICE.' By the end of April there was no market at all for the wool in warehouses (or still on the sheep), much of it costing fifty cents a pound. Half a million dollars had been laid out to pay for the spring shearings. Depression, then panic, came to wholesalers and wool growers.

George took some small losses on loans. The Australians continued to unload their wool at the fair prices the mills were willing to pay.

Rocco came into the bank late in the afternoon, newspapers in the pockets of his jacket, his bowler hat shoved back on his head. 'It's ruin for lots of greedy people. Ah *Dio aiutami!* Senator Kendrick is very hard hit, maybe two million pounds earmarked for his syndicate in warehouses. Bill Ralston got rid of his last week. Said you advised him to. The whole caboodle of silver kings took a beating, but can weather it. Two suicides, I hear, and Eddie Hayes has made a rush to Mexico.'

'That's the end of that,' said George. 'I never have figured out the whims and fancies of getting rich quick.'

Rocco straddled a chair, put his arms on top of its back. 'Irena, she is making offers of nine cents a pound for anything in the wool warehouses.'

George laughed. 'I'll be goddamned. Matt Gower was right. Unlike worm eggs, wool *is* needed; it makes a worthwhile investment, priced right. Rocco, we'll open banks in Sacramento, San Diego. I've noticed something, reading the eastern papers. The war has turned us from a nation of farmers into a country of manufacturing.'

This discovery and its evaluation shaped the turning

point of the career of George Fiore. He did not at first fully value what he had disovered, but it motivated his attitudes, his expansion from then on. He subscribed to eastern newspapers and magazines. Even to English, French, and German journals. He saw railroads spread out as the need for lamp oil expanded, as did need for steam-engine fuel. Certain men's names were being mentioned. J.P. Morgan (who had once sold condemned rifles to the Union armies) was starting to consolidate the rail systems. J.D. Rockefeller was seizing control of the vast oil-refining industries which kept the lamps of America and China alight. Carnegie, Gould, Fiske, Singer, Fields, Vanderbilt, Belmont, Astor (Yankees, Dutchmen, Jews) were known as 'Empire Builders' at the Bankers Club of San Francisco.

Twice, William Ralston had put George's name up for membership, and twice he had been blackballed; as one member put it, 'There's also another Italian banker. Let in one and we'll soon have two!'

'Never mind,' Rose said to George at breakfast on Maude's first birthday. 'We have our own little world right here.' Lupe brought in the whipped-cream cake and two burning candles (one for the birthday and one to grow on). Maude, a blue ribbon gathering her red-gold curls, plunged a hand into the cake and smeared her face as she gobbled.

When the baby's face and hands were washed and she was put away for a nap, George smoked his pipe on the terrace under potted oleanders. In the sunlight the shiny bay waters seemed paved with silver dollars. He drove *that* image away, not wanting anything to do with money today.

'I wish I could bottle what I feel when I'm here with you and Maude. I could uncork it in the bank when I needed a whiff of what's here.'

Rose said, 'Well, I'm rather proud, even a little haughty, at our stability. I'm breeding—*don't* look so frightened, mister—five hundred more chicks.'

Rose and Lupe had become raisers of special poultry—game birds, Cornish hens, ring-necked pheasants for the hotel trade.

George had at first been amused by this endeavor, but was soon aware that Rose needed to have a craft, something to keep her active. She rode, she had a small eighteen-foot sailboat, she read a great deal and he suspected wrote a great deal of poetry ('Sometimes the sunsets are of mustard and suicides' blood'). But she never showed any of it beyond a line or two. There was an overwhelming exuberance in her when he arrived, and another mood when he left late at night or the next morning. A gentle whisper, a last embrace, a wistful holding back of departure. He didn't like to call it a sadness. ('Lonely as a bell in its tower.') He wondered if after one of his visits Rose would sink into introspection, then spring up to attend her damn fancy poultry. He thought of elaborate strategies to mend the situation, to have *both* worlds, and would curse himself as indulging in fantasy.

4

Con Brio

18

Growing up was for the cousins a time of rapid evolution around San Francisco Bay, although they were not aware of it. They were adventurous youngsters who loved above all sailing on the bay, even in dangerous weather. Charles was the best sailor, Ramon the most fearful, and Fred didn't give a damn. Sailing wasn't the only activity that enticed them, of course. At fifteen, they knew all about the young Chinese whores standing there in open doorways offering their bodies provocatively, using their few words of English.

'Lookee, two bits.'

'How about all three of us lookee, two bits?' asked Fred. The girl was thin, almond-eyed, in a blue cotton gown slit at the side. She worked for Quong Lao Gaw, the boss of Chinatown, who ruled her life absolutely, as he did hundreds of other Chinese girls.

'Touchee, four bits. *Hi yung chi.*'

Their allure was so powerful to San Francisco men because, as Frank the coachman explained, 'Why, lads, they don't have ordinary cunts like white girls. No siree, theirs goes east to west, know what I mean? Not north to south like white nooky, no siree.'

However, the three cousins never investigated the offers of the Chinese crib girls, even after the final enticement: 'Dooee, one dollah.' They never discovered that the mysterious *Ni sihwan che ma?* merely translated as 'You

194

care for tea?'

Theirs were the shenanigans of the young: riding forbidden horses; putting a frog into the bed of Conchita Concepcion, Maria's maid; playing marbles (Fred had an enlarged thumb); and, on a day of rare excitement, sneaking into the morgue to see the bandit bank robber Kit Bluster, shot that afternoon by two Pinkerton men at London Jim's Saloon. Beneath a flickering gas flare near a back window, the boys stared in morbid admiration and awe at the naked body laid out on the mortuary slab.

'Look at the bullet holes!' said Charles.

'Dirty bastards, the Pinkerton men,' said Fred. 'Shot him in the back.'

'The cowards!' added Ramon, who was sketching with precision the features of the corpse. Ramon was hoping to join his father, Tomas, in Europe and study art in Paris. But Irena called it self-indulgence and had so far refused. 'It's bad enough I can't get your damn father to come back. You *stay.*'

The boys went obediently to dancing school once a week, water-wet hair combed down tightly, parted in the center, wearing patent-leather pumps. They trotted around on the waxed floor with covert hostility, dancing with girls in white stockings and white gloves, girls smelling of patchouli, girls who looked or tried to look complacent, bored with having to dance with 'just kids.' They were already, Irena insisted, forming interest in older men. As one girl told Fred, older men were 'so manly, smelling of cigars and whiskey.' Fred tried one of Rocco's cigars.

Two years ago, George had taken Fred and Charles out to Promontory Point in Utah to see the historic meeting of East and West, as the East Central Pacific joined the rail line of the Union Pacific in May 1869. George was in the party with the builders, bankers, politicians. Senator Kendrick, his son Judge Homer Kendrick— who had brought along his bride, Nellie Winthrop, one of the Boston Winthrops, niece to a former magisterially dull president. As George told Rocco as they descended from the East-facing train at Promontory point, 'The Kendricks have clearly outgrown Mormonism. I think the senator has his eye on the White House.'

'Well, he's fronted for the railroad bills—hand in glove with Huntington and his gang.'

Fred liked to listen to adult talk. It was no secret that the construction of the Union Pacific had been wrapped in perjury, fraudulent surveys, and creative bookkeeping. There were fascinating rumors of collusion with politicians and officials, to which were added land steals of millions of acres of public lands. Charles preferred to mingle with the roughneck work crews. Fred and Charles whooped and yelled among rail layers, gandy dancers, and engine drivers, drinking from bottles. Honored guests in frock coats and top hats shook hands and sipped sparkling wine. Everyone froze for a few seconds as a camera on legs recorded the event for future generations. The two steam engines moved slowly toward each other, almost nose-touching on twin rails uniting a nation. As William Ralston said in his speech: 'This close hug of East and West will never be parted. We tie forever the Atlantic to the Pacific! Two great bodies of water—a great nation in between.'

A polished walnut tie had been put in place, a hole drilled for the driving of the last spike, a gold one.

'Solid gold?' asked Fred.

'Maybe,' said Rocco. 'Could be just gilt.'

A dignitary lifted the heavy spike hammer but had difficulty striking the gold spike more than a glancing blow, and a brawny foreman had to finish the job as people cheered, photographs were taken, and a drunk fell off the cowcatcher of the eastern engine. There was later a rumor that the gold spike was missing the next day, but George told his sons, 'You can't drive a solid gold spike into hard wood. Gold is too soft. It must have been an iron spike covered with gilt.'

Charles was disappointed. 'Aw, shit.'

George did bring his eight year-old daughter a gift from

Utah, a bead-worked soft-tanned deerskin belt, set with silver disks and bits of blue stone. 'A gift from Uncle George.'

Maude had developed into a beautiful child, small and delicate. The cod-liver oil didn't seem to fill her out. She was so thin, George called her his furled umbrella. Her long red-gold hair, with uninhibited curls worn loose like 'Alice in Wonderland,' was angelically becoming. She would solemnly play exercises on the rosewood piano in the parlor, calling it 'kiss-kiss music,' and everyone had to press lips to one of her pink cheeks.

The impact of the railroad was immediate: Rose and Lupe were now packing dozens of their Cornish and other game hens in ice and shipping them east to Kansas City on the new railroad. Rose still got intimate comfort from George; but there was a private inner life she guarded, a precious solitude, like her writing that she kept for herself alone. The *ménage* had settled down almost casually to regular visits, making love, and gift-bringing. Their relationship was no longer heady with expectations; it had become one of serenity. They were in love, they faced the future (whatever it would be) with forbearance. Rose wrote her poems, but not as many and not with the ecstatic drive she had at first felt in coming to the cottage on the bay ('Love and all beauty has a strangeness in it'). She worked off her moods with her poultry trade, finding satisfaction in watching her business expand.

George had never fully recovered from his wartime illness. Attacks of malaria, chills, and fever would recur once or twice a year. He was thinner, had little taste for Rose's special food. He did swallow cod-liver oil when Rose insisted, or Lupe's noxious herbs in a brew. He rode less than he had; an open carriage with Frank the coachman became his regular mode of travel. He did go twice a week to the Neptune Swimming Club and Baths and had his body rubbed and slapped by Abdullah, the Turk. He enjoyed the steam room but didn't often swim in the frigid bay, as some did.

He was building a house on Nob Hill. It was the social thing to do to give confidence in one's business. It gave a family a bowing acquaintance with the Huntingtons, Crockers, Stanfords, and Hopkinses; the doers and shakers of the money tree. The house would be too big, with a pillared front, a ballroom, billiard room, and a den with sturdy furnishings, a stone statue of St Januarius in the garden, and a bathtub cut from a solid block of marble. The carriage house and stables held stalls for four horses.

Maria had over the years managed to be pious *and* a gambling woman. She was prepared, as she told Irena, for the last sacrament and expected to be forgiven for giving time to a good parlay on a horse race. She touched up her complexion and was increasingly prone to attacks of asthma in the night, which sometimes nearly suffocated her. She would gasp for air and frantically ring her little silver bell. Conchita Concepcion would come running with a mixture of boiling water and the oil of blue-gum trees, eucalyptus leaves. Maria would gratefully inhale the scented steam and slowly revive, lying back and feeling her heart pumping. Father Zorilla was summoned for the first few attacks, bringing ash and oil and all the materials for the last rites. But it was soon apparent that to avoid attacks Maria had just to avoid getting upset, angry, or shouting too loudly at the racetrack.

She no longer came to George's bed. As Irena told her when the gossip spread about the cottage on the bay and the young widow and her child, 'There are no secrets in any community. So they talk of Grego and this woman, so there *is* a brat, his or not.'

'He is a sinner, Irena, his soul is in danger. Marriage is ordained by heaven.'

'When a man has to decide between his soul and his prick, it's not even a close race. Tomas at least has a true belief in a soul. I expect him back for sure next month.'

Maria knew better. Tomas had escaped Irena, leaving her the duties of the Casa, the management of the Velasquez holdings. He was a well-known figure at Monte

Carlo, in the more permissive salons and brothels of Paris, with British sporting lords attending bullfights in Madrid. Claiming a fear of seasickness, he delayed and delayed the recrossing of the Atlantic. He wrote mischievously evasive letters—'Jules Verne is working on a great gun to fire me across the sea.' Irena paid his debts, his hotel bills at the Ritz, the Carlton, the Hassler, the Danieli. She gave him an allowance that he sometimes doubled at the casinos, but more often lost on the first day, living frugally until the next remittance. Tomas in the early 1870's sent Ramon sketches by Daumier, prints by Redon and Monet, and ukiyoe pictures by oddly named artists like Kitagawa Utamaro. His father admired the sketches Ramon sent him and wrote back: 'Yes, dear boy, Paris is the only place to study art. Had lunch with Degas, a feisty mean wit, ate at Des Lilas on the Boulevard Montparnasse. We ate: *escargots* and *langouste aux herbes*, the artist's favorites. Showed him your stuff; he said *Bon*. Insisted drawing was everything. Draw, draw, draw, my dear son. Père T.'

From his mother, Ramon had learned to play whist and discovered he had a keen skill with cards. From the Fiore coachman Frank (who claimed to have been a professional riverboat gambler) Ramon and his cousins learned to play poker. Fred and Charles lost their allowances, but Ramon grew skilled at the nuances of five-card stud, even second-dealing. He put his winnings away under a layer of loose brick by the old smokehouse. He pawned his double-lidded gold watch with its half-yard of gold chain and a Sutter's Mill two-ounce gold nugget (a gift from Uncle George when he was sixteen). A ferryboat captain bought his English-made double-barreled silver-mounted twelve-gauge shotgun that Tomas had left behind for him to inherit and a pair of ruby cufflinks. One spring day he decided he had enough to put his long-dreamed-of plan into action.

He was two weeks over seventeen when he boarded the east-bound noon train out of Oakland station and headed for Paris, carrying a small suitcase. There were various stops along the way, but he avoided New York and Boston;

As for the Fiore
seventeen. Fred w
Indiana, a strict,
General Sherman.
dragged a ten-pound
ferry station and firing
July celebration. The w
eggs and spoiled tomato
dignitaries, who were gat
making their long, self-c
was injured, just stained; bu
flask in the back pocket
shattered.

Rocco was in Los Angeles,
soon to open. George was not i
went off to Indiana, George
beginning to be called Chuck, in h
'I'm not going to stand any you
line. Lord knows I'm tolerant, but y
going to see what discipline is, and K
with his footloose father no bed of ros
knew what Rocco and I had to ... But n
'Ramon wrote of his study, drawing fr
'Naked, I'm sure. Now, Charlie, you
about, stay on call. I've about reached a g
with the Chinese *hong* leaders of Chinatown
know, means merchant company.'
'And *tongs* are the *bou how doy* hatchet me,
aren't they?' asked Charles.
'Yes—make sure you don't mix them up! Now,
hong leaders ... I've gotten some of the Chinese
advised them on land buying, import documents.
set with Quong Lao Gaw. He runs Chinatown and is
the white ward heelers, the political bosses.'

Irena would s
had left a simp

Dear Mama,
    I am now an
and, if you can,
shall miss you an
and Aunt Maria. I
may come to nothin
inside of me, wanting
    Mañana será otro d

He headed for Canada across
as good a poker player on a lak
money was stolen while he s
Halifax, and he had a choice
money to return to San Francisc
as a stablehand on a cattle boat, to
urine below deck for the two-week
It was miserable work in the reeking
crew were rough misfits, degenerate
roaches from his stew.
    At night after his stomach settled he
rail, the stink of cattle fainter; he grat
briny air, watching the moon play coy
clouds. His hands were raw from handl
wheelbarrows. He had no change of cloth
shirts. He slept in the foul atmosphere o
seasoned by farts, tar, damp unchanged b
powder and cheap tobacco. Ramon lay with a
under the mattress to repel the amorous Greek
    At the French port of La Rochelle he helped u
now desperate, sore animals. The first mate disa
and the unpaid sailors found him at the Christina C
paid them half what was due them and promised the
two days. Ramon didn't wait; he rode with the cattle

'Does he have opium dens?'
'None of our business. Now, no chink
no jokes about pigtails, and no "no tickee, no s
There is a thousand times more money for banking
investing among them than the other banks can imagine. So
pay attention when we're there.'
    Charles didn't feel it worthwhile telling George that he
already had a friendly acquaintance with Chinatown in his
own right; that he, Fred, and Ramon had been down to 'the
cowyards' to look over some of the region's sexual wares.
Although they had never actually gone inside, Charles
dreamed of evanescent Chinese singsong girls in silk pants
gently hinting at delightful aberrations, revealing their
charms through a swirling haze of opium smoke, which he
imagined smelled like dragons' sweat and the leather
binding of Aunt Irena's copy of Balzac's *Droll Stories*.

19

The morning mist still held the bay captive. From the
Golden Gate came the hoarse hoot of foghorns as ships
groped their way toward the city's wharves. Over Oakland
and Berkeley the sun was breaking through. Quong Lao
Gaw knew it would clear by noon. He gazed out his third-
story bay window overlooking weathered shapes of
Chinatown and thought of white bankers and George
Fiore.
    The Gaw Building was deceptive if one judged it from its
precarious outer appearance. Four stories, weathered and
faded, its style suggested oriental forms in the shapes of its
windows and a red tin pagoda on its roof, now home to

pigeons that laid down a chalky patina of their droppings on the tin cornices. The Pacific-Harvesters Bank was offering a forty-thousand-dollar mortgage on it at eight percent. On the ground floor was the Golden Dragon, its gilt-and-yellow sign proclaiming:

TRUE MANDARIN COOKING
The Best Peking Cuisine in Town

Which amused Quong Lao Gaw; it was low Cantonese, featured chop suey and chow mein, neither dish resembling the fine oriental cuisine the Chinese themselves ate. Next to the restaurant, he rented space to a barber shop. There was also a store of small windows full of 'antiques' and other tourist trash; beef bone (sold as ivory), next to paper fans, bundles of joss sticks, some copies of T'ang horses, and glazed pots with plum-blossom designs. On the window glass was lettered:

RARE MIDDLE KINGDOM ORIENTAL ART OBJECTS
Ivory, Jade, Porcelain—Quong Lao Gaw, Prop.

The second floor of the Gaw Building was the meeting room of the Hi Ling Hong, the merchant group, but it was also often used by the Kwong Sing Tong, a protective organization suspected by the police of many criminal activities. It was said to be controlled by the Hi Ling Hong, headed by the honorable Quong Lao Gaw. The third floor was the private residence of Gaw himself—furnished like a wing of the forbidden Palace in Peking, which he had an obsessive desire to copy. The decor was of silk wall hangings, screens, and low rosewood furniture. Because Gaw had begun life as a peasant in Kwangsi, he valued his exquisite furnishings not as art objects lovingly created by fine craftsmen, but rather he worshipped the very silks, the rare woods and gems of which they were constructed, as a representation of his wealth and power.

The fourth floor was used as a warehouse. The Hi Ling

Hong mainly dealt in dried foods, cloth, rice, abominable-smelling bottled sauces, and various ceramics and china painted with traditional willow tree and dragon designs imported from Foochow and Amoy. White visitors to Chinatown believed there were dark cellars beneath the buildings which harbored those who had committed loathsome crimes and practiced secret vices. Actually, Gaw paid off politicians and the police to run basements where opium was smoked, fan-tan and other gambling games were played, and white slavery was hinted at.

'This is all nonsense,' Gaw told George Fiore. 'Many white females live yes in Chinatown. Happy so.'

Police protection and payoffs permitted open gambling not only in Gaw's basement, but also in various halls of the *tongs* and *hongs*. Even George recognized the sweet scent of *gow* cooking in orangewood pipes emanating from the private quarters of prosperous merchants as well as in the backs of laundries.

There were, of course, Chinese slave girls, smuggled past bribed customs officers or brought down from Canada. Only the occasional reform group made any noise about the active trade in Chinese virgins.

George was making progress as a banker for the Chinese. He liked to have tea with Gaw, talk stocks, bonds and investments. He also enjoyed the company of Moon Orchid, Gaw's concubine. Gaw honored George by asking the girl, dressed in her finest white silks, to join them. White men, Gaw suspected, were animals about their sexual pleasures, displaying their lust in public; not like the Chinese, who did what one did in intimate detail in private, but whose dignity precluded revealing that side of human nature in public.

'So,' George said at his second bowl of tea, 'I would say railroad bonds could be your best investment for surplus funds.'

'You like, um?'

'It's a big thing, rail transportation, covering the nation with a network for shipping. I don't say it's not exploited by speculators, but for all the shenanigans, it's solid investing.'

The bland face of the Chinese broke into a small smile. 'This shenanigans, what that?'

George held up his bowl for more tea. 'What is called doing business by smoothing the way. Like Huntington, the rest, they give a little of a good thing *here*, a scattering of money *there*, like—'

'Like the *cumshaw* I give to police, city hall?'

'In a way. You know I can only advise, of course. There is risk in everything, but less in blue chips.'

'Ah, so, like playing pokah. Blue ships best.'

'I want the Pacific Harvesters to be the trusted bank of Chinatown. I have a son, Charles, young yet. I want to introduce him to you. To the other *hong* members.

'Ah, son good thing, son.' A very sad expression. 'I have no sons. Yes, I like you, Mistah Fiohe. I make a banquet, big doings for you, you son to meet the big people here.'

They parted on a handshake and the old man envied George his sons.

He had buried two wives, been unlucky in the death of very young children 'not destined to make old bones.' He had no direct heirs except for his nephew Kim Tai, his able assistant. In Gaw's time he had smuggled in many virgins from Canton, Shanghai, Hong Kong. Beautiful, slim, and wonderful girls of golden skin, and well-trained in their sensual skills for maximum sexual receptivity. But that meant little now—how sad—but for some futile caressing, someone to warm chilled old limbs or to hold close to inhale the pervasive scent of young-girl flesh before the opium took hold for the deep misty dreams. Gaw had smoked for fifty years. A moderate amount daily was good for him, he felt. And like the thousands of jars of rice wine, the hundreds of girls he had had pleasure in, he had not in his prime felt any strain. But of late, all his pleasures were tinged with loss.

Quong Lao Gaw sighed; the tea had tasted bitter. There was a tap on the teak door; it slid aside as Kim Tai, his nephew, entered: a fashion plate in a double-breasted jacket with padded Princeton football shoulders, pegged trousers like those worn by the touring actors at the Lucky Baldwin Theater and needle-pointed patent-leather shoes. His cheerful sleek face displayed even white teeth. Gaw saw his heir—and sighed again. Kim Tai was followed by the beautiful Moon Orchid, her hair done up in T'ang-style coils, her exquisite oval face—dazzling perfection, to his jaded eyes—a delicate tint of pale tan and pink. Her large eyes were outlined in black, and mutton-jade earrings hung from dainty ears. Her body at sixteen was not fully mature, but the old man looked at it with pleasure. So well-designed, graceful, the neatness of her long limbs showing under thin pale blue robe—yes, legs so long and graceful. Breasts just so—and the jutting of splendid buttocks. Moon Orchid was his last concubine, and gossip among the bawdy gamblers at *fan-tan* said that he no longer had the firmness to deflower her. She had been costly, bought to warm the lonely years of his old age. For Gaw, just to see her, to know she was not far away, sleeping, bathing, joking with her maid, Flower Seed, reading poetry, or practicing her music, brought some meaning to his life.

'Was it a good meeting, uncle?'

'It was. I want a fine feast for him.'

Kim Tai took a cigarette from a gold case but did not light it. He had learned many of the nasty white-devil habits, smoking foul tobacco when he could have opium. Kim had been to college at Oakland for two years, developed a wry disposition there, and had no trouble with his R's and L's.

'I will arrange everything, honorable uncle.'

The girl stood slender, silent; only her alert, searching eyes hinted at her true nature. Her interest in the white world was known to Kim. Kim had been born in Fresno—his father an herb doctor—and merged into white society as much as he could. He joked about baseball and drank bourbon with the whites who had to be bribed. He ran the gambling houses of the Hi Ling Hong and was himself a gambler of shifting luck and fortune. He insisted his uncle should own racehorses. His fondness for dice was a disgrace to the Chinese. (Quong Lao Gaw had told him, 'Any game where one has often to play on one's knees lowers one's dignity, insults one's ancestry.')

But now there were other matters to consider. 'Honorable uncle, I shall see Mr Fiore sees to our strength, our needs in the San Francisco business world.'

The old man smiled at the girl standing calmly waiting. 'The Italians, nephew, are the Chinese of Europe. Marco Polo showed them ways to be our equal in trade, clever in business, and they know the value of money. Be sure there is this whiskey they drink, the bourbon, the rye.'

'And a woman?'

'No, he keeps one, I hear.'

Kim Tai nodded, inclined his head in a short bow. He was not one to kowtow in the old style. 'Of course. I go now, good health, uncle,' and he went out.

For the first time Gaw greeted the girl, motioned her closer. With a woman, sham and pretension are best. He caressed her neck and shoulders, pushed aside the robe, petted her, handled her as one does a favorite dog, absentmindedly.

Gaw was aware Moon Orchid was already a Chinatown myth, described as the most beautiful Chinese slave girl ever brought to San Francisco. The old man's vanity about her had grown greater as his vitality diminished. He had the Chinese artist Cho Lee Lin, the last of the Ching masters, do a scroll painting of her on silk. The artist dressed Moon Orchid in full-length pale blue Chinese trousers, her rose-tipped breasts exposed, her hair done up in the style of a Mancho empress. The pose was natural, a girl turning into a graceful woman, her hands held in an easy gesture of repose directly in front of her. The young poet Kin Dee added some verse delicately brushed on rice paper:

> My songs of love
> have been made to dust.
> The earth fades from green
> I hear the night birds cry.

Dusk like Moon Orchid's robe
falls in my intimate dreams.

George Fiore was expanding his banking interests not only into the Chinese sections of San Francisco, Los Angeles, and Sacramento. In much of California he was building confidence in the Pacific-Harvesters Bank among orchard growers, the wineries, land developers, men looking toward the expansion of towns into true cities. Los Angeles still had a population of only eighteen thousand, but he saw that, unlike San Francisco—limited by space on its rocks and hills—the city of Los Angeles could spread out in all directions.

After his meeting with Gaw, he had brought Rocco up from Los Angeles and settled him into the Palace Hotel suite for a meeting of the bank's cashiers, tellers, and managers, including Tom Floyd and Charles. They sat around a long table in the suite's living room. Charles was fascinated by the skill, the sense of style, with which his father was explaining just what his plans were for the bank. He spoke clearly and with no ornate phrasing, estimating sixteen branches next year, double that the year after. He spotted the sites on a large map on a stand.

'Mining will peter out, speculation in land and dealings in stock and other securities will go on. But the major business will be in settling towns and cities, enlarging orchards, crop farming, cattle raising, pork processing, and items like Levi Strauss and his work pants for farmers. Then there are fish canning, bon tons, and general stores. Biggest will be trolley lines, gasworks.'

Rocco asked, 'Who will have the street rights to run trolley lines and the gasworks? I know we're not big enough yet, but these franchises have the public by the balls.'

'With luck they'll be friends of ours. But in the long run, it doesn't really matter all that much. Banking will always be needed. But we must also stay a bank for the little businesses, the small farmers and growers. There are a lot more of *them* than Senator Kendrick or Senator Hearst, or

Bill Ralston, Willie Sharon, or the silver kings.'

Tom Floyd, somewhat filled out since his war days, well-combed but still too lanky to be well-tailored, said, 'Speaking of Ralston, I hear he's overextended—living too high, and his silver-king friends on the board think he's getting too big for his breeches.'

George turned from inspecting the map. 'He can take care of himself. Let's stick to our own worries. Charlie, Rocco, Tom—I want you to come to a Chinese banquet one of the *hongs* is giving us next Tuesday.'

'Rat cutlets?' Rocco joked. 'Buzzard's nest soup?'

George waved a hand in protest. 'None of that. Bret Harte once told me long ago that the Chinese have the best cuisine in the world, better than the French.... Gentlemen, we want their mortgage business.' He picked up his hat and cane. 'And they are Chinese, *not* Chinks. Good day.'

George was developing a stern manner, he called it a 'pose,' the role of a man of business, of position in the city. He no longer felt it undignified (for reading a statement or some plans for the bank) to take out his spectacles in their silver octagonal frames. He also watched himself so there was no expenditure of useless energy. Near his mid-forties, he still suffered recurring attacks of fever. He was having lunch with Rose and their daughter, Maude, at a little French eating place calling itself Bon Louie. The city was expanding its taste, Rose thought, beyond Mexican dishes, Yankee camp cooking, Chinese bowls of pungent vegetables and other mysterious ingredients.

If Louie was short and his jowls shook, he did manage with his wife, Nana, who was tall and thin, to serve up a *soupe verte* and a sort of *sole Marguery*. He greeted Rose and Maude, a little girl in a pink dress with ruffles and wearing a little brimmed straw hat with a long blue ribbon trailing behind. George managed to have lunch with them once a week.

'The *gigot d'agneau?*' Louie suggested as he seated them in the corner of the six-table dining area. 'I get la lamb from Doña Irena herself.'

'Then it should be good,' said George, 'if it isn't a stunted ram. Irena is a smart businesswoman.'

'A lady, *une grande* lady. For the *petite chérie*, a crepe of ham, grated cheeses?'

Rose said, 'The *canotière* chowder last time was fine.'

'*Brioche, brioche! Apportez-moi des brioches,*' cried Maude. '*Comprenez-vous?*'

'Show-off,' said George.

Rose laughed. 'Mademoiselle Maude is studying French.'

'*Oui.*'

They ate with pleasure, Maude chattering about her cat Moumou, and how she could play a Chopin waltz if the score was simple. Rose and George nodded and said little. Madame Nana came out of the kitchen to accept their warm praise, wiping her face in a corner of her apron and making a shy little bow before returning to her pots.

After a *baba au rhum* for Maude (which she thought very daring), and *demitasses* for the adults, they went boldly for a walk along the Embarcadero. Most of the citizens didn't know who they were and didn't care, and those who *did* know who they were—gossipy friends and members of the merchant and banking class—shrugged and smiled at the *ménage*, and some of the women agreed with Irena ('Men are such bastards about these things').

'You're still too thin, George.'

'Rosie, I'll never be a fat man. A little paunch up front in time, I suppose, but that's a badge every prosperous man should own.'

They strolled along arm in arm in the bright weather.

'The banks are doing well?'

'They're on their way. It'll take a little time, and if there is no damn money panic in the East, and if silver against gold doesn't become a monetary issue, and *if* God doesn't make too many green little apples and—'

'Be serious. I worry, George.'

'Too sunny to worry, to be serious.' He turned to Maude. 'Right, kitten?' Maude had stopped by an old Mexican woman with a parrot on a stand and a tray of folded papers. 'Uncle George, give me a penny, I want a fortune.'

'Don't we all?' said her mother.

The old woman licked her lips. 'One cent, Juan magic bird, he pick the future of good fortune for the little señorita.'

The parrot scratched under a wing, the old woman took the copper coin from George and held a sunflower seed over the bird's red and green head.

'Juan, qué desea usted?'

The bird answered, *'Con mucho gusto.'* It picked out a folded paper from the tray with its beak. The old woman fed the bird a sunflower seed and handed the paper to Maude. She opened it, dancing about, shouting, 'My fortune, my fortune!'

Rose took it from her hand and read the sentence crudely lettered with a sputtered pen: '"It is better to be a crystal and broken than a tile whole on a rooftop."'

'What?' cried Maude, pouting. 'That's no fortune.'

The old woman and her parrot and tray of fortunes had disappeared.

'That's no real fortune. I want to cross water, meet a dark stranger.' Maude seized the paper from Rose's fingers, threw it down, and stamped on it, crying out, 'I am a Gypsy queen. I see dark deeds, cross my palms with silver!'

Rose said to George, 'She's been reading the Brontës. You stop that, Maude, or I'll slap you in front of everybody.'

The whole afternoon delighted George. There was a lot of Fiore spirit and oddity in his daughter. He introduced her to the Emperor Norton, who let her pet his dogs and offered to make her a princess. She was totally charmed, curtsied politely, and walked regally away with George and Rose.

20

The trip to Quong Lao Gaw's party was made in the Fiore
carriage. George leaned back in the carriage as it began to
descend one of the steep San Francisco hills leading to the
Chinese section. 'Remember, Rocco, Charlie, we're here
as guests of a group of major bank clients. We want to get
friendly enough to handle their investment.'

'Will there be women?' asked Rocco, looking at several
pigtailed figures in blue canvas gathered silently under a
lamppost, watching them pass. 'You hear things about
these mopsies.'

'Not true,' said Charles.

'How the devil would you know?' asked his father.

Frank the coachman turned around and pointed with his
whip to a building that housed curio stores, a barbershop,
and a hallway lit by gas flares inside glass domes.

'Here you be, gents.'

Gaw's nephew Kim met them at the door. ''Evening.
Please follow me.' They mounted steep stairs, entered
through a door opened by a small bowing boy, and found
themselves in a large room containing two long tables of
staring oriental faces. The tables were set with ornate
painted ceramic dishes. The guests were to be seated on
chairs of a red shiny wood, and hanging over all were
lanterns of various primary colors. Hidden musicians were
playing what sounded like the whine of music from some
far-off nation with different ideas of harmonious sounds.

George guessed there were at least two dozen Chinese present, mostly in oriental robes, including three women with shiny black hair adorned with tinkling ornaments. They were not young women, but middle-aged and nearly expressionless, with a kind of calmness suggesting, he thought, privileged pride.

Gaw himself came toward them, wrinkling features bent in a smile as he lowered his head in a bow and held out a hand that appeared suddenly, as if on a spring, from a loose sleeve.

'Much pleased, yes, much so.' Again he bowed his head, which was topped by a black silk cap set with jade buttons.

'My son Charles ... my assistant, Mr Bordone.'

'I am your host, Quong Lao Gaw. So other guests of Hi Ling Hong all ready to meet you.'

George took the offered hand. 'May I present to you a gift from the banking house of the Pacific-Harvesters, a token of our pleasure in being associated with you and your group.'

George couldn't read the expression on Gaw's face.

Rocco took a long black leather case from an inside pocket and handed it to George, who opened it. On a red silk pad was a round disk of ivory, bordered in gold, with a portrait of Abraham Lincoln painted on it.

'Ah, yes,' said Gaw, taking the little painting from its box. 'Who is fella man?'

'A great American,' said George, 'Press the little lever here so.'

The picture opened to one side to show a ticking watch and images of 'The Spirit of '76.'

'You fellas?'

'Our heroes,' replied Charles.

'So so,' said Gaw, laughing, his paunch quivering.

Gaw motioned at the seated guests, silent on their chairs. 'Let me introduce you some membahs of Hi Ling Hong. Kim Tai, I most depending on him. Chou Yi-Han, good with handling detail.'

It was hard for Charles to remember the names, and

Rocco didn't try—everyone bowed and murmured something that appeared lost in their throats. Kim Tai, young and sly-looking, took George's arm. 'May I add my assurance to Quong Lao Gaw's? You and your associates are most welcome.'

Rocco suddenly said, 'Holy Mary and Jose, will you look at *that*.'

From another door a group of Chinese women was entering. The first was a beautifully gowned girl, jeweled and graceful. She was tall for a Chinese maiden and her delicate headdress made tinkling sounds as she moved forward. She was followed by a young maid with large frightened eyes, and an old woman, tenacious-mouthed, hands up her sleeves, making painful progress on deformed feet. George suspected an impeccably planned entrance. 'Charming.'

'Ah, this is Moon Orchid, who honahs my household, and this guest is Mistah Fiohe and his people; son, helpah.'

The girl gave the three white men cool but not unfriendly glances. She tilted her magnificent head forward an inch or so and was assisted into a chair. Quong Lao Gaw indicated where the white devils were to sit, across the table from Moon Orchid and himself. George thought her rather too baroque in her costume, but still one of the most beautiful women he had ever seen. It was hard to tell her actual age. Rocco envied that lucky son of a bitch Quong, the old lecher, to have something like this exotic toy of flesh to play with.

They were handed small bowls of warm rice wine as Quong Lao Gaw recited some kind of greeting.

Rocco nudged George. 'They expect you to utter a few words.'

'Damn.' But he smiled, took a sip, stood up; the rice wine was strong as brandy. 'Gentlemen'—he added a nod in the direction of Moon Orchid—'and ladies, I am pleased to meet you, and I gather from our host'—a smile in that direction to Gaw, sitting back with his fingers laced across his belly—'we are to be involved in major business projects. I offer a toast to Chinatown and its citizens, and to whatever god we serve, may his blessings on us aid our plans, friendships, and associations.'

The toast seemed to go well, and soft-stepping waiters came in. Kim Tai offered the honored guests forks, if chopsticks were too strange for them. George declined, as he had used chopsticks and could handle them; but Rocco and Charlie were glad to accept the forks. Kim Tai explained the *chin chang peang* that began the meal: paperthin crepes with steamed duck and pork and various vegetables, covered with a spicy sauce, *moi cheung*, made of plums.

Next came steamed fish with hurt staring eyes, looking alive and rather angry as they were disassembled by busy chopsticks. Kim Tai spoke well of the *hoy cheung yau,* the seafood sauce, and suddenly Charles's mouth exploded as he swallowed some of it. 'It's goddamn fire!'

There was a sound of bell-like laughter from Moon Orchid, echoed by polite sounds of amusement from her servants.

Gaw spoke. 'Moon child, one not laugh at honored guests' humiliation.'

Rocco was laughing as Charles swallowed several small cups of tea.

'Jesus,' said Rocco. 'They'd laugh if you broke a leg.'

Kim Tai handed Charles a bowl of wine. 'This is *moi kwai lo*, a rosé wine; it soothes women in childbirth, or eases one from the pangs of lost love.'

'I'll stick to tea. You don't mind?' He felt he'd made a jackass of himself, and in front of the exquisite Chinese girl.

Moon Orchid had returned to impassivity, eating with pleasure, her chopsticks flying. This was no dainty girl, Charles thought, for all her perfection of body and features. By middle age she could be a fat dumpling wheezing for breath. He coughed as she gave him an amused glance and picked up a bowl of what could only be some sections of the stuffed gut of some animal. Holding the bowl just below her lower lip, Chinese fashion, she began to push the food into her mouth with the chopsticks. Charlie found it an exotic way to eat—but decided one should not question other people's customs. The classic fragility of her features was marred by a small trickle of grease sliding down one corner of her mouth. The wine came around again, some of it warm; Charlie and Rocco settled for tasting the procession of dishes still being set before them. There seemed no end to the cuisine. By the time the almond cakes and the *lai chee* nuts were served, Charlie had long since lost count of the number of odd dishes he had sampled.

His mind was aroused by more than food and wine as he let his sensual imagination flow. He noticed Moon Orchid didn't mind greasy lips and cheeks; her maid kept wiping them with a warm damp napkin. Waiters were handing steaming little towels to the guests, some of whom were thanking their host for an excellent meal in the old Chinese style, by belching and breaking wind. Charlie even thought he heard a tiny musical fart from Moon Orchid.

After the damp scented towels were collected, the guests sat back in their chairs, sated. Kim Tai was at George's elbow with a large cedar box holding long torpedo-shaped aromatic cigars.

'You will find these, Mr Fiore, the best Havana leaf.' George inhaled deeply the pungent tobacco. He realized that the dreadful dying-cat music that had caterwauled all through the feast had stopped. The air was stale and thick with both unfamiliar odors and some too well known.

He faced his host. 'I had hoped we could have a private talk.'

'That's fine, yes. You now seeing jugglahs and dancing womens.'

Three tumblers came leaping into the room, followed by three girls beating on some kind of oddly shaped drums. As the men threw themselves into cartwheel spins, Charlie noticed Moon Orchid and her escort had disappeared and that he had an erection. The other women guests had also gone. The men were opening sashes of their robes,

216

scratching and leaning farther back in their chairs. The girls with the drums began to undulate into sensual movements, turning to obscene gestures with outthrust stomachs, pubic areas rotating and thrusting.

Rocco grinned. 'More like it, Chuck.'

Charles nodded. 'It's amazing, twisting twat.'

Kim Tai motioned to George. 'Come this way.' The noise, sounds of satisfaction from the guests, increased as he left, followed by Gaw.

Settled into the small room hung with scrolls and set about with bronze figures of the meditating Buddha, George said, 'I have always been impressed by you as an art collector, Quong Lao Gaw.'

'No, no, I know nothing, me little old peasant. But one has investment, yes, in tings to show one has what Kim Tai call the culture.'

'Beautiful.'

'Yes, so, yes,' said Gaw as they settled into American club chairs. 'So now we alone, talk of mattahs of the bank.' He dismissed Kim with a wave of a hand. From below came the sound of wild drumming, muffled somewhat by the floors and walls. Still there were clear cries of women and the deep guttural growl of men in heat.

George inspected the end of his smoldering cigar. The wine was still affecting his thought processes, but he felt in control of himself, almost a benign complacency.

'Gaw, I am here to get the Chinatown banking business. I will pay one percent more interest and I will lend bigger sums.'

'So,' said Gaw, 'then we eat togetha same pot.'

George placed his cigar into a bronze tray. 'This is good for both of us.'

Quong Lao Gaw went to an ivory cabinet, opened it, and took out several bars of gold. 'You have give me sense of honest dealing. I foah Hi Ling Hong give something for deposit in bank.'

George pursed his lips, searched Gaw's face. 'I'd guess, Gaw, those bars now are worth ... say, five, six thousand dollars each.'

'You weigh deposit, yes? Twenty-five these?'

'Twenty-five bars?'

'That too many?'

'No, you'll get a weight report tomorrow. I'll write you a receipt when it's brought in.'

Quong Lao Gaw nodded, put the gold bars down on a rosewood table. 'When river makes new land, wise fella say, use soil from new channels to grow food. You will find you self much pleased with us.' Gaw bowed his head in a gesture of understanding.

'I'm sure.' George held out his hand, and it was shaken firmly. 'Have the gold at the bank at ten tomorrow morning.'

While Charles was waiting in the hall for George, he was met by a little Chinese maid, who handed him a small package. 'Lady Moon say gift for you for good ruck.'

Then she was gone in a hiss of silk garments. 'Ruck: Ruck? Luck! *Luck!'*

Charlie opened the soggy paper package and found a kind of fluted dumpling. He had read a travel book which described the cake called by the Chinese a *tow-fu*, a confection filled with sweet rice paste and shaped, although he was not aware of this, like the pudendum. Not that it meant the giver was offering her body to a lover; but it was an offering of a sort. The girl was interested in him. Still, there would be hell to pay if he were stupid enough to make advances to Gaw's prize slave girl. Just when the banks wanted, needed, everything from Gaw. Someone could be playing a poor joke on him. Most likely the sly Kim Tai.

As the white devils left, the noisy orgy was still going on in the great hall. Charles pressed the *tow-fu* in his hand, felt it squish between his fingers, and threw it into a corner.

The street outside was busy with white nighttime visitors, pleasure-seekers, hawkers of Chinese food, and offers of exotic pleasures. In the carriage, Charles wiped his fingers of the remains of the *tow-fu* before drawing on his gloves.

'What did you think, Chuck?' asked Rocco.

'Damn beautiful girl.'

'I mean the monkey food.'

'Oh, yes, very pungent.'

'That Chinese doll gave you the eye.'

George was still tasting the cigar. He had been polite in accepting it, but he'd carry a pipe on his next visit to the *hong* leader. 'Chuck, you listen. Don't get any ideas about that girl. She's property. Gaw has got some old drunk white woman teaching her English, reading, and writing. He has some fancy plans for her for himself. He wants to move about into some kind of white society, break out of Chinatown. He's using us as we use him.'

'He's smart,' said Rocco. 'Throwing that party for us.'

Charles rubbed his fingers together. 'She a slave girl?'

'Bought and paid for, he told me,' said his father.

Neither Gaw nor Charles had any true understanding of the unique quality of Moon Orchid's mind. She was more than a slave girl, more than decor at banquets. Even at sixteen, she had a clever brain, the kind of wisdom most acquire through hard experience, and an ability to see opportunities, take chances, and hope one day to achieve what she wanted. But she lived with an appearance of diffidence and humility. Mostly she wanted escape, wanted the gracious love one read about in poems, saw painted on silk panels, found in the white man's novels. Of her beauty there was no doubt; of her keen brain few had any hint. Her most flamboyant thoughts she kept hidden even from the old bitch her ancient servant, Hairy Lips, and her young maid, Flower Seed. Moon Orchid felt she was a hungry mouth hunting for something still elusive. Her English was progressing; her reading of Dickens, and Thackeray offered surprising revelations of western ways. In Charles Fiore she saw a hope of pleasure, satisfaction, and escape. But *how*? Impossible, it seemed. She was guarded by *tong* men, watched constantly. She was only permitted to read, to paint a bit, to gossip with the maids, to be caressed by an old man who could not get his flesh to rise even with the help of aphrodisiacs made from rhino horn and forked ginseng root.

This morning, Quong Lao Gaw found her warm to the touch, her skin smooth, hairless as an egg (he could gaze at her naked for hours), but it also gave him a sense of loss of his earlier life, of other times now long gone. He had bought her two years ago after a long wrangle; he was a keen bargainer, determined to buy the fourteen-year-old beauty. Old Hairy Lips, the former procuress, had examined her and vouched that her maidenhead was intact. Gaw never wondered about how Moon Orchid felt about him or asked how she enjoyed her condition in his household, nor did he care what her background had been or who her people were. In his youth and in his prime, he had not been curious about the many girls who passed from his sleeping mats to life in the cribs or to worse fate. The Chinese male, he insisted, is not entangled in moral alternatives about women. Now he lowered her robe, fondled the perfectly formed breasts, thumbed the strawberry nipples. Long months ago he had hoped there would come the moment when he could deflower this lovely object he owned, but that rigid moment, the provocative phallic stirring, never came. Never mind, one took what the gods of Kong Chow temple on Pine Street gave, much or little, and hoped for the future.

Moon Orchid tried not to show she was indifferent to his dry caress. She had slept well, had two bowls of tea with yellow and white jasmine blossoms, nibbled on *yow chein wuei*, and added slivers of fruit. Her face remained expressionless with just a faint smile at the corners of her bee-blown mouth. She disliked this smelly old fart, this 'nasty son of a bitch,' as old Hairy Lips would have put it.

Her mind turned away from him, to any distraction. She knew little of the world outside Chinatown. She had seen very little of it but for visits to some theaters, festivals in the streets, and one wonderful visit to a white seamstress when Gaw ordered that she have a wardrobe of western fashions as well as her traditional silk robes.

Old Hairy Lips had been educated before the pipe habit gripped her, and she and the seamstress (Molly the Diver, a white wreck) taught Moon Orchid to read and speak English. Her own curiosity prompted her to seek out news from beyond Chinatown in the newspapers she read daily.

Moon Orchid had read *Little Women* with joy, and *The Three Kingdoms* by Lo Kuan-Ching. She could recite Chinese poetry to her master by the hour; it seemed nonsense, but the old bastard liked it—his repellent smile showed that.

Moon Orchid, despite later myths to the contrary, was no romantic. She thought she saw life as it was, managed to have her way with the servants, those who served the old man in various enterprises. She knew of love and copulation, having observed her little lion dogs Yin and Yang. She felt the wonder of the idea and the act. When escorted through the streets to some *hong* banquet, she had seen some couples fornicating in doorways, and once she even saw Wie Pang, the doorman, copulating with Hai, the cook's daughter, on the rolled-up mats in the storage room where she had gone to match some silk for a robe belt.

The sight of those naked legs in the air, Wie's bouncing buttocks, the two emitting sounds like animals engaged in a battling war, had left Moon Orchid flushed and excited. Even the naughty caressing of Flower Seed, her young maid, one night had not been satisfactory. She had once dreamed of the sailors that visited Chinatown, their pants tight, their manhood worn lumpy on the left side. She often made plans to escape. What if the *tong* hatchet man, the Punisher, Chou Yi Han, recaptured her? And if the old man permitted her face to be torn open, scarred by the sharp iron comb? No, the old bastard would not do that. She was too costly an item. Oh, for the freedom to walk unescorted as Little Nell or the Little Match Girl, or Jo in *Little Women*. Free to shop foolishly in many shops, eat the white devil's ice cream, wear red-tasseled high-button shoes with little bells. And not be forced to give the old bastard the usual coagulated grin at his sterile gropings.

221

Moon Orchid was very young, and her desires were simple and direct. But she was not foolish. She knew she had great natural wit and wisdom, and she foresaw her fate could be dreadful when the old man died. Being the most beautiful Chinese girl on the West Coast was a danger. There were depraved Chinese heads of *hongs* in New York and Chicago, richer than Quong Lao Gaw. And their perverted lusts, if Old Hairy Lips didn't lie, were often beyond reason.

The old fart had said to her: 'You will look you best at a New Year's celebration.'

'As you say, honorable protector.' She giggled. 'I will wear the slit gown. The one that shows my leg?'

He cuffed her as one would cuff a pet, not at all painfully. 'Respect and decency. Your servants will know how to dress you. I again will have white guests.'

You son of a bitch, she thought (in English) as he kissed her neck.

As for Charles Fiore, young man-about-town, he saw Moon Orchid several more times that year, for Gaw and his *hong* members were building shops, warehouses, and dwellings in Chinatown, and the Pacific-Harvesters Bank was taking the mortgages and helping with the designs. Charles would take the plans for the new structures to be inspected by Gaw and Kim, arrange for the bank papers to be signed by both with their *chop* (red seal) and the white devils' version of their names in English. After the New Year's celebration, he caught two glimpses of Moon Orchid in a hallway, and once she waved to him from the garden roof of the building. This distant and uncertain communication encouraged him, enlarging his dreams to excessive excitability until he had at last to visit some of the sporting houses of the tenderloin. But the image of the Chinese girl dominated his dreams, intensifying the taut strain that grew daily. There was little hope of making any progress toward her. Becoming involved with Moon Orchid would have to remain a fantasy.

21

One morning at breakfast at Bay Cottage, George said to Rose, 'I dreamed again I was Emperor Norton. It shook me, Rosie.'

'Nonsense, darling. You don't even like dogs.'

He studied his soft-boiled eggs. 'My grandmother the witch said omens in dreams do have meaning.'

'Oh, damn your witch of a grandmother.'

Emperor Norton still lived a delightful reign, happy royal years with the obedient court, the two dogs. His own money satisfied his simple needs. He was a people's monarch. His scrip as payment was rarely refused; once for railroad transportation, to attend a session of the bribed, dishonest legislature at Sacramento. The Emperor was in the habit of giving the tainted lawmakers his honest advice on matters of running the state. He sat in a special chair held for him in the Visitors' Gallery. Once a railroad-car waiter refused his currency; the Emperor became angry and threatened to revoke the railroad franchise. The train conductor came forward to beg the Emperor's royal pardon, and the next day Norton was issued a perpetual traveling pass, good on all trains of the Central Pacific.

So that the Emperor could keep neat and maintain his uniforms properly, George asked the city's Board of Supervisors to vote him thirty dollars a year for life. Norton fed handsomely at the free-lunch counters in the better saloons and bars, tossing a tidbit now and then to his faithful retainers, the dogs. He took it upon himself—for he was 'a working king,' he told George—to inspect the wharves and markets, nod approvingly on his subjects' fish and fresh tomatoes. He expected to be bowed to on the streets, and usually was. Audiences rose when he entered (on the cuff) a local theater. He never abused his privileges or took a royal mistress.

Emperor Norton held his royal duties as a sacred trust. He spent days with pen and paper producing documents, issuing proclamations as impressive as the documents that came from the royal courts of Europe. The Emperor was a modern diplomat, using the telegraph and mail to keep in contact with other royal heads of state—Queen Victoria of England, the kaiser, the tsar of Russia. Emperor Norton always felt that his counsel had helped to settle the Franco-Prussian War. He was generous with his advice. During the Civil War, he was firm with President Lincoln, wiring him that it was his duty as president to marry the Widow of Windsor, Queen Victoria, 'in order to maintain western civilization by promoting mutual understanding between the two great English-speaking nations.' Lincoln's secretary replied that the president would give 'careful consideration to the command.'

The Emperor went on doing his duty by his city and his realm until one day, while passing old St Mary's Church, he was called to a higher kingdom and gave up his mortal rights. To his burial, the Pacific-Harvesters Bank sent a blanket of roses.

As the 1870's progressed, George Fiore became even better known in the banking circles of San Francisco. Some still saw him as a bit of an outsider, a banker with hardly the kind of clients their ornate structures catered to. But he was admittedly clever, honest, and 'one of the good wops.' The Italians were respected for their business savvy, and in the young city the names of other prominent Italians could be heard mentioned in the Poodle Dog Café, at the Palace Hotel bar, even noted in the *Chronicle*. Baldocchis, Cellas,

224

Alionons, Giannis, Ghirardellis, Petries, and Aliotos were men of power. These were not mere vine-trimmers or crab-catchers. They were investors in fishing fleets, chocolate, and one was George's fierce rival, a banker who backed a flower grower whose floral arrangements were all the rage in high society that year. The wives of these wealthy entrepreneurs dressed opulently, as befitted their station. The men ate *filet mignon aux truffes* during luncheon meetings and smoked Havana cigars.

But it was older money that maintained dominance over the city's finances. One major figure was William Ralston, a most respected man, still living lavishly with his wife in their mansion outside the city at Belmont, still entertaining in a grand style, still glorying in the Palace Hotel with its entrance lobby 'into which one's coachman could drive a pair of horses and a varnished carriage.'

George and he had become good friends during the many years since their first meeting, smoked together and drank blue blazers at the bar of the Palace. But their families never mixed socially; the Fiores and Velasquezes never went to the Ralston fetes to meet President Grant or Henry Ward Beecher. The two men did enjoy visits to the steam rooms of the Neptune Swimming Baths, to talk of financial deals and national panics, the doings of J.P. Morgan and his railroads and reorganizations, and the value of bank scrips and gold futures.

William Ralston recalled life as a clerk on a Mississippi riverboat. 'I tell you, George, running the river, the Big Muddy, in high flood with its snags and cutoffs, was like banking with today's sharpies, speculators, and shysters, and when I first opened the bank, I showed a lot of folk how to come along, clinging to my coattails. The Breckenridges, Tevises, Newlandes. Yep ... God, isn't this steam room great for sweating out problems?'

George mopped his head and shoulders. 'What about Mr Sharon?'

'Oh, Wallie? He came to me, didn't have enough money to buy a flea a dinner, all he had *was* fleas. He's a

225

millionaire now. And me, I lent him the first fifteen thousand dollars. He's running a branch of Bank of California for me, and running it damn fine, in Nevada. You don't like him, George? I feel it. What have you got against old Wallie?'

'I never dislike anybody who hasn't done me any harm.'

George wasn't generally one for evasiveness; besides, Anglo bankers like Sharon and Ralston stuck together. But as he had once told Rose, he had a kind of little tin whistle inside him. If it blew when he met somebody, it was a warning. He couldn't explain it, but he trusted it. And he heard it loud and clear around William Sharon. Still, there was no use pursuing the topic with Ralston now.

Back at his office, he couldn't get Sharon out of his mind, and asked Tom Floyd, 'That son of a bitch William Sharon, why does he stink up the air when I meet him?'

'He's a rival, and you are wary of rivals. He's a moneymaker, has silver mines, made millions. Your friend Ralston holds him to his bosom—lives at the Ralston mansion, Wallie does, when he's in town.'

'There was all that talk of him buying a United States senatorship.'

'Oh, that. It's the rule, so he bribed the Nevada legislators with shares of some of his silver stock to get the appointment. Everyone does it.' Tom laughed. 'The bastard, once he became a senator, he sold out all his shares of stock and it fell right down to the cellar. The boodle boys, the legislators, were sore as a bull's ass in fly time, but they couldn't do anything. Oh, that Wallie Sharon, he'd sell you his mother—and what's more, he'd deliver! He's dangerous! I mean, he runs with some sons of Sam Brannan's old Regulators who still handle shooting irons.'

George decided that Sharon was not his problem, but Ralston's fondness for the man continued to nag at him.

'Well, Major, Wild Bill Hickock used to say, "You need somebody to stand back of your chair so nobody can sneak up behind you."'

George agreed that these days one had to be adaptable to

a variety of experiences—and protect oneself the best way possible. The times were good, a panic now and then (like that of 1872) faded in time, and the silver millionaires of Virginia City dug deeper into the Comstock Lode: the Belcher Mine, the O'Brien, all shafts to fortune, the owners spending and enjoying the wealth the Cornish miners and others dug out.

George felt that banking, not mines, should be his major interest. And he was trying to slow down. He was now in his middle forties, and while he and Maria lived in the same Nob Hill house, the marriage was in a dormant state. It was his twin sons, his daughter, Maude, who gave him a sense of time passing and generations growing. Overall, he was pleased with them. Fred, the dark one, was a handsome lad with teeth a bit too large, clever in getting his way. He was a poor student but a good sport. His interests were varied; he was able to handle a frisky horse and gig with skill, raised hunting dogs, and played practical jokes—but never bad-tempered ones. The more serious Charles was blond with deep blue eyes, lean good looks, and a sharp, questioning mind. He was interested in the use of money and credits, fascinated by banking. As a boy, he played bank teller on the sun porch, writing checks on slips of paper, reading the stock-market reports in the papers. At seventeen, he 'played the market,' keeping accounts in a school notebook and making great profits (on paper) in pork-belly futures, spring oats, Central Pacific Railroad stock, even dealings in city trolley lines. All on paper—but George was amazed at his astuteness, and his profits.

'Well, I'll save you a place in the bank, Chuck, but I don't care much for gambling in pork bellies, oats, or wheat futures. They don't always go up.'

'Oh, I sell short at times. I bet I could corner something like corn or wheat by buying up the major share of the futures.'

'I'd beat your ass if you even think too much about it. It's been tried, can't be done.'

'I could. *Just* banking is dull, dull. The folks put the

money in, you lend it out, and the difference between is what *you* keep.'

'The bank keeps it, and it builds, has vision, gives people hope to better themselves.'

Charles wanted to sneer, but asked instead, 'What do you think of J.P. Morgan and his bringing all the railroads together in a combination? He's going to take over your shares of Pacific and Great Plains.'

'Go soak your head, Chuck.'

Despite their radically different personalities, both boys could have a future with him at the bank, George felt. Charlie would be the steadier, while Fred, who had been expelled unchastened from military school, was a gambler, sassy, with a rebellious streak. George Fiore didn't approve of gamblers. Not cards, racing, roulette, poker, or dice. He often said, 'The only toss in dice that's good, Fred, is to toss them away.' Maybe some of Charlie's steadiness would rub off on Fred, he hoped.

George's conservatism extended to his finances. He avoided deals in commodities futures, selling high or low, bull or bearish. George admitted he had gambled in backing Chinese building sites and, with bank credits, in erecting structures there. Yes, he also gambled a bit that the fishing fleet would do well with king crabs and Alaska salmon. It was a risk giving mortgages to the canneries at Monterey. What if the sardine runs failed, as they sometimes did? George saw a subtle distinction: *that* was business gambling. Ralston had gambled on building the Palace Hotel, must have put a couple million dollars into it. More recently, George backed clearing land for expanded vineyards and a winery Caesar Spinelli and his sons were building in Modesto. He worried, but took a risk with the rail line through Chuckaluck Pass—the Pacific and Great Plains railroad was building a line to bring crops and cattle down to connect with the Central Pacific. Maybe the bank had been too generous in financing its two hundred miles of track. Meanwhile, he'd keep a tight rein on Chuck and Fred, direct them with a gentle nudge. After all, he thought, they *are* my sons.

Fred had a sailboat, the *Sandpiper*, and on Saturday afternoons he would invite his brother and father to tack up and down the bay past the oyster beds to Vallejo. Maria would pack wicker hampers of food and wine, and warn Fred they were not to sail about in fog and be hit by the Oakland ferry and all of them killed. Often they talked of Ramon, missing his calm wisdom and dry wit. But he was still in Paris.

April days were their favorites for venturing about into the bay, and one day stood above all the rest for its perfection of sailing and camaraderie. The wind on this glorious afternoon was steady, and they tacked back and forth, bringing the boom around, all heads down. The sun was strong; other sailboats passed, exchanging shouts and waves. Heading for the picnic site, George sat with Charles against the dinghy and let Fred take care of the trimming of sail. George missed Ramon. Otherwise, it was a good picnic. 'A group of males,' Fred called it. 'Free of omniscient women, simpering girls.' They ate with relish the fried chicken, cold roast beef, chocolate cake, and sliced melons, and washed it down with two kinds of wine. Noses peeling, arms burned red, they docked the *Sandpiper* as the dusk was (as Charles said) 'falling like pollen over the city.' Fred remarked, 'Chuck is a goddamn poet.'

That night George had trouble falling asleep. The sun had badly burned his arms. Even more troublesome was the gossip about discord among the directors of the Bank of California. Was there any truth to it? Could Wallie Sharon and his silver kings toss their weight around, make grandiose plans, and ruin others by the outlay of their vast wealth? George muttered long-forgotten street oaths: *'Fesso! Coglione! Macche!'*

He should speak to William Ralston about the rumors and how they (or Sharon) could be stopped. Unable to sleep, George took a pillow and a book to the sofa in the sunroom. By morning he had lost his courage, deciding that

229

Ralston would be offended by any meddling. No, he would say nothing to Ralston. If a banking war between the millionaires took place, he should concentrate on the welfare of the Pacific-Harvesters Bank and its clients. He had the Chinatown projects to look after, though Charles was showing great interest there; and he would watch it closely so that Charles didn't get too reckless. Fred was not going to be of much use in the bank. He had been kicked out of the Indiana Military Academy a few years back for sending a huge box of candy tied with a red ribbon to the wife of the major who ran the academy. She had once described him at a tea as 'a really sassy guinea.' When she opened the candy box at a party before guests to offer them their choice, the box was filled with dried dog turds. The major figured that only Fred Fiore would have such an original idea and expelled him without a hearing. He was now enrolled at Berkeley, unenthusiastically pursuing a law degree.

Besides Charles, George depended on Rocco, who was doing well in Los Angeles, both in banking and with women. George was grooming Tom Floyd for a more permanent job at the San Francisco branch. He was loyal, earnest, a bit too serious, but very well liked by the people who worked farms, ranches, dealt in small crops, fish, a few head of cattle. Somehow, he'd have to encourage Tom to give stronger interest to land speculation, city building, canneries, shipping.

George looked at a framed photograph on his desk of a party at the Casa some years back. Irena dominated the scene, Maria seemed asleep, and Tomas—glass in hand—had an arm around Ramon's shoulder. Tomas would never come back, but Ramon could still have a good future in the bank, *if* he forgot about art.

22

The dawn was silver-gray, the sea fog drifting through the Golden Gate this morning near the end of August, the guttural *geek-geek* of sea gulls was becoming deafening over the wharves and the waterfront, where early cooks were soon to toss tidbits away. The sun appeared to burn away the fog just as the bark *Esmeralda* was entering the Golden Gate with a cargo of pineapples, twelve days out from the Sandwich Islands. Still far out at sea was the pencil scribble of smoke of the steamer *El Cid*. She was still below the horizon with a load of rare South American hardwoods, for mansions going up on Nob Hill.... Sweepers were removing the last of the horse litter from the streets.

Despite the early hour, a muttering crowd had already gathered in front of the Bank of California on Montgomery Street, two hours before it was to open its doors. First to arrive had been worried-looking workers in heavy shoes, then several housewives carrying large handbags. A tall woman dragging a wet-nosed child eating a large bun appeared. By the time Old Harry the peg-legged veteran of Gettysburg came out to polish the bronze letters spelling out the bank's name, there were a hundred people, some of them well-dressed. A man with an emaciated face, muttonchop whiskers, topped by a polished hard top hat (called a cylinder), was surrounded by several butchers in bloody aprons. Several Chinese standing silently made up yet another group.

231

'What the hell?' said Old Harry. 'Up early, aren't we?'

The woman with the wet-nosed child asked, 'Goin' to open this mornin'?'

'Open, that's what doors is for, ain't they?'

'Nothing wrong, I mean, Harry?' said a butcher. 'Nothin' real wrong?'

Old Harry grinned, wiped his hands on his trousers. 'You mean did I run off in the night with all the cash in the vaults, bags of silver, all them gold coins?'

But the crowd was not amused. More people were pouring into Montgomery Street from both directions, some in carriages and buckboards, one rider on a dappled horse with a dog yapping under its hooves.

'Open! *Open*!' someone shouted, and the mob moved forward, canes raised, and cried, 'Who's shoving?'

By the opening hour of ten o'clock, the clerks and cashiers were well aware that a run on the bank was about to take place. When the crowd grew louder, a clerk ran over to the Palace Hotel, where he hoped William Ralston was staying the night; there had been a ball, the Bay Area Cotillion, and he could have stayed over in his private hotel suite if the ball had ended too late for driving back to Belmont. The clerk felt a cramp in the side grab him. He clutched his ribs and ran on. The dog that had been molesting the rider now ran at his heels.

William Ralston was in the bathroom shaving his jowls with a long razor when he heard a hammering on the door of the suite and Mrs Ralston's maid, Nancy, tapped on the bathroom door.

'What's the damn commotion, Nancy?'

'From the bank, a fellow.'

'Well, no reason to get in a tizzy.'

The clerk blurted out his news, wiping his damp face, unaware he was using his soft hat for the purpose. 'It's the bank, sir. Mr Ralston, sir, a run, a bank run, street full of people.'

Ralston wiped his face with a small towel the flustered maid handed him. 'Well, Trumbell, don't look so bug-eyed. They'll calm down when they see we'll honor all requests for withdrawals.'

From the bedroom came Mrs Ralston's voice, still tinged with sleep. 'What is it, Billy?'

'Some bank nonsense. People acting like sheep. Come on, Trumbell, and Christalmighty, don't look like you're going to a hanging.'

When Ralston got to the bank, he figured there were at least four hundred people crushing their way into the bank, and the assistant cashier at the back door, carrying a shotgun, let him in.

'Put the damn gun down, Hendricks; we're not under siege.'

'We're running out of gold coins in the drawers, sir.'

'Get it out of the vaults, you dunderhead.' Ralston tried to appear calm. He went up to his office; the cigar he lit tasted sour. He asked for figures of withdrawals to date; they clearly showed a panic.

The reporter from the *Chronicle* asked for a statement, as shouts and outcries rose from the main area of the bank. 'A regular ruckus,' the reporter called it.

Ralston said, 'Now, Ned, you tell your editor, Mr De Young, your publisher is on our board—there is no danger of any sort, the Bank of California is not in trouble. Our assets are firm, our cash on hand is well able to meet any demands.'

The reporters asked, '*Why* do you think, Mr Ralston, there is this heavy run?'

'Why do birds shit on people's hats?' He had had two small bourbons already and his nerves were taut. 'Because it's the nature of things to act foolish, reckless at times. Yes, quote me as saying the smart citizens of this city don't lose their minds.'

'There are rumors, sir—'

'There are always rumors. Now, excuse me, I've a meeting of the board coming up. Nothing unusual, this was our regular monthly meeting. Yes, with men like William Sharon and Senator Kendrick on the board, it's nonsense to

233

think this bank is in trouble.'

When the reporters left, Ralston wiped his face and neck with a silk handkerchief, decided not to have any more whiskey. He had sent messengers on foot with notes to the members of the board; it was *not* the usual monthly meeting.

Hendricks tapped on the door, came in. 'George Fiore is out back.'

'Well, let him in, tell him to come right up.'

George, looking somewhat wide-eyed, held out his hand for the banker to shake. 'Jesus, Mary, and Joseph, Bill, it's like one of the old Regulators' lynchings going on downstairs.'

'I've called a board meeting for three o'clock. Christalmighty, this hit me like colic after a bean feast.'

George waved off the offer of the ritual cigar. 'How bad is it?'

'It's being carried to a ridiculous extreme, this run. Draining the cash on hand, we're dipping into the reserve vaults. I'm thinking of signing notes to get cash from the Merchants and the Ranchers and the Star State banks.'

'I might be able to come up with two hundred fifty thousand, Bill.'

'No need, old friend. These runs happen, as you know.' The banker's features remained firm. 'When the gold and silver markets fluctuate sharply or some zany prospector or speculator gives out that there is a new discovery, a big strike, the chicken-headed depositors rush the banks to withdraw the cash for investment, speculation.'

'No, Bill, it's somehow just aimed at *this* bank,'

George looked out of the window at the crowd still growing in the street below. Police were trying to keep order; glass was breaking someplace, by the sound of it. George turned to face the banker. 'Bill, this is caused by rumors that Senator Kendrick and several of the biggest mine owners, ranchers, and farmers are going to withdraw their deposits and open a bank of their own.'

'I've heard that rumor,' said Ralston dryly, 'but Wallie

Sharon and his friends will rally the bank's board.'

'That's good to hear, Bill. How do you stand personally?
I mean, credits and debts, you and the bank?'

'I've been an asshole.' The banker decided to have the
dram of bourbon, filled two shot glasses, offered one to
George. His hand was not shaky, but his forehead was
beaded with droplets of moisture. He wiped his mouth
carefully. 'It's come at a critical time, this run. I've been
cutting it too close for years, and now it's caught up with
me. That son of a bitch hotel cost a lot more than I figured;
only the best, I told myself, *always* first class. And my way
of life? Well, you never were at Belmont, were you? High
living for me and the missus. The best money could buy—
only often it was never bought. A structure of indulgences
covered by only fancy bookkeeping—big borrowing,
George, *big*.'

'How much are you in the hole?'

Ralston unbuttoned his waistcoat. 'I owe the bank four
million dollars. Oh, yes. I'm into Wallie Sharon for two
million more, and then, well, there are creditors for this
and that. Running, say, three and a half million more.' He
swallowed the drink and peered into the glass, as if, George
thought, it were a crystal ball able to offer a change of
fortune. 'I'm up shit creek and no paddle.'

'What are your own personal assets, Bill?'

'Oh, I can rack up maybe four million, less than half of
what I owe. Where do I turn?'

'It can blow over in a few days. If you put a good face on
everything. But right now, close the bank a half-hour early,
announce the bank will meet all demands in the morning.
That half-hour will keep a lot of money here overnight in
the bank.'

'That can't hold back the deluge of withdrawals.'

George began to pace the priceless dusty-rose-and-pale-
blue Persian rug. 'Get your lawyer to work out a deed of
trust for you to sign. To convert all your real and personal
assets to a trustee who, if things get real bad, can use that
deed to reach a settlement with the creditors.'

The banker moaned, 'It mustn't come to that.'

'No, most likely not. A deed of trust is a kind of insurance of your assets aiding the bank assets. Sounds good, gives the board confidence.'

'I'll name Wallie Sharon as trustee of the deed. I made the man, and he's smart. Smarter than I was, that's for sure.'

'You have full faith in Wallie?'

Ralston looked up, mouth slightly ajar. 'Yes, of course.'

George looked at his watch, snapped the lid shut. 'Good. I have to be going. Got a bank of my own you know, Bill.' He smiled, patted the banker's shoulder. 'I had a grandmother who was a witch. People said so, anyway. A wise old biddy in her way, she told me once, "When you face desperate problems, big ones, shove your thumb up your ass and lift yourself off the ground."'

The banker laughed, the men shook hands, and George left by the rear exit, which was by now also surrounded by a huge crowd.

George woke early on August 27 to the cawing of a crow in the garden tree. He had dreamed it was *his* bank that was in trouble—the Pacific-Harvesters Bank going up in flames, the gold coins in the vaults melting, flowing like yellow water into the street, and somehow the face of Moses Kendrick was shouting at him and quoting from some old book that George had once read long ago on a sailing ship. *'Every man has the right to utter what he thinks truth and every other man has a right to knock him down.'* Kendrick was intoning all this in evangelical tones punctuated by blows delivered with ebullient satisfaction.

And then he was eating *zabaglione* with a black-draped witch riding a goose—the two of them, the goose and his grandmother, flying in a sky of a perishing violet. *'There is a magic spring, Grego, guarded by a giant, and when you ask if you may drink, the answer is yes—the price is your right eye.'*

He came awake shaking, thinking of all the damn unpredictable stuff of dreams. He went into the kitchen, stirred up the fire in the cast-iron stove and added wood, made a pot of coffee. He sat in his dressing gown, barefoot, slippers forgotten, sipping the brew without sugar.

He had been wrong, so wrong, to tell William Ralston to sign a deed of trust. If things went wrong, the Ralston family would be stripped bare. George had to talk Bill out of the idea. Life was only desire and despair. What if dissension among the board took away Bill's lifework, his bank? 'Moses Kendrick could be the deciding voice in Ralston's fate. He's changed since the early days, when he and I marketed farm produce,' George said to himself. 'He's grown more smug. As Irena would say, God is his classmate. He hides a deficiency of pity for his fellowman with his role of public service as a senator and a trustee on Ralston's bank's board. Honest in his own way, good as his word; but a hard word is more likely than a generous one, I'm afraid.'

George gulped more coffee. He'd dress and go warn Ralston not to issue any deed of trust. Hearing sounds in the front hall, he went out to investigate. Fred was just coming in, top hat cocked to one side of his head, his cane held over a shoulder like a rifle, and he was trying to whistle. His smile was weak; clearly he had a fierce headache.

'Just coming in, Fred? So late?'

'Late?'

'It's about seven in the morning. You need some coffee.'

Fred gratefully accepted the steaming cup, explaining that he had attended the Bachelors' Ball sponsored by the Breckenridges. After that he and some of the Tevises and Mosses had gone down the coast to see the dancers at Lil's, then to the Alhambra to watch them gamble at faro.

George watched his son sip the coffee. 'And were you drinking the whole time? And gambling?'

Fred rolled his head, blinked. 'Not so much. Well, I played a little. I was copping my bets with a six-sided black chip on top.'

'And you lost. Sign any papers? Any IOU's?'

'Lost?' Fred fumbled in a jacket pocket and pulled out gold and silver coins, a fist full. 'Didn't lose, old man.'

'Call me "father," you insolent pup. I hope it's only one wild night because of the damn Bachelors' Ball. Never mind what I think, but there's your mother, Chuck, the family, *and* the bank. I'll ship you to Mexico, damn you, if this becomes a habit. I don't mind fun and I don't mind a young man doing a little deviling. But gambling, no. This family can't have that.'

'There was talk Billy Ralston gambled a bit on the roulette wheel in Virginia City.'

'The trouble he's in isn't from gambling.'

'There is nasty gossip. Louie Blue is offering six-to-two odds that the bank doesn't open this morning.'

George pursed his lips, looked at his dark handsome son and, like all immigrant fathers, thought of how hard he had worked in his own youth, the filth and dirt he had lived with, the agony of survival. But he held his peace and suppressed his opinion of youth's deficiency in common sense, of the self-indulgence of the young.

'Go take a hot bath, Fred, eat something solid, and sleep it off. Ralston isn't going under.'

Fred looked at his father put down the coffee cup, and hugged him. 'It's such a feeling of release, going reckless, doing crazy things. It scares me, Dad. I can't accept things the way others do, like Chuck.'

'Hell, the idea of faith in oneself may be the only reality any of us have, Fred. Now, don't wake your mother clattering up the steps and don't let her know how you spend your time when not at Berkeley studying law.'

'The law ... oh, yes. I'm learning how to flay people alive in the courts and make waistcoats out of their skins. Lawyers!'

'That's why I want you to be a lawyer. To protect the family's hide from *other* lawyers.' He patted his son's shoulder. 'Upstairs, git.'

He was proud of his two sons, and tried to recall the irresponsible comedy of his own coming of age. He had

238

once been like young Fred—full of piss and vinegar.... *Six-to-two odds the bank would not open? God damn!*

He dressed and wrote some letters he had to get to New York, and crossed to Montgomery Street at ten. The crowd could be heard even before he came in sight of the Bank of California's Roman-Greek facade. The people were curb to curb, tangled with horses, carriages, and buggies. Police were failing to keep order. Stones were being flung at the bank's windows. Next to losing your health, he thought, the worst is losing your money. Clearly the bank would not open this day. The shades were drawn. The crowd was getting violent. Pickpockets were working it already, adding to the confusion and anger. A police officer with apprehensive features had his helmet off and was wiping out its lining with a red bandanna.

'Hello, Mr Fiore, you too wanna get some of your cash outta the bank?'

'I have my own bank, Captain Hayes.'

'You do, you do, Mr Fiore. It's not goin' to open here. Notice on the door: "Closed for Audit. Reopening to Be Announced."'

'Yes, an audit.'

'There's a meetin' goin' on, all the big muckamucks goin' in the back looking a bit chalky, if you ask me.'

'That so?'

'No skin off my ass, Mr Fiore. My old woman keeps whatever we has in the mattress.'

23

George felt it was time to look after his own interests, take care of his own bank. There was a nervous contraction of his shoulder muscles. The streets seemed more dangerously restless than he remembered seeing ever before, but for some long-ago street fighting. Even people who had no accounts at the Bank of California were carrying on as if it were a national holiday, or even, George thought, a lynching.

The Pacific-Harvesters Bank had a small run of depositors of its own; more people than usual were moving cash about. Tom Floyd was opening the doors wide and holding them agape, holding them in that position with felt-covered bricks. 'Thought we'd show *our* depositors they didn't have to push the doors to get in.'

'A good idea. How are withdrawals?'

Tom adjusted the brick with a polished point of his shoe. 'Oh, a little bit more than usual this morning, but no panic. And when they see how calm things are, some don't pull any money out after all.'

There was a bit more activity than usual for such an early hour, but no signs of frightened clients. George waved to those he knew, spoke with an elderly Chinese man who imported dried herbs (and, it was suspected, smuggled slave girls). In a way, George's clients—the depositors, borrowers, and note signers—were different from the people who used Anglo banks. Pacific-Harvesters served mainly the Italian, Latin, and oriental communities, and the poorer of the orthodox Jewish businessmen. George knew most of his customers from years of contact; he had even encouraged some of them to make their first deposit in any bank.

He motioned to the head cashier, Peter Watson, an impressive man with a magnificent equine head.

'Get some bags of gold and silver coins out of the vault, Pete, and stand them around behind the tellers' windows, along with some packets of greenbacks. Let them see the real thing, not just penpushers and ledgers.'

'Yes, sir, Mr Fiore. What's doing at Ralston's?'

'They didn't open this morning. The trustees are meeting again. How much more in withdrawals this morning than usual?'

'About ten or fifteen percent.'

'Get me a full report by noon.'

Seated at his desk, looking at a vase of tea roses (Irena's offering from the Casa), he felt that banking was turning into a grotesque dream, that the rules by which he played no longer applied. It was enough to give you vertigo. How could things go so wrong? This was America, not the Italy, the Europe, of the landless, the voteless, the inarticulate living in wretched sheeplike obstinacy. True, every place had its ignorance and pretension; one could so easily be trapped on the flypaper of greed, entangled in moral misdeeds.

There was a money panic in the East which demanded George's attention. He examined last month's report of the bank's assets, its loans and investments, a report only he and Rocco knew existed. Money was tight. There was a seesawing around the zero point in bank profits—bad months, profitable ones—all in all, he was overloaded by outstanding loans to small vineyards, mortgages on old, uninsurable fishing vessels, and that damn hundreds of shares of railway line, the Pacific and Great Plains Railroad. It didn't get to the Pacific itself, but connected at Kingston Junction with the Central Pacific. Still, it should

241

show a good profit someday soon, hauling mine machinery into the foothills, carrying farm products, cattle, swine, sheep. He had been generous there because he wanted to show his faith in the stock to some of the richer Chinese like Gaw who were stockholders in the Pacific and Great Plains Railroad.

There was a tapping on his ope door (Never close yourself off from the people).

It was Hendricks, the assistant cashier of the Bank of California. He was panting through his open mouth, and a rather too small bowler hat was perched on the back of his head. Hendricks was usually calm. Now there was a tic in one cheek and the quivering of his hands—St Vitus's dance?

'Mr Fiore, Mr Ralston sent me.'

'Sit down here, have a drink.' It was best to ignore the twitch. The man sipped the glass of port George poured for him. He began to talk of the bad day, the bank not opening, the hostility of the crowd.

George held up a hand, shook his head. 'Never mind all that. Just *what* is happening? Did the trustees meet with Mr Ralston?'

'Well, may I have just a bit more of the wine ... usually I don't, you know, thank you ... Near noon Mr Ralston opened the meeting of the trustees. I was there to take notes, but Mr Sharon said no, just listen. You know Mr Sharon?'

'Not really. Seen him around town. Bill, Mr Ralston, introduced him to me, or me to him in the lobby of the Baldwin Theater. Shook hands. No, can't say I know William Sharon, but I'm aware of his career. Go on.'

'So, Mr Ralston outlined the bank's and his own situation to the directors. It wasn't new to me, not all of it. I knew of the four million he owed the bank and the two million he owed to Mr Sharon, yes. But holy gee, I didn't know the four million he also owed other creditors.'

'He had told me that.'

'Yes, he told me you knew his situation when he sent me

to see you.'

'Why did he do that?'

'Because of the meeting. Oh, he's a talker, I guess you know that, and he was serious and pretty grim as he explained he had only about four million of his own assets, just about half the bank was liable for. But he told them straight, the banks here in San Francisco have weathered other runs and panics. Hysteria, he said, mob hysteria causes a run *and* rumors. He told them a crowd has a hair-trigger reaction. A whisper can set them off.'

'What did he propose the bank do?' Out in the main lobby of the bank, there was chatter and other sounds. There was still a small run at the Pacific-Harvesters.

'He asked the board to give him time, Mr Fiore. He said the bank could remain closed for a little while; it has a good honest history and the business climate will improve. The bank doors would open again and things would go on as usual. All he wanted from them, he said, was faith and trust. He'd bring the bank through.... Well ...'

'He could be right. Things usually calm down after the first panic passes.'

Hendricks seemed to be counting his fingers. 'The men all listened poker-faced, known what I mean? No smiles, nothing but blank faces.' Hendricks gulped the rest of his drink, ran a hand across his brow. George noticed the man still wore the rubber fingertip that aided in the counting of a stack of bills. 'Senator Kendrick asked us, me and Mr Ralston, to step out of the room for a few minutes. And so we did. Mr Ralston, he had an unlit cigar in his mouth, but didn't light it. Just kept tearing little bits of paper off the notes he'd brought to the meeting and saying, "Wallie Sharon will kick their asses if they take too long."'

George half-closed his eyes and leaned back in his chair. Hendricks suddenly seemed calm, as if in talking he had regained his control. 'Senator Moe Kendrick came out and stood there facing Mr Ralston, hands behind his back. You know that voice he has for speech-making, the one that comes out of his gut and throat. He said, "William, the

243

directors have voted and demand that you step down." Mr Ralston, he stood there and then he said, "Who presented the motion?" and the senator said, "Sharon did and the vote was a majority agreement!" I near shit in my pants, hearing that, I tell you, Mr Fiore. Cold as Kelsey's nuts, the senator was. Yes sir, Mr Ralston just looked at the senator and motioned me to hand him a sheet of our good letterhead stationery. The kind with the steel engraving on it.'

George frowned. 'He wrote out his resignation right then and there? Wrong, wrong! He should have stalled, played for time.'

'He did resign, and the senator nearly offered his hand to shake on it, but then just took the letter and went back to the trustees, closed the door.'

'Jesus, did you know about Ralston's deed of trust? Giving the bank creditors everything he owns, land, home, everything?'

'No, I didn't. Mr Ralston was kind of walking in his sleep. He took his hat and cane, wound his watch, asked me to get him a hack. Any kind of carriage and horse.'

'Where'd he go?'

Hendricks took a folded bit of paper from a soft leather wallet and handed it over. 'I was to let you know how things went and give you this.'

'You know what's in it?'

'Yes, Mr Fiore, I looked. A letter … and some sealed papers to hold for him. I was afraid it was maybe, well, showing he was going to do some harm to himself.'

'Not Bill Ralston. He's copper-lined and steel-riveted.' George looked at the note he had unfolded. The handwriting was calm enough, looked almost like an engraving. George thought of a man who had been a billing clerk on the rough hard runs of a Mississippi riverboat. It read:

George,
  I need a cooling off. Going to the Neptune Baths at

five; please meet me there. And put this sealed packet away. I might need it some day and I'd feel better knowing you are keeping it safe for me.

Bill

George refolded the note. 'Thanks, Hendricks. No use lamenting—from here on, survival is all. Bill will come through somehow, and give those cocksuckers their comeuppance. As for you, if the bank doesn't reopen, I can find a place for you with the Pacific-Harvesters.' He smiled. 'We're not fancy with marble and bronze, but it's a good place to work.'

After Hendricks departed, George sat for a long time thinking about banal things like destiny, failed faith, and small souls in power.

George had little time that afternoon to brood over Ralston's fate. There was a crush in the bank that afternoon by a group of Italian vineyard owners, with Caeser Spinelli the spokesman. *'Benvenuto benvenuto, come sta?'* With this happening in the Bank of California, would the winemakers be able to get loans they needed for wine kegs, bottles, repairs to their grape presses? Could a panic result and money become difficult to arrange for with the banks? They trusted George, but premonitions of austerity and rumors of failure were rampant, and they needed him to assuage their fears.

George reassured them; loans would be arranged as usual. They all toasted with glasses of last year's wine, and agreed as to its goodness, *di molto*. After a round of proclamations of friendship and loyalty, and enthusiastic hugging, Tom took them to the front doors for the last *'Arrivederci.'*

It was four o'clock, and George decided to go to the Neptune Baths and Swimming Club at North Beach. It would be best for Ralston not to be alone on this cursed day of his personal crises. George took a hack to the Neptune and was surprised to discover a crowd milling around its entrance. Several police were pushing people back. It

245

hardly seemed possible that there would be anything around a bathing-and-swimming club to attract a crowd. George told a bulky policeman that he was a club member, and asked what had happened. The policeman stroked a broad thumb across his mustache. 'No information bein' given out.'

The crowd could scent trouble but had little information. George went into the club, to sounds of caustic derision offered the police. Sam Crowley, the lobby attendant, unlocked the door to let him in. Sam had a habit of clicking his set of china teeth together when excited, and they were clicking now.

'Took 'im away just ten minutes ago by the side alley. He was covered.'

'Who the hell are you talking about and *what's* happened?'

Sam clicked, inhaled. 'Mr Ralston, sir. He took a bathing suit and went for a swim in the bay.'

'When was this?'

''Bout three o'clock. Thereabouts. Two hours later a sand barge finds 'im floating. Drowned, suicide they said. All his troubles eating at him. Unbalanced his mind. People what come for the body, the morgue people, talked that his bank drove him to it.'

'No, I don't believe it. Did it strike you he was going to do … that he was thinking like that?'

'He was just like usual, Mr Fiore. Said, "Hello, Sam," changed to a suit, said, "Water looks cool, Sam," and he swum out like he often did …'

George felt disbelief turn to anger. William Ralston wasn't the kind of man, even under stress, to take his own life, and especially not by drowning. Even in defeat, under pressure Bill Ralston would exude vitality and pride. Not a man, ever, to drown himself. Just a month ago in this very club after a session in the steam room, they had sat sipping cool drinks and Ralston had insisted to some pessimistic member who had taken a beating in commodities that life was unique and precious. George felt giddy with an eerie

246

apprehension that something was out of whack.

He asked Sam, 'The family ... has Mrs Ralston been notified?'

'Cap Hayes said they'd notify the family. He was a good man, weren't he, sir? Sensible?'

George said he thought so and made his way down the narrow lane to the city morgue, an unimpressive red brick building. He had never been inside, but forced himself past the glass-paneled doors into deep-green-painted hallways smelling dreadfully of some chemical and the odor of something else he didn't want to give a name to. There were flaring gas lights in a small office and behind a desk sat a wide little man with a brown beard, gold-rimmed glasses, wearing a gray smocklike garment.

He waved George away. 'No statement to the papers, nothing.'

'I'm not a journalist. I'm a friend of William Ralston. George Fiore.'

'Banker? Oh, yes, well, I'm Dr Semmel, coroner.' The doctor had a Teutonic accent and dark eyes magnified by his eyeglasses. 'He's dead enough, *ja*, or he woodend be here.'

'Could I ... I ...?'

'Vant to see the body, of course, this way.'

The room George was led into was damp, taps were running, a gas light hissed, a wall of storage doors gave off the chill of melting ice. A Mexican-Aztec-faced man was swabbing the wet concrete floor with a tangled mop. On a marble-covered table lay a shape under a gray sheet. The little doctor whipped off the sheet as if unveiling a public statue. The dead people George had seen before had always seemed asleep rather than dead. But the body of William Ralston looked *very* dead, the face a sadly fixed freezing of features in some last consciousness. The fingers were rigid and extended indecently; the thick pubic bush showed genitalia, somehow tragic but not offensive.

George identified the odd smell of embalming fluid. 'He

was a powerful swimmer, Dr Semmel; it could have been an accident of some sort. As for talk of ...'

'We'll not know for sure till I do a more detailed autopsy. Such a death of a prominent man calls for one to be sure, and there is the insurance company. They will insist we autopsy. A suicide they do not pay, *nein?*'

George handed over a card. 'Will you send me a copy of your report? I'd be grateful.'

'But of course, Mr Fiore.'

It was two days before the autopsy report reached George. He had gone the morning after the sad event out to Belmont, to enter for the first time the elegant mansion of the Ralstons. He had met Emma Ralston twice at some public events, a mere greeting of 'Pleased to meet you' after an introduction. Now she sat in the bay window of the front parlor, the shades drawn, velvet drapes half pulled down. George was aware of the gilt frames of large oil paintings, mostly landscapes. The furnishings were exquisite, a grand piano crouching in one corner, a tall Chinese vase filled with some kind of dried branches in another. Emma Ralston was not dressed in black, but in a deep gray gown. On the right sleeve was a wide band of black. She was a large-boned, handsome woman in middle age; her gently waving hair was showing gray. A black-piped handkerchief was neatly folded and held in one hand. She showed some traces of weeping—a reddish outline around her eyes, a tired corner to her tight-lipped mouth.

'Sit down, Mr Fiore,' she said in a low firm voice, indicating a highbacked chair by a delicate marquetry table.

'Thank you, Mrs Ralston. I suppose everything I could say about losing one's closest friend has been said.' What an ineffectual remark, he thought.

'It's good of you to come.' She made a wry gesture with her mouth. 'Not too many have. The trustees I refused to see.'

'You know how things were?' George felt perverse, sweaty under his collar. 'I mean ...' He couldn't match her

248

stoic acceptance.

'Yes, Mr Fiore. The morning of the board meeting, he came to me and said, "What the hell, Emma, if everything goes, I can start all over again." He added, "Remember we once lived on fifty dollars a month. We can again if we have to." Then he went away to the meeting.' Now she was silently weeping.

'That sounds like Bill.'

She recovered, sniffed, and used the handkerchief. 'Yes, he was still a man in his prime, my husband. Oh, the shock of Sharon and that Kendrick leading the vote to ask Bill to step down … The sons of bitches! Excuse me, Mr Fiore. We faced a lot together since the early days; it wouldn't have caused him to …' She didn't finish, just waved a hand in the air.

George wanted to bring up the matter of the deed of trust that would take everything away from her, even this mansion. And insurance—surely a man like Ralston would have life insurance of sixty to a hundred thousand dollars. Wouldn't it be paid? He left after a handshake. He looked back at the mansion, a bit too massive and proud, but one man's idea of a reward for himself and his family after a life of accomplishments…. And how well had he known William Ralston? A surface friendship, a mutual liking for each other, but between them a veil of inscrutability, a discreet avoidance of probing into each other's agonizing dilemmas, forbidden thoughts and emotions. And, in the other direction, they had failed to express to one another their intoxication with life, their visions of delight in tawny mountains and blue distances; to confide those moments when all seems a void of unanswered questions.

It was Police Captain Hayes, a close friend of George's, who brought him Dr Semmel's autopsy report.

The captain refused a drink but took a cigar, sniffed it, put it away in a jacket pocket. 'For later, thank you. This is just between us two, of course. No one must know I've shown this to you.'

George read the two-page report quickly. Semmel's

handwriting was in a calligraphic European style, and some of that in a medical Latin beyond George's skill to translate.

The captain was seated well back in his chair, his eyes steadily focused on George. 'You get the gist of it?'

'Death by accident.'

'That's malarkey for the New York life-insurance johnnies. There is a sixty-five-thousand-dollar policy they'll have to pay Mrs Ralston. The half-sheet of the report is *only* for you, George, because we go back a long time together.'

George looked down at the separate half-sheet and read: *'The subject's lungs contained no water, indicating that he had not drowned. There was also congestion in the brain, which suggests he could have been suffocated.'*

The captain made no comment as he stood to leave. George asked him, 'Nothing more to say, is there, Hayes?'

'Not by me, and not by you. Higher-ups are involved. When two of the trustees, John Mackey and Wallie Sharon, were asked to identify the body, I took them into the morgue where he was laid out, and Mackey said to Sharon, "Couldn't they have revived him?" and Sharon whispered—I was close and I've a keen ear—"For a while, I was afraid they would." That's what Mr Ralston's best friend and turncoat said.'

George cried out, 'But something must be done about this!'

'Hold your water, George. I'm just doing you a personal favor even by telling you this. You'd be pissing up a rope to try to do anything more. I'll not swear to what I heard, Mackey won't. Like a sick cat who's shit in the flowerbeds, we'll all have to kick the dirt over it.'

'Murder! The trustees were all old Regulators, or their supporters. It *was* murder!'

'Accident,' said Hayes. 'Death by water. Good day to you, George, and thanks for the cigar. I know you understand that my career depends on your keeping quiet about all this.'

250

Tom Floyd found George standing at the window long after the bank had closed, the lamps lit over the vaults. George pointed to the autopsy report, indicating that Tom should read it. After he put the papers back on the desk, Tom gave a short whistle. 'Lock it away. Better still, Major, burn the fucking thing. You keep your nose clean ...'

'You're a hard-hearted bastard, Tom. I feel I should bring all this into the open. Jesus, all his so-called friends just ganged up on him. I'll demand a hearing. If only I could be sure it wouldn't backfire on Hayes ...'

'You're not going to do that.' Tom came closer. 'It would tear the city apart, bring in bank investigators, maybe the feds. The doc could claim somebody forged his writing on that private note, and the townspeople will turn against you for bringing this up, even close down the bank. And you'd ruin Captain Hayes, who trusts you to keep this confidential.'

'I know all that, but I have to do something!'

'You know, I've been studying law a bit, knocking Blackstone and other books around. Why don't you write a private letter to the attorney general in Sacramento? You know him personally. Put all this before him, Major, to take note of.'

'What will he do?'

'Do? He'll do nothing, nothing at all. He's not going to open the privy. He's one of the Native Sons. He's no jackass. He's going to run for governor and will need backing and lots of money from all bankers. Also, there is no evidence that will really stand up in court. Who will you accuse of foul play? Maybe Senator Kendrick? Or millionaires and "respectable" men like Sharon, Mackey, O'Brien?'

George said bitterly, 'So I'll be off the hook with one letter. I can say to myself, I did *something*.'

'Believe me. You once said survival is all.'

The attorney general praised George's interest and did nothing. The deed of trust took every last asset of the Ralston estate. In time, the panic had abated and the Bank

251

of California reopened to a brisk business of deposits and withdrawals. There was a banquet at the Palace Hotel at which the press reported: 'William Sharon and Senator Moses Kendrick were cheered as the heroes who saved the Bank of California.'

George Fiore did not attend the banquet. He was away in the High Sierra Madres with his sons, teaching them the finer points of dry-fly trout fishing.

24

'The Ralston Mystery,' as some called it, was mulled over in bars for months. Evil plotting was hinted at by journalists hoping for a free drink at the Palace or the Poodle Dog. Gradually other events took precedence—talk of congressional investigations of the railroad swindles involving the Big Four, for example. Moses Kendrick retired from politics when Sarah died, and his son Judge Homer Kendrick became senator. There was even talk that in a few years he'd be running for the presidency, but Kendrick's support was not national in scope, his boosters being mostly from the West.

The Fiores and Velasquezes had tragedies of their own. Tomas Velasquez had died in Europe. Rumor said that he fell dead by the roulette wheel in Monte Carlo, surrounded by *filles de joie*, at a gambling party hosted by the Duke of Devonshire. The truth was that he died in his sleep after a very happy decade in Europe, living in style or borrowing until his next remittance came from Irena to buy an early Pissarro or a few good bottles of wine. Tomas was always a favorite among the demimonde, with his love of good food, good drink, and the good life.

His son, Ramon, was in Brittany painting seascapes when Tomas died. Ramon came back to Paris, buried Tomas in a Catholic cemetery at Lagny, where the padre accepted Tomas without questions as a faithful son of the Church.

Ramon wrote to Irena that he was coming back with his father's last will, a gold watch, six walking canes (one a gift from the Prince of Wales), and some unpaid bills from merchants on the Rue des Beaux Arts.

Irena had taken the news of Tomas's death very badly, to everyone's surprise. It had been assumed that she was well rid of him, glad to have him gallivanting about in Europe and out of her way. But she had loved him, even when it proved impossible to mold his personality to her desires. His refusal to accept responsibility infuriated her, yet she accepted—even enjoyed—his irreverence.

'Always a gentleman,' she told George and Maria, who had come to console her. She waved a black handkerchief in the air. '*À poco, à poco!* Little by little, we are all slipping away.'

George figured she must be fifty years old, or almost that. Village records were not too accurate. Now she sat large and corseted, feet a bit swollen. But George saw a great deal of the old fire still burning in her, even if it now flared in odd directions. She took such strange postures! She favored votes for women, castration of rapists, and the training of apes to pick fruit.

Irena's strong impulses were usually under control. She attended the mass for Tomas's soul—*Iais Hominum Salvator*—which Maria insisted be said. George was aware that Irena had taken lovers, often gentlemen riders at the local horse shows or a navy captain from a coastal-survey vessel. They were always men with 'a gloss of gentility,' as Irena confessed to Father Zorilla. 'A Velasquez wife, even one with a weakness in the flesh, can't disgrace the family name by being in sin with just *anybody*.' Father Zorilla sadly ordered Hail Marys and Our Fathers....

Charles and Fred met Ramon at the train station as the Overland came in spouting smoke and cinders.

Ramon, too, had grown. He was still slim, but his face was longer with the more angular planes of maturity. He sported a thin mustache, a blue travel cape, and a flat wide-brimmed hat. The proper figure, he hoped, of one of Henri Murger's characters from *Scènes de la vie de bohème*. The cousins' greetings were warm and boisterous.

Charles asked, 'How is your painting going?'

Ramon smiled, waved a hand with a blue-stoned ring on it. 'It's gone. I'm a very good painter, but not a *great* one. So ...'

'What's the difference?' asked Fred. 'Girls, wine, Paris ... Being good is enough, Ramon. Who cares who smears the most paint?'

Ramon shook his head. 'No, it's the angle of vision, Fred. You look at the art in the Louvre, meet men like Monet, Degas. After that, you can accept only the very best as worth following.'

Fred whipped up the horse. 'You're like Chuck here, loving working in the bank and driven always to be the best.'

'If Uncle George will have me, that's what I'd like to do, too. I can still paint for my own satisfaction. And there's art in all of life. After all, the Rothschilds have made banking romantic. And Balzac tells us that the deep desires for fame and wealth drive most of us.'

'Balls-who?' asked Fred. 'Never mind, we'll have a night on the town after things have settled down. Chuck'll set up some fancy Chinky quif for us.'

'Shut up, Fred. Papa doesn't like disrespect for the Chinese, and neither do I.'

'I think Chuck's got a tootsie down in Chinatown.'

Ramon looked over the hills, green from rain, the lofting landscape. 'It's all so much bigger, wilder than the little farms of France.'

The buckboard moved on upward past the start of the Velasquez land, passing sheep browsing, rows of grape vines heavy with fruit. Ramon said, 'Not too bad to come home a failed expatriate. Mama taking it hard?'

Charles replied, 'Aunt Irena is taking it dramatically.'

Irena wept and cried out, *'Bambino! Benvenuto! Come stai!'* as she embraced her son, and yelling at the servants to see to the food, the wine. 'So tall, so handsome the face, like dear Tomas.' Wiping her nose with the black lace handkerchief: 'You speak French?'

Before Ramon could prove it, Uncle George arrived with Aunt Maria, said it was sad about Tomas and that it was good to see Ramon back home. Would he come to the bank in a few days to talk things over?

Ramon asked about Uncle Rocco.

'He's in Los Angeles,' said Charles. 'Running the branch of the Pacific-Harvesters Bank down there. He's still Rocco.'

'He's mentioned in Papa's will. Rocco gets a pair of Louis XIV dueling pistols.'

Two days later, Matt Gower gathered the family in the parlor of the Casa to read the last will and testament of Tomas Velasquez. Tomas had made this new one in London just a few months before he died. The old lawyer sipped from a cup of black coffee and fingered the stiff sheets of heavy paper.

'It's a good valid will, replacing one on file with me. Heavy English language but quite *proper* under our laws. Tomas Velasquez wrote it out himself with some legal help. Well, to begin: "I am Tomas Orvando Velasquez of the Casa Cuesta in the state of California of the United States of America, and having retained my citizenship in that nation and being of sound mind and aware of mortality, time, place, and world events, this is my last will and testament."' The lawyer looked up. 'Interesting phrasing. "I leave much love to all I know. To my dear wife, Irena, great affection and admiration; also to George and Maria Fiore, good people, on whose shoulders I have often brought my problems. I thank them for being close and friends. To my nephews Alfredo and Cesare, the hope they

255

will always retain and return the love of my son, Ramon. That takes care of saying farewell to the family who, when I was with them, showed how close in affection true relationships can be. Of others, people the family may not know, I leave in an added page some little things consisting of my Escoffier's, *Guide Culinaire*, a tie pin, a snuffbox, meerschaum pipes."'

The lawyer looked up and took a sip of coffee; he motioned to the servant. 'A little hot coffee, please—this has cooled.'

Irena shook her head. 'Tomas was a kind man, he was a man *di molto*, who made everything seem easy, casual.'

The lawyer sipped the replenished cup. 'Yes, now to the actual beneficiaries. You can all examine the document later, but to strip it of the legal jargon, I'll simplify. The entire estate of Velasquez holdings, land, herds, vineyards, all else, whatever shares of stock certificates, all go in trust to his wife, Irena Fiore Velasquez, who will arrange for five thousand dollars a year to be paid their son, Ramon, and a provision that any stock of the Pacific-Harvesters Bank be divided between the two of them. To George and Maria Fiore, he leaves the collection of Callot and Goya prints in the library. To his dear nephews Alfredo and Cesare, a shotgun each, to be picked from the collection in the Casa tack room, as well as a Henry and Winchester rifle each. They are to divide the fishing tackle with his son.'

The lawyer slowly sipped coffee. 'There are, as mentioned, certain gifts, small sums of money, snuffboxes, rings, some sets of ... well, *odd* engravings and photographs to go to certain friends and ... *hmm*, women in Europe ... You can read it for yourself. He claims Ramon is his only legal issue and anyone making claims of any sort is to be paid one dollar. His only legal marriage is by court and Church to Irena Fiore Velasquez; to any other claims, the same dollar is to be paid. Oh, yes, to Old Julio and Young Julio, the pick of a horse each from the best stock at the Casa Cuesta.'

Irena picked away at her handkerchief. 'The man Tomas

was also often a bit of a fool.'

Maria asked, 'Nothing to the Church for novenas?'

'I'm sure he knew the family would arrange for those.'

The next Monday, Ramon joined Charles at the bank, to learn a multitude of ways of making or losing money; how to get along with clients, whether they be farmers, ranchers, or widows; and how it all related to commodities, markets, and the game of dealings and double-dealings on Wall Street.

As he told Charles, 'If I have any regrets about giving up art, I have no remorse.'

He had a vulnerable innocence about banking and soon learned under George's tutelage that banks didn't really put one's money away in vaults for safekeeping, that all that existed were inky recordings in ledgers; the money itself was long gone as loans, as expenses and sometimes as dead losses never to return to the bank.

He and Charles got along well. He saw Fred less often and had less in common with him because of Fred's lack of interest in banking.

Fred and his Aunt Irena were breeding dogs and raising horses. Ramon enjoyed living with his mother, but it was time-consuming and often difficult to cross over to the city. One day Charles suggested they share a flat he had his eye on near Pioneer Park on Telegraph Hill.

'I want to get away from Nob Hill, Ramon. I don't want my comings and goings picked over.'

Ramon agreed. 'It would be a bit like Paris.... Hell, I've got to stop comparing things to life there.'

'If you miss it, you should go back.'

'No, there's the estate to manage, and I don't want to be like a few hundred half-assed American failures there. Second-rate painters, writers; mooching drinks, living in attics, keeping up the romantic notion that they are talented.'

'I like your painting fine.'

'Covers holes in the wall.'

They hung several of the pictures in the three-room flat

that they took in the second story of a tall lean house with fine bay windows overlooking the water.

Charles loved the paintings they hung of trains entering the Gare St Lazare, the Seine with Notre-Dame dark against a brooding sky; and a view of the Butte's *boîtes* and cafés on a festive day with crowds and flags.

Ramon was more objective. 'Too much Cézanne, too much Monet, *not* enough Ramon.'

'Never heard of those blokes.'

'God, to be able to see everything new. Show the world as it's never been seen.'

Charles got some discarded furniture and kitchenware from home, Ramon provided a round-bellied stove for heating and what little cooking they would do. Fred lugged over an old set of Mexican chairs and sofa made of woven rawhide and polished piñon wood. The bank came up with an old Turkey-red carpet. Various items such as tables and a little bar were improvised from slabs of redwood and ships' hatches found in the bay.

Charles bought brass beds the dealer swore had once been used in a luxury brothel. Ramon liked simplicity; a pine cupboard, a solid chair, a green-shaded lamp furnished his room. Charles had a Chinese screen, framed woodcuts from *Harper's Weekly*, lamps of stained glass, and cushions of various colors. The two young men thought of themselves as gay young bachelors, original wits, *bon vivants*, men-about-town, unaware that they were following a pattern, hardly original, of the young male in society, based on physical needs, ideas of amusement and entertainment. They gave a beer-and-rarebit party for young men like themselves and several 'fast girls.' It was a noisy and boisterous gathering. Ramon sang *'Oui moins p'r aller!'* and *'Mourir pour la patrie'*, and Fred tried what passed for Gilbert and Sullivan. The party lasted into the early hours of the morning, when Tom Floyd began dancing on the table and had to be helped to his boarding house by two guests.

George usually went sailing with Rose and Maude on Sundays. Maude at twelve years old was lively. She was learning to handle the small sailboat, how to tack, to duck the boom, and to handle the tiller—all with help from 'Uncle George,' who had been a sailor long ago and had a tattoo to prove it.

'Do you think Ramon did right in giving up painting, George? He has a marvelous color sense.' Rose clasped her knees, gazing out at the water.

'Nobody twisted his arm to stop; he just felt if he couldn't be the best, he didn't want to be second best.'

'Second best in Paris is better than being top dog here.'

'You don't mean that, Rosie—my true blue Californian?'

'Why not? I keep thinking if Maude's music shows signs of real progress, I might want her to study in New York or even Europe.'

'Rosie, Rosie ... ' He grasped her hand. 'All we have is each other and Maude, of course. Let's not rush the future. She may want to be a sailor—hard aport, honey!'

Rose smiled. 'Just dreaming out loud. But what if Maude *is* a genius?'

'Grab that line!' George shouted.

'The genius nearly fell overboard ... Maude, get over to starboard.'

George watched his daughter and frowned. He was troubled by Rose's grandiose, if understandable, ambitions for Maude. Rose was deeply affectionate, resourceful, yet her independence made her seem somehow apart. When acting like a woman (he thought), she could be fractious, often as if she were hiding a part of herself away from him. That would be her poetry-writing side, he thought, like Ramon's integrity about paintings. These damn artists, always playing the game of the conflict between the two sides of human nature, with their whims and fancies, as if a banker doesn't have them, too.

It was at times like this that George felt outside Rose's and Maude's life. His life was so dominated by business and

259

the booming city. Business was good or bad, there was crime, there was political power—often in the wrong hands—but there was also, George knew, a greatness in this city, a beauty of hills and bay. It was the people he most admired, though, always striving and forever curious. It distressed him that as the city grew, the pioneer spirit which had made its people unique was slowly waning and the social stratification of the East was becoming more apparent, though the backgrounds of the upper crust would make an Astor shudder.

A society of exclusiveness was forming, based as the old song 'The Forty-Niners married the Barbary Coast whores and sired the Native Sons.' 'Nouveau riche' was the expression applied by easterners to miners and beanhouse waitresses who had made their pile and now ate off Spode. There were even, as Ramon discovered, copies of Burke's *Landed Gentry* and Debrett's *Peerage* in the public library.

Though the nation scoffed at California's gentry, Washington recognized the state's political value. Homer Kendrick was making quite a reputation as a United States senator. 'Earnest, rough-edged, with the cool, calm grace of a mountain eagle,' as the Chicago *Tribune* wrote of him at the Republican national convention, there was talk of his being nominated to the 'highest office in the land.'

Well, thought George, then why not *any* American-born boy? Even my son Charlie. He's steady, responsible, and intelligent. Couldn't do better than him if you look for a hundred years. But, no, I guess he's moving in other directions. Well, we'll just have to see.

25

Charles liked the busy streets, the world of Chinatown bordered by Bush Street and Pacific Street. He knew Kearny and Powell and Grant Avenue running through it. A world isolated and foreign; dried ducks nearly as flat as cardboard banging in windows, the pungent smell of Chinese herbs, and shop signs of great gold-and-red letters, their words like spiderwebs to occidentals. He loved the bright mounds of golden oranges, kumquats, lichees, and bags of crystal rice: the odors of sesame oil and ginger, and everywhere men with pigtails carrying bundles wrapped in matting.

Though the streets were calm now, he recalled how wild Chinatown had been during the seventeen prodigious days of the New Year when the Chinese Consolidated Benevolent Association, Gaw's rivals, with their Six Companies, had brought their long dragons into the streets and scattered goodies and coins while the smoke of incense was everyplace. And the Chinese girl, Moon Orchid, had stood on the balcony with her maids, tossing down coins and colored streamers of red and yellow paper.

There was an emotional confusion in him. In fantasy he imagined a meeting, in reality he knew he was a fool ever to dream of it.

Still, he continued to visit Chinatown and meet with Gaw, hoping in vain to catch a glimpse of the Chinese girl. The final arrangements for the mortgages were being approved, and he would no longer have excuses to go to Chinatown. George was talking of sending him to Sacramento to work with Zimmerman, a former cashier, who was to open a new branch of the Pacific-Harvesters Bank.

Six months after he and Ramon had moved into their flat, Charles was returning in late afternoon from inspection of a vineyard asking for a loan from the bank. Ramon was visiting his mother at the Casa, and Charles was feeling a bit depressed. He had been reading Emerson: *'Beware what you desire, you will get it'* and *'Things are in the saddle and ride mankind.'*

He was washing up, drying his hands, when there was a light tapping on the door. He called, 'Come in,' but the tapping continued, more a sort of enigmatic scratching. He threw down the towel; he opened the door and a small Chinese girl stood there, wide-eyed with doubt, or was it fear? She wore a dark coat and flowered hat that didn't go with her moon face, large precocious dark eyes. He recognized her as the little maid who had attended Moon Orchid. Was it another erotic dumpling to be delivered? No, it was an envelope fragrant with sandalwood. The object was thrust at him, and as he accepted it, the girl turned and fled.

He sniffed the envelope, baffled, turning it over and over in his fingers. He closed the door slowly, as if expecting a return of the Chinese girl. Carefully he tore off a corner of the envelope and ripped it open. There was a stronger, spicy smell from the very thin pale green paper, folded over twice. The handwritten note looked much like a schoolchild's first efforts at putting words together with printed capital letters. It had been lettered with red crayon: I MUST GET AWAY. YOU FIND ME MUCH ATTRACTIVE, I FOUND YOU TOO SO ATTRACTIVE. I AM A WOMAN, YOU A MAN. MEET ME TOMORROW TWO O'CLOCK AT THE ENGLISH SHOP GRANT STREET. MOON ORCHID.

The message seemed strangely emphatic, but like a bad jest. It sounded (he frowned) earnest, with a touch of desperation. Was it genuine? Or was it some wily trap by Quong Lao Gaw to test him? He tried to imagine some sinister motive only an oriental mind could figure out. He, of course, had no intention of being at the English Shop at the time named. He poured himself a drink. It could even be a bribe. He swallowed the drink slowly. Yes, a bribe of a beautiful girl's body, a delicate or mischievously clever bride. Was Quong Lao Gaw the type who would offer such a cherished possession? Hardly. Charles envisioned the splendid body of the girl spread-eagle on his bed. She was a puzzle, bewitching him. The scent of perfume was strong. Certainly she was amazingly beautiful and desirable. He carefully returned the note to its envelope and locked it away in a metal box that he kept in his trunk, placing it between two bags of gold.

He grimaced at himself in the mirror and decided he would do nothing. If it was a trap or a bribe, hints would come to him. If it was truly a plea for help from a valuable slave girl of the most powerful Chinese merchant and businessman on the West Coat, Charles had better avoid it. In the back of his mind, the popular San Francisco poem came to mind:

> That for ways that are dark
> And for tricks that are vain,
> The heathen Chinese is peculiar ...

Old Hairy Lips often thought about, and liked to tell Moon Orchid and Flower Seed, how there had been a time in her distant past when she had been young and the pampered mistress of a great house in Lanchow, the favorite of the great scholar Ku-Hung-Ming, he who had edited an edition of that Chinese classic *Mustard Seed Garden*.

Gaw had put her in charge of Moon Orchid and she was much trusted. Moon Orchid had been extraordinarily kind and had procured—stolen from Gaw—for Old Hairy Lips—a two-ounce ball of black pitch opium. In the outer room that protected the inner portal of Moon Orchid's quarters the old woman was preparing the *yeng-tsiang* pipe of polished orangewood. She reclined on her couch facing a *ken ten* lamp on a small table, where a blue flame burned steadily. From a little silver box she lifted up a soft round pellet of the drug and with great care rolled it between thumb and forefinger.

Skillfully rolling the *gow hop*, making it ready for the needle, she held it over the flame. The *gow hop* sizzled, giving off the sweetish odor of heaven and the key to the gate of dreams.

Moon Orchid appeared, dressed in an American dress and coat of dark blue. On her head sat a flowered bonnet.

'The old dragon sleeps?' she asked Flower Seed.

'Like a stone chow dog. But must you still plan this mad meeting with the white devil?'

Moon Orchid stood very still as she looked down on the drugged old woman. It was now that she must decide. As Moon Orchid stood by the old drugged body, she knew she had to come to a moment of final decision. To go? To stay?

Flower Seed whispered in ludicrous quavering tones, 'I am not going.'

'You are. You are my servant.'

'I am much filled with fear.'

The old woman stirred. Moon Orchid bit her lower lip. Her eyes betrayed her fright to Flower Seed, but Moon Orchid's stance was also one of determination.

'Come, get your cape and accompany me.'

'I'm scared. The master will comb our bodies with steel claws. He will hang us on the wall hooks like smoked ducks!'

'I'll strangle you myself, Flower Seed. I don't intend to die of old age here.'

Flower Seed flung herself at Moon Orchid and they stood hugging each other. They listened to the sounds of the servants below them, going about their morning duties. Wide-eyed, mouths half-open, courage returning, Flower Seed and Moon Orchid wiped their tears away and, still trembling, went down a steep staircase that led to a storeroom of silks, special bales not kept with the other merchandise. Moon Orchid produced a long thin bar of brass, a bar divided down the middle, a Chinese key that fitted the intricate metal lock. She opened the door slowly and found herself looking down on the narrow outer staircase that led to an alley. She and Flower Seed carefully descended the iron steps and hurried along the dark alley which ran between two overhanging structures.

Behind a small window, an old man with a saffron-colored face was pushing noodles into his mouth from a blue bowl, working his chopsticks with greedy skill. Moon Orchid pulled Flower Seed back and they waited, crouching. The old man finished his noodles, wiped his face with his meager beard, broke wind, and sighed. Then he rose, tottered to a stand where a teapot stood over a pan of glowing charcoal.

Moon Orchid whispered, 'Now!' and pulled Flower Seed along with her. The alley took a turn to the left, and thirty feet ahead was a stout wooden door topped by a timber beam into which was set broken glass. Moon Orchid cursed, touched the latch on the door. At first it resisted, but there was no lock, just a latch lever, and the door opened inward. She and her maid found themselves in a weed-strewn lot. They ran past a boy with a bundle of reed baskets on his head and were soon on Grant Avenue. Here Chinese and white shoppers mixed, crowding the stalls and gossiping. Moon Orchid stopped in the doorway of *'Dr Chew, One Flight Up—Herb Medicines.'* She was breathing hard, her face damp.

Flower Seed clung to her. 'Oh, Moon, Moon, what shall we do now?' She plucked at pots of mimosa and oleander.

'Get to the English Shop.' Moon Orchid tried to speak calmly but her heart was a fluttering caged bird in her chest. It was fine enough to be romantic and bold and project dreams, even to try to put one into reality. She wondered at her daring foolishness. What was she but the unused toy of a revolting old man? A slave girl. Yet, out in the open, her truculence was melting; she was tempted to return the way she and the maid had come—back to Quong Lao Gaw. Give it all up as a dream, a mad dream. Yes, go back to be handled by old swine. Dress well, eat well, and accept a future like Old Hairy Lips's.

Moon Orchid felt the reality of her perceptions crumble. What did she know of the big blond man? Only that he looked handsome, genial, substantial. He had given her that interested series of male glances that she knew so well. Only glances. He would not be at the English Shop. Flower Seed with a keening murmur pulled on her sleeve. 'I am full of fear. I shall wet my clothes.'

'*Damn!*' Moon Orchid said in English, then added in Chinese, 'Go back in the hallway, lift your clothes, and get it over with. Go!' She slapped the maid and laughed at her woebegone expression. Somehow this natural reaction of her maid with her frightened little bladder gave Moon Orchid the courage to proceed, to go on to the English Shop.

The English Shop, which Moon Orchid often patronized, was run by a florid-complexioned cockney, Agnes Gilray. The long narrow shop featured robes, ribbons, buttons and cotton stockings. A section of the shop in the back served a '*Cup of Tea with Scones—25 Cents,*' or, if one knew Agnes well, a local whiskey brewed only God knew where.

The entrance was two steps down from the street, and the shop had one window made up of eight small panes of glass, under a sign:

THE ENGLISH SHOP
NOTIONS, DRY GOODS, ALSO A TEA SERVED

Charles looked at the blue bonnet displayed behind the panes. He had not intended to come this far, intended just to stand across the street and wait and see if the Chinese girl actually did show up for this mad adventure. He pulled his watch from his waistcoat, snapping up its double lids. Charles crossed the street carefully, using a board laid across the mud, remembering the story Rocco had told him of the man found stuck up to his hips in the mud during the early days of the town. When asked if he wanted help, the man replied, 'Yes, but I'm safe enough, I'm sitting on my horse.'

The jest took Charles's mind away from the fact that he was keeping an appointment, one he had definitely decided not to keep. It was ridiculous, letting his body betray his mind, the fact the bank could suffer because of this exploit.

He entered the shop, a bell tinkling overhead. The large woman with red hair was behind a counter measuring off some yellow cloth by extending her arm, while gripping the cloth and holding the other end to her nose—under the impression, Charles decided, that this was a yard.

'In a mo,' said the woman. 'Just finishing my measuring.'

He noticed the two figures seated at a table in the back. He nodded to the woman and walked back into the shop where three oak tables, round and scarred, were placed around a brick fireplace in which sections of some cut-up ship's mast smoldered. Moon Orchid looked up at him boldly. She felt for him great desire—and saw him also as an escape from the oppression of Gaw's world. Perhaps one feeling was stronger than the other, but right now she didn't know which.

Her cowering maid was seated at her side. A teapot covered with a cloth cozy was on the table, teacups, milk pitcher, and a plate of some brown crumbly little cakes.

'How fine of you to come, Mr Fiore.'

'Damn fool, more likely.' He smiled and was aware of the large woman at his elbow.

'A nice cuppa in this weather, sir?'

'Yes, it helps,' said Charles, sitting down.

'If you'd care for a drop of the strong … '

'Tea will do.'

Charles sat staring at Moon Orchid and Flower Seed. He seemed unable to begin. What frivolity did one talk to a Chinese beauty? 'I'm, a … be goddamned if I know what you're up to, Miss Moon. Damn if I do. Mr Gaw isn't a man to like this.'

Wide-eyed, Moon Orchid said simply, 'I am coming to you in my bad situation, to be the woman of your own. Do you not find me of desire?'

'That has nothing to do with it. You go back home where you belong—to Mr Gaw.' He looked around the shop, past the door into the street. 'Before he finds you two crazy girls are gone.'

'I often shop here, we are safe.'

Flower Seed, speaking Chinese as she gnawed on a cake, said, 'Master will kill us, master break our limbs, tear our face open with sharp iron combs.'

Moon Orchid leaned over and slapped her, then turned to Charles. 'I beg pardon for the noise of my stupid handmaiden.'

'Whatever she said may be right.'

Moon Orchid took his hand, her voice sweet and firmly serene. 'I have for you love, admiration. You are built as a man in size and limbs. I want you intimate—yes?' She paused, thinking of some term from a novel or newspaper to express herself, gave up, and added, 'You understand? You manhood and myself together, the yin and yang?' Her hand gestures made her meaning even more explicit.

'Oh, murder,' sighed Charles as Agnes set down a fresh pot of tea.

'If the gent and lady would care for a room upstairs, very private. Just say the word.'

Moon Orchid said, 'Know your place, woman. Please go.'

Charles felt caught between levity and lechery.

'It's open,' said the big woman, leaving as the bell clanged over the door and two women with feathered hats came in.

Moon Orchid laughed. 'Mr Fiore, I offer myself not just for the need to escape a bad life, but because I wanted to make love with you as soon as I see you at the banquet. I have never been had, is that the right expression?'

The confession was enough to make him choke on his

tea. *'What?'*

She lowered her eyes, telling herself her sexual impulses were not just a way of convincing this man to help her. But how was one to know? The devils in one's flesh play at more than one game at a time. Certainly it would help persuade him—but she knew she wanted him for more than that.

She took his hand, put it between her thighs. Through the silk he felt her body warmth, the yielding of young flesh under gentle pressure.

'Yes, *so*?' she whispered.

'So, what?'

'I mean, yes, I am the virgin.'

'You mean the old bastard Gaw didn't … hasn't … I mean, he … ?'

'He cannot gather the lust to make him stand up. Am I saying this clear?'

He waved a hand in the air, gulped his tea. 'Oh, yes, you are just fine.'

'Yes, fine. We go upstairs.'

'I'm not going to get into Gaw's bad graces, dammit! He may be having you watched right now.'

'I am like the girl in Jane Austen—I have made my mind up. You will find me wise as a woman. I have the pillow books, the pictures of Japanese masters, Utamaro, Hokusai, art of all the positions of man and women, the fine games.'

God, even if she spoke insanity, she was such a beauty! She sat with such grace, such a tilt to that magnificent head. And she was so earnest, even if she shocked Charles a bit. Jane Austen? This glorious girl had an unexpected and mysterious personality. He removed his hand from its warm nest and felt Moon Orchid reach for his crotch. He stood up hastily like a schoolboy suddenly caught in a forbidden act.

'Now, look, you two have me boxed into a situation that isn't as simple as you think. Maybe if I were not in San Francisco, if I were … Oh, damn, too many ifs, maybes.'

Moon Orchid stood up, her head tilted forward, her dark

searching eyes focused on his face. 'Maybe it's not just right at *this* moment. Yes, I am for you whenever you want. Remember, I want for you.'

Charles felt sweat roll down his armpits. God's balls, she was attractive! There was something in the sight, the odor of her that was painful to lose. But he was, he told himself, a hardheaded banker. He wasn't going to test her love in a tacky teashop. Or get the bank in trouble in an amoral moment of tight pants.

'We shall see,' he said.

'Yes.' She took his hand and slipped it under her loose clothes and he grasped a warm breast, felt the stiff nipple, noted her slightly open mouth, the message of her eyes, a ready woman. Wrong woman, wrong man, wrong place.

Her voice broke a bit. 'You swear as you hold me here you will send for me when the time is right? My maid will be in touch with you.'

'I'll do what I think is right.' He released the breast, his loins aching with desire. Damn! *Élan vital*, Ramon would call it.

Moon Orchid bowed. 'I wait.' At these final words she gestured magnificently with her head and walked to the door of the shop, Flower Seed staring back at Charles over her shoulder.

He puffed air out through his mouth. Unreal, *unreal* he told himself. This is not the Arabian Nights, no, this is the modern era, 1879. There was still a trace of her musklike perfume. Fred had been so right when he said, 'A man chases a woman until she catches him.'

Charles handed the woman two silver dollars. 'Very good tea.' He went out into the street, trying to relax mentally, physically. It was a tiger-bright day. Carriages and drays were splashing mud, people were coming out of saloons and stores. The sun shone and the town was going about in its confident manner as if every day a beautiful Chinese virgin offered up her love, her body.

He went into the Shipmates Saloon and had a three-finger tot of bourbon in a shot glass. Three Negro minstrels in red coats and high gray hats were plucking their banjos and singing a ballad about a yella gal and a randy preacher. The crowd listened, drank, gambled. There was a faro table open, and two tables were active in poker. Charles had another bourbon and almost asked if he could sit in on a game.

But instead, he just stared at the bar mirror and its scrollwork, and up at two oil paintings of nudes hung low over the bar. The stomach of one was pulsating, the navel moving in and out. God damn, he was bewitched, everything was a sexual image. Moon Orchid was so desirable, and perhaps in him it was not the mere itch of lust but wanting someone to love. But he was certainly feeling strange. Animated paintings! What had been in that tea?

The barman watched Charles staring at the reclining nude. 'Damnedest thing ain't it?'

'What?'

'That whore's belly button and them stomach muscles twitching. It's all done by clockwork, a key you wind up in the back of the picture. See, it beats the picture back and forth ... think she's breathing, don't-cha?'

'You certainly do have an illusion there.'

'First one of the coast. Come round the Horn with some engine to make steam beer. Yep, I wouldn't mind puttin' my shoes under her bed.'

Much relieved that he wasn't hallucinating after all, he put down some coins and went out into the street. All the way back to the bank, he replayed his meeting with the Chinese girl. He tried to remember what she had said, tried to rearrange the scene so he dominated the event. But it always came out that it had been the girl's play. Not that he intended ever to get intimate with her. No, a fool might, a milksop romantic who read Bryon, a man who sniffed at petticoats and let his prick act as his compass in life.

Charles felt better in his firm resolve not to think of Moon Orchid. Beauty, grace, the trap set by nature, a longing for something solid in human relationships—they had ruined many a man, he thought as he entered the

271

Pacific-Harvesters Bank.

As for Moon Orchid, despite her haughty exit, she had not left the English Shop as much in control of herself as Charles had imagined. She had spoken boldly in a language still alien to her. She had spoken firmly as much to convince herself as Charles Fiore. She could only hope that in appealing to his evident desire for her as well as to his kind nature, she had captivated him completely. There were still circumstances to overcome. Big ones with dangerous consequences.

She and Flower Seed walked to the Tin How Temple at Waverly Place—not her usual place for prayer, so Gaw's associates would not see her—and bought six joss sticks. Yes, there was much danger, but one had to take risks to be a bold lover. She would burn more joss sticks in the Kong Chow Temple on Pine Street, for she believed it best to worship the Queen of Heaven image there, as she was also the Goddess of the Seven Seas. It was not that Moon Orchid was a great believer in scrolls relating to the gods: only the Buddha impressed her. But this way she would be protected no matter what. If it was all true, she was being properly pious. And if it was all nonsense, as she said to Flower Seed, 'What have I lost?'

Moon Orchid was very practical and was adept at analyzing any situation with perception—which surprised many people, who expected a girl of such beauty and grace to be a fool. She had not yet accepted what Old Hairy Lips said, that 'to live, one must compromise with logic.' There was no morbid subtlety in her seeking an escape from her situation and in questioning her desires for Charles. Mr Charles Fiore: how did he feel about her? And if lust was also strong in him, as it was in her, why didn't he drag her upstairs at the English Shop?

Just before the two girls returned to Gaw's building, Moon Orchid bought a packet of *tow-fu* from a sidewalk stand. When they entered the building boldly, they were chewing on cubes of it. Cheerfully they climbed the stairs. Yung Fat, who kept his one eye on goings-on in the building, was seated on a low chair one flight up, banging the counters of his abacus. 'Where have you two been?'

Moon Orchid chewed and held out a handful of goodies. 'We had this desire for some *tow-fu*. Have some, Yung Fat.' He waved off the idea.

'My teeth ache and I am waiting for the noon rice bowl.'

'You should have a set of the white devil's false teeth.'

Once back in her section of the house, Moon Orchid exhaled and licked her fingers. 'I felt like the victim of Ching Kee, the great beheader of criminals whose swift sword strokes were famous. Once the man kneeling, waiting, said to Ching Kee, "Begin, begin, don't let me wait." And Ching Kee said, "Bow," and the man did and his head fell off. Kee was *that* swift.'

'Please, I am frightened enough.'

Moon Orchid knew she was chatting away from nervousness.

Flower Seed added, 'The Old Dragon is stirring.'

They entered Old Hairy Lips's room; there she was, snoring loudly. The little lamp was smoking, the orangewood pipe lay flat on the floor mat. The old woman muttered something unintelligible. Without opening her eyes, Old Hairy Lips added, 'I have a great thirst ... very great thirst.'

'Flower Seed, get the honorable lady some water. Did you have a good smoke-sleep?'

'Ah, what can it mean to you, my recall of my youth? The dream of great love I've had in these frivolous times is lost.' Old Hairy Lips lay quietly, her eyes lost in reverie.

'That is true,' Moon Orchid said.

5

Capriccio

26

'Are you listening to me or catching flies?'

'Of course I'm listening.'

'You have the look on your face as if you're a million miles away.'

'I'm here, Father. You were talking about the Sacramento Bank.'

'Zimmerman will head it; you'll be his assistant.'

Charles looked down at the gray cloth tops of his pearl-buttoned shoes. 'I've got this flat with Ramon, as you know. To pull tracks now when we haven't lived there long and we've furnished it and ... '

George looked up over his eyeglasses at his son. 'Well, Sacramento isn't too far off. You can come down for weekends, and it will keep your tomcatting under control.'

'I'm not tomcatting like Rocco.'

George was listening pleasantly to the hum of bank activities going on below. He looked pale and thin—another bout of his recurring fever, his son suspected. A great surge of love for his father filled Charles, a feeling of more than just sympathy, of just wanting to express himself.... My remarkable father, so sure in times of national panics, or market manipulations, keeping the bank afloat, even expanding. And he has this woman someplace on the bay, and a child, a girl, my stepsister; the man has never fully recovered from the war.... Charles started to say something, to say how much his father meant to him, but he drew back. One never knew how George would take any overt signs of affection beyond a hug or a peck on the cheek. 'Slopping over,' he called it.

'I'll keep Ramon here. He's a quick learner and has an amazing knack for banking. I suppose that comes from Irena's drive and head, and not Tomas. God rest his soul. I'll keep Ramon and Tom here and see how they develop. Fred? I don't know. He may come to his senses someday.' He pointed to a red-marked map on a wall. 'In the next few years, all things being equal'—he smiled—'and the wind in the right direction, I hope to have branches of the Pacific-Harvesters Bank everyplace I've marked. To begin with, Salinas, Monterey, Fresno, San Luis Obispo, Santa Barbara, Ventura, and San Diego.'

'You'll end up on the moon.'

George laughed, gave Charles a quizzical look. 'Haven't you read Jules Verne? Why not by your grandsons' days a Luna branch of the Pacific-Harvesters Bank?'

'We were planning a few days to go salmon fishing, sail up the coast to Gold Beach, but now this damn Sacramento thing.'

'Take the trip. Marvelous salmon season there. I don't plan to send you upriver to Sacramento for another month. First I want you to clear up all your Chinatown business. Gaw likes you.'

Charles scowled. 'Fuck him. I don't like him exploiting slave girls. Why doesn't the YMCA or Christian Endeavor do something?'

'They're working to change the underworld customs in Chinatown. And they're *not* slave girls; they sign some kind of papers, a servant's contract. Christ, Chuck, Gaw had political protection from City Hall, and elections are coming. Homer Kendrick is going to the national convention again, and he may get the Republican nomination. This fellow Bryan is scaring the shit out of the big guys. And Gaw and his merchants have been ponying up cash in a big way for Homer's political fund, based on some promises by Homer to help change the laws against the Chinese. Old Moses has set his heart on Homer in the White House! Have a good fishing trip. Pack a few salmon back on ice. Your mother is a handy woman with a sweet-and-sour planked fish in aspic.'

It was good to put on scratchy rough flannel shirts, to go unshaved, camping under the big trees on the Gold River bank. They rose at dawn, washed a bit in the creek, smoked pipes, drank strong coffee, and devoured huge stacks of wheatcakes. They hired a ketch under Cap Olson with his nicotine-stained whiskers, and he knew just the right place where the biggest salmon, the steelheads, were running. At the start of the salmon run, the fish were fat and fought hard. It was good to hook into a ten-pounder. Every evening they came ashore, sunburned, noses peeling. Ramon would hack and split open a salmon and roast it over hot embers. Nothing as tasty ever existed, they agreed. They sang songs and drank a native beer with more hop to it, Cap Olson said, 'than a six-foot bullfrog with a hot coal up his ass, *ja?*'

While Fred occasionally did go into the small lumber town of Tollifer to seek 'some female companionship,' Ramon and Charles stayed by the fire to talk of deep subjects: the true nature of cats, the moral beauty of the soul, the merits of peach brandy over hard apple cider, the ties between genius and tragedy. And as so many young people at the time did, they sat by fire reciting *Omar Khayyám* aloud to each other:

> A moment's Halt—a momentary taste
> Of being from the Well amid the Waste—
> And Lo! the phantom caravan has reach'd
> The nothing it set out from—Oh, make haste!

'Make haste!' they howled to the treetops and the river, feeling pleasantly sad about nature, about life.

Fred came back one afternoon with buckshot holes in his jacket. Some husband had returned early from barking logs, he told them. 'Half-Indian girl she was, you never saw such tawny skin, glowed like candlelight.'

The last day of salmon fishing they shared a bottle of Old Crow, exchanged fish yarns, and Cap Olson lied outrageously about the last Indian war. The cousins returned to San Francisco with four salmon on ice, a sense of comradeship and deeper love for each other, a promise of going forward shoulder to shoulder in life's work. They were young and would grow old together, and next vacation they would go after wild ducks at Mono Lake.

Charles saw there was gray in his mother's hair when he went to the dinner of the salmon in aspic that Maria had made. Somehow the big house on Nob Hill seemed too big for her and his father, but she led an active life, she told him when they had a minute alone—between card parties, attending race meets with Irena, and mass and a *novena* now and then. She seemed to be accepting her relationship with her husband.

'A good man, your father. Yes, I pay no attention to gossip. So how is life with you, Charlie?'

'I am working hard at the bank.' He looked into his mother's face; older than when he was a small boy. She sat by his sickbed the year of chickenpox, counting the beads of her rosary and smiling as she moved her lips in silent prayer for his soul and recovery. She was a stranger to him now, or had he never been able to see the woman behind her virtue, her honesty?

'You have a girl?'

'Now I have several.'

'I would like grandchildren. Go confess to Father Zorilla and be again in a state of grace.'

He didn't say he would or wouldn't go to confession. As for girls, marriage, and grandchildren—Moon Orchid, half-yellow babies? No, that was a crazy thought. The sooner he got to Sacramento, the more quickly her image would fade. The musk odor of her scent mixed with sandalwood would soon be beyond recall. Should he have gone upstairs with her at the English Shop? Would he, if there was ever such a situation again, resist temptation?

A week later he found a letter addressed to him in the brass mailbox labeled 'FIORE-VELASQUEZ.' He sniffed—musk and sandalwood. He read:

I have made up my mind if I do not hear from you in the next month on the tenth day of the tenth moon, I shall drown myself in the bay. All I desire is some notice, a written word left at the English Shop that you regard me as alive. I have cast the colored stones of fate, *shii hing*, and they speak of good fortune for us to be together soon. I have made such progress with English speech and talking. Have you read *David Copperfield*? It is very sad, telling of a person alone with no one to love him. But do not despair, for in the end he finds happiness. Amusing too is the story and the people. The bay water is very cold this time of year.

Your only one,
Moon

He shook his head. Damn, God damn all women. Yet her beauty was so close and real—as if they were standing close, exchanging breath. There was an ache in him, a palpitation. His mind filled out the image of her, the grace of her body; an amazing work of living art. But he thought not of art but of her as a woman. Sexual images began to form and he put his hands in his pockets and was very still.

Was he really foolish enough to be in love? That damn irrational tyranny? That desire to see one particular woman as different from any other? He moaned aloud at these thoughts.

Was he still too stubborn to admit it fully? He would try to fight it. But looking at the letter raised his pulsebeat and caused a sexual pulsing through his veins. Clearly this Chinese girl was a ready woman and a realist, at least when it came to facing the drive of a hopeless passion.

He took up his pen and a sheet of paper:

Miss Moon:
I do not desire you to leap into the bay but I do not

think you understand my position professionally and my way of life. There is no way by which we can come together. There are problems that would result if you were daring [he scratched out 'daring'], determined [he crossed that out, too], foolish enough [that was better] to try to make more of our friendship [scratch 'friendship'] meeting than it is. I offer you the thought that I admire your beauty and I understand your situation. But have we both built up our meeting into more than it can ever really be? Let us remain friends.

Yours truly,
Charles Fiore

He reread the letter. Cold as Kelsey's nuts. No, don't reject her so cruelly. He balled up the letter and put it into his pocket to burn later in the stove. He wrote quickly on another sheet:

Dear Lady:

I accept your friendship. Do not think of the bay. Spring will come, and many things happen at such times. Writing a letter, I can't express why all this is wrong. I'll explain it better at the English Shop. Tuesday, two o'clock.

Yours truly,
C.

He didn't like that letter either … a schoolboy fumbling about. That's what it sounded like. He addressed an envelope, care of the English Shop, Miss Moon Orchid. As he wet the flap with his tongue, the sharp glue edge cut his upper lip. He bled slightly and thought of it as a symbol of the deflowering of a virgin.

He decided not to keep the meeting. Then he felt that would be wrong, cruel. He decided he'd be there. Tuesday morning he decided *no*, but by noon had changed his mind again. Ramon asked if he were feeling all right. At ten after two, Charles was in the English Shop. Agnes, the owner, and Flower Seed were drinking tea laced with rum. Neither

281

said anything. Agnes pointed to the staircase. He wanted to retreat; instead he took the stairs two at a time, hesitating only when he reached the door behind which he knew would be Moon Orchid. He turned the doorknob slowly and entered into a dimly lit room. He did not notice the peeling wallpaper, the motheaten curtains, or the scarred chest of drawers. Facing him, legs exposed, wrapped in a blanket, was the Chinese girl. High smooth forehead, amethyst eyes.

Oddly enough, he was struck first not by Moon Orchid's beauty but rather by the warmth he felt at seeing her, the pleasure he took in this intimate moment. He looked around, taking in the shabby setting. 'This is not the right place for you.'

She said simply with no bewilderment, 'Does that matter?'

'Does it?'

She took him by the hand, and if she had any qualms, she didn't show it, except for a slight quiver of the lips. He kissed her, almost without thinking, as if it were the most natural thing. Her arms went around his and she raised herself on her toes in order to place her face next to his, at the same time molding her naked body to conform to his.

She covered his mouth and chin with tiny dry kisses; then, when he was least expecting it, she darted her moist tongue between his parted lips and made thrusting movements that caused him to tighten the grip of his hands at the small of her back. He saw the curves of her breasts and belly where the edges of the blanket no longer met.

They had said very little, and now he cupped her face in his hands and looked down at her, closer than he had ever seen her. She blinked at him, assuming no air of coyness, just breathing quicker, mouth half-open. Suddenly he felt her fingers making featherlike strokes on the fabric of his trousers, which tightened over his swelling erection. He groaned, and as he did, she increased the pressure of her strokes, essentially exciting, infinitely pleasing.

He forced himself to break away from her. 'Will you be

282

missed?'

'I took trouble to procure for Hairy Lips more *gow hop* than she is accustomed to having. Master Gaw never calls for me until after his evening business is completed.' Her eyes sparkled with delight at her own cleverness; then fear entered them.

'You must be careful, Moon. Things could go badly for us if Gaw suspected. He regards you as his property. Hell, you *are*.'

She curled her lip. 'Now that we are here, I am your property.' As if to prove the veracity of this statement, she stepped back a single pace, and making a sound deep in her throat, she dropped the blanket around her feet.

A groan escaped from Charles's mouth. He had come to the English Shop like a man mesmerized; he had climbed the stairs imagining that he could solve this lunatic idea of Moon Orchid, keep her from her folly. A lie—he had come in lust. Now, seeing her pale ivory body standing before him, he knew that she was honest and he had been dishonest in his thoughts. He marveled at what was being offered to him. Those high, perfect breasts, her smooth belly, the silky texture of her arms and legs, the sweetness of her warm breath.

She turned her head away and said, 'There is a bed.'

He saw it in the next room through an open door, a brass bed piled high with pillows next to a nightstand holding a pitcher, basin, and towels, all dominated by a huge pier glass in an ornately carved frame. It presented a scene of a naked couple.

He gathered her up in his arms, legs tucked over the crook in his elbow, her hands laced around his neck. She murmured in his ear; he knew the strange soft sounds to be Chinese endearments, words of pleasure and encouragement, and they made the scene somewhat unreal.

He laid her gently on the bed and began to kiss her, beginning with the arched insteps of her delicate feet. He had known women since age sixteen, but he had never before been so stunned with a sexual reverence, so astonished by the intensity of his evolving arousal.

Moon Orchid whimpered as his mouth gently brushed the inside of her thighs. Her back curved instinctively off the bed as she thrust her pelvis up toward his lips ... . After a while, he raised his head and looked at her, feeling the blood pounding in his head. He ran his hands from her forehead to her ankles, wondering at her beauty, at every spot he touched. He launched himself at her and began to kiss her again, rolling his tongue along the dark pink labia. Suddenly she thrashed beneath him with sounds like a wave on the shore, drawn-out noise issuing from deep inside her body. Without losing her rolling rhythms, she stretched out her arms, pulled him up, raking his chest with her nails.

'Now, oh, *now!*' she commanded him, and he changed his position, penetrating her moist tightness with a single thrust that seemed to have all the effort of his life behind it.

'*Aaaah,*' he heard her cry, and then he no longer knew what he heard. The waves broke again and again. Their pleasure was total and unthinking, no other images penetrated the whirling, pleasant pressure in their lungs.

He watched her wash later. She stood with her fine back to him, humming that Chinese noise they called music as she scrubbed. He saw the towel she discarded was bloodied, and noticing his glance, she laughed. 'You are pleased at what we have done together?'

'I was sure of that when we were doing it.'

'That is not good enough,' Moon Orchid told him severely, waving the towel. 'You are now my lover, forever.'

'You're so damn young!' he reminded her. 'And as a young girl, you think that way. We're in a tight spot.'

'I have plans.'

'Christ, I haven't.' He looked down at his sweated body.

'I wish you to take me away. We go someplace far.' She came over and sat next to him on the bed, leaning her head on his shoulder.

'Can't you see it's impossible?' Yet, even as he spoke

harshly to her, Charles pulled her down to him. Catching his fingers in her hair, he brought her face up to his. A tear slid from one of her eyes and she began to shiver. Her voice was not at all girlish, but firm, angry. 'I have been strong, to get you here. You must now be strong to keep me. You can! You want to? You must!'

The day, he thought, had taxed her reserves; Moon Orchid's fears now were in danger of overwhelming her and were rendering her incoherent. Charles cursed softly, feeling his nakedness as a kind of shame. 'I may wish to take you away, but there are complications. You're such a kid ... and ...'

Moon Orchid flared her nostrils and said evenly, 'I felt you would have answers.'

He chuckled at her single-mindedness even in fear and he confessed to himself that she was certainly a risk worth taking, but his common sense saw the impossible situation clearly. (Rocco had crudely put it to Fred and him one weekend at the Casa: 'Fuck 'em and leave 'em, it's the best for them, best for you.')

'Too much talk, Moon.'

They made love again, and this time her skills made him a voluptuous victim of her hands and mouth. He was stirred as he could never remember having been before. They were both spent with delight.... Agnes found them asleep in each other's arms and wakened them. It was twilight and Flower Seed was weeping in the kitchen. Moon Orchid dressed quickly, asked Charles to depart first by a side door. He gave Agnes a twenty-dollar gold coin. Once in the street, he wondered if all San Francisco would know, just by the expression on his face, what had been done. He felt as if slightly drunk. He recalled the scent of her and the timbre of her voice. He trembled as he recalled Moon Orchid's hands on his body. Yet she had no place in his other life. Could he—would he—abandon her now? No, but what a hell of a pickle he was in. An evaluating mind that was no help at all. Clearly mind and body were in conflict.

27

'You can't change your mind!'

'The hell I can't. When I'm running things, I'll change my mind any day I feel like it—and *twice* on Sunday.'

'But now it's San Diego. You said Sacramento before.'

'I've decided Ramon will go to Sacramento. You'll do better in San Diego. You've had more experience. Sacramento is closer, so I can keep a close eye on Ramon.'

'I don't mind going to San Diego,' Ramon said.

'I'm not going,' said Charles, sitting across the table from his father and his cousin in the dining room of the Palace Hotel. They had begun the meal cheerfully enough until George had announced he was sending Ramon to Sacramento to assist in running the new bank, and Charles was to go south instead.

Ramon felt he would be ineffectual entering the verbal conflict arising between father and son. He removed a bit of crab shell from a mouthful of salad and wondered at Charles's ludicrous grievances at the change in where they were to go. He wondered if his cousin was involved in gambling debts or hated the idea of leaving San Francisco for such a distant place. Or, more likely, whether there was a woman.

'Nothing more to talk about,' said George, getting out his pipe as a waiter poured coffee. Charles clenched his fists, looked from his cousin to his father, stood up, pushing back his chair with a backward kick. It fell over with a clatter.

286

He said, 'The hell with banking!' turned, and went out.

The waiter widened his eyes and George lit his pipe, sucking it into life. From a nearby ballroom came the staccato chords of percussion and woodwinds. 'They make a good pie here, Ramon. Apple, from fresh fruit, not the dried stuff.'

'Just coffee. Chuck doesn't mean it, Uncle George.'

'Of course he doesn't. Leave the bank! He's got this damn stubborn streak. Talk to him, Ramon. I don't say I know what is best, but I think I know.' He laughed, took a sip of coffee, a puff on his pipe. Why, he thought, do fathers lack the ability to talk to sons decently and naturally? ...

Ramon did not speak to Charles. His cousin was not at the flat that evening and did not sleep there that night.

In the morning Ramon found that Charles's two small suitcases, a carpetbag, his outdoor clothing, and his Colt pistol were gone. It was no sudden impulse, he discovered; Charles had withdrawn five thousand dollars, all his deposits at the bank, and taken certain securities he kept in one of the strongboxes.

'Uncle George, we must do something.'

'It's his catastrophe, Ramon. If he wants to sulk, go off someplace, let him. He'll come back when he finds out the hard kicks in the ass the world has waiting for him.'

'He may be in trouble in some dive below the Slot, or in a shanghai dive on the Coast.'

George waved off the idea and added in agitated tones that he didn't care to talk of Charles's silly action. 'If he thinks he's punishing me, he isn't.'

Six days later Ramon received a letter postmarked Carson City. It was written in Charles's usual irregular hand, the G and Y endings a little wild:

Dear Ramon,

What I have done may appear to you foolish, and to others completely despicable. Well, the devil take them. I write you in the hope you will understand. Please tell my mother and whoever else might be interested that I am traveling and will not be in touch with them for some time. Nor am I alone.

As there will be questions as to my sanity and stability, I do say I did what I did, if not with a clear head, perhaps in outrage at my father and because I love, with extravagant passion, a Chinese girl.

Yes, read on. We are now together. Both have cut ourselves adrift, and though it may sound too romantic, we have run away. Her name is Moon. She is a slave girl owned by Gaw. I can't go into details of how we met, what steamy potion worked between us. It's come to a climax, and problems are cascading over us from all directions. When my father made it clear that she and I could be parted for long periods of time and I (as you were witness) made it clear I would not go to San Diego, Moon herself was finding life in Gaw's household dangerous. There are spies and informers, so if the old goat had found out we were meeting, were lovers, he certainly would have killed her after some dreadful oriental torture. I'm not being melodramatic in the style of Wilkie Collins—I know Chinatown's codes and the consequences when they are broken.

What shall our future be? We shall survive. I know you will not be condescending. You may think that when I say I feel now the presence, the consistency of life, that I'm talking like a schoolboy. Didn't you say once that in all farce there is hidden some tragedy? I'll face what I have to. I have been thinking of this action for some time. But it was only fantasy until my father tried to force me to take on the San Diego position. I wasn't in control in my rage; my despair and anger won out over what some call reason. I made contact with Moon, and we made arrangements to flee.

That night we crossed the bay, and while you know we were in Carson City, from now on you most likely will not hear from us. It sounds, I know, like something out of a novel, but there is danger to our lives, as Gaw has his networks of *hongs* and *tongs* everywhere. He will not accept the situation. Moon is not only a costly property (what a dreadful thing to write about a wonderful girl), but this also means a loss of face for himself in the community as the orientals see it. Vanity, pride, the fact that he may become a laughing stock in Chinatown all mean he will make every effort to find us. I know the comic absurdities all this suggests, but dear Cousin Ramon, the danger is real enough. It's like a dream— I'm not here and yet I am.

What can you tell Maria and George and your mother, Irena? Just tell them that I love them and respect them, that I hope they in turn will not think too badly of me and my actions. I don't expect them to understand about the girl. We exist in a dense, complicated society where the idea that I may marry a Chinese girl is as grotesque as the mating of dogs with apes. Wish us luck. If I am the fool for all the absurdities, I am at the moment a happy one, aware of the problems ahead. Your cousin,

Chuck

Quong Lao Gaw thought he knew how to control his emotions. He sat alone on a low chair drinking oolong tea from a Sung bowl, savoring each sip with a sigh releasing inner tensions. He wore a splendid dragon robe and white-soled slippers. For visiting his various interests, he dressed in white-devil style, very much the sport: yellow shoes with bulldog toes, a well-cut suit by Grant Avenue tailors, a shiny black top hat on the remains of his graying short hair. Gaw was sixty-two, a man of small stature, with no particular grace or distinction in appearance but for his dark eyes that seemed sad and brooding. Those eyes were always observant, as if wary of the precarious condition of how one lived in this strange city.

He thought back on his life—now so shattered. He had come to California long ago as part of a cargo of peasants, little better than slaves, under contract to work for the railroad being built east to meet track coming west. He had dug and pushed carts of broken stone, drilled in rock hanging on the end of ropes to plant explosives. And when he was injured in a premature blast, losing two fingers from his left hand, he had taken what was paid him for his injuries and set himself up as a seller of dried fish, pickled nuts. He was a scurrying figure catering to the track layers. He soon expanded into whiskey, on paydays operating a small gambling tent with Bou Yi-han, his cousin. He progressed from moneylending (those who did not pay were dealt with harshly) to importing rice and curios. He began buying up buildings, exporting cotton, cutting railroad timber. He always bought through a network of shady white lawyers to circumvent laws forbidding orientals from owning certain things. His next big business ventures were in opium and women. Gaw did not consider these enterprises sinful or disgraceful. They were simply additional commodities to be bought and sold.

Now, a cruel blow, and who could help?

There was a tap on the golden-oak door and Kim Tai came in, followed by George Fiore and Ramon in informal black, as if for a burial. The men looked at each other, and Kim motioned to a yellow silk sofa.

George said, 'You had faith in me once, Gaw.'

The Chinese did not answer, but put his hands up into his robe's sleeves. Kim looked up as if waiting for a signal. When none came, he turned to George. 'There are two parts to relationship with our world. The personal relationship of men who trust each other, drink, smoke together. Yes?'

'May I say something?' asked George.

'In good time. The other side is the business way, the business world. Master Gaw is much involved with you in that way. Your family has dishonored his house by carrying off his girl, Moon Orchid. It does not seem possible that a man as wise and knowledgeable as yourself would have any part of this.'

'Goddamm it!' cried George. 'Let me get a word in edgewise! I came here to express my horror, my dismay at what my son has done. I came to you, as you put it, to *kowtow*, bow, and I speak my humiliation at this.'

'As expected,' said Kim.

'Also'—George took a dispatch case from Ramon—'to account for *all* our dealings. Figures, dates, holdings. I want to know to whom Quong Lao Gaw wants to turn all this over. Our books can be inspected.' He held the case out to Gaw, not to Kim Tai. His face registered pain and a smoldering but controlled anger.

Gaw removed his hands from his sleeves, rubbed them together as if he were cold. 'I want none of that. No talk of making other fella take care of mattahs of business. No. You be a man of honah and I have faith in dealing with you.'

'Thank you, Gaw. I must express my sorrow of what has been done, I can only—'

Gaw held up a hand. Ramon noticed the fingers lacked the extra long fingernails a master Chinese was supposed to cultivate. Gaw said, 'Do not go on. A man can talk to salve his wounds with words. So we go on, you, me. But now it must be known both girl and man will die when we find them.'

'We've tried,' said Ramon. 'Detectives, Pinkertons, posters to sheriffs. We've not found a trace.'

Gaw gave a wan smile. 'Kim, get hot tea. Fiore, I have means to find them, have much ways of doing it.'

Ramon shouted, 'I'll be damned if you think Uncle George is going to let you murder Chuck.'

George put a restraining hand on Ramon, forced him to sit back on the sofa. 'Gaw, if you do this, you will destroy yourself. I am witness to your threats, but I shall forget them.'

'No threats. I do not forget.'

'This is not Imperial China. Even the politicians who protect you will not accept murder. You'll be deported, if not hanged. Your assets will be seized.'

A bowing girl entered, carrying trays of tea. Kim poured tea and Gaw lowered his head and closed his eyes. Both George and Ramon accepted the cups but did not drink. Gaw lifted his head. His face was calm, but not expressionless. 'I am ignorant peasant, but no one come shit on my doorstep. When the lightning flashes, who can know if it will strike him? I have no sons, much sadness of that. Now, whatever was to add some joy to my life is all gray and without color. I am alien to the place, but I am a man, I am a way of life, yes, that make me feel good, high and good within.' He turned to Kim and said something in Chinese. Kim answered, 'Dignity, pride in being Master Gaw, he says, not a dead dog you throw on a dung heap.'

Gaw nodded. 'Go now. We do banking as was, we respect you honest way like was. What else is done outside what we do against.' He turned his head to Kim and spoke softly; Kim nodded. 'He said, "White people are barbarians and it is not your fault. There are some things you don't understand."'

George handed the dispatch case to Ramon. 'I shall serve him and his interests to the best of my ability. I do have commitments to him, I respect his faith in me, and I will manage his investments better than anyone else in San Francisco. But I match my threats to his if any harm comes to my son.'

Gaw had closed his eyes and seemed to be deep in thought or, Ramon thought, asleep. Kim saw them to the door. George leaned over the young Chinese's head and wanted to tell him to go fuck himself. He didn't.

Gaw opened his eyes and smiled. 'Not wise to part with bad talk.'

In the street, as they made their way to a coach stand, Ramon said, 'The old bastard doesn't really mean that about Chuck?'

George frowned. 'I don't fully understand what goes on in the minds of most people, and I certainly don't know what populates the mind of a Chinese who's been humiliated all over the city. Jokes are being made about what has happened, and Chinese humor is ribald and coarse. Chuck has poured shit on the old man's head.'

Ramon saw his uncle was feeling as humiliated and hurt as Gaw.

Years later, a journalist trying to trace Charles Fiore and Moon wrote:

By the middle of the 1870's mapmakers and railroad surveying crews had penetrated beyond the Indian sites, muddy towns, gone into the wilderness along the Gilà and Snake rivers, climbed Pikes Peak, eaten beans under the buttes of the Black Hills, and been mildly menaced by the last of the red hostiles being pushed into reservations or hunted down for butchering at Wounded Knee. There was still much uncharted wilderness around the Teton Mountains in Wyoming and to the big Timber below the Birdtail Divide. Here among the big cone pines, wild lilac, and squaw cabbage it would seem the banker's son and the boss of Chinatown's slave girl found refuge.

It made good reading twenty years after the event, but hardly suggested the hardships. Moon Orchid had been dressed in dark tailored clothes and heavily veiled. They had taken a stage to Ukiah, where, after outfitting themselves at the Solid General Store with a buggy and horse, they raced to Mendocino. Here, the rig sold, they went north by small schooner to a bay called Trinidad. Gaw's agents traced them this far. But from here on no clue of their movement was ever on public notice.

They traveled east past almond-colored rocky places in a covered buckboard pulled by two half-tamed broncs. Charles kept on east and north to Montana, to a certain spot where at age fifteen he and his father had once gone with a government survey team; they to chart a river's course, and he and George to fish for steelheads. They had found an abandoned stone ranch house in the wilderness where, a generation back, a daring young Frenchman and his bride had built a cattle station to raise prize steers, and failed.

For the last hundred miles the lovers rode horseback followed by a packhorse, Moon in divided Indian buckskin pants, a logger's flannel shirt, and beehive hat.

'You sorry?' he asked her as he studied a penciled map he had copied from an old survey.

Under the big hat he could just make out her chin. She laughed. 'No, no, just my ass very, *very* sore from the horse. But is a good time.'

'You're a game one.' He cuffed her lightly.

'I don't understand. Game one? We are playing something?'

'No, no darling, it means showing stamina.'

'Good.' She kissed him. 'You stamina to make love?'

'In daytime?'

They did. They made love very often. It seemed to Charles the Chinese were a very erotic people.

For two days it rained and they holed up in a sandy river cave and they shared their most intimate interlude with fervent intensities.

On the morning the rains stopped, they caught the horses and packed gear to head northwest toward the upper river and the standing timber where the Frenchman's house was. Glancing at Moon Orchid, who was swinging herself up in the saddle, Charles thought how fragile she looked, decked out in Indian garments and bulky woodsman's clothing. The oddly fitting gear emphasized her delicacy, and even the floppy leather hat tied by a scarf under her chin enhanced her charm.

'Oh, if Flower Seed could see me now.' She giggled.

They went on some days, past loblolly pines, ivory-billed woodpeckers, wild bees in the shagbark trees. The forest changed suddenly to tall birch and thick oaks; soon after, the cliffs and ridges were topped with hawthorn and sycamore. There had been no smoke, they had encountered few settlements and no other travelers, and Charles did not believe them to be hostile Indian lands. They followed a river, the Ripadippy, swelling with spring meltings and rains, rippling over the rocks beside their trail. They felt at peace, far from danger. As a boy Charles had learned the names of trees and plants, and he reeled them off for her. The smell of swamp rosebay permeated the air, and Moon Orchid, clasping her lover's wrist, delighted in their surroundings.

Then, as they rode by a formation of reddish crumbling rock near a clump of cottonwoods, they came to a clearing where, set against pale pines and sumac, the Frenchman's stone house stood, the river below it.

One corner of the roof had fallen in a bit but the house was otherwise in good repair, blending comfortably into the landscape. They rode toward it, dismounted, and Moon Orchid hung back while Charles knocked on the door. No one came, and after a few minutes he opened the door to reveal a deserted interior, no signs of human habitation.

A flash of intuition seized Moon Orchid and she began laughing excitedly. 'You *knew* this was here!' she challenged him.

'Yes,' he confessed. 'But I didn't want to tell you in case I couldn't find it. It was built by some Frenchies who tried to make a cattle ranch.'

'We can stay here?'

Charles smiled at her. 'As long as we like, until we think they're not looking for us anymore.'

28

In a corner of the stone house was a room where there had once been a wall mirror (by the marks left there), and most likely the space had been a lady's dressing room. Moon Orchid made it her own. She created a kind of shrine with her little brass Buddha set up on a crate. She surrounded it with fragrant pine branches and cones, wildflowers in season, and burned a fragrant sap of some aromatic tree she found nearby.

The stone house had three rooms with an assortment of rickety furniture: a wooden rocking chair with one rocker missing, a child's bed, some chipped crockery, and a small table. However, the fireplace was practically ready for use.

Charles found shelter for the horses. An acre or so of land was cleared behind the house; it was too risky to let the horses roam free and they weren't going to be saddling them on a regular basis. After settling in, he chewed on a long piece of sweet grass and was amused when he looked over at Moon Orchid, to see her imitating him, rolling a blade of grass between her lips.

This had not been easy for her, he damn well knew. At Gaw's she had been petted and spoiled and waited upon; she had never washed her own hair or prepared her own cups of tea. And she had changed her clothes as many times a day as whim demanded. Certainly she had never been without a large looking glass! She was learning. After two months their diminishing supplies was a subject he preferred not to think about, preferring instead to discover new sources of food around the Frenchman's house. The river solved the problem of water. There were deer and rabbits everywhere.

He himself was not a seasoned woodsman, nor was he a particularly good cook. But he was a good shot. What he could do, he told himself, he would do. 'Improvising for survival. After all, Moon, it's pretty much the same wherever you are.'

'Do they have lobsters?'

With Moon Orchid by his side, he was profoundly glad for the safe haven offered by the stone house. He hardly ever thought of George, Maria, Ramon, Aunt Irena. Just a few times, late at night.

Part of the floor had once been wooden but much of it had been ripped up. With care, it was possible to negotiate the three rooms safely. While he collected kindling and chopped wood, Moon Orchid had set about arranging the objects that came out of the saddlebags, and if she did things badly, he heard noises like Chinese curses. He knew, like himself, she was making the effort to live in the present, not to dream of the past.

They were careful to keep in reserve most of the items and supplies the packhorse had carried. They kept them on a high shelf built under the eaves and doled them out with restraint—sugar, salt, flour, cornmeal, beans. Small game and fish were plentiful and Charles's skill at catching these enabled them to stretch their rations of dried meat.

There were wild onions and berries and mushrooms. As a child, Charles had gone mushroom hunting at Aunt Irena's and remembered some of the lore governing the ingestion of the potentially deadly fungi.

Sitting at dusk, listening to the sounds of the river, they would hardly speak. Both realized that this was a present existence that was not related to the past—that it was a gift to them, she insisted, from benevolent gods.

Sometimes Moon Orchid would beg for stories of white-society gossip in San Francisco. 'One day we shall go to Paris. My cousin Ramon says it is beautiful.'

'Good people there?'

'Oh, yes, a beautiful city. Full of remarkably beautiful women, Ramon said, and ...' She bowed her head to hide her laughter, to postpone showing her wide smile. He added, '... but none so beautiful as you.'

They embraced, their contentment in each other deepening with the twilight.

So they spent the summer. No one approached them, and if there were Indians or hunters, they did not show themselves. Day faded into day as they swam, walked, ate, slept, made love, and made plans for a life untainted by the troubles of the past.

The days started getting shorter and the nights colder. The mourning doves left, as did the geese, and the horsetail reeds turned brown and brittle. The swamp maples began to change to crimson bowers and the animals began to grow their winter coats.

Charles's face was now defined by a mustard-coloured

beard, which Moon Orchid occasionally attempted to trim with a dulled razor. Her own hair lay like a blue-black mantle down her back. He loved to see her lying entwined in it as she waited for him to join her on their raised pallet.

City dwellers in new surroundings. There were moments of doubt, for neither had known before what it meant to live in a wilderness. But Charles insisted the solitude comforted and nurtured them. Moon Orchid's curiosity about the flowers and plants, the birds, the animals, the fishes, and the rocks ruled her days. After her chores, which she did badly, she rushed outdoors from one thing to the next, exclaiming over the wondrousness of everything she saw, heard, and touched.

'It is as Buddha said.'

'Good for him.'

Her attempts at cooking improved as she learned how to make a decent coffee just as their supply of it gave out. She was bee-stung, not badly, when she tried to purloin some wild honey from a seemingly deserted hive. She swam naked and shivered, she wove the river reeds into mats and into extra padding for their deteriorating clothes. Charles watched all this, encouraged her, and affectionately called her his 'little Indian wench.'

Charles knew that time was running out on them, that Moon's Chinese gods would just as lief scorn them in the winter. Evenings were turning to cold nights. Their supplies were just about gone. Moreover, he was running out of rifle ammunition. Before too much time elapsed they would have to find a town along a railroad line to replenish their near-empty sacks of meal and sugar and beans. They could show themselves, see if there were any signs that Gaw and his gangs were hunting them and if Pinkertons were also in the game.

Surely enough, months had passed. Charles wanted to believe that they were forgotten, the chase was called off; but there was no way he could be sure.

One morning, coming back with a section of skinned-out

carcass of a small deer, Charles found her before her shrine, bent over, deeply involved with her godheads. More than usual, he felt. A length of scarlet silk was spread like an offering over the little altar.

He said, 'You sure are involved this morning.'

She did not turn her head, remained kneeling, eyes closed 'I am offering a special prayer to Chung-li Ch'uan.'

'Who's he?' Charles took off his hunting jacket.

'Chief of the Eight Sages,' she said.

'What does he do … I mean, what's his special job?'

'Keeper of the Elixir of Life.'

'I'll be damned.' He went up behind her and put his hands on her neck, rubbed the firm column of flesh, and felt the spine solid under it. Moon Orchid did not move or respond. Charles felt ardent. It had been a good hunt; the doe had played him through thickets and he had followed and wished he had a dog. At last, by a red oak he had claimed his meat with a good hundred-yard shot.

She had her eyes tightly closed and was rocking back and forth on her knees, her hands clasped in front of her breasts. As he waited for her to finish, he was impatient. Suddenly, in a graceful flurry, Moon Orchid gathered up her makeshift shrine, placed the objects under a cloth, started to return to the pallet. It was a moment before she realized that Charles was watching her very closely.

He started to question her, feeling remote and alien from her. What was happening, it occurred to him, was happening because they were different; he could not bring himself to resent the very things which had so charmed him. It was a miracle that they had been in such harmony during the months they had spent together.

'Moon, darling,' he began, 'you are hiding something from me. Do you think I give a damn because you pray to Chinese gods?'

'I pray for a special reason,' she answered him. 'I had wished to be certain before I told you about this new thing in my life.'

Misunderstanding, and thinking that she, too, was

concerned with their dwindling supplies, he sought to reassure her. 'We'll be leaving here soon. We must move on before winter sets in.'

He motioned to her, and she came to him, lying down beside him and fitting her body into the curve of his. She had said nothing in response to his words, and he felt the stiffness in her neck and shoulders as he stroked her. With her back to him, it was difficult to catch her words. Then he heard her say simply, 'We need celestial blessings.'

'The hell we do!' He continued to caress her, running his fingers down her straight spine. 'We're doing pretty well by ourselves.'

She whispered, 'But we are no longer on our own. We have made a baby.'

'What? Are you sure? Oh, Moon, how wonderful you are!'

'Oh, so sure. You're happy?'

'I could dance in the streets, if we had any streets! But you'll need a woman here to help, and ...'

She looked at him scornfully. 'I do not need anyone to help.'

One night Charles reached for Moon Orchid, and instead of acquiescing, she moved away. He tried to understand the state of her mind, and wished that he could surround her with her own kind. He was not changing daily, as she was. He had heard about pregnant women, their whims, their often sullen resentment at their growing bellies, and the morning sickness. He fled to the horse barn when she began to retch, and he had placed a basin within her reach.

When she was feeling better, she said, 'It is a crowning event in a Chinese family, but we shall not celebrate with ducks, plum sauce, warm wine, and fireworks. But it is good to have made this joy.'

Fear overwhelmed him, as he exclaimed, 'But we must get you a midwife!'

She took his hand in hers. 'No, have no fear. I have the knowledge, and I helped when Kim Tai's woman, Blue Jade, had her child. I assisted Old Hairy Lips, and she explained it all to me.'

'But you'll have no one here but me.'

'In China, the women often have babies in a corner of the field between daily tasks, and in a few hours they are back harvesting.'

'You're not a peasant. You're my dear joy. We are together and this child will mean so much— a new future and a final break from the past.'

She leaned her head on his chest, amused. 'I am a peasant, my dear Charles. I am the daughter of a lantern maker and of a mother who had magic with paper. I am not grown fat sitting on silken pillows.'

'Damn the poetry!' Charles found he was smiling. A man's world, after all, differs from a woman's world. He felt a guest at some sacred mystery. His lust had brought this girl to this condition—and hers as well, he supposed. Such is nature's way. He lifted her in his arms.

In the next days, Charles felt she seemed to become more a woman, more a mother-to-be. She put up her hair, worn in long braids, Indian fashion up till now, and wrapped it in a chignon knot. She got out a pair of rhinoceros-horn chopsticks from her blue Chinese bundle and offered them to her shrine.

'They belonged to a poet who once wrote a verse about me. They are very old, these sticks, and have magic, great virtue in the matter of our yin and yang, the doings of men and women.'

'I hear the old Chinese grind up the horn and drink it in their tea to make them potent.'

'Gaw paid much money for some of the horn powder. But it did him no good. This poet Wei Pang only saw me twice, but he wrote so beautifully:

> No bird sings
> Free them from the cages
> I dreamed I went to Moon Orchid
> To join her on the mats for love
> Then they woke me.'

301

Charles said, 'If Gaw had found that, there would have been a dead poet.'

He recited to her some verses he had learned at school, one of Petrarch's sonnets of Laura.

She said she preferred Ch'in T'ao-yu, and she recited 'A Poor Girl':

> So year passed year
> She sewed with golden threads
> The bridal garments
> For unknown girls.

He decided they'd stay the winter at the Frenchman's house. They'd survive on smoked deer meat and fish.

29

George Fiore was a believer in family solidarity, for all his family's deficiencies. Rose and Maude were part of his secret life; he wished his sons had turned out differently. Fred was a town sport, a horse fancier without enough brains or ambition to work in the bank, and Charles was more than a disillusionment—an ache that bordered on fear. George was aware that he himself was going through a tumultuous period of transition; he was no longer a young man, and as he brooded over Charles lost somewhere on the North American continent, he was shocked to feel a loss of exuberance, a loss of interest in the bank—*his* bank. Was Maria's sadness and anguish over Charlie's vanishing a deeper grief than his; could a mother's heartache be more agonizing than a father's? They so rarely talked about such things, their lives and hearts so separate.

Was George just being morbid, or was there some pressure turning him inward to look closer at himself? For all the closeness he felt for Rocco, Tom Floyd, and his sister, Irena, when he was at home with Maria in the enormous house on Nob Hill, he felt a stranger in his own home. They got along well enough, with a limited rapport. But any vestiges of intimacy between them had been shattered when that fool Charles had run off with that bit of Chinese fluff. Gossip was that Gaw had sent his Suey Sing, the feared Boo-How-Doy Tong men, to find the runaways. But then, Ramon insisted, one always heard such romantic nonsense about sinister Chinatown's hatchet men.

George had terrifying dreams; his appetite was nonexistent. He knew he had to get away for a while, go on some sort of search for Charles—who had now been gone for three months. He called together Rocco (who came up from Los Angeles), Tom Floyd, and Ramon for a Saturday-afternoon meeting. He was deeply worried about Maria. Silent and mournful, even Irena's comforting arm and all the prayers for her son didn't lift her despair.

The men assembled in the dull light of gas flares tinting the office a hazy yellow. George faced the men he trusted, had trained, formed. Ramon was the best, the wisest, the most astute in banking. Sensible, well-adjusted ... Irena and Tomas's son had turned out well. George thought of this with a pang—Ramon was what he'd hoped Charles and Fred would be. He thought of Gaw's Chinese saying: 'Prosperity never lasts three generations.' He disliked the word 'dynasty,' but his had failed early.

As for Rocco Bordone—loyal, cunning, wise to the seamy side of human nature, too many women in his life— he was too much the pleasure-seeker, given to after-hours card games and drinking. There could easily be a disaster in Rocco's life. He would be and remain a splendid vice-president, but nothing higher. Tom Floyd? George looked at Tom—husky, neatly dressed, a good and faithful servant, hardworking but limited.

303

'Well, I've become a pain in the ass to myself. I'm going on a vacation. Need to be free to blow the cobwebs out of my head.'

'Going east to New York?' asked Ramon.

'No, I just want to wander around the West a bit. The bank is in fine condition. I drop it on your shoulders. We have some problems with the Chinese. If they should suddenly begin withdrawing their accounts, we'd be a far bit up the creek, but we'd still have paddles. Ramon takes over here. Rocco stays in Los Angeles. Zimmerman will move to San Diego. Tom comes along with me; after all, he's the great army-camp cook.'

'What about all the new branches you were talking about?'

'When I get back. I'll try to stay in touch by telegraph and—'

There was a battering on the locked front door, and Tom went down to let in Tony Mendoza, the stableboy at the house on Nob Hill. He was thin and small, had been a failed jockey, and he seemed now awed by the office, the glare of gaslight as he rotated his cap in his hands.

'Come quick, oh, *very* sick the lady.'

'What lady?'

'Missus, your missus, she very, very sick.'

'Maria?'

Ramon said, 'I've a rig outside. I'll drive you, Uncle George.'

The dusky streets of San Francisco near George's office were still bustling, but in the more respectable residential sections the lamps were already lit in most windows. Ramon's gig on its racing wheels and pulled by one of Irena's best horses (a birthday gift to her son) managed to do well even on the hilly streets, and while the climb up Nob Hill slowed the animal, they were at the house at last. George ran up the stone front steps. In the hall were two frightened maids.

George yelled, 'Have you sent for Dr Norris?'

The youngest maid sobbed. 'We have sent for the priest.'

'Goddammit!' He turned to Ramon. 'Just a block downhill, Dr Norris, yellow house.' He took the stairs on a run, felt his heart pound as he came to Maria's bedroom door. Once inside, he was met by the overheated air, the odor of blue-gum oil mixed with steam from a big boiling kettle set over a gas ring. The cook, Mollie, was bent over Maria, and the sound of his wife's struggle to breathe was frightening. He had been through several of her chronic asthma attacks, and they were usually of this nature— suffocating, the struggle to get air into the lungs.

'When did it start?' he asked, bending over the bed.

Mollie pointed to a silver bell on the rug. 'I hear the bell ringing and I know it is the poor creature's attack. So I put the kettle to steam, get ready the oil. It's no help.'

'Maria, Maria ...' He took her hand, and her eyes were enormous, her lips pulled away from her open mouth, and the dreadful gasping was shaking her body. He felt guilt, a long list of misdemeanors passing through his mind.

He lifted her up, felt the damp tension of muscle spasms racking her body.

'Get the damn kettle closer! Closer ... Maria, easy, *easy*. I've sent for Dr Norris. Don't tense up ... try to relax, *relax*.' She looked at him directly, her face set in a puzzled stare. He wiped her mouth with the back of his hand as she struggled to make sounds, producing at last a caricature of her voice. 'Charlie, want Charlie.'

Then suddenly, with a restraint and a delicacy in contrast to her struggle for air, she was very still, eyes open and no longer desolate. George knew his wife was dead.

Dr Norris said it was her heart giving out after too many attacks of asthma had put a strain on it. The doctor nodded with solemnity and told George it was God's will, and left.

Father Zorilla had been found. He had arrived just before the doctor and had given Maria extreme unction and added, 'May she be protected by the four good angels, Michael, Raphael, Uriel, and Gabriel.' He took a glass of wine afterward with Mollie the cook and did not claim it was God's will but rather 'we must all bear our burdens.'

Mollie told Tony the stableboy the last rites were impressive, even as she claimed Maria had been dead for twenty minutes. Irena arranged for a high mass for Maria's soul, and the church was well filled, for the Fiores were now important citizens of San Francisco, and Maria had done good work for the Convent of the Sacred Heart. Present too were some of her whist players, several of the track people who knew her as an advocate of the sport of kings. Father Zorilla praised Maria as a good woman, with a blameless life.

Irena, looking older, took George's arm after mass. "I feel scoured like a pot. We came here together, she and I. What for? What for?'

'To be.'

'It's all predestination and damnation. Poor George.'

'Poorer in some ways, but not poor.'

He could sense Irena was being dramatic. He hugged her. She smelled of snuff and brandy. He wanted to be alone. No, he wanted to be with Rose and his daughter, but it would be unseemly, the new widower seeking the consoling arms of a lover. He shook hands with his son Fred, with Ramon, and the rest.

It being a Sunday, he went back to the empty bank, up to his office, and filled a favorite pipe. He sat smoking, thinking of his wife, with wonder at her image, her placid life, of Father Zorilla preaching, 'We are all strangers in Egypt. We are God's own, or we are nothing, doubly alienated.' He fell asleep in his chair, and it was nearly dark when he awoke, creaking in the joints. In the streets were a few people and overhead a scud of dark clouds turning to a cold tea-colored rain.

Two days later he was at Bay Cottage being greeted by Rose (who tactfully did not mention Maria's death, but tenderly urged him to take care of himself). His complexion, she said, was bad, and he ate hardly any of the food she put before him. Maude was maturing, growing up. At thirteen his daughter was pert, lean, and buoyant. 'Uncle George, I'm going sailing with the Bensons and going to handle the tiller.'

'You're a fine sailor, sweetie. Just remember, starboard from the other side.'

'Silly, I knew that before I could talk.'

She gave him a hug, kissed him on the cheek, and stuck out her tongue.

George sipped a pale wine. 'She's growing. I'll want to stop being "Uncle George." I want to be Papa. She can't go on believing her father died a soldier defending the Union.'

Rose looked at him closely, did not smile. 'I was expecting some sort of reaction like that. I mean, a marriage offer.'

'Dammit, I'm saying we're going to be married—within a decent time, of course. Say, three months?'

'No, George. I love you, I'm grateful for Maude. As for me, in a hemmed-in way, I've been happy. Very happy, but—'

'No buts.' He tried to seize her hand over the terrace table, but she withdrew it. He wondered. Was it true that as we know more, we feel less? No, of course not, not between them. 'We're getting married.'

She looked at him and he thought: Rosie, Rosie, how mysterious and palpable you look. 'George, I don't desire to get married. You don't owe me that. This, our relationship has gone on so long, there is such a conscious acceptance, why—'

'But dammit, there's Maude. She'll have a father, legally. I may die a very rich man. Also, what of the shock to her in the word "bastard," very popular around here? We could explain you're marrying Uncle George, who loves you both. Rosie, listen.'

She stood up, walked to the railing of the terrace, and looked out over the bay, the triangle of sails tacking in a light wind and the shimmering water. She spoke without turning. 'George, I've made a life enclosed in parentheses. You've been comfortable, happy within its boundaries. I hope so anyway. Now for me to refresh the gossips who knew about us nearly from the start, to move into that big

307

fancy tomb of yours on Nob Hill, and be pointed out as the whore who outwaited the betrayed wife ... No.'

'Christalmighty, what are you saying, woman? Who gives a damn what the whole fucking town thinks? Rosie, whatever I thought of my wife, I've lost a human being. Charlie has gone off, most likely to be killed. And now this, *you*.' He stood up and lifted his arms as he shouted, 'No, *no!*'

She came to him, put her arms around him. 'Calm down, darling, you're going to bring on an attack of fever. For myself, I could face it. But for Maude to hear San Francisco gloat and whisper, no.'

'We could move to Los Angeles, San Diego.'

'Just hoping to outwit what? Maude's a very fine pianist—all promise now, true. But she's been studying with Kolokoff in town, and he's excited. He talks of her going to New York to study with Boris Thomkin.' She didn't seem to be talking to him, but rather exposing some inner vision. 'I want her to have a fuller life than mine, wider horizons, a deeper sense of the whole world rolling through the universe. Paris, Rome too. St Petersburg. To see royal processions at Buckingham Palace, climb the Leaning Tower of Pisa, walk down the Champs Elysées, the Place de la Concorde, touch marble carved by Michelangelo, and ...'

She stopped speaking, caught herself with an intake of breath. 'Sorry, darling. It doesn't change my love for you. I'm just'—she gave a quick short laugh—'I'm just turning down the title of Mrs Fiore and a big house full of dust-catchers.'

She tried to embrace him, but George moved back, anger turning to unreason. 'You're just a damn Jewish mother. You can't help it, I suppose. I've seen it with the Hellman family, and the Newmans and the Harrises. The mother keeps tight hold of the children, the husbands become castrated ...' He stopped talking, feeling a touch of the recurring fever, lightheadedness.

Rose looked closely at him. 'That's unfair. Bringing up

my Jewishness, as if it's clutching our child out of your reach. Don't you feel the same about your sons? Your own Italianness. The love of the *bambini?* I've seen them being stuffed with *pasta* by the Italian vineyard workers. What's so fraudulent in me, in thinking of the child?'

He said softly, 'Jesus, all I did was ask you to marry me.'

'Yes, you did. I should have been more gracious in my refusal.'

'Yes, Rosie, when you feel like shouting, you write a poem.'

'Oh, God, God ...' She was suddenly weeping, her face streaked with tears. He put his arms around her and kissed her damp cheeks, he petted her neck, put his face down in the curve between her shoulder and throat. He, too, wanted to weep, but one didn't do that. He was aware that there was something impregnable about Rose Rodman, an inner serenity, her people's alertness to the need for survival. Maybe it was an inner awareness of godliness, of moral values, values held to more than lip service. No wonder her people had such difficulties; they were vulnerable these Jews, strong and vulnerable at once.

Rose said, 'Let's dry our eyes and have a drink.'

George left Bay Cottage with a renewed wonderment at his lack of knowledge about women.

At the Casa, Irena was carrying on as usual. The sheep herders took their flocks into the hills, the dairy and the vineyards were busy, the steers fattening for market. Irena sat under her wisteria arbor, looking old and gray, a bit too bulky, but she could still erupt with all the vigor of youth, cursing and yelling at her servants and foreman. But the physical drive, George could see, was slackening and she had traded her frisky horse and Hancock saddle for a Springfield rig with red-painted wheels and overpadded seat. She looked up at him, a thin dark cigarillo smoldering in one corner of her mouth. 'So, you're going on a wild goose chase, with Tom and two of my best horses.'

'I'm going to round up Charles.'

'Are you? Where to hell-and-gone can he be?'

'I've been thinking, maybe he got on a ship for Japan, China. If so, there's nothing to do. Or maybe he made for Mexico. But the Pinkertons watched the border. I've got a feeling, a crazy vision, Irena, he's in a place we both enjoyed, deep in the Montana wilderness, an abandoned stone house some damn fool Frenchman built to raise blooded cattle.'

'And when you find him and that Chinese ragbag he trotted off with?'

'I don't know what *then*. I just want to see him, touch him, talk to him. I need to get away from the bank, the city for a while.'

'From the big house, the bastard you were there to Maria. Suddenly the bank isn't the only vital toy in the whole wide world?'

'I've put Rocco and Ramon in charge. He's a big help to me.'

Irena laughed, her haunches and belly shook.

'You can thank me, not Tomas, for the boy's abilities. And he wanted to be a paint dabbler.'

'He still does, but he feels he isn't a genius.... So look in for me, Irena ... and now give me a big Italian hug and an *arrivederci*.'

They held each other close, aware they were growing old and that what they accepted as reality was often as nebulous as dreams.

30

The country George and Tom were moving through had an arid, hard beauty, a starkness as if nature had set up its patterns not for man but for its own unsolved purpose. There were great difficult slopes to descend, narrow passages among wild shrubbery to move through. After topping some ridge, they would stand, panting from leading their horses, to look upon the next ridge and beyond.

Tom's travel sense and companionship were invaluable to George, and Tom had been delighted to come along, pleased at being asked. Though George hadn't told Rocco or Ramon why he was taking this trip, he had confessed its purpose to Tom. The two men had shed their city bankers' clothing, trading their suits for long linen suitcoats and wide-brimmed hats. Behind their saddles were packs containing buckskin shirts, camp gear, a pair of rifles, a Smith and Wesson six-shooter, and foodstuffs.

George felt he was moving into a new world, and though he sensed he might be foolish to search, he felt exhilarated as he moved away from the burial of a wife, the rejection of a mistress, the problems of banking, and the enmity of Gaw.

George regained his ability to recover energy quickly, to face physical obstacles. Wilderness, tragedy, and time had hardened him but had not weakened his intensity, his tenacity.

They were husbanding their supplies. George managed to shoot several large rabbits, and a good blast from a shotgun collected half a dozen sage hens. They became soot-smudged, grease-stained from campfire cooking.

After two weeks they came upon signs of habitation, circles of firemarked stones that had been campsites, clearly a deserted farm; they found a leaning cabin, a plow with its handles polished by sweaty, hardworking hands, even an attempt at a well. They found, too, the remains of a child's rag doll, its features sketched with charcoal.

'Sad, Tom, very sad. Someone tried to make a home here and failed, had to leave.'

'Soil's all wrong. Not enough rain.'

George was looking at a tattered map. 'It's not a very

311

good map, but we should be near a town called Hard Flats, and then on to the Frenchman's house.'

A day later they came across some cornfields blistering in the lime-white heat of the sun, the plants tattered by wind, the tassels not developed fully; a scarecrow made of rags stood guarding the failed crop.

They rode on ten miles and found a little stream, green-scummed in the shallows, a pool made by some dead brush barrier. They shucked their clothes, and wading out past some reddish rocks, they found moving water. They filled the water bottles and dunked themselves in the cool water, sputtering and yelling as they dripped water from their hair and faces. Their entire bodies, to the very insides, cooled and felt refreshed.

George felt renewed, felt his zeal for the quest revitalized. They lay on the bank, on a flat sandy area among the reeds, and smoked their pipes. The horses drank and blew air from their rubbery nostrils, setting up bubbles in the water that flowed past. Tom fried lake bass in the last of their bacon that night. George got out a flask of whiskey and they had some dollops with water, drinking from tin cups, seated cross-legged by the fire. They could hear the tethered horses cropping grass.

'It's cleared my head, Tom, this trip. I can see what the bank has to do to meet the future.'

'You always did.'

'No, I mean not just expanding, opening branches here and there. We should study the crops, the cattle, the value of farmland. Don't just barge in and put up a sign, "Pacific-Harvesters Bank," but make a survey.'

'A survey?'

'Talk to people, see how the other banks are doing. Find prosperous towns and avoid the failed ones. Study villages the railroads have opened up—there are big futures in those towns, and we should get in there before anyone else has the sense to. Study the tax and bankruptcy records.'

'That's smart, Major.'

George smiled. 'Not really, just paying attention to

details.' He banged his cup on the ground. ' I needed this change, time to scrape off old ideas. Get a good look at the stars, feel anything is possible.'

Two days later they rode into Hard Flats, a dismal place, hardly a town—a dusty hundred yards of main street full of potholes and discarded wood ash, three cross streets that lacked wooden sidewalks. Every structure in the place was unpainted, even Portus Klein's General Store. A blacksmith forge stood out in the open under a canvas awning backed up by a barn. There was a water tub in front of the building announcing a saloon, and several hitching posts. A half-dozen horses, tormented by flies, stood heads down, twitching their tails whenever the flies bit. It was a town populated by rough farmers, drunks, diseased Indians, the dregs of the westward migration, who would later become folk heroes.

It would be banks like his—moving away from the coast—that would produce change and growth in these wastelands. George noted no bank, just a grimy shed lettered 'Hiram Ash, Farm Loans, Auctions, Wells Fargo Agent.'

On one side of the street there was a two-story building with a wide porch. There were clean curtains on its two windows and tin cans growing geraniums on the sills. 'NEW WEST HOTEL, TRAVELERS' REST/MEALS.'

The interior was clean. At a burnt-oak counter, under a huge mounted elk's head, stood a wide man with great mustaches testing a pen he had pulled from its resting place in a potato. He looked up. 'Ah, yes, I can offer shelter.'

George took the pen from the man's fingers. 'Just for the night.'

'As you say, sir.'

'We want a hot bath, and some well-cooked food free of grease, and a clean room—no bedbugs, no spiders.'

'Just sign.'

George cleaned the pen and wrote their names with a flourish.

'Is there a stage that goes north?'

313

'Wells Fargo passes through every two days on its way to Porter Springs.'

'No, we're heading northeast. Ever hear of the Frenchman's house?'

The man smeared ink on his fingers from the pen George handed him. "Seems like some Frenchy did try to work cattle up among the sugar pines. Off to hell and gone in the direction you speak of. Petered out, the frog, he pulled tracks.'

'Two people, a couple pass through here in the last few months or so? White man, she Indian or a high yellow?'

The man wiped his inky fingers on his oiled waistcoat. 'Well, now, Injuns, they are mostly settled away on them reservations. High yella, or Chinks worked on the spur line up near Mettysburg. They passed through here some. A couple you say, hey?'

'Tall blond man and a girl, could be Indian or something.' George slid a five-dollar gold piece across the scarred countertop. 'Settling an estate.' He added a card. 'I'm a banker, as you can see.' He held a forefinger on the coin, waited.

'You see a lot of odd mixings, squaw men, hoors in silk, three-card-monte dealers.'

George took his finger off the coin.

'Yep, about yer couple, they just bought supplies and went on. Didn't stay here—town gossip, you know, mixed pair. They seemed kind of rabbity, like they were not so happy to attract attention.'

'Thanks.' The coin was slid off the edge of the counter and into an open drawer. 'Now, I can git you elk steaks, fried chicken, hash-browns. I'll just roust out the greaser that cooks and have it coming up hot in half an hour.'

'Have someone feed and water the horses, bed them down for the night.'

'I'll get the saddlebags, Major,' said Tom.

'Military man, sir?'

'Long time ago. Anyone passing through ask about the couple?'

'Oh, maybe a couple months ago or so. Let's see, yes, a big fuck of a Chink. *Really* big, I mean all of six-feet-three or four, did ask around, with what small English he had.'

'What else he do?'

'Well, now, he didn't stay here. We have a respectable policy about color, you understand. He bought a packhorse, loaded up, and went on.'

Clearly Gaw's men had been active.

George and Tom left the hotel in the morning after a breakfast of ham and eggs. They took the road north at nine o'clock in the morning. Two miles from the town, the road, mere wagon tracks, rose to rocky ground and wound around ravines, wild growths of hardy plants that survived dry summers and hard winters. Tom was in a good mood, watching some birds circling a green strip below the road, pointing to a patch of wildflowers. He hoped the horses had been properly fed; it was wild country ahead.

Charles and Moon Orchid had decided to stay in the Frenchman's house for the baby's birth. Moon Orchid feared any idea of revealing themselves at this time, even to a backwoods village. But the strains brought on by the prospect of Moon Orchid's coming confinement and by Charles's edginess about their condition cracked the facade of their lighthearted attitude toward their dwindling supplies. Both, Charles felt, were spoiled enough by civilization to crave coffee and sugar and other items. But game and wild fruit would see them through. Both, feeling vulnerable, drew closer together.

Something else added to Charles's anxiety. He had come upon the tracks of a man's boots a mile from the house. There they were, in plain sight, heavy-footed and disappearing into the wet leaves and brush. But no person made himself known. It was almost as if a lurking figure was daring them to find him, for the tracks began to show up, over a period of four or five days, nearer and nearer to their refuge. Charles did not tell Moon Orchid of this ominous development: how could he announce that a snake had invaded their Eden?

He tried to convince himself that the signs of the presence of another human being, where heretofore there had been none, did not have to signify menace. After all, the wilderness country around was gradually being explored and settled. God knows, he thought, there's plenty of room, and yet people are going to brush up against one another. Moon Orchid and he were intruders, as had been the Frenchman and his family before them.

But lurking, nagging danger was staking out a claim on his peace of mind; his sixth sense of trouble hung on. One gray dawn while Moon Orchid slept, he set out to stalk their unidentified visitor. He spent several hours, testing to the limit his woodsman's skills, finding nothing concrete and yet nothing to allay his fears. No fresh tracks, no recent campsites, only some rabbit heads near the remains of a long-abandoned wire-loop trap.

As he was heading back down a piny ravine, he heard a rifle shot, followed by the sting sound of a chunk of bark pried loose by the slug. He threw himself on the ground and crawled into a small thicket, lying there until the afternoon darkness began.

Charles was at a severe disadvantage, aware that his adversary had time and patience on his side. Instinct told him that he was being toyed with and that the single shot had been a purposeful near-miss. Anger and revulsion rose up within him, and moving as quickly as he could in the deepening twilight, he made his way back to the house.

Reaching the door, he called out for Moon Orchid, and when he heard her answer his summons, his heart gave a glad leap. At least, for the moment, they were safe.

'What is happening?'

He hesitated, then decided that he could no longer pretend that nothing was wrong. 'I don't know for sure,' he said, reaching out to stroke her silky blue-black hair. She did not resist him, but her eyes grew wary.

'It may be that there are some trappers passing through this part of the country. We had better lie low until they move on.' He could not bring himself to mention the rifle shot.

'They could be friendly.' She pouted. 'We could trade with them. Deer pelts for some supplies.'

He shook his head and drew her close to him. His inability to be explicit about his fears communicated itself to her. In the silence that had become familiar to them, they ate and then went to sleep. Or at least Moon Orchid willed herself to do so. Charles lay tautly awake, her thickening small body nestled into his side, his hand outside the cover clenching a loaded gun.

31

The next morning he announced his intention of looking around. Still, he did not mention what had occurred the day before. The idea of leaving her alone again was torture to him. Charles hated even more to be leaving Moon Orchid unprotected in the house. But he had to trick the intruder into showing his hand.

'You must stay here ready with the shotgun,' he warned her, and embraced her tightly. 'Keep the door barred and do not open it on any account.'

Moon Orchid assented, without saying a word. As he was leaving, she uttered one short question. 'Do you fear outlaws or Gaw?'

'I don't know,' he admitted. 'Whoever it is, he's someone rough.' And he went out, listening for the sound of the wooden bar being pulled across the door.

'I'll be back around the middle of the morning,' he called softly to her, tapping on the heavy door. She tapped back her assent. Putting his ear to the door, he could just hear her murmur his name. A chill seized him, but shaking it off, he struck into the trees.

A few hours of making larger and larger circles around the dwelling turned up no more than had his search of the day before. His sense of unease, however, increased by the minute. Cautiously, trekking his way back to the house, by way of the spring where they went for water, he stopped short when he noticed a thin trail of red droplets on the dirt. Blood, without a doubt. Throwing caution aside, he followed the blood as it lead to the stone house. His hair itched on his scalp, and the sweat falling from his forehead clouded his vision; it was hard to quell his panic, hard to convince himself he had done the right thing by a second reconnoiter instead of keeping a constant surveillance on the house.

'Moon! Moon, my darling!' He was a few yards from the door, pausing in the shelter of a tree. Never had a deep panic been so perilously close to the surface.

After a while—a few minutes that seemed like hours—he heard her. Then he heard the door being unbarred and opened. Moon Orchid stood there, the shotgun in her hand. He ran to her and held her as she, trembling and laughing, and crying all at once, dropped the gun.

'You hurt?'

She gave a sob and a hiccup. 'No, I shot somebody who started coming in through the window. I didn't get a good look. I got the gun up as he ran ... I let him have it. Such a loud noise, and it threw me backwards. I missed.'

'No, you hit him. There's blood out there.'

Moon Orchid clung to Charles with all her strength, then pushed him away. 'We must move on.' He bit his lip, struggling with himself so that she would not see his feeling of helplessness. 'We might get ambushed if we left now. He'd just lay for us. We'll wait until dark, then sneak out of here and spend the night in the hollow tree.'

'If you think that is the best course.'

He looked at her, gauging her confidence in him and

318

finding it stronger than his in himself. He only said, 'You'll be safe in the hollow tree with the shotgun. No one can find you there. But I have to go out after the son of a bitch just before the sun comes up.'

'Don't!' Moon Orchid stifled her cry of terror.'You will be killed.'

'We'll see it through. Rub your little brass Buddha.' Charles forced a smile from her.

Together they gathered blankets, some dried meat, and a flask of water. They waited for dark, then built up the fire, and when it was sootblack outside, ducking low, they went into the bush. They froze when suddenly a hoot owl sounded too close, but they covered the remaining rocky ground to the hollow tree without incident. There was only room enough for them to press inside and sit locked together with the blankets cocooning around them. The hollow smelled of field mice and beetle dust. It was a cold night and they could feel the warmth of each other's breaths on their faces, although they said little, afraid the sounds would echo in the night.

The morning found them stiff and damp. Putting his finger to his lips, Charles checked Moon's shotgun, put the pistol in his belt, and took up his rifle. He kissed Moon Orchid and held her close, her woman smell practically overpowering him. She was breathing hard, but just said, 'Go.'

He got out of the tree just before the dawn came, cold and gray-blue, and headed first for the blood on the path. It stopped soon, too soon. Pausing to survey the broken underbrush, Charles sat on an old rotting log. Some blue jays came jabbering, then flew away. A spotted doe trotted out into the clearing, her ears up. She jumped over a log draped in wild melon vine, her white tail flashing, and was gone.

A voice came to him from behind. 'No move or you dead fella.'

Charles said, 'No move.' There was a choking giggle, a body moved, and a barrel of a gun was poked into Charles's back. He turned his head, and there was his stalker, a Chinese named Chiang, the boss of Gaw's Chinese work gangs. His long greasy hair hung over slit eyes; the mouth was open, revealing black snags of teeth as he cackled. Charles swiveled his head around and said, 'Gaw sent you?'

The Chinese grinned and pressed the gun barrel harder into Charles's flesh. 'Nevah give up, Mastah Gaw say. You go, he said, find Moon woman. I find, yes.'

At this Chiang drew the gun lovingly around Charles's side and stood facing him. Then, lowering his bulk, he squatted on his hams, shifting the gun against Charles's chest. 'Other places take time to look-see. So now I catch.' He seemed satisfied by his speech. He squatted in comfort to enjoy his victory. Charles felt he had been a fool to let himself be trapped. Moon and he should have run for it the night before.

'I kill you, take Moon back to Mastah Gaw.'

Charles remained silent. The thought of Moon Orchid being returned to Gaw was obscene. He could not suppress a shudder.

Suddenly a squirrel scuttled overhead. Chiang was startled for a split second. It was Charles's move. Tensed and ready, he kicked out both his legs and knocked the squatting man off balance. The gun fired into the air as Chiang fell back on one hand. Charles rolled fast to the right of Chiang, grabbed his own rifle from where he had let it fall by the log, aimed it at Chiang, and the slug tore into the leg.

But even this did not stop the huge Chinese, already incapacitated by the still-fresh arm wound inflicted by Moon Orchid the day before. With a horrible cry Chiang leaped upon Charles, knocking the rifle out of his grip, and seized Charles by the throat. Charles felt a brief second of resignation to fate, but then the remembrance of Moon Orchid and their child gave him the strength to exert a final desperate effort. Chiang's hands were closing around his windpipe when he reached beneath the coat and pulled out his pistol. Shoving it into Chiang's stomach, he pulled hard on the trigger before the grunting Chinese had time to realize what his victim was attempting.

Chiang's fingers loosened their hold as Charles heard the blasting sound of the shot burying itself in the giant's innards. He pulled back and watched coldly as Chiang's eyes rolled up into his forehead as he sank to his knees, blood flowing from his mouth, a crimson spittle. He collapsed quickly, his expression disbelieving to the end, that he could have been bested.

Charles all of a sudden felt his stomach rising. He tasted blood in his own mouth, heard a rushing whistle in his ears. He got to his feet and noticed that his heart was racing, his lungs were burning, the skin on his chest felt tender and bruised. In the deepening twilight he could see Chiang's bulky shape lying on the ground in front of him. The eyes of the corpse were bulging open and the smell of blood filled Charles's nostrils.

It was a dizzy walk back to the hollow tree where Moon Orchid continued her vigil.

She began to weep when she saw him, whether with relief or with distress at the way he looked, he could not tell. "It was just,' he tried to comfort her, 'a berserk trapper.'

'No, it was Gaw,' she contradicted him. Her face was set in an expression he could not fathom.

He nodded, having no strength left to hide the truth from her. 'One of his men. I killed him.'

'Good. Now we rest, sleep.' Her calmness at his announcement that he had just committed murder startled him, causing him to realize for the thousandth time that there were facets of Moon Orchid's character that he would never comprehend: that she had chosen him, had followed him into the wilderness, yet she was hardly more than a girl.

'We go away.'

'Not now. He was alone, I'm sure. But if Gaw sent him, he must have sent others, perhaps offered rewards to bounty hunters?'

'Bounty hunters?'

'Men who seek other men for money.'

She clenched her fists and frowned, set her mouth tightly. Charles, cushioning her in his arms, felt her trembling.

'We're safest here, at the house,' he said to her.

'We are together. We will not fear,' she murmured as he picked her up and carried her to the house, to the room where the fire had died out.

He was fanning the new flames in the fireplace, and he realized that both of them were aware that their private world was spoiled, that it would never be the same.

They slept, but Charles woke in the middle of the night. Moon Orchid was moaning in her sleep, despite her earlier calm acceptance of the day's horrors. Was she having a nightmare? He lit a candle stump and saw that her face was contorted in pain and that the bed beneath her was stained with blood.

She looked wild-eyed, like a trapped animal snared in a loop of wire. Alternating panic and blankness. A cry escaped her, but she was barely aware of his presence.

'It's too soon for the baby,' he said helplessly.

Her moaning intensified. Suddenly she grabbed his arm, squeezing it with an inhuman pressure. 'Hold me, hold me!' she screamed. 'I must *not* lose our child!'

'No, no. It's not time yet.'

An hour later she miscarried. What would have been their daughter arrived lifeless in the world. He bathed Moon Orchid's forehead and gave her the remains of the whiskey in hot water. Then he bundled up the small shape of the infant's body in a piece of blanket. It was so small, seemed so perfect, each little fingernail breaking his heart. He went out to a far knoll, while Moon slept, worn out and drugged with the drink. He dug a little grave, deep between two great stones, putting down his burden. He filled the grave, sweating as he piled heavy stones over it. He was more than half mad, and he found that he was yelling meaningless shouts. Then he wept. This would not do, would not do, not do, Charles kept repeating. He went back to the Frenchman's house, limbs aching, cursing Gaw,

322

who had brought this tragedy.

Moon was sitting up when he came back; wan, she asked nothing.

For two days they hardly spoke. It was gone, the joy of their private world, private isolation. Safety was also gone. Charles saw they would have to move away from the stone house. Neither could bear to go on living in it.

He got out some old maps from a pack and looked them over, pondering routes, while Moon sat by his side as the fire burned bright and the outside world was dark and a sinister place.

'Canada,' he said. 'We'll make for Canada. The horses have loafed long enough. They're strong.'

'What is Canada?'

'Safety for a while. And they have law there, the Mounties. We'll head for Vancouver and get a ship across the Pacific.'

'The Pacific?'

'Away from here.'

'Will we ever come back?'

'Ask one of your gods.'

She began to laugh. He took her in his arms and rocked her back and forth. They both knew this was the only way. They didn't dare try to get to the East Coast with Gaw's spy network covering the country all the way to New York.

In the morning, Charles went to hunt up the horses, which were feeding in a nearby clearing.

It was a week later that George and Tom came in sight of the stone house. No smoke came from its chimney, and along a path they found the dead, putrifying body of a huge Chinese. George said to Tom, 'One of Gaw's *tong* men.'

'Been dead a few days, by the smell of him. Ants all over the place.'

'Best to get to the house. Go easy, Tom, and rifles at the ready.'

'Think there are more of them?'

'Could be. Or there might be a couple more corpses up there.'

323

Once they reached the house, they could see it was deserted. There was old ash in the fireplace, a tattered waistcoat which George recognized as Charles's and a bit of Chinese writing done in charcoal on the wall. And there was still a trace of musk and sandalwood in the air.

'They've gone.' George sat on a low bench, gazing around him as if he could conjure up his son, Tom thought.

'Maybe we'll catch up with them.'

'No,' George said. 'I'm dog tired, and they want to do what they're doing. It ends here for us, Tom. I need a drink ...'

'We've got a few slugs of bourbon left.' Tom went out to the horses, and George sat, eyes closed, inhaling, absorbing the atmosphere of the place, sensing his son and the mysterious woman Moon Orchid. For a moment he understood Charles's audacity and felt almost exhilaration, mixed with fierce love for his son he feared he'd never see again. He drank whiskey with Tom, who had built up a fire and was studying his torn boot.

'I'm a banker, Tom. That's my work, and that's what I should be doing. It was a crazy idea, this damn trip. But it did me good. Yes, it did. We'll start working out the branch banks as soon as we get back.... The Devil had me, Tom, and my grandmother always insisted his power is strongest when we do not believe he exists. The cunning son of a bitch! Have the horses ready early in the morning, Tom.'

'Yes, Major.'

6

Agitato

32

As the 1880's swung into place, George Fiore felt the burden of his half-century of years. He was still too thin, ached in the joints, but the recurring bouts of fever no longer came. They had disappeared on his return from the journey to find his son. He thought it odd that nothing had ever turned up about Charles and Moon Orchid's whereabouts since their departure from the Frenchman's house deep in the wilderness. There were rumors, of course. They had been seen in Canton, Charles acting as a tea merchant for a British firm. George also heard that they were deep in the Yukon territory in Canada, as agents for Hudson's Bay Company; that a trunk containing a dispatch lettered 'Pacific-Harvesters Bank' and an added 'C.F.' had been found among the wreckage of a ship near Nueva Imperial off the coast of Chile. For George, hopes, doubts, and apprehensions remained; Charlie would someday return. But for now, dead or alive, Charlie was no part of his life .

He hoped Rose and Maude were still close to him in spirit. They had been in Europe for two years now. Could Maude really be nineteen? That brisk, slim, bright-eyed child, who at first could barely reach the piano pedals with shoetips was now studying with the masters and giving concerts. The last letter from Rose had contained disturbing undertones:

Darling George:

We are here at Baden-Baden at time of Heulen and Zähneknirschen. Maude and I are just beside ourselves with delight with the concert she gave in St Petersburg. She played Chopin as she had never done it before, the Waltz No 6 and the Scherzo No 3. in G sharp. The czar and czarina attended and we met them later at the reception at the Hermitage and there were flowers in our suite at the Metropol. No more public concerts this season.

We are going to Italy to stay with the Baroness Gazarette at her palazzo. And Maude will prepare herself for her appearance with the Nacionale for the South American Tour. She is adding to her Chopin, Schubert's *Seligkeit*, and Mozart's Piano Concerto in F.

She has become very mature, a bit too feisty, and tries to take the reins in her own hands. But I manage to shoo off the idle young men with titles, the hangers-on of the arts. If all works out well with the South American tour, we hope to get concert bookings in New York and Chicago, perhaps even in San Francisco. I don't know if Maude is ready yet for America. She must arrive home at her very best, and her Brahms *Capriccio* in B, Op. 76, is not yet right. I agree with Signore Cabaldi in Rome, with whom she has been studying. She must work harder and not attend so many fetes and social events.

I know all this may seem perverse and strange to you, our world so far removed from the bank and your life in the West.... I do miss you. I think back to the times at Bay Cottage, the blooming crocuses , and feel again the uniqueness and direct simplicity of our love. I want to be in your arms again, but I also want something for your—*our*—child. Genius isn't given to everyone. We must nurture it, watch it grow, direct it properly in a young girl. I use the word 'genius' as some of the critics here have, but it's too soon. Maude is not fully mature as an artist and she could go wrong, seek popular adoration, play the wrong music. You see, I am divided between

327

settling down with you, and my sense of duty to Maude. Didn't you once call me Duty's Child? I have not written any poetry for some time. The project of a little book, *On the Bay*, seemed to need more poems of a mature nature. But someday, *some*day, I'll work on it and I'll be with you. I must close this letter. We are going to Bayreuth; there is a private party for Chancellor Bismarck at the Countess Witka-Eizheimer's and Maude will play Liszt. The Germans are such a wonderful people, so sentimental about things, and so clean, so *gemütlich*. It's important for Maude's career she be accepted in the best circles. Try to understand, my love—*Il divolo non è così brutto come si dipinge*.

Love,
Your Rose

' "The devil is not so bad as painted!" ' George flung the letter from him. God damn *all* Jewish mothers!

There was widening national interest in the wealth and political power of the West. As Rocco put it to some members at The Bankers' Club, 'There is a damn good chance we can even have a California president.'

Senator Homer Kendrick was prominent in his party, a powerful voice in national affairs. 'The coming man from the West' was a phrase often heard. Yet there was a small dark cloud appearing on his horizon. Investigations were heating up in Congress, lawsuits were hinted at, commissions were formed to look into the affairs of the western railroad builders, who had put down hundreds of thousands of miles of rails, and, it was suspected, swindled the public out of hundreds of thousands of dollars. The Big Four—Huntington, Hopkins, Stanford, and Crocker— were under serious investigation. 'Their tainted wealth,' cried one Fourth of July speaker of San Francisco, 'pours over them in a golden flood. They swim in a sea of millions stolen from you!' There was talk of their buying congressmen, senators, and judges to pass railroad bills, giving them free public land and federal aid. Homer Kendrick had spoken in their favor. 'It is only fitting for a Californian to speak of our great enterprises that benefit *all* of the people of the Golden State.'

Proof was elusive. There were hints that letters existed incriminating the Big Four, but the letters had yet to surface.

Kendrick's chance to get the nomination at the Republican convention was aided immeasurably by the assassination of President Garfield, the twentieth president of the United States. There was talk of a new kind of candidate from the West. Homer's campaign chest was overflowing; Gaw and other Chinatown figures had contributed heavily because of Kendrick's fight against a permanent ban on Chinese immigration. The senator had managed to limit the ban to only ten years by intense lobbying. A Chicago newspaper editor (the convention would be held there) looked over the field of candidates and wrote, 'Not all politicians are corrupt; not all heroes are only successful thieves.' Presumably he had Homer in mind.

'That's faint praise,' said Rocco to Ramon at a fund-raising lunch. 'The boys think if they are smart enough to be able to rake in the boodle, there's a future in politics.'

'That's so cynical, Rocco,' said Ramon. 'We find the best men we can, and hope. Saints don't smoke cigars and kiss babies. I think Homer is a better man than Cleveland or McKinley, or any other easterner trying for the office.'

Rocco shrugged. 'Those letters people are talking about—supposedly Ralston once had them.'

'What about them?' asked Ramon.

'Remember when his "pals" dumped Bill Ralston and the Bank of California, and maybe did Ralston in because of secrets he knew? I think that ghost may walk, might come out of the woodwork to haunt that scum!'

George, reading the morning *Chronicle* while sitting in the warm morning sun on his veranda, noted a sharp increase in muckraking stories focusing on the Big Four as the convention drew nearer. He sipped his coffee—black, as his doctor had advised.

Alicia, niece of the late Conchita Concepcion, came out to the veranda, retying her apron strings. 'Mr Kendrick to see you, sir.'

'*Who?*'

'Mr Moses Kendrick, he said I should be sure to say Moses.'

'Christalmighty!' said George, rising. 'Moses?'

He buttoned his morning coat and went into the library, then out into the main hallway, where he had placed a stuffed bear holding a tray for visiting cards. The stained-glass panels in the fanlight of the front door threw gleams of red and yellow on the wallpaper. Moses Kendrick, looking old, was leaning on a heavy cane and stood staring at the bear with fascination.

'Where the hell'd you get this grizzly, George?'

'Fred shot it some years back and gave it to me as a birthday gift. His idea of a joke … Moses, how are you?'

The old man made an effort to straighten his back, fingered his short white beard into order. 'How can an old man be? Gout, a heart that plays tricks, my joints stiff. How are you?'

'I'm getting by.' He held out a hand and put an arm around the old man. 'Forgive an emotional wop. It's been years and years, we should have—'

'—made up years ago. Never mind. I come because I want a favor. There. That's a fact and I've said it.'

'Come sit down in the library.'

'Don't offer me your arm. I'll make it under my own steam.'

It was a slow walk even with the cane, and at last the big man sank into a deep leather chair and sighed, 'I'm aware of what Sarah used to quote from some damn book, "the skull beneath the skin"—old Mortality. I miss Sarah. And Maria, she too is gone. I wanted to come to the services but was laid up by some heart pains. The old ticker plays tricks.'

George poured two small glasses of bourbon from a cut-glass decanter. Moses sniffed his glass. 'Good. I don't fancy this new habit of drinking Scotch.'

'No, this is good mash Kentucky-style bourbon, and if you like branch water ...'

'Skip the water.'

They sipped and stared at each other, thinking of their ages, of time passing, George recalling all the banal truths of mortality.

'George, I wanted to see something before they pat a shovel of dirt in my face. It's Homer in the White House.'

'I like Homer. We worked together when he was young. He's a bright new penny, a man with a feeling for the poor, and he's ambitious. But then, so was Caesar.'

'You're hedging.'

George refilled the little glasses. 'You didn't come here to ask me to vote for Homer or march in a torchlight parade for him.'

The old man lifted his glass near his lips but didn't take a sip. He said slowly, 'The Ralston files.'

George sat well back in his chair, half-shut his eyes. 'You've been hearing talk.'

'How the hell can anyone avoid it? I hear Ralston turned over some private files to you.'

'I'm not saying yes or no. I'll only discuss this on one condition: either crap or get off the pot ... You don't lie. Tell me who murdered Bill Ralston and why.'

Moses sighed, chewed on his lips with a nearly toothless mouth. 'I don't know.'

'Did you know at the time it was murder?'

'No, George. By all that's holy, no. I may seem to be a son of a bitch to you, and maybe I've done things against my creed at times, but I've never condoned murder.'

'You were one of Sam Brannan's Regulators, and so were some of the trustees who kicked Ralston out from his own bank.'

'About the Regulators, *that* was Law and Order. And, yes, you could say I gave Ralston the message he was out. The man was acting too big, spending too much, stripping

331

the bank of some of its assets. But that's all, George. I'm
sure two or three of the directors who backed me wouldn't
murder a man.'

'But you knew that *some* would.' George wondered why
he wasn't more angry facing Moses, why he was
questioning a man about a murder as casually as he might
discuss the stock market.

Moses tugged on his short white beard. 'Some who
might, yes—that's a guess.'

George stood up and rubbed his fingers together as if
warming them. 'Someone needed to get rid of Bill Ralston
because he did have certain papers that would implicate
them in the big Huntington railroad swindles.'

'Still, that's not murder.'

'The coroner sent me a private report swearing that
although the body was found floating in the bay, there was
no water in the lungs. You can't drown without inhaling a
hell of a lot of water.'

Moses Kendrick looked at George, anxiety plainly
showing on his face. God, George thought, Moses *is* old—
that thin, arthritic neck, the half-controlled tremor of the
bony hand. I could show a little mercy to the old bastard.
After all, he built the foundations for my own success, and
Bill Ralston's been dead a long time now.

George went to a tall teak bookcase and lifted out a set of
red-bound books. 'Sarah gave me this set of books, *Decline
and Fall of the Roman Empire*. I'm no longer much of a
reader.'

Behind the books was revealed the front of a small black
safe set in the wall, its dial and handle shining dully. George
spun the dial one way, then the other. The safe door swung
open. After looking over several bundles of paper tied up in
yellow linen ribbons, he picked one out and brought it over
to the library table.

'These are some papers Ralston sent me the day he went
to that trustees' meeting, his last.'

'He tell you why?'

'No, Moses, he just noted that he might need these

someday and asked me to keep them safe for him. I went through them after he was found dead. Personal notes and camera copies of certain original documents and letters.' He picked up a sheet of yellowing paper and read from it:

The directors of the Union Pacific contracted with themselves at costs which were inflated from $80,000 to $90,000 and $96,000 a mile, twice the maximum estimates. The total cost was $94,000,000. No one could ever figure out why the railroad had cost more than $44,000,000 to build; leaving $50,000,000 unaccounted for, save in the private pockets of the Big Four. It is estimated that the cost of building the first hundred miles was $30,000 per mile; for the second hundred miles it was $37,000 per mile. A head bookkeeper resigned. The contract was then given to one of Union Pacific's dummy companies, who expanded the cost to three times as much as originally called for. Money was paid to some congressmen, one of whom became a senator to push for special railroad decisions in Washington favorable to the Union Pacific.

Moses said, 'No names? That senator?'

'Not given in these notes.' George picked up several other letters. 'I'll just read you from some letters sent by Huntington to Washington.'

It will cost money to fix things. I believe with the $200,000 to start we can pass our bill, with you paying out the funds.

'Who's the letter to?'

George ignored the question and read from another Huntington letter:

Congress took half a million dollars a year from me so far. I am fearful this damn Congress will kill me. It costs so much money to fix things with them. We were very careful to get a US senator from California, disposed to use us fairly, and have the power to help. You are friendly, there is no man in the Senate that can push a measure further.

'Damn Huntington,' said the old man, banging his cane on the side of his chair, adjusting his calcified joints.

If you have to pay money to have the right thing done, it is only just and fair to do it.... If a politician has the power to do great evil and won't do right unless he is bribed to do it, I think it is a man's duty to bribe the politician. A man that will cry out against them himself will also do these things himself.

George looked up. 'Here's another Huntington letter.'

I received your telegram that B. has received for his services $60,000 in S.P. bonds and is asking how much more I think his services are worth in the future.... In view of the many things we have now before Congress, it is very important that your friends in Washington should be with us, and if that could be brought about by paying $10,000 to $20,000 per year, I think we could afford to do it, but of course, not until you had controlled his friends. I would like to have you get a written proposition from C. in which he would agree to control his friends for a fixed sum.

The old man made a painful effort, stirred himself, ripped the letter from George's hand, leaving a corner of it still in George's fingers. Moses peered at the paper. 'It's addressed to Senator Homer Kendrick, Senate Building, Washington.'

'Huntington asked several times that these letters be destroyed.... Ralston has noted, "H.K.'s bribings of Congress, commonwealths, courts, were disbursements listed on company records as 'General Expenses,' 'Legal

334

Expenses,' and when the going was hard and the costs painful, as 'Extra Legal Expenses.'" '

The old man shook his head.

'The letters weren't destroyed,' said George. 'They were kept as a threat over Huntington. I don't know how Ralston got them—he must have had to pay for them. There are about two dozen letters in which the greeting "Senator Kendrick" becomes "Dear Homer," and Homer is told "you promised the people through whom we pay you that you would stay in line."'

'You sat on these papers so long now. You wouldn't release them, would you?'

'No, I'm giving them to you, Moses. But they're only copies.'

'I know.'

'These letters can do incalculable damage to Homer's hopes of winning the nomination and were clearly written to him by Huntington in a rage. The originals, I'd guess, are being held by someone—maybe someone on whom Huntington once played a nasty game, double-crossed, cheated. So if there is a commission or investigation of Huntington and his partners, the letters could be part of the evidence.'

The old man rose, clutching the bundle of papers to his chest. 'You know that Homer is a good man, a practical man. To become someone, a power in the party, he had to have the right people behind him.'

George nodded. 'In return, he did favors.'

Moses shouted in outrage, 'Wouldn't you, if it meant saving your bank? Sure you would—as quick as shit goes through a goose!'

George thought, frowned. 'The world is whatever we decide it is in our heads, *not* out there; only the moment of deciding counts.'

'Well, would you piss on ethics to save your bank?'

'I'd be damn tempted, but I think not. I wouldn't do what people in Sacramento and Washington do with such casual ease.'

The old man coughed. '*You* wouldn't, George ...' He held out a hand. 'Maybe we can stop the original letters now I know what's in them.'

George took the offered hand. 'Stay well, Moses. I wish you that. And to be frank, I hope you don't get the original letters. The country is in the grip of Homer's friends, cartels of coal and wheat and gasworks, steel, tariffs, schemes, trusts, legislation for certain people that Homer might have to do favors for *if* he got to sleep in Lincoln's bed in the White House.'

Moses Kendrick didn't answer. He turned, grasping the papers, and shuffled towards the hall, thumping his cane down on the floor to assist him. George followed him to the front door and saw him move across the slate sidewalk toward a waiting carriage. The coachman helped him in, and the last George saw of the old man, he was slumped over in the carriage, head down.

Two weeks before the national convention an investigation was opened, and some of the Huntington letters were published. Senator Kendrick did not attend the convention. Grover Cleveland became president in 1884. Homer did not run for reelection to the Senate and retired to raise cattle and plant vineyards on the vast acreage of the family holdings in Napa County.

The congressional investigators of the railroad scandals filed their ineffectual reports, and nothing much was done to punish anyone or recover the millions lost. George, visiting Washington with Ramon, sat in the Visitors' Gallery of the Senate and heard one voice cry out: 'When the greatest railroad in the world, binding together the continent and uniting the two great seas which wash our shores, was finished, I have seen our national triumph and elation turned to bitterness and shame by the unanimous reports of three committees of Congress that every step of that mighty enterprise had been taken in fraud.'

Moses Kendrick died in 1887 and was buried by the side of his wife, Sarah, in the family plot in Santa Clara. The Pacific-Harvesters Bank sent flowers, but not in George

Fiore's name. George had not told the whole truth when he said he did not know who had many of the original Huntington letters. He suspected it was Mrs William Ralston and that it was she who made them public.

33

As the century drew to its close, George and Irena commiserated, Irena bemoaning her advancing age. 'The years go rushing by like telegraph poles while you're riding in a fast train,' she would sigh to George.

She felt badgered by betrayals, confidences, indiscretions she suspected were going on all around her. She often confused her son with his father. Though it was 1898, to her Ramon was still a boy, the youth she had cherished, not a man in his forty-second year and president of the Pacific-Harvesters Bank. The former aspiring painter was now a confident banker and heir to the chairman of the board.

Ramon was amused by what the Spanish clients called him—'The Comendador.' He didn't mind at all.

George had achieved the expansion that he had envisioned for so many years. There were now twenty-three branches, and more were planned. And if the damn horseless carriages were really to be the transportation of the future, the bank might give loans to certain carefully controlled oil drillers. As for that thing to be called 'the movies'—those scraps of flickerings projected on borrowed bedsheets, viewed for a nickel in a store holding two dozen folding chairs from the undertaker's parlor—it didn't seem likely to amount to much. Still, it bore watching.

George often discussed bank matters with Ramon in George's bedroom in the big house on Nob Hill; the doctors felt he should rest more. There was nothing much the matter with his heart, just a little murmur, but his blood was a bit thin as he neared seventy. 'A rest in bed for a week or so every six months,' said Dr Bronson, 'would do you no harm.'

Ramon brought over a huge black portfolio containing sketches and plans for the new Pacific-Harvesters Bank Building. It was going to take up most of a block on Montgomery Street.

'Damn doctor thinks all I have to do is lie here and go through self-scrutiny. Those the Sullivan plans?'

'Came by express from Chicago this morning.'

'Open them up, open up.'

The portfolio contained several watercolor sketches, two feet by three feet, presenting the imposing structure from different angles. There were also two dozen draftsman's layouts of facades, floor plans, details of staircases, main banking areas, offices, and details of the roofline, the tiles and ironwork around the windows.

George looked like a happy child, Ramon thought. He huffed, chortled, looked pensive at times and became engrossed in details.

'You think we did right to hire this fellow? He drinks, they say.'

'You picked him over Standford White's firm, some of H.H. Richardson's boys.'

'Hell, yes. I saw his Sullivan's Auditorium Building in Chicago, and I liked the pictures of his Guaranty Trust Bank in Buffalo. What do you think of all that glazed terra-cotta?'

Ramon said he liked it … George had fallen in love with the work of Louis H. Sullivan, his Carson Pirie Scott store, and even with the fact the man had studied at the Ecole des Beaux Arts in Paris. The architect had come out to San Francisco, looked over the site that George was buying up bit by bit, drank a lot of George's brandy, smoked his cigars, and said: 'Fiore, I'll design for you the goddamnedest structure Frisco has ever seen.'

George refilled their glasses. 'We don't like to call it "Frisco."'

'I'll do something worthy of the Golden Gate, that glorious body of water. None of the fancy crap we had a few years ago in ninety-three at the Columbia Exposition. Christ, everything since that damn fair has gone neo-Renaissance.'

They enjoyed the brandy, each other. 'Roomy, easy, not too much gold and vomit-colored marble, Louie. I'm giving you a free hand.'

'George, I always wanted to do a structure from which you could spit right into the Pacific Ocean.'

Now, as George flipped over the finely inked plans, he kept nodding. 'Telegraph to Louis it looks good, at least at *first* sight. We'll keep in touch. We break ground right after New Year's, 1900.'

Ramon put the sketches back in order. 'Look, Uncle George, maybe 1902? Maybe 1903? We need to study foundation stone, water table, rock resistance. We've got contractors to find, contracts to draw up, the City Hall boys to entertain. Abe Ruef and Mayor Schmitz decide *everything* in this city.'

'I don't want to know about payoffs to unions, political parties, or boss boddle men. Those are Rocco's contacts. Leave the plans here. I want you to give a dinner at the Casa when Louie gets here with the final plans. Who's this fellow Sargent, this painter Rose Rodman used to write me about? Maybe a mural by him? A red sunset, a batch of real people, Indians, Spaniards, mountain men, miners, fruit growers, sailors, all along the walls. The true West Coast. Want them all in it. Everybody.'

Ramon laughed. 'You want Barbary Coast whores, opium-den owners, bread-lines below the Slot?'

George was not listening. He had fallen back on his pillows, eyes closed, and he waved a thin hand at Ramon in farewell. Yes, the damn years like telegraph poles flashing by and we're all riding a fast train. He didn't feel old, just tired at times. How preposterous and yet lucky too, his past seemed. He saw it all with lucidity and precision. Life is not just facts but a more important relationship with what lies behind the facts.

Fact: Rose had been killed six years ago in one of those romantic train wrecks of the Wagon-Lits: Paris to Constantinople. Preposterous that they hadn't seen each other for so many years; their love perhaps was still there, hovering over the Atlantic. The Rose of those ecstatic times on the Rodman Rancho, and later the years of weekends at Bay Cottage. Gone now in a smear of bone and blood after a train plunged off a bridge into a ravine someplace along the Bosna near Majiaj.

Fact: their daughter remarkably precocious, a bit gauche as a child, seated at the piano or holding a tiller in a brisk bickering breeze. She never did give concerts in America. There were some good years as the celebrated 'Maude Rodman, Chopin in Concert.' Then she married that shave-necked Prussian Baron Heinrich Eisenlohr von Zollern-Boxberger; a horse's ass, judging by the image in the wedding picture sent him; spike helmets and crossed sabers in front of an ugly church in Ortelsburg; grandchildren now: Konrad, Hedwig, Siegfried, Mathilda.

Fact: Ramon had turned out well. He was actually running the bank, the whole organization, well assisted by Rocco, who was being featured in the Hearst and Pulitzer Sunday sections as 'The Playboy of the Western Coast.'

Fact: Tom too had shown his ability to work hard, organize staffs, watch over the small vineyards, fishermen's loans, the families that had been the original basis of the banking empire. (George didn't like the word 'empire.')

Fact: that you could now buy stock in the Pacific-Harvesters Bank, listed on the New York and West Coast stock exchanges. But he and Ramon and Irena held controlling shares. Rocco, Tom, the rest of the board had their bit of stock, too.

Fact: there was no direct Fiore heir to take his place as head of the bank. Charles was probably long dead. He'd never know. And Fred? While he had some shares as gifts, he was always in need of money to run his racing stable, hoping for the Triple Crown, for one of his horses to win the Derby, the Belmont, the Preakness—Fred, the *bon vivant*, tinkering with gasoline-driven horseless carriages and stinking up the Long Island countryside's back roads.

Fact: I'm drag-ass tired, lying here under a ceiling colored like wine dregs, my rheumatic joints aching, and again thinking of my Charlie. Why do I keep thinking he'll come back?

George dozed off, dreaming he and Irena were both young. They were barefoot on a hilltop, standing by a huge net and thousands of birds were flying toward them, already plucked and roasted, and he and Irena were shouting, 'No, no, fly away.' General Grant in muddy boots, smoking a cigar as the ironclads, the gunboats, ran the river past Vicksburg ... and a little girl whose feet couldn't reach the pedals played 'Beautiful Dreamer' on the rosewood paino, playing for the minority of the living, perched on millions of years of the dead ...

After a night of contradictory winds, the Golden Gate sky was at dawn turning the color of the inner skin of a plum. Old man Julio (who used to be Young Julio) came out onto the gray-stone drive of Casa Cuesta. He called loudly to the two dogs that ran loose inside the grounds all night. They were savage-looking animals. They leaped about the man, droplets of night dew gleaming on their pelts, well aware that Julio had some tidbits in the pocket of his worn tweed jacket with its dark leather patches at the elbows. The dogs, in a dry season, kept the deer from devouring the blossoms and leaves of the gardens. Julio's jacket had belonged to Ramon many years before, and the faded remains of a gilt-and-silver crest of the house of Velasquez were still barely visible over the right shoulder.

Standing by an herbaceous border just beyond the dog

run, Julio could see across to the distant city. The man smiled. *Eso es lo que es.* It was a good omen when the city was visible; he would play one of Señor Fred's horses, put two dollars on the nose. A good long shot. He nodded, and as he was old and a bit hard of hearing, he talked to himself in his own mixture of Spanish and English: '*Hijo de la gran puta*, it is time you won a good race at some damn fine odds, eh? And tonight is coming from Chicago the big man who makes the plans for the new bank building, and we give big grand dinner for him.'

The day was as yet evocative, vague but brightening. Soon the hard, bone-white sunlight would take over from the morning mists.

Ramon Velasquez was still sleeping off one of Rocco's parties. He had had too much to drink, and had been dreaming of lonely wives of lost fishermen copulating with seals on empty beaches. He had been awakened by the barking of dogs. He sat up, legs dangling over the edge of the bed, naked and lean, not showing his age—he was too aware that he was past forty. He scratched his ribs, smiled.

He continued to smile as he moved toward a bathroom tiled in egg-yolk yellow, a color he remembered from a yellow brandy at the Café Flore when he was still a hopeful young painter in Paris. He had recited, with satisfaction at his romantic despair, Baudelaire's lines: 'I am at the end of my nervous resources—at the end of my courage, at the end of hope.'

What a callow young prick, and with that bohemian bluster he had disparaged life in those days! And now the impressionists were gaining favor—might he have been one, could *he* have achieved their vibrancy, their insights?

He stood in the tepid shower with a bit of a hangover, not lathering himself but enjoying the comforting flow, remembering Irena's warnings: 'Daily washing of the whole body, Ramon, takes away its needed natural oils, opens the skin to various ugly infections.'

He turned off the shower to a sound in the plumbing like a flute with plaintive stops. He saw a good enough body reflected in the hazy mirror, a man a bit over six feet, overlong legs, delicate hands, still a reddish tint to his thinning hair.

Wrapped in a blue robe, he lit the first cigar of the day and walked toward the balcony of the bedroom, ignoring the wall of portraits and landscapes his great grandfather, then his grandfather and father had collected. Not a Titian, not an El Greco, a genuine Kyriakos Theotokopoulos among them. The paintings were good enough, the crop of minor talents, but how fine it would have been to have picked up a Goya duchess or a Rubens faun!

He inhaled, exhaled on the balcony, stretched, not a man given to the fetish of disciplined exercise, but rather to occasional horseback riding or engaging too often (when younger) to some amorous exchange with another naked body.

He pulled the wall cord that signaled the kitchen he was ready for breakfast.

As he descended the stairs, he could hear Julio around the corner by the clumps of arbutus and privet roaring blasphemies at the dogs. Hard to believe the old bastard had once had a beautiful young cousin? Or was it a niece? When he was fifteen she had introduced him and Fred to the game of two becoming one. He grimaced, grinned, and looked forward to his morning coffee. His thoughts turned, inevitably, to the shape of his life.

He had been so involved with the bank when Uncle George was so ill seven years ago, that his courtship of Consuelo, a prominent citizen's only daughter, had been an afterthought. He had grown tired of the amorous excesses of his youth, and Irena's persistent desire for grandchildren had persuaded him. He and Consuelo had married, found it neither good nor bad, and when it ended in her death in childbirth, he buried both her and the infant with perhaps a shamefaced hint of relief. He was full of shame now, thinking back; so unfair to poor Consuelo, so unfair to himself.

The huge ranch stove was lit in the long gold-and-blue

tiled kitchen. Breakfasts were being prepared at the Casa. Claudia, the heavyset cook with her black Aztec hair tied up in a blue band and buttocks quivering, was yelling at the two kitchen helpers, barefoot giggling girls awkwardly handling the plates and sorting the silverware.

'Don't scratch your heads, you empty brains! You got fleas, a touch of dog mange? Now, set the proper trays or I break your heads, *hasta el infierno!* We have a big dinner tonight.' The cook turned to Julio. 'Señor Morus, I need strong backs to move the big tables. Señor Morus, I am speaking to you!'

'*Dueña Crispi?*' Julio cupped a hand over one ear as if he hadn't heard clearly. 'Two? Strong *macho* studs for you? Claudia, for me a mess of *chorizo*, two eggs, and very strong coffee.'

He looked up at the wall fixture of room numbers, each bearing a buzzer. One was rasping persistently. 'The Comandador has signaled for his breakfast. And the big guest tonight is Irish—what do they eat?'

'Potatoes boiled in beer? Not *here!*'

Miss Munday, the personal nurse and maid of the Comandador's mother, Doña Irena, came down the back stairs to the kitchen bearing an armful of sweaters: 'To be washed with care and not to be put into the laundry hamper.'

Miss Munday was what the gardeners called *güeras chingadas*, an obscene reference to Anglo blonds. She was a solid, cheerful girl, in her late twenties, with a sharp tongue when riled. She felt superior to the kitchen help. She read Henry James, Jane Austen, and successfuly covered up Doña Irena's worst lapses of memory.

Julio watched the breakfast trays being prepared. He feared loss of domination below stairs more than death. He knew he had to maintain his position as majordomo, the oldest family retainer, house tyrant, and general supervisor—one who reported directly to the Comandador.

Upstairs, Ramon looked at the maid setting down his

344

tray; a small smile, a slight flush of the skin, fine teeth. She shyly handed him the folded newspaper. 'Good morning, Comandador.'

'Ah, good morning, my girl.' His sense of etiquette hunted for her name. Memory must be weakening, just couldn't remember her name. He liked large-hipped women. He adjusted the unfolded paper for easier reading while he inspected the tray, and looked up at the maid. 'Maria?'

'No, Isabella. Maria, she married,' she replied, just a touch of archness in her voice.

'Of course.'

Of course, they were all beginning to look alike to him, but no less desirable. He ate slowly, taking full sips of strong black coffee. He read the New York Times; trouble in South Africa, the Balkans. People were so needlessly cruel to each other.

The great teak-and-silver hall clock just off the kitchen rang the hour. Julio checked the fact with his watch and wound it slowly as he issued orders: 'Gardeners, move tables, polish chairs, clean silver, rake drive, burn old rosebush twigs and vine stalks—big dinner tonight for the *tonto* Anglo fella from Chicago.'

He took a bit of folded paper with drawings from a pocket, swung black-rimmed glasses over his nose. 'So, we serve a fish, *gazpacho andaluz, cordero con salsa boribcha*—leg of lamb—a beef dish, *ternera mechada*, and'—he looked up over his glasses—'apple pie, *oye*, with Yankee cheese.'

Claudia the cook made a mock sad face. 'Dogshit in aspic next, maybe Yankees will like it.'

Irena Fiore Velasquez—'Herself,' as some called her— never rose before noon. She had stiff hip joints, a loud gong-like voice, and a failing memory. She had never been a beauty, she admitted, though she remembered her vibrant youth fondly, herself a healthy young girl, fresh from Italy, who rode wildly on unruly horses, swore strongly vile stable oaths. She did not believe in the Pope as God's vicar, only in Jesus. She never looked back, claiming as her philosophy, 'Nothing on earth can bring back the minute before this one.'

Now in old age, she was voraciously consuming her breakfast from the tray spread over her too ample lap, spotting her pale blue dressing gown with food. Her reddish-brown wig was set a bit too far back, and from time to time, between swallows, Miss Munday wiped her mistress's mouth while it chewed with strong yellowing teeth in what the nurse thought of as a consummate performance of gluttony.

Her son came in smiling. Ramon had not feared Irena for over thirty years, even if there was still a small scar on one cheek where she had hit him one hot day with the butt of her riding crop for refusing to jump a brook. For all that, he had always admired her, and in time he had grown to love her deeply, a wonderful old rip who had always avoided the rut of mediocrity.

'Good morning, Madre.'

She looked up and grinned as the maid swabbed her chin.

'Good morning, Ramon.' She tilted her head to one side for his expected—almost demanded— kiss as he bent over the tray. She smelled, he thought, like overripe stored fruit, of bath powder, and just now of the hot buttered toast.

'Good appetite.'

'And what have you done so far this morning?' she added, adjusting the too long sleeves of her robe.

'Eating a filling breakfast. Soon I shall inspect the dining room for tonight's fete.'

'In your grandfather's days he would be out on the *rancho* rounding up the big horned cattle to sell the hides and the tallow to the Yankee ships.'

Her memory was fallible, unanalyzing at times.

'Perhaps it was the great-grandfather.' She frowned, bit into a bit of toast. 'It's his bed I'm lying in, Ramon. As many whores as wives I'm sure have been here before me ... Oh, I ordered that necklace to wear at the party tonight for that Irishman.'

Ramon smiled. 'The jewelers wanted fifteen thousand dollars.'

'I am not marrying again. I'll wear it at your wedding.'

'I was married. I'm sure you remember.'

'Call it a marriage? Call it a solid effort at making Velasquez babies? Two withered skinned rabbits she produced, and both dead. And your wife, Ramon, that Consuelo, following them. By the disposition of Providence, soon enough. Women aren't what they used to be. Bodies like boys.'

He felt a desire for a fresh cigar, the good Havana smoke. 'You picked her, you insisted Consuelo was a proper bride. It was a sin what we did, you and I, Madre, a thing done without love to produce heirs. We share that sin, you and I.'

'Ramon, I have confessed it often enough. Father Balbac said it was pride and arrogance in us. The sin to want to keep a great house, a God-fearing dynasty alive, and—'

He kissed her cheek again. 'It's all past. You will be at your best at dinner tonight?'

'It's still my house, I am its hostess.'

'You can make a new will again. Your lawyer is one of the guests.'

'When the Devil becomes a nun, Ramon, you'll find honest lawyers … My joints ache so, maybe I'll stay in bed tonight.' Her constant rewriting of her will was a Casa joke.

'As you desire, Madre,' he said, knowing she would be at the dinner. She was still greedy for pleasures, living in a surge of anticipation. It was one of her good days. She had called him 'Ramon,' not 'Tomas.'

Her stiff-limbed condition at times prevented her from attending as many masses and horse sales as she once had. Cardinal O'Drood had assured Ramon that Father Mackin, a plump, short priest with a low center of gravity, would come twice a week to Casa Cuesta for a private mass in Doña Irena's small chapel.

Irena was convinced that Father Mackin was too young, had been removed too early from his mother to be worthy of the honor of hearing her confessions. Her confessions mostly dated from the past, when she was younger and full of 'the devil's overweening impulses' and a vitality and obstinacy that led her at times to mortal sin (long since paid for and, she hoped, forgiven by the Church). Using Father Mackin as a confidant, she would confess to eating chocolate against her doctor's advice, and having dreams of wonderful clarity 'concerning certain lustful acts with men now long dead.'

Never in her life had Doña Irena been a pessimist. She liked horses and dogs and riding at fences; she was a good shot and loved the excitement of harvesting a good crop. True, Tomas had been a bad husband in the end. But she had accepted with good grace this man of hedonistic nature, who had loved her in his own casual way. Now he was dead—God rest his soul—and tonight she would wear the necklace for someone important. But who?

34

As he dressed for the dinner at the Casa, taking more care than usual, George was more aware than ever of his isolation in this huge Nob Hill house he had built for Maria and his sons. Now they were gone from him; he lived with the servants and with Mollie, who was the cook and housekeeper—as he ate little and simply and entertained rarely, there was little to do in the kitchen. In addition there were Tony his stableman and coachman, and two maids. He had no idea if the place was well run or not.

All he felt he had left was the building of the new bank. It would be higher and bigger than any other bank in San

Francisco. He would pick up Louis Sullivan and his young assistant at the Palace Hotel for the dinner. He knew he had to move forward. Time never stands still to be studied; one can only participate and move on. He had learned to face time's passing with a calm facade. As he put it once to Rocco, 'Never show your lining.'

He looked at himself in the pier glass, seeing not the man, but the starched white shirtfront with its black pearl studs, the well-cut (just a bit baggy) dark evening dress, the waistcoat which he now adorned with a large heavy watch and a set of gold chains.

Tony tapped at the door and announced the carriage was ready.

At the Palace, Sullivan, cheerfully shaking hands, appeared to have had a few bourbons.

The once great dinners of the past, so much a tradition at Casa Cuesta, were rarer now since Irena's decline— those patriarchal dinners of twenty to forty people: businessmen, political figures, always available for some special holiday or event.

By 1900 the dinners were smaller affairs, a dozen people at the most, polite affairs of wine, wild game, and reminiscenses by Irena of how fine and good it had once been.

Julio Jesús Morus, in too-tight Edwardian dress suit turned blue-green with age, inspected the *sala de recibo*, the formal dining room. He studied the long teak table brought from China in the days of the clipper ships returning from the tea port of Canton. Now the vast surface was covered by what seemed a half-acre of crisp damask, a cloth rarely used, for it took a week to wash and starch the tablecloth and napkins. Julio cursed the gardener Mike, serving as an extra waiter, for getting the forks in the wrong order. Mike, the more alert of the gardeners, often was drafted to help serve. He was limping in a pair of patent-leather pumps.

'In the old days,' Julio said, 'when Señor Tomas was home, six waiters were hired from the hotel, three chefs below in the kitchen, also a pastry cook and fish cook. Where the devil are the fish knives?'

From his balcony, Ramon watched Father Prado's rickety old carriage climb the ridge. The priest, as usual, was the first dinner guest to arrive, just as Julio lit the ground lamps.

Ramon stood at ease, feeling a singular lucidity that night often brought him. There was a cooling breeze from the Pacific. Nightfall also released in him the springs of sensibility, an awareness of the fallibility of humanity.

Ramon went down to greet Father Prado and other guests not far behind. Carriage lamps flickered up the great stretch of road leading to the Casa's drive. He descended the creaking staircase to find servants rushing frantically about. Irena, dressed in regal deep blue and leaning on a gold-headed cane, was imperially issuing orders in thunderous tones. 'Respect and order, damn you clods!'

He advanced to greet Father Prado. 'Good evening, Father.'

'*Buenas noches, Comandador*.'

Father Prado, old, tanned, like leather, had long since filed away in his memory the major sins of many of the old Spanish families and now devoted much of his time to the *barrios*. He presented their poverty and misery to the surviving old families who bought God's grace by giving to Father Prado's causes.

'Ah, Father O'Hara!' cried Irena as she took the priest's arm.

'No, no, I'm Father Prado.'

'I knew it all the time.'

Julio Morus stood on the great stone porch, viewing the guests as they arrived, directing one of the gardeners to see to the horses. He had had two tots of brandy and was rapidly sketching.

The arriving guests would have been surprised, perhaps even insulted, if they could have seen Julio's perceptive pencil drawings: Father Prado—a skull drawn wearing a

350

clerical collar; Owen Devlin, the family's personal and business lawyer, accompanied by his wife, Mary Jennet, a pig with a shamrock on her rump; Rocco Bordone, a rather realistic drawing of a penis in full erection.

Julio put away his guest list and took a deep breath of cooling air. The night was a sooty velvet, a sky sugared with stars, large and small, an omen of a good night for the Velasquezes.

The carriage of George Fiore pulled up before the steps and Julio ran forward to open the door before the coachman could. He greeted Señor Fiore, who was followed by Louis Sullivan and his young assistant.

'How are you keeping, Julio?' asked George.

'Keeping fine, Señore Fiore. I welcome you and your honored guests.'

Sullivan, in a ruffled evening shirt, ornate tie, and opera cape with red silk lining, looked at the facade of the Casa. 'Ah, real California, Spanish, lots of Iberian doodads. But honest ... very honest, Chester.'

The assistant agreed, 'Very honest.'

Ramon came out and stood on the steps, greeting his guests, shaking hands.

'Welcome to the Casa, sir.'

Sullivan nodded. 'Grand place, don't add any goddamned steamboat Gothic to it. No wooden flying buttresses.'

'It's finished, Mr Sullivan, just aging.'

'Good. A bit of a chill in the air, a tot of whiskey wouldn't do any harm, eh, Chester?'

Chester agreed it wouldn't. They went inside for more introductions, and wine cups laced with good rye whiskey.

Irena was at her best, talking of several trips she had made to Chicago. 'When we shipped beef there on the hoof in the first steam trains, the city was all mud and smoke and stockyard stink.'

Sullivan nodded, looked over the hand-hewed raftered ceiling, the iron railings of the stairs. 'Those ironworks came from Spain. *What ...?*'

'My husband's grandfather brought them around the Horn. Tell me, is the Parker House still standing after Mrs O'Leary's big fire?'

'Been rebuilt in a dreadful style.'

'We don't burn cities here,' Irena said, adjusting her necklace so it caught the light of the candles, the great hanging lamps. 'I'm hungry. *Julio!*'

But there were still guests arriving. Rocco came alone, Devlin the lawyer and the mayor with their ladies.

The best silver shone on the long table. Crystal glasses in groups of four stood ready for the wine. The guests took their places, Julio pushing the chair in for Sullivan. Ramon sat with the guest of honor on one side, George Fiore on the other, Irena at the far end talking to Mrs de Souza and Father Prado.

Father Prado waited for a signal from Ramon to offer a prayer. The signal was given and the guests' eyes lowered.

The dinner service was nearly flawless. The dishes arrived, were served, Julio standing to one side signaling, ordering, pouring out the correct wines for each course: Bodega Bay oysters, *gazpacho andaluz, carne asada,* tender roast beef, and finally apple pie and a Grand Marnier soufflé.

Irena was eating with great relish, telling Father Prado of a holy relic she had been offered in Mexico at a bargain price—the mummified finger of St Apicius, patron of sufferers from St Anthony's Fire. The priest wrinkled his nose. He said he found the trade in relics repugnant.

Sullivan ate hungrily but with dainty care, insisting he didn't eat this well every day or he'd be 'as big as an outhouse.' When Owen Devlin, the lawyer, asked for details about the new bank building, Sullivan insisted, 'No, no, never talk of business when honored with such a grand feast. This is a very fine wine, Ramon.'

'The last of it, Louie, I regret to say.'

All conversation ceased as the guests became aware of some excitement from the serving pantry. The door burst open dramatically as two of the waiters marched carefully

352

into the dining room, balancing a huge cake in the shape of a new bank, Julio, following close behind in agitation. It was a tall structure of layers set with candied fruit, icing, and nut meats. Julio, fearing it would topple adjusted the flags of the United States and California waving from the top layer. In three-colored icings at the base, a bit of misspelling featured the legend: 'THE PASIFIC HARVESTERNS BANK.'

There were cheers, and Julio, wiping his brow, smilingly signaled for the champagne to be served.

Irena inspected the cake. 'Too garish, no almonds.'

Ramon stood up, glass in hand. 'We shall soon see this in brick and stone and'—bowing to Sullivan—'in terra-cotta, so let us toast our architectual genius, Louis Sullivan, and our founder, George Fiore ...'

There was a clanging of fine crystal as the crowd toasted, amid cheers and applause. Rocco demanded a quick refilling of glasses.

George pointed to the guest of honor. 'Speech, Louie?'

'Hell, yes, I suppose so.' He stood up, his assistant alert in case his swaying boss needed assistance. 'Your hospitality warms me, your food and drink cheer me, and I just want to say that it took courage for your founder to hire a man whose work is still frowned upon by many. You could have had a Greek temple, a Roman jail, a pious Michelangelo fruit cup, or a cast-iron General Grant frontier fort. Instead you faced the rising sun and saw a new century needed new visions. But enough. I'm a builder, not a speech maker. So I'll just add to the good priest's words, God bless.'

He swallowed his drink and admired the cake. Irena, as the hostess of the Casa, was asked to cut.

As the last bit of cake was consumed, the last sip of coffee swallowed, everyone agreed it had been a splendid evening. Later, Sullivan, inviting all assembled to join him if ever they were in Chicago, said good-bye. Only his assistant, Chester, had to be carried out to the carriage.

As the last coach lamp dimmed, Julio began what was to

be the real work of the evening, as he barked orders to his sleepy staff.

Irena had taken her shoes off, and bowed to guests who had already departed, protesting at Miss Munday's attempts to get her upstairs and into bed. 'There is the dancing, we *always* have dancing after dinner.'

'Not tonight.'

'I must talk with Father Prado.'

'Father Prado has already left. He gave you his blessing.'

'Of course he did. I know *that*.'

Ramon stood on the front veranda smoking a cigar, thought of his Uncle George, so thin, so thoughtful, saying little. Ramon envied him, his ability to decide without hesitation, or so it seemed, on this radical new building—decided as if he had knowledge of a truth no one else possessed. Ramon, as a painter, likened it to an artist imbued with a kind of desperate clairvoyance, rebuilding reality into something magically new and special. George, too, was an artist of sorts—in the matter of money, credits, organizing of institutions. He had vision.

Julio joined Ramon. Julio looked tired, a bit bowed with fatigue and age. 'It went well, *Comandador*.'

'With your help it always does, Julio.' Ramon laughed and handed the man a cigar, lit it for him. They stood silent, puffing smoke into the night's moist air. In the distance a tugboat gave its sad, shrill call, and from the dog kennel came the answering barks of the animals anxious to begin their night patrols.

'Doña Irena looked her best,' Julio said.

'You liar, Julio. None of us looks our best anymore. We're getting old.'

'God grant us many years more, *Comandador*.'

'Go let the dogs out.' Alone, Ramon stubbed out his cigar and thought of the work ahead—the hours to be spent with contractors, masons, designers of the new vaults which were on order from England and purported to be the biggest in the West. Unlike the rest of the diners that night, he did not feel that the new century would be as wonderuful as prophets predicted. There were too much technology, too many steel battleships, and too much saber-rattling from the kings of Europe, Asia, and Africa—the greedy, the empire builders (some called them robber barons), and always the dishonorable politicians, here and abroad.

One late-fall day in 1902 was declared Pacific-Harvesters Day by a rather disreputable mayor, and as a bit of morning mist dissolved, the majestic new structure was officially opened. It was a work of great beauty, most agreed. The dignitaries sat on a flag-draped platform in front of the new building with its builder and designer. Except for a few diehards who wanted this temple of progress to be based on designs of the Greeks or Romans, the city honored the building and its builders. Even President Teddy Roosevelt was there, and as Rocco commented later, he didn't once say 'Bully,' shout 'By Godfrey!' or mention the 'carrying of a big stick.'

Irena attended in her own way, seated in her nephew Fred's new Simplex-Mercedes, chain-driven, with red running gear and an enclosed top. Ramon didn't want her to risk the steep steps to the platform. She sat in light furs and looked up at the structure in doubt. 'George was always foolish when he didn't take my advice. God didn't mean anyone to build any more towers of Babel. I tell you, Fred, comes a good strong wind, a quake, and it will *all* tumble down.'

'I hope not while I'm in it.'

'Who's the red-faced man waving his arms?'

'The president.'

'I once danced with General Grant. He couldn't waltz worth a damn.'

Miss Munday, at her elbow, said, 'We've seen enough. It's time for our nap.'

'Not today, Munday. Why aren't you out there getting next to some fine well-hung man?'

Fred winked at Miss Munday. He had gotten portly and had lost most of his hair, for which he compensated by a long pointed mustache. He sported horsy tack-room clothing, bold checks, and a little hat with a feather in the band.

On the platform, Rocco was leading the band, having pushed the leader aside. The music was drowned out by the bay ferries, sirens, foghorns, the tugboats, factory whistles, fire bells ringing out, all at the cutting of the ribbon by the big bronze doors, which George, in a shiny top hat and yellowish gloves, did with aplomb.

George ceremoniously removed his top hat and handed it to Tom; he then took the symbolic gold key that would unlock the doors.

'If,' he said to Tom, 'I made a mistake, it's a hell of a big one.'

'Never, Major.'

35

While Ramon was pleased to see cousin Fred, and the attention he paid Irena, he was also worried that Fred was sweet-talking the vain old woman who controlled so much bank stock and the vast Velasquez land holdings. He suspected that Fred, like so many sportsmen, had no morals above horses, cards, and the fast life. Ramon knew that Fred was desperate for money, and Irena wasn't as canny as she had once been. Ramon wondered how to protect Irena's bank stocks and the land values from Fred's plans. *If* he had plans.

Doña Irena's mind was not entirely sunk into wandering pleasantly between the present and the past. There were long periods when she seemed fully alert to events around her—not at all given to vague or rambling allusions. Miss Munday insisted Irena was 'bright as a polished dime. It's just she *does* have, you could say, a *certain* perversity. Yes, well, true; she does hoard the most daffy things.'

For some years, Ramon had been aware that his mother would furtively hide bits of breakfast toast or a jam jar under her pillow, and that one had to remove old magazines and newspapers without her knowledge, or she would build towers of them in her closets. At her worst, when she and Miss Munday went out to shop, or to lunch in her favorite tearoom, she would set off for the ladies' room and, sneaking away from Miss Munday, rummage through the trashcans in the alley, in search of chipped dishes or old boots.

As the new bank prospered, became a landmark, Irena would raid it for pens, blotters, calendars, and carry off brass rulers and inkwells.

When she was under such a spell, her son never chided her. He would visit her during her afternoon rest period.

'There is no danger, Madre, of the Casa being sold by a foreclosure mortgage. We are not poor.'

'Times must be hard; you have closed my bank account.'

'Only because as a great lady, you are *too* generous. You make large gifts to total strangers. You buy four of everything when the mood is on you.'

She gave him a quizzical, derisive look. 'They are not strangers, they are my cousins. And right now that the war is on, tell me'—she took Ramon's hand, put her head close to his, and whispered with an inflection as if of great pain— 'has Richmond fallen?'

'I fear so.'

'Ah, I must prepare for the victory ball. Send for Julio.'

'He is busy somewhere else.' He felt ineffectual with his mother, as it had been when he was a boy.

In the gentle afternoon light, his mother didn't look her age. Her facial bone structure still revealed how handsome she had been. There was a proud self-assurance, assertiveness in her, even if her memory at times did not separate the past from the here and now. Her features held

357

the firm solemnity of a person satisified with her own aggrandizement as if, he decided, she had discovered her real commitment to life. He leaned over and kissed the dry cheek with just a hint of added color. He wished he could feel tenderness for his mother, once such an exuberant personality. But beyond great respect, admiration for her skill in managing land, cattle, and money, the vivacity of her youth, he could not do so.

Rocco, George, and Ramon were lunching on the terrace of the Hispano Club, facing a blue-green lazy surf. It was not the grand club of the Native Sons, not splendid and white brick like the restricted Jubilee Club. The Hispano did have a membership that George felt was in its way as restricted as the Mayflower Society; it catered to those Latin-American families with money or a historic past. Some members still held now worthless bits of parchment representing long-lost land grants.

Ramon rarely came to the club, but as his father, Tomas, had been one of the founding members (his portrait in oils now hung in the main room), he still maintained his membership.

Rocco said, 'Fred is not *my* relative.'

George nodded. 'We must settle things. Now, we can't commit Irena or declare her incompetent to handle her assets, control her wealth and holdings.'

Rocco asked, 'Then why is this meeting being held?'

George smiled. 'Because we want to share the blame. No, we can't do it.'

Ramon sighed. 'I just couldn't decide by myself. She's my mother, but you knew her when she was at her height— powerful, wonderful, opinionated, usually right. Now ...'

'Now,' said George, 'she is old and senile. For too long we've called her only odd, eccentric. But it's more than that. Her holdings in the bank go back to when I first started, and they've grown greatly, quadrupled in quantity and value. She owns about eight percent of the stock, and dammit, that's voting stock, which she could sell. We were all young then. Who ever thought of getting old?'

Ramon sighed. 'There are the Velasquez Land Company, the Napa vineyards, the Casa, and the Bay Holding Companies. She's at least a forty-five percent holder of the assets. I own a quarter, including Tomas's share. There it is, as they say, on the table.'

They ate slowly, thinking, tossing out suggestions, only to reject them a moment later. After the meal, George flicked a fingernail against his brandy glass. 'Let's try to see my son Fred's side of it. He's a fast liver, a yea-sayer. Fred loves to live well, and that takes money. Horses, cards, fancy women—these all call for funds. But in his own way, a sportsman's way, he has a sense of honor. Maybe if we put it that way to him, he'll promise to keep his hands off Irena's holdings.'

'Why should he?'

'Because we are going to pay his debts and give him a generous allowance, up to a certain limit. We'll give him a bank title, improve his image of himself.'

Rocco looked at George with admiration. 'I'll be goddamned, George Fiore! You're a genius. Why didn't we think of making Fred a remittance man?'

'He's not that, and I'm not a genius. We love Fred, *all* of us do. We can appoint him to some honorable bank position—say, adviser on our printing. We do a lot of it. Something like that, yes, so his pride isn't bruised.'

They left the club in a cheerful mood, although Ramon felt this was only a temporary solution. What if Irena's will favored Fred?

On a certain Tuesday in May 1904, a well-dressed young woman neatly attired in fashionable tones of gray and black and a veiled wide-brimmed hat trimmed in dark plumes boarded the two-o'clock bay ferry at its San Francisco dock.

There was a light load of passengers bound for Oakland; only a dozen people were on the lower and upper decks. The sun was clear and bone-white over the dimpling bay, the early-morning fog had burned off. The walking beam that drove the paddle wheels performed its steamy task as a faint breeze rose. From below came the odor of old wood, engine grease, ancient horse piss.

Nearing the Oakland landing, the woman mounted the worn steps to the upper deck. An old man sat on a stool playing a weathered cello and a barefoot young Negro boy sat on the deck beside a shoeshine box. Leaning on the railing at the bow was a broad-shouldered attractive man, neat dark mustache ending in needle points. There was something a bit daring in the cut of his dark pin-striped banker's suit. He stared intently at the drift of the bobbing debris in the bay.

'Rocco.' The woman's voice was firm, but not loud.

The man, as if breaking away from some thought, turned slowly. 'What the hell ...?'

The woman casually drew a small silver-plated pistol from her handbag, one gloved hand on the butt and a finger on the trigger. She repeated, 'Rocco ....'

The man made a tentative move toward her, an expression of panic on his features, his mouth open as if ready to plead for mercy.

The woman fired, standing steady, then fired again. The man uttered four words: 'You fucking stupid bitch!' Slowly he sank to the deck, quivering, holding his stomach and clutching his groin at which she had so unwaveringly aimed. Satisfied, expressionless she tossed the pistol over the side, the sun catching a highlight of its silver barrel and the sheen of its mother-of-pearl grip.

The old man with the cello stopped his bowing motion, the shoeshine boy opened his eyes very wide. Blood ran in a little rivulet along the deck. The man lay inert, still clutching himself. People were running up from the lower region of the ferry. Up from the wheel deck of the boat the captain appeared, his face transformed by alarm and wonder.

The woman stood erect and still, her face still hidden by the veil. Three blasts of the ferry siren sounded overhead, a signal for police to head for the Oakland ferry terminal. No one approached the dying man.

The siren blasts were repeated, but the woman seemed not to hear them or to sense the presence of the gathering passengers. She faced the shore, approaching rapidly, her handbag now firmly tucked under her left arm. Three answering hoots came from the ferry station.

The San Francisco *American* headline blazed: 'MYSTERIOUS WOMAN MURDERS PROMINENT BANKER AND SPORTSMAN ON FERRY! ROCCO BORDONE, VICE-PRESIDENT OF PACIFIC-HARVESTERS BANK, SLAIN BY VEILED WOMAN'S PISTOL SHOTS.'

At 12.32 p.m. today, as Rocco Bordone—well-known San Francisco socialite, sportsman, and vice-president of the Pacific-Harvesters Bank—was standing on the upper deck of the ferry *Bay Queen*, he was approached by a fashionably dressed young woman who, according to eye witness Anthony Pagona, called out his name as she shot him twice with a small pistol, which she then tossed overboard. Mr Bordone fell to the deck bleeding profusely from the lower abdomen. The woman made no attempt to escape. Captain Montrose Welton signaled the Oakland ferry police, who met the *Bay Queen* when she docked.

Officer Dan Coffee arrested the woman, who remained silent to all inquiries. She is being held at the Oakland police staion, still refusing to give her name or state her reasons for the assault. Rocco Bordone was carried into the ferry-station waiting room, where unsuccessful attempts were made to stop the bleeding. He was then driven to Bay City Hospital. Dr Royal MacIntyre pronounced Bordone dead on arrival. He is survived by no known relatives.

As vice-president of the bank, Mr Bordone was responsible for financing vineyards, crops, commerical fishing activities, and new town developments springing up in the bay area. For many years his racing colors won at Bay Meadows and other western tracks.

His assailant appears to be about twenty-five years of age. Her handbag, according to one police source, held a flask of French perfume, two large handkerchiefs, a hand mirror, two ticket stubs to Gilbert and Sullivan's *The Mikado*, a wallet containing little money, and one of Mr Bordone's business cards, with a pencil notation which the police refuse to divulge. There are rumors that a valuable diamond bracelet was also in the handbag. And in a bank folder, sources say, were Union Pacific railroad bonds running into thousands of dollars.

District Attorney Carter Lipton refuses to confirm or deny the last two items. A Jane Doe warrant for murder is being drawn up.

We have not been able to contact George Fiore, chairman of the board of the Pacific-Harvesters Bank and close personal friend of Mr Bordone. His nephew, Ramon Velasquez, president of the bank, issued a short statement on Mr Fiore's behalf: 'We at the bank are deeply sorrowful at the senseless death of our senior vice-president. Our long personal frienship goes back many years and was stronger than any business relationship; a deep and extraordinary business friendship. Rocco Bordone was a citizen of San Francisco who took pride in this city, and as part of its early history, he will not be forgotten ...'

Two days after the murder, following a private funeral at the Hill of Grace Cemetery, George and Ramon sat in the library on Nob Hill. They could hear steet noises from the front of the house, the sounds of gathered reporters and cameramen with the three-legged tools of their trade. Attempts by the journalists to bribe the servants had failed, and four of the city police were on hand to push back the crowds.

Ramon and George were sipping white wine as George looked over the bank papers. 'There has been a slight run on the bank, the shares are down two and a half points. But we'll weather this, unless an audit turns something up.'

'I have the accountants in now checking Rocco's most recent loans. They are very large, perhaps too large, but mostly safe, I'd judge. His personal accounts are rather shocking.... J.P. Morgan's firm holds loans against his bank stocks, his racing-stable losses are very big, and he'd been buying bad stocks on a bear market, all on margin. I found bills from specialty shops for women's items, wine merchants, house furnishings; nothing's been paid for over six months. Of course, his credit was good and—'

'I'll see personally it's taken care of. Within reason.'

A maid announced, 'Mr Hummel is here, sir.'

'Oh, yes, send him in.' George said to Ramon, 'Our Pinkerton.'

Mr Hummel was a solid-looking man with large brown eyes, heavy shoes with bulldog toes, and a derby hat that seemed hard enough to be made of black metal. He carried the headgear in the crook of an arm.

'I've brought the stuff you wanted, gents.'

George pointed to a chair, but the man shook his head, put down his derby, and took out a small notebook from an inner pocket. 'The police are about to discover the identity of the woman who committed that crime on the deck of the ferryboat on its third trip of the day, between—'

'Skip all that' George said.

'Yes sir ... *hummm*. Her name is Audrey Crane, age twenty-seven, educated at Mills and Vassar, daughter of the well-known Oakland Brinkley family. Her father is president of the West Coast Grain and—'

'Yes, yes,' said Ramon. 'What about the woman?'

'She is married to a Norton Crane of the Crane shipping people, and—skipping all *that*—yes, they have been separated for nine months. Mrs Crane has been living for the last seven months in the flat of Mr Rocco Bordone at 242 Van Ness Avenue. Audrey Crane was in residence there until a week ago, when, according to the janitor, there was a series of rows. Yelling, furniture breaking, objects thrown, and then, sirs ...'

'Yes?' said Ramon.

'Well, I guess you could say he gave her the bum's rush. Tossed her and all her things out. The janitor helped her get the gear into a hack, and where she went from there, Mrs Crane that is, until she was taken off that ferry after the crime, I have not yet ascertained.'

George rubbed his chin. 'Damn! Mr Bordone led a rather too open life.'

Hummel turned some pages in his notebook. 'He visited at least three times a week at her Clark Street flat, one Lily Vendon, known as "Frenchy" in the theater trade. Mr Bordone was paying for the upkeep of a little four-year-old girl, Mandy Condon. Her mother is a portrait painter. Parentage proceedings brought against Mr Bordone two years ago were never pushed.'

'Thank you, Hummel. Keep us informed if anything else turns up. I mean of a legal nature; we don't care to go into *too* personal matters, you understand? You say the authorities will soon identify Mrs Crane?'

Hummel smiled for the first time, picked up his hat. 'The Pinkerton office felt you should have this information first, Mr Fiore, before we passed on our knowledge to the Oakland district attorney's office.'

After the detective left, George strode to the window, looked out at the crowd still gathered in the street. He turned to Ramon. 'It's going to be a circus. I can't believe Rocco is dead. I just *can't*.'

'George, the citizens love this sort of thing. Let them sensationalize it. The bank will keep a dignified face on it. Whatever happens, we'll keep quiet. In six weeks it will be replaced in the news by some Barbary Coast stabbing or the elopement of an heiress and a stable groom. God, George, I loved Rocco too. My Uncle Rocco.'

'Murder? No, manslaughter will be the most likely charge, by a woman seduced by a rogue, a womanizer. Lured away from her home and husband. If she has a golden-haired little child crying "Mommy," so much the better for the defense. Poor Rocco. He was too open and foolish in his love of women, but he never meant to be cruel to anyone.'

In the following weeks, the bank did its usual business, and George saw to it privately that Rocco's debts were paid off and the child Mandy Condon would be provided for till she reached the age of seventeen.

As George predicted, the jury of twelve fairly decent men was swayed by the story of Mrs Crane. She was impassive and demure in black, wearing elbow-length gloves and a wide dark hat with just one touch of color, a small yellow rose. The jury agreed with her defense, that because of her great trauma, she was of unsound mind at the time she shot Rocco—a broken woman, mistreated by a heartless brute. The verdict: not guilty.

Mrs Crane went into a sanatorium for six months, after which she and her husband (there had been a full reconciliation; he was an understanding man) took a trip to Italy.

George felt the loss of Rocco for a long time. He would often turn as if expecting Rocco to be there within call when he had some question to ask him. Also, when he and Ramon or Tom would go to the theater or some social affair, George would see Rocco in opera cape and hat, cigar in his mouth, laughing at some jest he had just made. But it always turned out to be someone else, a stranger. Rocco's death had taken away his last real link with his youth. Irena lived more and more in her dreams of the past. The children were now vital, forceful personalities in their own right—if only Charles and Moon Orchid were there too. Perhaps it was time for the new generation to step forward and build their own lives, George thought.

The death of Rocco Bordone made for exciting reading in the city's newspapers, but other sensational news stories gradually seized the headlines. Leland Stanford, former governor, had won his twenty-five-thousand-dollar bet that a galloping horse had all four legs off the ground at one time—to prove it, he had a running horse photographed by a dozen cameras simultaneously. And a month after Rocco was buried, during a 'celebration,' Nell Kimball's upper-class sporting house in the tenderloin had a small fire when one of the guests tried to set a girl on fire by pouring brandy on her head and igniting it. There was also talk that Mayor Schmitz and political boss Abe Ruef were to be indicted for defrauding the city of thousands of dollars—as George said, shaking his head, 'There's *always* that rumor going around!'

More exciting was the news that five Chinatown *tongs*, led by the Suey Sings, offered a reward of three thousand dollars to any man who would kill Gaw. Once called 'The Mayor of Chinatown,' Gaw had fallen upon bad days. His *tong* had declined in power as he had grown older. Gaw himself had not changed with the years, except to become more demanding, wanting bigger shares in Chinatown projects. Gaw refused to retire, refused to share or hand over his power. In answer to the threats to his life, he had steel doors installed throughout his building, and savage dogs were set to prowl the hallways at night. He also employed three tough, strong-arm white men besides his *tong* men. He had a long coat of mail made, which he could wear beneath his regular clothing.

The most notorious attempt on his life, was made by two Chinese gold hunters, Lenn Jung and Chew Tin Gop. They had learned that once a week Gaw went to a Washington Street barbershop to have his long gray hair washed. While his bodyguard was in the public part of the shop, the two would-be assassins entered the private area through a cellar door and crept up behind the victim. One seized Gaw's long hair and pressed a revolver under his robe, firing five shots. The coat of mail saved Gaw's life, but a week later, whether from shock or the usual illness of advanced age, he died.

George and Ramon joined the mile-long cortege, following in their carriage behind the mourning, shuffling priests *hong* and *tong* men. They eyed the huge display of baked funeral meats and special dishes, the crates of hard drinks, while firecrackers notified the gods who was coming to join them.

The body was sent by steamer to Canton, carefully swaddled in a huge red varnished casket.

As George said to Fred and Ramon the next day, 'Gaw was a remarkable old bastard. He once said to me that if he'd been white he would have been another J. P. Morgan. And dammit, I bet he would have, too!'

Fred laughed. 'Then we'd all be eating rice!'

That night George dreamed that Charlie had come back, not a bit older, and with him he had brought a tiny Chinese bride who somehow did not look like Moon Orchid. In the background were at least two dozen yellow children, all apparently the same age. He awoke in wonder and poured a shot of bourbon to steady himself. He felt sure there was a message for him in that dream.

Two weeks later, as he was having breakfast with Fred and Ramon (who was often a houseguest), the maid brought in a telegram. George adjusted his glasses after reading the simple message; he could not believe his eyes. 'FATTEN THE BIGGEST CALF. PRODIGAL RETURNING WITH FULL FAMILY. CHARLES.'

Fred whistled. 'Must have gotten the news about Gaw. That was fast! What kind of grapevine does he use?'

Ramon studied the bit of yellow paper. 'Sent from Portland. But why hasn't he let us know before this that he was alive, and where he was?'

George took the telegram, folded it, and placed it carefully in his waistcoat pocket, patting it as if to make sure it was securely put away. 'Gaw had worldwide connections, wherever Chinese people live. Letters can be traced, and Charlie knows that. We should be glad that he's managed to take care of himself so well.'

'Charlie …' said Fred. 'Ke-rist! We keep thinking of him as young and frisky. Hell, he's as old as we are, Ramon— middle-aged and doddering!'

The homecoming was celebrated by a huge feast in the Nob Hill house. Even Irena and her nurse came, as did all those who had known Charles as a young man. The Sum Yep, Gaw's group, had dissolved completely with Gaw's death. Still, Mayor Schmitz had been kind enough to send two helmeted police to guard against any intruders.

There were not two dozen yellow children—but only Gregory aged ten, and April, aged eight: 'a beautiful mixture of features and colors,' George said, hugging them.

Charles had grown stouter, his hair was thin and gray; but Moon Orchid was as slim and luscious as ever. Her eyes searched the faces of people around her, and her serenity seemed to cover an inner tension, as if she wondered what everyone must make of their unusual family.

As Charles explained late that night when he and George sat up in the library sipping brandy and talking: 'The last few years, since the kids began to grow, we've been living way up north in Canada, running a branch of the Hudson Bay Company. We've been elsewhere, but Moon was always afraid that Gaw's *boo how doy* would find us.'

'It's been cat-and-mouse for you all these years?'

'Not really. As you see, we made a good life for ourselves. We had lost one child and wanted more. ... Dad, this has been something I wanted, needed so deeply. And it's been so good. There aren't many women like Moon.'

'Damn sure of yourself, aren't you? I've known one woman who ... But never mind. Damn, it's good to have you back! But you could have trusted us to help you for all that time.'

'I never trusted anyone. Anyway, *Grandpa,* we're here now.'

'You can help Ramon run the bank. I'm getting on, you know, and we've gotten big, real big.'

'Not in San Francisco, I won't—I'll go anywhere else you say. Maybe we're out of danger now, but Moon still feels too close to Chinatown. You know.'

'All right. How about Santa Barbara, then, just down the coast? The manager there, old Tom's son, isn't doing too well. But he's earnest, so go gently and do what's needed.'

Charles rubbed his chin, smiled at his father. 'I'll give it a try. Great place for the kids, too. God, dad, I'd dream I was back here and wake to find I wasn't.'

'I had dreams, too. They're crazy things, aren't they? Somehow they can give you the creeps, and you feel maybe there is something mystical in them. Supernatural.'

'Or an undigested lobster.'

Later, as he and Moon prepared for bed, Charlie watched her brush out her sleek black hair. He still felt that ache of wonder and love that had sustained them through so many hardships. 'It's all going to be fine now.'

She smiled. 'I always knew it would be, even if the pressures were sometimes too much. Even if you had doubts.'

'Yes, I was afraid. I didn't want to try again.' He put his arms around her. 'Now we'll grow new roots in Santa Barbara, raise two American kids. Maybe Greg will be president!'

'He can't be—he was born in Peru, remember.'

'Oh, well, old lady. Come to bed, and we'll dream that Greg's son will get to the White House. After all, Dad says we're a dynasty, and that means we have a future to beget!'

Epilogue

In the San Francisco vaults of the present Pacific-Harvesters Bank Building, in a safe-deposit box, lies a handwritten manuscript in a brown leather binder. Page one is titled 'The Great Quake and Fire: Memoirs of Ramon Velasquez.' Page two begins:

I shall set down the events of these horrifying days and nights as they affected the city of San Francisco, the Pacific-Harvesters Bank, and naturally, myself.

At dawn on April 18, 1906, I was awakened by a feeling of oppression, an incomprehensible uneasiness. I looked at my old double-lidded gold watch left me by my father, had difficulty seeing the hands. I was staying at George Fiore's mansion on Nob Hill. Getting out of bed, I walked to the window, drew aside the shade, and saw by the street light that my watch said it was 5:08 A.M. As I stood there watching the streetlights dimming, I could hear the early cable cars already making their groaning noises.

I had the feeling I was at sea, as the street below suddenly seemed to undulate, ripple like a pond, then an ocean. I didn't move, just saw the shiver, the dance of rooftops. Chimneys toppled over, bricks fell, and I could feel the jar of the shock right to my bones as the violent fury shook the world. I heard the servants screaming, and George's son Fred ran into my room, also still in his nightclothes.

'A damn good shaking we're getting.'

'It's a big one, all right. I don't think I've ever felt one this powerful.'

'I'll go see how Dad is, although he's such a deep sleeper now that he probably hasn't even been awakened. What do you think I should tell him?'

'Just tell him it's a tremor.'

We timed the shock. It began at 5:12, ran itself out in one minute, four seconds. The house itself was protesting, making excruciating sounds, doors rattling. Outside, dust was beginning to rise. It was as if something, someone, was punching a great fist up from underneath. Fred went off to see George. I began to dress and heard for the first time the roaring, the grinding of the city in shock. A gust of wind swept by and made tearing sounds, as the whole house shook. The sound of shattering glass lasted for a full minute after the tremor had ceased. Somehow the colossal silence that followed was more frightening still. A last brick falling, then the awful sense of unreality, that this must be a nightmare. I heard people crying in pain and fear, yet I couldn't leave the window. South toward Market Street I seemed to see buildings huddled in bent shapes ... knew the dismal hotels there—Valencia, Brunswick, and Cosmopolitan—from my youth. Wondered whether the new City Hall had survived, with its six million dollars' worth of stone and style. Banal thoughts seemed to push aside the horror outside.

I finished dressing and went down to the street. All was confusion. People were milling about, beating their hands together, and a pale gray-green light was stippled with little puffs of dust; the air seemed to be growing thicker. George was calm, grim. 'All that land which was once under water ... Montgomery Street is all filled in now, right out to the bay.'

Water was rushing, and a dark stain seeped into my boot soles. Could this be the city in which we had grown up, gotten middle-aged, grown old?

'Is the Ferry Building still up?' Fred asked. Somehow that tower had become a symbol of the strength and vitality of San Francisco. Whatever else happened, if that endured, perhaps all of us would, too.

We all looked to George as if he could explain the chaos and disintegration. He was not in the best of health now, but the urgency of events seemed to revitalize him. He had a new color in his face and he turned and pointed a finger at Fred with some of his old comic vigor, incongruous with the tragedies and horror surrounding us.

'You still have that smoking stink bomb of an autocar in the stables? I want you to drive me to the bank so I can see what damage is being done. Ramon, you stay here at the telephone. Keep calling the

371

newspapers for any facts about this quake and what it's doing to the city.'

Tony the stable man came out to the sidewalk to join me. 'Telephone's not working. Central doesn't answer. You think the fire-alarm system could be out too?'

Smoke was rising on Market Street. I wondered idly if the City Hall building would burn. I soon discovered City Hall had burst apart with the thrust of the shock, its columns falling away with the grim weight of tons of stone, one slashing off the face of a Larkin Street rooming house. The land wrinkled like a prune as the earthquake shivered the peninsula and the houses built on the fill sagged and bobbed about in all directions before sagging all out of kilter. The market district, not much populated at sunrise, saw millions of bricks separate themselves and strike out in all directions. The hill streets seemed to survive best, but plate glass and chimneys shattered, dishes tumbled off shelves, pots banged against each other, and art objects dissolved in fragments as they vibrated off their stands. The crash and clatter seemed to gain in volume after the first shock had passed, in some capricious whim of balance and counterbalance.

The shock left the city in a bad condition. But worse was to come. The gas mains were bursting, and soon fires were breaking out. I tried to collect information for George, but cable cars and telephone services were still out. Heavy columns of smoke settled over the waterfront and the Mission District.

General Funston, who commanded the local militia, was said to be out inspecting the damage. Grace Church and Old St Mary's appeared to have withstood the shock, and the pious were going there to pray. Sansome and Washington streets seemed to have the worst of the spreading fires. Fire horses were running and bells were clanging, the grind of wheels loud on the streets, inordinately fear-inspiring sounds.

I walked to Bush and Taylor streets, to the firehouse of Engine 38; the men had the gear out and gave me the news that Fire Chief Sullivan was dying in the ruins of the station. I found the engine crew fighting a fire on Stuart Street. The hydrants were all useless; just a few muddy drops came from them. Firemen cursed, and for the first time I was seized with fear for the city. There was no water anywhere. The only thing we could do was to form human chains and try to rescue the people still trapped in the smoking ruins. In many cases, the flames were too strong. I broke two fingers trying to pry up a granite step beyond which lay a man with a beam across his back. He died as I struggled to reach him; he was crying, 'Come get me, for the mercy of God, please save me!'

No one could; the smoke was choking, the flames bright yellow with red edges.

My fear and the devastation around me numbed the pain in my hand. I helped load injured people into empty laundry wagons. The driver shook his head. 'Them hospitals ain't takin' nobody. They're moving out the sick and dying to safer places.'

Later I heard the Central Hospital was itself a ruin. The shock just tore it apart like paper and it fell back on the doctors and nurses. They had little chance to survive in the dust and fallen ceilings.

By this time I was near panic and I made my way past the fugitives, the desolate, homeless people, the firefighters, to the bank. Fred's autocar was in the alley behind the bank. He and two clerks were loading metal containers and black japanned boxes into its backseat. I found George inside the main vault packing currency, gold, and silver coins into more boxes. He had the quiet tension of a chess player in the final moments of a championship match.

'Dammit, George, these vaults are fireproof. There's no need for this.'

'They may be fireproof, Ramon, but they could certainly be buried for weeks if the building falls down around them.'

'You don't expect *that*, do you?'

'The hell I don't.' He seemed amused. I hadn't seen him so animated in years. 'Every *other* bank in this city may go out of business. Now, help me carry this stuff to the car.'

'Where are you going to take it?'

'The old Hawk dock. Isn't the *Sandpiper* still there?'

The *Sandpiper* brought back to me the memories of picknicking, those joyous days of sailing and adventuring so many years ago.

'You're going to try to get all this across the bay to Oakland?'

'That's the idea, if there isn't a mad throng at the waterfront. You stay here and don't get killed. Just get about as much as you can and see how the other banks are doing. And what they're not doing. They're sitting on their fat asses, most likely, wringing their hands with despair.' He chuckled.

Shaking my head, I turned and pushed my way through the milling crowds, racing wagons, and frightened horses. Water was being pumped from the bay and there was talk of dynamiting buildings to stop the spreading fires. It was nine o'clock at night before I realized how tired and bedraggled I was. I went back to George's house, which was miraculously still standing; I changed into some hardier clothes—a hunting jacket and checked Scots cap, and heavy shoes. Mayor Schmitz had ordered the police to close every saloon and bar. He had seized all autocars he could find to carry messages, and a Committee of Fifty was appointed to stop the looting that was ravaging the city. The reek of burning soot and carbon filled the air. Plumes of smoke rose in new places, and here and there the dawning sky glowed orange with the flames. Hours later, exhausted and disconsolate, I walked down to the Hawk dock. Fred was covering his autocar with canvas to protect the paint.

'Dad got across to Oakland in the boat with the loot.'

As the telephones were still out of service, I continued my wandering, trying to get news of the rest of the city. I was told that the wharves had held up better, being cushioned in water; but Long Wharf, loaded with tons of railroad coal, was crushed like a stepped-on fruit by the violent shifting of the coal. The Ferry Tower had been whipped back and forth by the fury of the shock, wavering like a needle on a compass. But it still stood. Smokestacks fell, killing five people, and a fireman died when he was hit by a section of falling roof. There was little awareness yet of the full scope of horror, just fear and disbelief.

It was later estimated that the shock covered thirty to forty miles in its widest part, and extended two hundred miles, from Fort Bragg up north to Salinas in the south. Millions of dollars in property were destroyed, even as far away as San Jose, Berkeley, Oakland, Santa Rosa, Gilroy, and Sebastopol.

The streets were still sending up smoke signals. Huntington and his railroad partners lost four thousand feet of steel rails in one gulp; they just slid off the cliffs into the blue Pacific. One train that remained on rails had its wheels knocked off by the shock and fell over on its side.

I found a bar still serving liquor (it had somehow evaded the mayor's notice) and had a drink of bourbon and a Denver egg sandwich. Then I went to find the new Fire Chief, a man named Daugherty, who told me that the units were all out and at least fifty fires were raging. One had only to look up at the red sky to know the city was doomed. There was no water. No one had ever thought the water mains could be broken, snapped by an earth tremor. All that water in the bay, but not enough pumps or lines to carry it to where it was needed.

Small boats had managed to keep traffic moving across the bay. Back at the bank building I found an ink-smeared note from George, apparently left by a seaborne messenger: 'Got across safely. Keep eye on bank and tell Fred I will break his ass if he doesn't stand by with autocar at dock. George.'

What was amazing was the variety of reactions to the disaster. Some reacted with absolute impassivity, staring stone-faced as if in shock. Others seemed restless and uneasy, as if they were somehow guilty. And some (very drunk) cheered as the flames roared and hissed.

There were voices crying out that San Francisco was a city of sinners and that God was finally punishing it. One preacher ranted, 'First cast out the beam of thine own eye,' while the crowd cried and prayed in fear.

The *Slocum*, the army tug, was bringing in the Twenty-second Infantry. Commanders had been alerted as far away as Fort Baker, the Presidio in Monterey. The mayor had posted notices all over the city:

PROCLAMATION FROM THE MAYOR

The Federal Troops, the members of the Regular Police Force, and all Special Police Officers, have been authorized by me to SHOOT AND KILL any and all persons engaged in Assault, Looting, or in the Commission of Any Other Crime. I have directed the Gas and Electric Lighting Companies not to turn on any utilities until I give the order. You may, therefore, expect the city to remain in darkness for an indefinite time. I request all citizens to remain at home from dusk to morning every night until order is completely restored. I WARN all citizens of the danger of fire from damaged or destroyed chimneys, broken or leaking gas pipes or fixtures, or any like cause.

E. E. SCHMITZ, MAYOR

April 18, 1906

The rapidly spreading fires were awesome to behold. Everything south of Market Street was destroyed. I went to find Fred at Hawk dock, to see if he had any further news of George.

'At his age, I hope all the excitement doesn't hurt him.'

'Hell, Ramon, he's as lively as a flea in a fat lady's corset. Just look how this damn ash is ruining the finish of my autocar.'

'You going to try to get out of the city?'

'Dad said I'm to stay here and wait.'

'What for?'

'He didn't say.' Fred offered me a flask; I took a sip and left, deciding to check once more on the bank. Flames were surrounding it. The vaults were sealed; the place was beginning to burn. Louis Sullivan's fine terra-cotta tiles were falling from the facade. Sadly I went back to Nob Hill.

All night the fires and looting continued. The next morning at 7 A.M. I saw the troops, armed with bayonets on their rifles, marching down Market Street. The Presidio army detachments reached the city an hour later, made up of horses, guns, batteries, infantry, and stubborn army mules. Seventeen hundred men were ordered out to bring order to the city.

The houses on Nob Hill were doomed, George's among them. Headlines in the Oakland papers announced: 'PALACE HOTEL ON FIRE, CLIFF HOUSE TOPPLES INTO THE OCEAN/FERRY TRAFFIC STOPPED, ST.

377

Old China, the Chinatown of fake opium dens (and real ones), the nest of shacks and cellars of slave girls—were all gone. Afterward there was talk of forbidding a new Chinatown from being erected. I strolled down to Kearny Street, where I was amazed to find that Mother C's brothel was still standing, the iron horse tie (a jockey figure) cleanly painted.

Back at the Palace Hotel, everything was deep in debris. Enrico Caruso, the famous tenor, fell out of bed on the first shock, I heard, covered with fallen plaster. He escaped by train, saying he'd rather face Vesuvius.... The most dreadful rumors circulated: hundreds shot as looters, rapists, terrorized the streets; wide chasms swallowing up dogs and ponies; criminals from the Coast cutting off ring fingers and earringed ears from the bodies of the dead and injured.

The Pacific-Harvesters Bank Building was burning furiously. I almost found myself offering up a prayer for the doomed structure. Dynamite squads were blowing up buildings in front of the fires, trying desperately to hold back the advancing walls of flame.

George arrived, ash-covered but excited, looked at his burning bank with composure. 'It's best the bank burns,' he said.

'Why?'

'The vaults are strong, but who knows what a dynamite charge might do? It's the records I want to save.'

'What do we do, just wait?'

He grinned. 'How Rocco would have been thrilled by all this.... What else is there to do for the next couple of days? Just wait.'

'Then?'

He winked. 'Our Father in heaven, bless our

survival, and for the Redeemer's sake, amen.' He was as vigorous as he had been a generation or so before, alert, elated by the challenge. I couldn't fathom him. He didn't seem to mind when word came that his big home was on fire. 'Never liked the damn barn anyway. I only built it for Maria and the boys.'

The Big Four mansions, some already public institutions, were going up with a roar. Mark Hopkin's towered, gingerbreaded Victorian fruitcake architecture burned, as did the mansions of Stanford, Huntington, and Crocker; all were soon ash. Arguments raged; many people claimed the whole business of blowing up buildings was stupid and did little to stop the fire.

Nob Hill and Russian Hill were devastated. Everyone was sooty, looking for water, something to eat. Children cried, women wept, men looked numb as they drank warm beer salvaged from ruins

The soldiers were ordering thousands from their homes, giving them no time to pack or carry off more than the barest necessities. People were cursing the troops they had been cheering just the day before. As the fires advanced to Portsmouth Square, the bodies of victims were being buried in shallow scooped-out graves, but the survivors, the families, drew some comfort from the burials.

George and Fred went back to Hawk dock. I slept that night in Jefferson Square, where a strange kind of picnic atmosphere prevailed. A couple of tarts sat on a piano in the street, sipping whiskey and singing 'A Hot Time in the Old Town Tonight.' Tents and blankets were distributed and jugs of whiskey were passed around freely.

Saturday, April 21: All is over now. Smoke remains in our hair, clothing and food, but all the fires are out at last. The last rush of fire was down the south ridge of Telegraph Hill the night before.

379

The city's buildings are charred, steaming ruins. Fred, George, and I drove out to examine the gutted corpse of our bank building. As we walked amid the rubble, George turned and called to me, 'Come on, Ramon, get me two barrels from over there and a big plank or a door.'

'You'll see. Just do it.'

As Fred and I scavenged for the required items, we became aware of a sooty figure approaching—a battered hat shading an unshaven face. The figure waved and ran toward us.

Fred cried out. 'I'll be a son of a bitch—I don't believe it! It's Charles! Charlie!'

'Dammit,' said Charlie, shaking our ash-smeared hands and hugging us all, 'you all had me worried. I couldn't just drag my ass in Santa Barbara when the city was burning—and I didn't even know if you were alive or barbecued.'

'But how did you get here? There aren't any more trains running—everything is in ruins.'

Charlie kissed George, put an arm around him. He could feel the old man trembling. 'Willie Hearst has a fast steam yacht—just forty feet long, but *fast*. I borrowed it. I have to admit I wasn't easy about it— steam was escaping from every vent. But I made it, landed at North Beach and walked the rest of the way. And here we are, almost like old times—a real gathering of the clan. And what on earth are you all up to, digging around in this mess?'

Fred laughed. 'Dad wants two barrels and a plank, but he won't tell us why.'

'You're both idiots. I want to build a counter and put up a new sign, of course.'

Charlie said, 'Come on, Ramon. Let's find them!'

They lugged a six-foot white-pine plank from the backseat of the car, its newly painted foot-high letters bright and clear. Nearby the street preacher was reasonably delivering his message to the burned-down city: 'Who shall ascend the mountain of Yahweh? And who shall stand in this holy place?'

Charlie walked around to see the legend on the plank: 'TEMPORARY OFFICES, THE PACIFIC-HARVESTERS BANK. DEPOSITS ACCEPTED, HOUSE AND BUSINESS LOANS TO REBUILD SAN FRANCISCO QUICKLY PROCESSED. GEORGE FIORE.'

George admired the sign. '*That's* how one faces the unexpected! Now, boys, let's get the boxes of cash out of the car and get back to being bankers!'

That's how it happened. The miraculous, incorrigible ingenuity that was George Fiore recreated his bank from its very ashes. People stopped to shake his hand. Some gawked, a few smiled and a woman who had lost her clothing shop came to ask about a loan.

George handled his business at the makeshift counter we had set up for him. 'Business as usual, at the usual rates. No loan too small, and try us for any credit you need. Times are hard, and we don't want to make them harder.'

'He's overdoing it,' I said to Charlie and Fred. 'He's an old man. Maybe we should make him rest.'

'Hell, Ramon,' said Fred. 'You can't stop a runaway steam train. He had me ruin two tires and blister the paint off the car. He didn't even listen. Just said something about "secure assumptions" and "solid business justifications!" But, Charlie, we didn't even get to ask how your lovely family is doing. That April is going to be a beauty one day.'

'They're fine, Fred. The kids are getting sassier every day, and they love Santa Barbara. I've started teaching them to sail—remember our great adventures? Look at all these people—word must have spread fast. Looks like people think we're *giving* money away. But, Ramon, I don't think you need to worry about George—he hasn't lost his touch at all!'

George was talking to a plump man who was

speaking with a German accent.

'Meyerhoff, forget temporary calamity. We need bread from your bakery, so go get flour from the army; there's plenty of firewood around. Credit?' He opened up a tin box. 'The hell with references. Meyerhoff, go bake bread!' He counted out several hundred dollars into the man's hand. 'What do you mean, sign for it? Meyerhoff, forget it. You have an honest Dutch face. We understand each other, right? Now get out of here and bake!'

The preacher was still crying out: 'WHO SHALL ASCEND THE MOUNTAIN OF YAHWEH? THE CLEAN HANDS AND PURE OF HEART: WHO HAS NOT RAISED HIS MIND TO AN IDOL NOR SWORN BY A FRAUD—HE SHALL RECEIVE BLESSINGS FROM YAHWEH. …'

For some time, I had been aware that the old man was no longer the Uncle George of my youth, but still a man who accepted a life of duty, compassion, loss—a man true to his own principles, values, visions. He was no mandarin of ultimate wisdom, but was just what he had always been—only older and growing somehow more removed from the interests which had once so consumed him. The earthquake disaster was like a rolling-back of time, a return of the young George we had known as we grew up but whom we hadn't seen for so long.

He began to waver with fatigue. Charlie helped him to sit down on a crate. I knelt beside him, held his thin hand. He was close to weeping now, and I thought: Perhaps he is rejudging the past in all of us, in the changing shapes of the present. Or maybe it's the realization that he is again an old man, who rallied the last of his vitality in the crisis, but who no longer has the youth and strength to sustain it. I love this old man—my uncle, whom I must now care for as he once cared for me.

The preacher came over to us, holding out his hand in a begging gesture. George motioned for us to give him something. 'It's up to you now. I'm too tired, too old.'

I handed the preacher a silver dollar.

STAR BOOKS BESTSELLERS

FICTION

THE PROTOCOL	*Sarah Allan Borisch*	£2.25*
SEASON OF CHANGE	*Lois Battle*	£2.25*
LET'S KEEP IN TOUCH	*Elaine Bissel*	£2.50*
DANCEHALL	*Bernard F. Conners*	£1.95*
DREAMS OF GLORY	*Thomas Fleming*	£2.50*
DEAR STRANGER	*Catherine Kidwell*	£1.95*
PHANTOMS	*Dean R. Koontz*	£2.25*
THE PAINTED LADY	*Françoise Sagan*	£2.25*
LAMIA	*Tristan Travis*	£2.75*

FILM TIE-INS

EDUCATING RITA	*Peter Chepstow*	£1.60
TERMS OF ENDEARMENT	*Larry McMurtry*	£1.95*
PARTY PARTY	*Jane Coleman*	£1.35
THE WICKED LADY	*Magdalen King-Hall*	£1.60
SCRUBBERS	*Alexis Lykiard*	£1.60
BULL SHOT	*Martin Noble*	£1.80
BLOODBATH AT THE HOUSE OF DEATH	*Martin Noble*	£1.80

STAR Books are obtainable from many booksellers and newsagents. If you have any difficulty tick the titles you want and fill in the form below.

Name _____

Address _____

_____

Send to: Star Books Cash Sales, P.O. Box 11, Falmouth, Cornwall, TR10 9EN.

Please send a cheque or postal order to the value of the cover price plus:
UK: 55p for the first book, 22p for the second book and 14p for each additional book ordered to the maximum charge of £1.75.

BFPO and EIRE: 55p for the first book, 22p for the second book, 14p per copy for the next 7 books, thereafter 8p per book.

OVERSEAS: £1.00 for the first book and 25p per copy for each additional book.

While every effort is made to keep prices low, it is sometimes necessary to increase prices at short notice. Star Books reserve the right to show new retail prices on covers which may differ from those advertised in the text or elsewhere.

R SALE IN CANADA